Readers love
B.G. THOMAS

Getting His Man

"Honestly, I found the story refreshing and August and Artie adorable, even pretty hot at one point. I'm more than happy to be able to recommend this one."

—Jessie G Books

"I can honestly say this was another one of my favorites…"

—Love Bytes

Blue

"The book touched my heart, at times it was happy and other times sad but through it all there was love."

—Paranormal Romance Guild

"…B.G. Thomas doesn't tell stories. He writes about lives. REAL lives that have real people."

—*Divine Magazine*

New Lease

"If you want a short story that will tug at the heart strings, then this might be the book for you."

—San Francisco Review of Books

"This is a really short read, but I loved every page."

—OptimuMM

By B.G. Thomas

All Alone in a Sea of Romance
All Snug
The Beary Best Holiday Party Ever
Bianca's Plan
Blue
The Boy Who Came In From the Cold • Anything Could Happen
Christmas Cole
Christmas Wish
Derek
Desert Crossing • A Different Perspective
Do You Trust Me?
Grumble Monkey and the Department Store Elf
Hound Dog and Bean
How Could Love Be Wrong?
It Had to Be You
Just Guys
With Noah Willoughby: Mele Kilikimaka
A More Perfect Union (Multiple Author Anthology)
New Lease
Orange
The Real Thing
Red
A Secret Valentine
Sometimes the Best Presents Can't Be Wrapped
Soul of the Mummy
Editor: A Taste of Honey (Dreamspinner Anthology)
Until I Found You

Published by DREAMSPINNER PRESS
www.dreamspinnerprss.com

By B.G. THOMAS (CONT.)

DREAMSPUN DESIRES
GETTING HIS MAN
#48 – Getting His Man

GOTHIKA
Bones (Multiple Author Anthology)
Spirit (Multiple Author Anthology)
Contact (Multiple Author Anthology)

SEASONS OF LOVE
Spring Affair
Summer Lover
Autumn Changes
Winter Heart

Published by DREAMSPINNER PRESS
www.dreamspinnerpress.com

ORANGE

B.G. THOMAS

Published by
DREAMSPINNER PRESS

5032 Capital Circle SW, Suite 2, PMB# 279, Tallahassee, FL 32305-7886 USA
www.dreamspinnerpress.com

Trade Paperback ISBN: 978-1-64080-230-8
Digital ISBN: 978-1-64080-231-5
Library of Congress Control Number: 2017956595
Trade Paperback published February 2018
v. 1.0

Printed in the United States of America

This paper meets the requirements of
ANSI/NISO Z39.48-1992 (Permanence of Paper).

This one is for Noah Willoughby.
Friend, coauthor, researcher, and "Voice in the dark."
This book would not have happened without you.
At least not on time!

CHAPTER ONE

"HEY," FRANK Sinclair said to the stranger. "You want a blowjob?"

And then he waited for the answer.

Everything would depend on the next few seconds. There would be either a smile or a snarl, and sitting there in his red Mazda MX-5 Miata, Frank's left foot was on the brake and his right hovered over the gas in case he got a hostile answer.

Thing was, though, a surprising number of men said yes. Even the straight ones. Odds were, most of them *would* be straight. Statistics said nine out of ten. Yet still he got to give those blowjobs.

Frank figured his good luck hinged a lot on the fact that he was not only good-looking but well-built and masculine also. He'd always been able to fit in anywhere he went. Be "one of the guys." This was not conceit on his part, and he thought it was ridiculous, stupid even, when an attractive person pretended they were unaware of their looks. Knowing you were good-looking and being conceited about it were two entirely different things.

Come on, say yes, he beamed to the hottie standing there.

Wait.

Waiting….

The man stared back at him, mouth agape, clearly taken by surprise.

He was hot. *Fuck*, he was hot. Both figuratively and literally.

Figuratively because the guy was a *stud*—younger than Frank by five or more years, muscular, with a mop of brown hair, a thick, almost-wild beard, and huge—simply huge—blue eyes. He was wearing nothing but a thin-strapped tank top and bright Lycra biker shorts so revealing he might as well have been naked. Frank could clearly see the length of the guy's penis, the flared head, and two significantly sized balls nestled beneath, one a little lower than the other.

And literally because it was in the upper 90s today, as it had been for unrelenting weeks, and the man was sweaty, hair stuck to his forehead, the wide-open sides of his tank top dark with perspiration. Frank thought if he stuck his head out the window, which at this point he dared not do, he could smell the man, and he knew it would be a *good* smell. Not acrid or nasty, but all man. That's what his imagination was conjuring up, at least.

All of which was the first (no, second) reason Frank had made his blatant offer.

Of course, it certainly wasn't the first time he'd proffered such an unashamed solicitation, and it certainly would not be the last. Coming on to strangers, especially those as hot as this, was one of his two fetishes, and one he'd been able to fulfill many times.

God, this guy was hot. Even better up close. Frank liked what he saw, and he wanted to see more, even though the man's shorts were so revealing. Frank was from Missouri, after all, the Show-Me State, and Show Me was his motto.

A quick glance (and it had to be quick because he didn't want to take his eyes off the guy's face for long) down past the bulge in those shorts revealed muscular, hairy legs and big feet, the latter encased in tennis shoes, sans socks. Certainly not those fruity ankle socks with the little pompoms on the back that Frank would forever associate with the kind the high school cheerleaders used to wear. On a girl they were fine, if not a bit silly. But on a man? The thought practically turned Frank's stomach.

Anyway, the guy's whole outfit, what there was of it, was a wet dream come true—

(although not as hot as the man had looked in orange)

—and Frank found he was holding his breath in anticipation.

Say yes. Say yes. Say yes!

Frank had been parking his car in front of his apartment building—a virtual miracle that the space had been open and he hadn't had to park in the lot around back—when he'd spotted the man in the bright (and very tight) shorts at the gas station kitty-corner across the street. Even from that distance, he could see the guy was built. And since Frank had been horny all day, his balls actually *heavy* with need, he impulsively drove over to see if the guy was as hot up close as he was from across the street.

To Frank's great surprise, the guy was the "man in orange."

He'd been so surprised he had simply stared for a moment, his come-on unsaid. Holy shit! Not only was this guy a jerk-off fantasy, but he was the man to whose image Frank had already jerked off to more than once.

Better and better.

God, who would have believed it? Frank's cock had started to harden the second his lewd offer had sprung from his lips.

But now? Now he was steel hard and throbbing in his jeans. What would the dude say? It had taken him a moment to realize that this man was that man. His hair had been very short the first time he'd seen it. Marine cut. And his beard shorter. Much shorter.

But God, it *was* him.

They locked eyes. Those eyes! Bordering on unreal. Almost like eyes from some character in one of those Japanese cartoon movies everyone was so crazy about.

The man swallowed. So hard his Adam's apple bobbed. And…

This is it!

"O-okay," he said quietly.

Yes! Christ, Frank couldn't believe his fucking luck.

Wait….

Was the guy blushing? *Adorable.*

The guy trembled. Looked around nervously. Licked his lips. Changing his mind?

Don't let him change his mind.

"I live right across the street," Frank said quickly.

"You do?" Dude asked, voice cracking.

Frank nodded and finally took his foot from its position above the gas. The guy wasn't going to punch him. "I was parking my car and saw you."

"From across the street?"

Frank nodded again. "Yeah. And you were *so* fucking hot, I had to ask."

"You thought I was hot from over there?" Dude's Adam's apple bobbed again.

"Fuck yes," Frank said, his voice almost a growl.

Dude's eyes flashed. "Let's do it."

THE FIRST time Frank saw him, the man was walking in the grass alongside the road.

He was wearing orange.

The traffic was crawling along I-70. Frank had taken the top of his Mazda down so he could enjoy the breeze through his thick, wavy hair and the skin on his bare chest. He was wearing his jeans shorts—the ones he'd made, not those horrible nearly knee-length shorts that were popular today. He blamed *those* ugly things on that motherfucker Michael Jordan, who'd turned the only sexy American sports uniform into something that looked like bathing suits from the 1910s.

Frank's shorts? They weren't cut so high his balls would hang out, but they showed off his muscular thighs, and as hard as he worked on them, he wanted them to be seen!

But none of that made a bit of difference when the traffic came to a total stop. Or close enough. He was just thinking it was time to put the damned top up so the air conditioner would do some good when he saw the men along the side the road. The men in orange.

His friend Cody had a little fantasy. He liked UPS men. "I'll tell you what brown can do for *me*!" he'd said one evening after too many cosmos.

Cody wasn't the only one. Turned out a lot of guys thought men in those brown UPS uniforms were hot. And Frank had to admit they often were. The shorts *were* short, for one thing. And the men were usually fit. Their jobs involved a lot of driving but a lot of running as well. Leaping in and out of those trucks, running to a front door lugging packages of various sizes and weights, and then dashing back to their vehicle. He'd had to laugh when Cody suggested it was dirty old queens who did the hiring for UPS.

"I mean, have you seen a UPS man who isn't hot?"

Frank had to agree. He understood the appeal of the color brown.

But for him, it was orange.

The only difference was he didn't know anyone else who shared his interest.

Frank didn't know what it was about those men in their orange jumpsuits. Maybe he didn't need to. Evaluating such a thing was something Cody would do. Frank only knew those men turned him on.

And that hot day, he laid his eyes on one who put iron in his cock in about thirty seconds.

The man was around twenty-five, give or take a year. He was very fit, slim, and wide in the shoulders, and he gave the almost-shapeless orange jumpsuit a run for its money. Tight. Like he was wearing one a size too small. His beard wasn't quite as full that day as it was today, but trim, shorter, and his hair was in a buzz cut. He was carrying a bag and a pole with a claw at the end, and he was picking up garbage. Then—as if Frank had been a remarkably good boy and Karma was rewarding him—a man in a police uniform handed the guy a bottle of water. Frank still couldn't believe what had happened next. The man in orange—the hot man Frank was taking back to his apartment right now—opened the bottle, drank about half of it, his throat working, working, working, and then—*oh Christ!*—he poured the remainder over himself, tossing his head to either side as he did. It was like something out of a sexy bottled-water commercial. Time seemed to slow down as the water ran right off that buzz-cut hair. Some of it spread through his trim beard and then went flying out in a fan. The rest poured down his front over his bare, *very* muscular chest—his orange jumpsuit had been unzipped scandalously low—and where the water touched the edges of his garment, the fabric turned almost red.

And then—

(oh God, and then!)

—he turned his head and looked at Frank.

Their eyes locked.

Frank wasn't sure he'd ever seen eyes so blue. So *big*. Eyes that belonged on an elfin character in a fantasy movie.

The man licked his lips. Gave another toss of his head. Water droplets flew. But he still looked. *Still* stared back.

Frank thought he'd have an orgasm right then.

A loud horn sounded then—*honk!*—and Frank had jumped in his seat, and then he was no longer locked eye to eye with the stranger in orange. He looked around to see the traffic had moved on a bit, and someone behind him was impatient. As if he could pull more than about ten feet ahead.

Sadly, the team in orange was going the opposite way. Frank didn't get to play fuckeyes with the stranger any longer.

He sure came hard that night, though, thinking about him. Thinking about swinging the passenger door open and telling him, "Quick! Jump in!" and then hitting the gas, tearing down the shoulder of the highway, and zooming up the next off-ramp, and taking the sweaty man home and fucking the Jesus out of him.

Cody and his partner, Harry, had enjoyed the story—which surprised him because they were *such* a couple, so saccharine sweet in their couplehood, and always telling him he needed to find him a man and settle down. Despite that, they had cheered after he'd told them about Mr. Orange the next day.

That's when they told him their "Google for brown" story. How they'd found a uniform online and ordered it, and how Harry had "delivered" a package.

It was pretty hot, actually, that a couple that had been together for five years could still get up to such antics. Could almost make you think….

No. No way.

"That's what *you* need to do," Harry said. He was a stocky bear, though not too big, and had he not been coupled, Frank would have taken him for a spin. But Frank did not do married men—even if the two of them hadn't made it legal yet. There were 4.5 billion men in the world. He wasn't going to help someone cheat on some poor, innocent, unsuspecting partner.

"Google you up one of those jumpsuits. Hell! You could get one from one of those Halloween places easy! And I'm sure a guy like you wouldn't have a bit of trouble getting someone to help him fulfill a little fantasy."

But for Frank, a costume wasn't going to do it. For him, it had to be real.

Now after years of waiting, it was going to happen. He was going to blow a man in orange. And while the guy wouldn't actually be *wearing* the jumpsuit—for that Frank would have to draw on the memory of that hot summer day—at least his man du jour was *real*.

"Just picture him, see him in that orange jumpsuit…," Frank told himself aloud. *Picture* it! The sweat, the bottle, and the thrashing of his head with the water spraying out in a fan, catching the sun like diamonds, the rest of the water running down his torso.

The thoughts, memories, had Frank so hard his cock hurt. But the pain wouldn't last. It would soon transform into delightful pleasure. Why, he'd probably cum the minute he got the guy's cock in his mouth. Luckily Frank wasn't a guy who lost interest in sex the minute he'd had an orgasm.

It hit him that he still didn't know the guy's name. Not that it mattered. He'd had sex with lots of men whose names he never knew. Who cared what their names were? He usually forgot their names a minute after they told him. It didn't matter. This was sex. He wasn't planning on marrying them and bearing their children. Love didn't have anything to do with it, to paraphrase Ms. Tina Turner.

No. This was about fulfilling a fantasy he'd had for as long as he could remember. One that was rooted somewhere around sixth grade, when he'd seen some men on the side of a different highway one of the many times he and his father were on the road. One of the few times they'd been in the US.

"Who are those men?" he'd asked his father.

His father had looked. They were in a convertible that day as well, and funny that he was suddenly remembering that. Dad was smoking and Frank remembered the smoke curling out of his mouth as he squinted at the men on the side of the road, focusing on them for just a moment.

"Those are bad boys," his father said then. "They did something they shouldn't have done, and they got caught, and now they're being punished."

"Those are bad boys."

The words fired up something deep within him. Something... *exciting.*
Bad boys.

And now, at last, he was going to get his bad boy. At long last.
Please God. Don't let him change his mind and run....

CHAPTER TWO

He didn't run.

In fact, there was a fire in his eyes when Frank met up with him in front of his apartment building, the Oscar Wilde.

They took the elevator to the sixth floor. The whole time, the dude's eyes were doing crazy things, going wide and dark. Frank actually saw it happen because those eyes were such a bright swimming pool of blue that he could see the pupils dilating. The guy's nostrils flared. His mouth was open, and that throat was working again, as if he were drinking from that bottle of water once more.

Then, having still not spoken since Frank's offer and the dude's acceptance at the gas station, they left the elevator, walked down the hall, and went into Frank's apartment.

Inside, Mr. Orange stood on the threshold, breathing with audible huffs, his legs wide, those eyes staring. Frank figured he better get this show on the road before the guy chickened out and ran. That had happened. More than once.

Please not today.

Frank glanced down at the man's crotch and saw—holy shit!—the dude was hard. *Rock* hard. The bright Lycra shorts were too wet from perspiration for Frank to tell if the guy was leaking yet. But goddamn, what a feast!

Before Frank could go to his knees, his visitor grabbed him by the collar of his shirt, slammed him against the wall, and kissed him. Kissed him rough and firm, mouth open, tongue thrusting. And *fuck*, he wasn't a bad kisser!

Now his hands were at the side of Frank's face, and he pulled back ever so slightly and stared at Frank, eyes crazy with lust. Frank couldn't help but think of the scene from *Brokeback Mountain* where Ennis Del Mar and Jack Twist kissed after years of not seeing each other. That had been one of hottest things Frank had ever seen.

So why not continue the scene? Jack Twist had kissed Ennis back. And that's what Frank did. He kissed back as good as he'd been given.

Jesus H. Christ it was good. Frank didn't know when the last time was he'd been kissed like this. Such fervor. Such fever. Such—*God!*—passion. Mr. Orange ground against him, moaning into Frank's mouth. His tongue darted, dived, danced with Frank's.

Who is this guy?

Suddenly, Frank's trick pulled away. Gazed at Frank. There was so much happening in those eyes. Lust. An animal wildness. And was that fear?

"I'm awful sweaty," he said in an apologetic tone that Frank found humorous. "It's so damned hot, and I worked out this morning…."

"I love workout sweat," Frank growled.

The guy blinked and then nodded and growled right back, "Where's your bed?"

"Back that way," Frank said, gesturing with a bob of his head. He led the way, Mr. Orange on his heels. They'd no sooner crossed the threshold of his bedroom than he was on Frank again. But trembling. Nervous? Scared?

So Frank put his arms around him and pulled him close, rubbed his upper arms reassuringly. He did not want the guy to freak out and run. Not this close.

Please no!

But then he kissed Frank again. This time some of that wild sureness was gone. He was hesitant at first—one breath at a time, moaning, gasping, almost… whining. But slowly the aggression came back. Frank took a chance, ground his erection against his trick's, and yes! The guy was moaning even more.

The time had come.

Frank carefully nudged him back to the bed and sat him down, put a hand on his chest, pushed him back. Finally—at last—he went to his knees. Down between those muscular legs. The guy wasn't wearing the orange jumpsuit. He wore shorts instead. But that was okay. They were hot as fuck, and his cock was even hotter. Frank laid his hand on those hard, powerful thighs, then grabbed the waist of the shorts. Started to pull, and—

"Wait!"

Frank looked up. *No! I don't want to wait!* He was looking into those eyes. Mr. Orange was leaning back on his elbows, propped up so he could stare down between his legs at Frank.

"Wait?" Frank asked.

"What's your name?" the man said with a panting gasp. "If I'm going to have sex with you, I want to know your name."

Have sex with me? Is that what this guy called getting a blowjob? Or was he saying he wanted more?

"Frank," he said.

"I'm… I'm Roy." And then, of all things, he blushed. Or was that just the color of desire? "Suck my cock, Frank. *Please.*"

Only too happy to oblige, Frank grabbed the waist of those ridiculously bright Lycra shorts and pulled them down. Urged Roy to lift his ass. Pulled again.

God, there it was. Roy's cock.

God! Hot. But it was also beautiful. Big, uncut, and below the thick shaft, large testicles in a satiny scrotum. His pubic hair was a light, short bush above. Had he trimmed it? Why, Frank thought he had.

Enough looking!

Frank lowered his face, pressed it against that warm column. Kissed it. Kissed it again. Kissed down between his balls and pressed there too, then went a little lower and placed pressure against that one spot *outside* of a man that was so close to his prostate. Roy moaned and put his hands in Frank's hair, wound his fingers in it. Frank mouthed the spot hard, and Roy cried out God's name.

Oh, Roy smelled *so* good. Musky and very strong, but fresh and all man. Frank's cock began to throb at the scent. The fragrance of a man.

Then Frank began to lick, swirled his tongue hard and made Roy moan all the more.

Gonna give you the best blowjob of your life! So I better stop fucking around and start sucking.

He ran his tongue, wet as he could make it, up the shaft. And when he reached the head, half-covered in lovely foreskin but damp with need, he wrapped his fingers around the fleshy column, gripped it (more moans), lifted it, and took it in his mouth.

"*God!*" Roy shouted.

Took it deep. Massaged the underside with his tongue. Flexed it. Did those things guaranteed to make a man cum. Never sucked a man he couldn't get off with his mouth. Ignored those men who said they couldn't cum that way and showed them that, oh yes, they could!

Frank bobbed up and down on that thick shaft, deep-throating him, making himself a wet, tight tunnel of pure pleasure. Roy cried out and curled his fingers in Frank's hair so tight it hurt, but Frank didn't mind. It turned him on. Drove him on.

Cum for me. Fill me. Drown me!

Roy's cock began to throb in that way that told Frank the orgasm could be no more than thirty seconds away and then—

"No! Stop!"

Stop?

Roy pulled his cock out of Frank's mouth—

What are you doing!

—and when Frank tried to take him back in, Roy actually pushed him back.

"No! I don't want to cum yet."

Wait. What?

Oh, the fire in those eyes.

He doesn't want to cum yet? Because so many straight men wanted it over fast....

"If...." Roy's throat began to work again. His mouth opened. Closed. Opened. Closed.

If? If what?

"I don't think I can suck you if I cum." His cheeks went red again.

Wait. What? *Suck me?*

"Roy... you don't—"

"Frank. Stand up!" Commanding him. Not asking.

"You don't have to, man. I'm fine with—"

"I want to, Frank. Oh *God*. I *want* to!"

He wants to. Holy shit. And looking into those blue eyes, Frank saw Roy meant it.

Stand the fuck up!

So he did, nearly shaking, thinking, *Is this really happening? Please tell me this is really happening!*

Frank stood, and while he wasn't filling his jeans quite as full as Roy filled *his* shorts—certainly didn't show through thick denim like Roy through his Lycra—he could see Roy liked what he saw. Then he sat up and reached, paused, reached, and... touched. So light Frank could barely feel it, but still a shock shot through his whole body, and he gasped. Good. *So* good!

But wait. Was it him who had gasped? Or was it Roy? Because now Roy was shaking. He gave a little moan. He pulled at Frank's jeans, opened them with a *pop* and a *ziiiiiiip*, and Frank's cock sprang out. He never wore underwear. Not in years and years, and his father hadn't cared. His old man thought it showed that Frank was a *real* man.

Roy gasped, "Oh God," and grabbed Frank's erection.

Later, Frank wasn't sure how he hadn't shot off immediately. The pleasure was a shockwave, and then Roy started jacking him, staring, whispering to himself, and Frank had to grip his own ass hard with clawed nails to keep things from ending too soon.

"God," Roy said. "Your dick…. It's so…. It's so *hot!*"

Frank wasn't sure if Roy meant *sexy* hot or *temperature* hot, and through the pleasure haze suspected maybe he meant both. But before he could ponder it any further, logical thought was driven from Frank as Roy sat up and took Frank's cock into his mouth.

"Christ!" Frank hissed, and it was from pleasure *and* pain. "Teeth," he warned.

Roy caught on miraculously fast after that. Lips folded over his teeth, he began to bob. Maybe not wet enough, but who frigging cared? A straight man was sucking his cock. Why the hell had he even cared about the fucking teeth? Roy could do whatever he wanted as long as he kept sucking and… *God*… he was doing good. He was trying to imitate Frank's patented tongue-massage technique and was doing it well! The wetness was here now. Roy was practically slobbering on his cock, and oh God oh God oh God, Frank wanted to cum but….

But Roy'd said he wanted this to last.

Did he?

Frank stepped back, pulled out of the delicious mouth. Roy let out a sound that could only be a whimper, and Frank laughed. He couldn't help it. When Roy looked up, Frank surged into his arms, pushing him down and back onto the bed. He used his legs, feet firmly planted against the floor, to push Roy even farther up on the bed and then scrambled on top of him and kissed him again.

Now they were both moaning and rolling, and their legs and their half-pulled-down pants were tangling, and it was so hot and funny and sexy and *great*! When Roy was on top, Frank pulled that wet tank top off of him and flung it—*flung it!*—away, and when Frank was on top, Roy did the same to his polo shirt. One of the few buttons popped free and zinged off to parts unknown. Now their bare chests thrust up against each other, crushing, their nipples hard like pebbles, touching, sending more delightful zings out to toes and fingertips. They rolled and fought with their pants, used hands and knees and feet to get them low enough to kick off, and finally it was all skin. Skin against skin, muscles grinding, cocks thrusting.

Oh, this is so damned hot. So hot. Thank you, God! So hot.

He remembered that he had told himself he would fantasize about that orange jumpsuit, that he'd forgotten to... and then he forgot again. Oh well.

Frank was on top again, and he wanted Roy in his mouth once more. So he did it. Took him deep. Sucked his cock and licked too. Licked everywhere. Sucked his balls and then licked down and darted under to... God yes, taste Roy's hole.

Roy stiffened, and Frank did it again. Oh, it was clean. He could tell. It was all sweat and that wonderful new-penny-copper taste, and he wanted more than a quick lick. So he reared up and pushed Roy's legs back and wide and attacked with vigor. Licked and sucked and licked some more. Roy yelled, and Frank knew his neighbor on the other side of his bedroom wall had to hear, but hey, at least it was the afternoon, right?

Oh, and how nice that Roy's hole was opening to his ministrations, and when he peeked at it, he decided that Roy's pucker was perhaps the most beautiful he'd ever seen in he didn't know how long. Perfect and pink, and as he licked it more, it opened like a flower.

"Frank!" Hearing his name like that was incredible, and Roy said it again and again before he realized Roy was calling *to* him and not just shouting.

Frank lifted up and looked at Roy, and then surprisingly, Roy wrapped his legs around Frank's waist and pulled him tight, shifted so that his wet ass was pressed against Frank's throbbing cock.

Roy's next words stunned him. "Frank...?"

Frank looked into swimming-pool-blue eyes.

Ever so quietly, Roy whispered, "Fuck me?"

Wait. Had he heard that right?

Roy's eyes were incredibly wide now.

"You want me to…? Are you sure? I mean, it can really hurt the first time, and—"

"Please don't talk me out of it. I want to do it all. I know, but I don't want to regret *not* doing it. Because this is never going to happen again."

Frank didn't know what to say. He was indeed quite stunned.

"Please, Frank. Fuck me. I want to know…."

He almost asked, "Know what?" but then realized he understood completely.

Frank reached out to his bedside table, opened the drawer, fingered through it, found what he was looking for, and pulled out the little square foil packet.

Roy saw it, registered it, and said, "You don't have to use one if you don't want—"

"*Yes*," Frank said quite firmly. "*Yes*, I *do*. And don't you *ever* let a man fuck you without one." Then, driving his point home, "Do you understand, baby?"

Baby? Why the fuck had he said that?

Roy obviously heard it too, and his eyes widened ever so slightly. His cheeks went pink again—God, Frank loved that Roy could blush—and he nodded.

But Frank saw disappointment. *He wanted me to fuck him bare. Sorry. That is the one thing you* can't *do. You can't do it all. But God yes, I will fuck you.*

He sat back, opened the packet, pulled out the condom, and rolled it down his length while Roy watched with such goddamned—*wow*—lust!

Then Frank positioned himself, spread Roy's legs carefully, and lined his cockhead at that perfect, slightly open, and flexing hole. Looked down at him. So fucking hot. Those eyes. That chest, lightly hairy, the six-pack and the tight little navel, his hairy tummy. God!

"Try to relax. Take a deep breath and push out. I know that sounds weird, but it will help. And *relax*."

Roy nodded. Took the deep breath.

Frank reached down, touched his cock against that flexing hole… and gave Roy one more chance. "Are you sure?"

He got a sob for an answer and then a quick, hard nod. "I'm sure. *Please*, Frank."

No man could resist anymore.

He pushed and was surprised at how easily he slid in.

Roy's eyes flew wide, and he cried out and then locked his ankles behind Frank's ass and pulled him all the way in.

"God!" they both shouted as he bottomed out, and then Roy kissed him and told him to "Fuck me. Fuck me, Frank. Oh Christ! *So* good. So much… *better* than I *ever* thought. *God*!"

He went slowly at first, but not for long. He couldn't hold back, not with Roy fisting his own cock and begging Frank to fuck him, *fuck* him harder!

Frank fucked him harder and faster and ever so much deeper, and then Roy was cumming. Shooting between them in forceful blasts of bright white, splashing them both, one shot landing on Roy's cheek. As he came his ring of muscle and his tunnel clenched tight, and that was all it took—the squeezing and the sounds and the splashing—and Frank joined Roy. Cumming. Cumming so hard his vision went gray.

The orgasm seemed to go on forever, and when it finally ended, he fell on Roy, a puppet with its strings cut. He lay there, knew he had to be heavy, and told himself to roll off, but he couldn't. Not quite. Finally, using all his will, he started to move off Roy, but Roy's legs went tight again, and he said, "Please no. Not yet. I want you in me. Just a little longer."

Frank nodded, not wanting to be anywhere else.

Eventually, though, he couldn't hold himself up like that anymore, and he shifted them to the side. As his cock softened at last, he slipped out of Roy's exquisite warmth.

Roy rolled with him, threw a leg over Frank's groin, and laid his head on Frank's right bicep and the side of his chest. Then he sighed.

It was incredibly sweet.

CHAPTER THREE

AFTERWARD, ROY didn't leave. Not right away. It surprised Frank more than just about anything that had happened today. Not only did Mr. Hottie turn out to be the Man in Orange, and not only did they have great sex—no, frigging fantastic sex—but he didn't leave after. Straight men left. They might be bicurious, but they were saturated in Catholic—or whatever—guilt. They would get more and more and more curious until finally they could stand it no more and were driven by forces they couldn't understand to try to find gay sex. They usually had to get drunk first—how many of his tricks were from out of town and picked up in either a gay or hotel bar? Frank wasn't sure, but he bet the number was high. Those drunks would take him to bed, and about ten seconds after they came, the guilt would hit them like a runaway train.

This moment was very important. It could go one of two ways.

A man might turn into a blubbering, weeping fool, pacing, begging God for forgiveness, begging Frank to tell them this didn't mean they were gay—Frank usually did that for them, absolved them, whatever. It allowed him to exit, stage left, as quickly as possible.

But another man might get violent, blaming him for their fall from grace, screaming, shouting, swinging their fists. He'd gotten popped once on the jaw so hard his face hurt for a week, thought the guy had broken it. Men had even accused him of slipping them a roofie. Ridiculous. He was all the roofie he needed.

Roy didn't get hit by a trainload of guilt, and he didn't get violent. He... snuggled. Which could be the worst scenario yet.

Because sometimes men got all gushy and romantic and declared their undying love after a half-hour tryst. And Frank wasn't interested in committing himself to any man. He wasn't looking for happily ever after.

On the other hand, this was... well... kinda nice.

He wasn't sure why. Usually he liked it when his trick left. The sooner the better. Unless maybe he stayed to get dressed, pop open a six-pack, and watch the Chiefs. Man stuff. And if the home team won, that was an excuse for round two before Frank kicked the guy out.

Man stuff. Not gushy chick-flick stuff.

Roy shifted. Somehow got even closer to Frank without suffocating him. Their bodies... *fit* together. Very well. Like the Legos Frank had spent endless hours playing with as a kid.

What the fuck are you thinking?

But hell. It was true. He was propped up a bit on a couple pillows gazing down at their entangled bodies, Roy's body, and he was struck by how good it looked. Why, it was tempting his dick to get hard again. Roy's back, unlike his chest, was smooth, and he had a big rose tattoo on his right shoulder. Funny that Frank hadn't seen that until now. He contemplated that expanse of muscles and hairless ass, lightly hairy legs, big feet.

For some reason, Frank was reminded of a lady who had once asked him if he knew God, if he had found Jesus. She was telling him how it wasn't right or natural for him to be gay. That the final proof was that only a man's and a woman's bodies fit together. That two men's bodies could never fit right.

She needed to see this, he thought, and laughed. These two bodies fit.

I fucked this hottie.

Hot sex. Really hot sex.

Here all he'd wanted was to give the guy a quick blow-and-go. Instead it was the best fuck in he couldn't remember when. He thought about telling Roy that he'd jacked off thinking about him; it was the kind of thing that turned some men on. Thinking that you were so hot for them you masturbated, picturing them in your mind. An ego thing. Hell, it turned Frank on when he'd been told the same thing.

But then he would have to explain why. And he wasn't sure Roy was ready to know he had been recognized. And there was still the question of why he'd been working by the side of the road in that orange jumpsuit.

"Those are bad boys" came the echo of his father's voice. *"They did something they shouldn't have done, and they got caught, and now they're being punished."*

Bad boy.

I just fucked a bad boy.... It made him grin.

But then—geez, Frank had actually been slipping off to sleep—Roy finally said something.

"Wow. I just had gay sex."

Frank paused before responding. Wanting it to be the right thing to say to cover as many bases as he could.

"Well, my friend, *I'm* gay. This doesn't make you gay."

Roy looked at him, thickly bearded chin propped against Frank's chest. "It doesn't?"

Those eyes of his looked so... childlike. If a man *could* look childlike after what he'd just done with his body. What he'd done to Frank with his mouth. His ass. His hand and fingers and words.

"Please, Frank. Fuck me. I want to know...."

Somewhere between begging and a command.

Know what, Roy? What did you want to know? Did you find out?

"You're gay?" Roy asked, and there was incredulity in his voice.

"Kind of the reason I wanted to suck your cock."

Roy's eyes went wide, brows went high.

Then ever so quietly, "*I* wanted to suck your c.... Your c-cock."

"How could you resist?" Frank asked, grabbed himself, and winked. Chuckled. Joked it away. "I got a nice one."

Roy cleared his throat, looked away, laid his cheek once more on Frank's chest. "Yes, you do," he whispered.

Frank couldn't help but smile. Liked that little zing Roy's words gave him once again. What man didn't like his dick praised?

"You okay?" Frank asked. "I mean, you took quite a fucking there." *Took it better than just about any virgin I ever knew.* "That was something else." It was unbelievable was what it was. And he couldn't help but wonder if maybe, just maybe, Roy had....

"I'm okay," he said.

After a little while, Roy moved, propped himself up, looked down Frank's body, focused a minute on his half erection—

I'll get it back up for you again if you want me to, pretty man.

—and then sat up.

"I should be going."

You don't have to, Frank tried to say with his eyes. Because there was no fucking way he was going to say it out loud. He didn't say *that* out loud.

"I'm supposed be at… my mom's in…." He looked around and spotted the little alarm clock on Frank's bedside table. "Shit. Is that right? I should be there already. I told her I'd come early and that I'd bring potato salad. Red-skin if I could find it. Do you know where I can get some red-skin potato salad?"

The question was so sincere Frank almost laughed.

And here he worried about tears or fists or declarations of love. All Roy here wanted was some potato salad. Red-skin if he could find it.

"We could make some," he offered.

"No time!" Roy got up and glanced around for his clothes. He looked so damned good. That big chest, lightly hairy. Those arms. That little bit of pubic bush over that lotta bouncing cock. That ass—so smooth. He bent and picked something up, which aimed his ass at Frank, and Frank *knew* he could get it up again.

Roy stood and pulled his tank top over his head, revealing lightly hairy pits. Then he sat on the edge of the bed and pulled on his bike shorts.

"You're really going to your mother's house dressed like that?"

Roy gave him a curious look in response. "Huh?" he asked, standing again.

"You are downright scandalous in that!" He grinned and pointed at Roy's dick.

Roy peered at him and smiled—so cute—and blushed and said, "Well, I have something to change into in my car. I was going to take a shower when I got… to her place and then change. I was doing a job this morning, and I got all sweaty. Sorry about that."

"Sorry about being sweaty?" Frank grinned. "I liked it. Like it. But you know you can shower here before you go. For your ma."

Roy paused, seemed to think about it a second, and then shook his head. Laughed. "Naw. I don't think that would be a good idea." He shook his finger at Frank. "I know what *you* would want. You'd just try and f-fuck me again." He blushed furiously. "I gotta get out of here."

Frank gave a half shrug and smiled. "You do have an amazing ass," Frank said, surprising himself. He never tried to get a trick to stay. He wanted them out when the cumming was done. But he was surprised when it occurred to him Roy was right. He would like to climb in the shower with Orange Boy. Wash his back. His ass. Get another shot at it. Who knew? Maybe let Roy have a shot at his.

Then, surprising himself again, he said, "You could fuck me." Not that he didn't like being fucked, but there he was trying to get Roy to stay. "You did say you wanted to try *every*thing."

Roy's Adam's apple worked. "Gosh," he said, and his eyes told Frank he was thinking it over. "That's certainly tempting. But I really do have to go."

"Maybe next time," Frank said and then remembered there wasn't going to be a next time. Roy had said that, and it wasn't like Frank did "next times" all that often anyway.

Roy trembled for a second or two, then shook his head. "I can't."

Ah well. Potato salad.

"There's a Cosentino's on 13th," Frank said then and climbed out of bed. Scratched his balls, then sniffed his fingers. Sex. Pure sex. "Or the Sunfresh in Westport. I bet either one of them would have what you're looking for. Cosentino's is closer, but Sunfresh is cheaper."

Roy eyed Frank's crotch. Frank liked that. Then Roy looked him over from head to foot and back up again. He liked that even better. His dick twitched.

"You sure you don't want that shower? You do smell like sex. You might raise your mother's eyebrows."

Blush.

"She won't notice. I could walk in there naked and she would hardly notice. But thanks." He nodded. "Thanks for everything."

And then he did something that was the most surprising of all. He held out his hand.

He wanted to shake?

Frank looked at Roy. Once more there was that complete look of sincerity. He thought about how different Roy's expression had been while he was being fucked.

Why not? He shook Roy's hand.

And then Roy nodded and turned and walked to the front door. Frank followed him naked, opened the door, stood there just out of sight of anyone walking down the hall.

Roy looked at him again.

"You know you could have any woman you want, right?"

Frank shrugged. Thought better of it. Roy was leaving, and Frank would never see him again, and for some reason he cared what Roy thought of him. Of all this. The woman comment was a compliment. Roy was a man telling him that he, Frank, was a man.

"Roy." He smiled. "I don't want women that way. You know that, right?"

He blinked. "So…. So, you're *totally*… g-gay?"

"I am." He smiled. "Roy, after an afternoon like this with *you*—" He held out a hand to Roy. "—personally I can't imagine being anything else."

Roy regarded him. "You're just so…." The words stopped, but there were a million things going on in those eyes. Decisions being made? After a full minute, Roy sighed. "Cool, man," he whispered. And then, "Thank you for…."

Frank nodded. Because he didn't think Roy could finish saying it. "Thank you, Roy. I won't ever forget this."

Roy's eyes widened. "You won't?" Still a whisper.

"God no. It was fucking incredible."

The corners of Roy's mouth flickered upward.

And then he left.

CHAPTER FOUR

ROY SAT behind the wheel of his Jeep.

I just let a man fuck me.

Jesus….

I just let a man fuck my ass.

His ass was sore. *Of course it is. You just let that guy* fuck *you.*

And God, he'd never felt anything like it. Nothing had prepared him for this. Nothing. His skin was tingling. The hair on his arms would move now and again. It was like there was this tiny little electrical charge running through his body. He looked out the windshield. Everything seemed so much more… colorful. Clear. Detailed. It reminded him a bit of the Adderall he'd taken with Ramona.

Except this was natural, wasn't it? No drugs. This was real….

As if letting a stranger fuck you up the ass was natural.

He closed his eyes and gripped the steering wheel. Let his forehead rest against it. Took a long deep breath. Let it out very slowly.

I did it, didn't I? After all these years of not *doing it?*

After all those months in a place where lots of guys did it? He'd resisted that. Fought guys off.

And then I let stranger do it to me?

He looked up at the big redbrick apartment building. Knew he would never be able to drive by it again without knowing what had happened there. Thought that maybe he would find a way never to drive by it again.

He let out a long, shuddering breath. Saw Frank in his mind. As crystal clear as everything was around him. So…. Gorgeous. That was the word. The one he'd tried to say to Frank when he said, "You're just so…."

But men didn't call other men gorgeous, did they? That was a girl's word.

It was Ramona's word, and she used it too goddamned much.

But it was true. Frank looked like a movie star. He was unreal he was so good-looking. Better-looking than Channing Tatum. More manly than Jason Statham. More handsome than Hugh Jackman.

And he wanted me! Roy trembled. *I sucked his cock. And I liked it.*

The Katy Perry song came to mind. All about kissing a girl and liking it. But he'd done a lot more than that, hadn't he? *I sucked a guy, and I liked it.* Somehow he didn't think they'd be playing that on the radio anytime soon.

I sucked a guy, and I liked it.

He shivered again, and the hair on his arms moved, and it felt *good*.

It had felt good. Having a cock in him. He couldn't deny it. He'd never experienced anything like it. Nothing any girl had ever done to him had been so intense. Nothing that kinky Ramona had done to him—and oh the things she liked to do to him!—could equal what he'd just done with Frank. God, oh God. And it was more than having something there, inside him *there*, or touching his "sweet spot" as Ramona liked to call it. His "man-clit" when she really got going.

No. This was different. It was so… so… so *real*. Real flesh. Warm. Part of a *human being*. Inside him. And on top of him. And over him. And holding him.

Roy started to tremble, and tears sprang to his eyes as he thought, *I can never do that again. If I do I'm screwed.* Then he laughed out loud thinking of that. *Screwed.* He *had* been screwed.

I can never do it again. Because if I do, I'm gay. And I just can't do it. I can't be gay. I don't want that life! I want to be like everyone else. My friends. My buddies. My family.

He looked back up at the building again.

He smiled.

His ass hurt.

He wiggled, trying to get comfortable. Looked at the seat beside him. The one in back. There was a hoodie there. He reached back and got it, folded it over a few times, and then climbed out of the Jeep. He laid it down on the seat and sat back down, and it was a little better.

Not totally. But that was all right. Because he'd been fucked. He *should* feel something, right?

One more look.

He smiled again.

Thank you, Frank.

He started the Jeep, checked over his shoulder, pulled into traffic, and went to the Sunfresh. Frank said it was cheaper.

"*FINALLY*," HIS mother exclaimed as Roy walked in the kitchen. "I was wondering when you would get home!"

He always came in through the back door. He had since he was a kid. His mother put these pink plastic flamingos in the front yard, and the kids made fun of them, and he didn't want anyone to know he lived there. So he would get off the bus and walk past his house, then double back and come in through the back door. Turned out he didn't fool everyone for long. But he was good in a fight, and he coldcocked the first guy to say a word about them. That wound up making him cool.

"Did you bring the potato salad?" she asked, and he pulled it out of the bag—*ta-da!* She told him to hurry up and put it in *this* bowl—she put out a clear glass bowl that was just the right size—and told him to put some Saran wrap on it because Granny wouldn't be happy if she knew he brought some store-bought brand. As if he could make potato salad. As if Granny *thought* he could make potato salad. As if he were even *using* Saran wrap and not something called Kling-Tite.

"Okay, Mom," he said and did what she asked quickly, then went out on the tiny back porch and threw the plastic container away.

"Did you cover it up?" she asked when he came back in. She crossed her arms and nodded, and her jaw-length blonde hair moved like a drawn curtain. "If she sees, she will know. She's eighty, not *stupid*!"

"No, but I will." She smiled, and it was a nice smile. He'd always loved her smile, especially when it was directed at him. She reached out, patted his cheek, and said, "I love you, Roy."

"I love you too, Mom."

She smiled again in one of the ways she always did. But this was her amused smile, not her I'll-love-you–no-matter-what smile, probably because she was stressed. Stressed about Granny's birthday party, and why on earth should she be stressed? Granny would be happy. She wasn't always totally with it anymore. She would be happy no matter what. All the guests would be family, and it would be pretty much the way it always was on Sundays, except there would be a cake and a few more people.

"Do you want to see the cake?" Mom asked, and he told her yes, he did, and he flexed his ass and thought, *I got fucked up the ass today!* It was sore, but not terribly so. Enough that he couldn't, at least for now, forget what had happened to him today. At last.

Would you still love me if you knew what happened to me today?

"Is everything all right, honey?" That tiny furrow appeared between her eyebrows. If he went blind and reached up and felt that, he would know it was her.

He stiffened and then realized this was just Mom stressing and *looking* for something to stress about. Roy shook his head. "Everything is fine, Ma."

She rolled her blue eyes. "You know I hate it when you call me that."

"*Ma!*" he cried in a braying honk.

"Oh you!" She gave him a playful smack and then turned and opened the refrigerator, bent, and pulled out a sheet cake with white frosting and great big bows made out of pink icing. "Happy 80th Birthday Granny!" it announced in matching pink.

"Wow, Mom!" Roy said with great pride. "You've outdone yourself. How did you do the ribbons?"

"It's this stuff called fondant icing. A least that's what I think you call it. It comes already made in sheets. I just cut it in strips and laid it down, easy-peasy. Looks *just* like ribbons, doesn't it?" She smiled happily.

"Easy-peasy, *right*," he replied. "For *you* maybe. For the rest of us, not so much."

She rolled her eyes again, and he was struck for about the millionth time how she could be one of the girls from *The Brady Bunch* all grown up and a sixty-year-old. Not that she looked sixty. No way. Men hit on his mother at shopping malls and grocery stores all the time. She was oblivious. Roy was charmed—as long as the men weren't rude or lecherous.

"It's the stuff I used to make the underwear on Janet's cake," she said as matter-of-factly as she'd said the word "ribbons."

Janet being his cousin who'd turned twenty-one a few months before. When she'd come to visit him and showed him the photographs, it had shocked the shit out of him, his mother making such a thing (and it had already shocked the shit out of him that Janet, of all people, had visited him)! It had been one of those men's torso cakes, usually used for superhero birthday cakes for kids—Batman, Superman, Spider-Man. Except this man was wearing only underwear, and there was a Twinkie under them, looking just like a barely concealed straining erection.

"Oh you!" his mother had cried and patted his cheek. "It's the twenty-first century, my sweet *naïve* boy!"

Naïve. Right. *Sure.* If she only knew, and he caught himself rubbing his ass.

"Oh," she said now, eyeing him from top to bottom. "You did say something about showering and changing before people got here? I can't imagine how shocked Mother will be if she sees you in that—all, well, on display like that. You sure didn't get your father's genes!"

Roy's face blazed. He couldn't believe she'd said that, and he quickly pulled his tank top down to try and cover himself. He'd told Frank that he could arrive naked and she would hardly notice.

Frank. He smiled, seeing the handsome man in his mind's eye.

Stop it! You gotta put that behind you.

"Behind me," he whispered.

"And can you imagine what *Donald* would say about your getup?"

Donald. His uncle. Her brother. He could imagine. And it would be worse than embarrassing. It would be crude. *Gross* crude.

"I hear you," he said and grabbed his tossed-aside gym bag. "Ma!" he added and fled the room.

"Oh you!" came her voice.

He went to the bathroom he'd used all his life and quickly stripped down, then caught his reflection in the mirror. His heart sped up. He was looking at the reflection of a man who'd been fucked. Up the ass. Staring at himself he couldn't help but think of a different naked man. *Man.* Frank. And how his body had meshed with that other man's. Frank's. Having sex. And then the way those bodies had fit when they cuddled. Like the Lincoln Logs he'd played with as a kid.

He started to get an erection.

Geez, he thought. Hadn't he gotten any itch he could possibly have scratched for about a lifetime? Which made him think about that scratching, and that pumped his cock up all the more.

God.

Roy trembled.

What's going on? What was going on with him? *Can't think this way. It's done. Done and never to be done again. You did it.*

It was… yes… *hot.*

But done!

Not gay.

Roy studied himself closer, avoiding looking at his now fully erect penis. Did he look any different? He didn't think so.

Because I'm not different.

He'd read about this. When he was looking up… stories. That quite a few straight men had tried gay sex at least once: 6.9 percent.

The number was emblazoned in his mind—6.9. As big as the Hollywood sign.

Which was pretty normal. Why, more men were beginning to identify as bisexual than ever before.

Don't go there.

"Hurry up in there, son!" came his mother's call. "Everybody is going to start getting here soon!"

He froze, covered his erection, then laughed at himself for it. She couldn't see.

Except couldn't she, maybe? Didn't mothers have X-ray vision? Like the eyes on the back of their heads?

Roy shook it off and climbed in the shower. It was nice and hot and felt good. He washed and rinsed and… he was still hard. Almost hurting hard. He thought about turning the water to cold, but then…. Hell, why not do something about it?

Frank leapt to mind, and he took himself in a soapy hand and began to stroke himself. But no! He conjured pictures of Ramona instead. Pretty, sexy, ginger-haired Ramona, always willing to try *anything.* Pictured her taking him in hand and… and then he thought of where she led him, and that started other *horrible* thoughts, and God…. He stood there under the water (that wouldn't stay hot forever), his cock in hand, and then he closed his eyes and saw Frank down between his legs, looking at his cock as if it were water in the desert. More than that. With lust. Had any girl ever looked at his cock like that? He couldn't remember if they had.

He saw his hard-on slip into Frank's mouth and, *God*, the pleasure doubled, tripled, even though all he was using was his hand.

Fuck it. What difference did it make that he was picturing a man? It wasn't having *sex* with a man. What did it hurt?

So good. *So* good….

Then he reached back, slipped his fingers into his crack, found his tender hole—

Tender because I got fucked *today.*

—and toyed with it ever so slightly and—

Aaarrghh!

—he was cumming. Cumming hard, shooting in jets even though he'd had such a powerful orgasm only an hour or so ago. His legs nearly buckled from the pleasure of it, and it wasn't even as good as the one he'd shared with Frank. When Frank was holding him. Kissing him. Looking at him with beautiful blue eyes in such a fucking handsome face.

He shook the image away, fell back against the tiled wall, and somehow didn't fall. When the shocks finally passed, he could only marvel at it all.

Wow.

Roy's eyes went wide. Had he made that noise out loud?

But his mother wasn't knocking on the door asking him if he was all right, and she would be if he'd shouted as he thought he had. No. Somehow, he'd instinctively held his tongue. And at least his cock was going down now.

Quite suddenly, another pair of eyes came to mind. Staring at him from across a span of grass. Intense eyes. Eyes that had seemed to look into his soul. Why, he hadn't thought of that since…. That day, maybe. That night. What made him think of it now?

He rinsed quickly and turned off the water, got out—remembering the thousand million times his mother had told him to dry his feet first so he didn't make the pink furry bathroom mat all wet—and wiped himself down with the equally bright pink towel. Then he scrambled into jeans, a T-shirt that said Fear the Beard, socks, and tennies.

It was time to join the party.

CHAPTER FIVE

ROY STEPPED back into the kitchen as the first group of people arrived through the front door, the group probably being most of who was coming; Uncle Donald, Aunt Audrey, his cousins Nicholas and Janet—would wonders never cease?—and of course, Granny.

They were big people, all of them, although Granny had *lost* some weight over the last few years. Big and wide and always made sure that they didn't have to sit on any of the kitchen chairs behind the table, against the wall. They wanted to be able to sit back from the table. Which made getting to the refrigerator a bit of a problem. And Jesus, Uncle Donald hadn't even shaved. If he had a beard it would be one thing. But he was just scruffy in a nasty way. And his stringy graying hair didn't even look washed.

And Mom was worried about the way I looked?

Granny's eyes lit up behind her oval glasses, and she reached out and patted his cheek like his mother did. Or more likely, his mother did it the way Granny did. Her strawberry-blonde hair (not a hint of gray, and Roy had no idea if she dyed it and knew not to ask) was cut in a style similar to his mother's (or was it the other way around?) except a fair deal shorter, and she was wearing (lo and behold!) a light pink pantsuit. "So good to see you, Roy! I haven't seen you in forever. Where have you been?"

Roy's stomach lurched a bit at the question, Uncle Donald gave a "*Ha*," and Aunt Audrey made a sniffing sound. And his cousins?

Janet looked at him with… what? Pity? He remembered so clearly the day she'd come to see him while he was… away. How weird it had all been and how he'd wondered why she was there. Surely not just to show him pictures of her birthday cake.

And Nicholas, *wow*, nodded and gave him a fist bump. "Go, man," he said.

At least one of the four wasn't an asshole. And he supposed only two were total assholes.

"I told you, Granny," Roy's mother said. "Roy went away for a bit. But he's back!" She smiled radiantly in her *Brady Bunch* way.

Uncle Donald muttered something like "Away, my ass," but Mom glared at him and hissed, "There'll be *none* of that today!"

"Look at that," Granny said and tapped the edge of the glass bowl holding the potato salad. "And with red skins! My favorite."

"I know," Roy said as his relatives put several bags of chips, a pie, a vegetable platter, and a huge bowl of spaghetti with the meaty sauce already stirred in (he hated that) on the table.

"Oh, Audrey," Granny said. "You mixed the sauce in. I just hate that."

"It's because some people *hog* the sauce, Granny," his aunt snapped. She spared her husband and Roy a rather scathing glance, especially for so early in the proceedings. "And then some of us don't got nothing but noodles."

"*Have* nothing but," Granny whispered. She had been a school teacher for forty-eight years, had retired only two years before, and had wanted to wait until she'd taught for fifty years, but a heart condition had nixed that, to her displeasure. Correcting English was as much a part of her as flying was to a bird.

"It'll be fine," said Aunt Audrey.

"Fine as paint," Mom said.

And then Granny noticed the cake, big and glaring pink and near impossible to miss, but then there was a lot going on, wasn't there?

"Why, just look at that!" she exclaimed and reached for it, and for a second there, Roy thought she'd dip a finger right into it. He wasn't the only one, as several people reached out as if to stop her, but before they could, Granny raised her hands instead and gave a clap. "Just beautiful, Phyllis! It's just lovely."

His mother beamed, and then Granny *did* touch the cake, but ever so lightly. Touched one of the ribbons and then marveled as she realized it was made of icing. "How did you do that?"

His mother explained all about the fondant once more as everyone chose a chair around the table. Roy gave a quick glance and was relieved when he saw that at least one with a pillow tied to it (with dark pink ribbons) was available. The thin, plastic-covered cushioning of the chairs could be a problem.

Which made him think of Frank *again*.

"Why look at you!" Granny declared and reached out to pat his cheek again. "Why, you're just a-glowin'! What's got you a-smilin' so?"

Roy stiffened—*shit!*—and forced his smile all the bigger. "*You*, Granny. Happy birthday!"

Now she was the one glowing, and she said, "It's about time *somebody* wished me a happy birthday. *They* haven't." She swept a hand out to indicate her son and his family.

Said family glowered, but Granny seemed to be totally unaware.

"Now that's simply not true," Mom said. "Why, I wished you a happy last night *and* this morning on the phone. And I can't believe they"—she nodded at her brother and his family—"haven't. I bet you just don't remember in all the excitement!"

Mom. The eternal diplomat.

There was a knock on the kitchen door, and then it opened. "Hello" came a voice, and then in walked Mrs. Kelly, the neighbor Roy had known for a thousand years. Or at least it seemed that way. As long as he'd known anything or anyone, Mrs. Kelly had been around. With her big, funny, dark-rimmed glasses and her mop of gray-black hair, she'd watched over him many times when his parents, and later only his mom, were at work. Her last name was Wowereit, but he'd never been able to pronounce that as a kid, and so he called her Mrs. Kelly. He'd been delighted by her story about how her last name meant squirrel and was a nickname given to young men working in beekeeping. In the old days, she explained, beehives were kept in pine trees about fifteen feet above the ground, and the young beekeeper had to climb the tree to collect the honey, like a squirrel climbs trees for nuts.

She had lots of wonderful stories.

"Happy birthday, Billie Dee," she declared as she handed Granny a brightly wrapped flat box that was about nine by nine inches.

"Well, look at this!" Granny said and showed it to everyone. "Isn't this just as pretty as can be?"

Mrs. Kelly had also brought her famous meatballs in wine gravy he'd gotten such a kick out of as a kid. Hey! He was having wine, and he swore he felt all wobbly after eating it. It wasn't until years later that he found out the alcohol evaporated as it was cooked.

When she spotted Roy, Mrs. Kelly's eyes flickered, and her smile did as well, and then she hugged him and said, "It's so good to see you."

This was the way it was going to be, of course. He'd served time. It didn't matter what it was for. He was Al Capone. The Birdman of Alcatraz. The Teflon dude—or whatever he was called. At least, Roy felt he might as well be. But the hug was still tight, and he could feel how warm it was.

I'm such a disappointment.

Which made it all the clearer that he could *never* have sex with a man again. Then he really would be a disappointment to everyone.

God. I did it. I really, really had sex with a dude! I avoided it for six months. I fought for myself for six months. Had to do the full time because of it. And then I let some dude pick me up at a gas station.

Then, as if on cue:

"Hey!" exclaimed his uncle, grinning from ear to ear. "Why are faggots happy that they have nutsacks?"

A deep dread hit Roy. Deep and awful and twisting. *Faggots....*

Then, before anyone could answer, his uncle called out, "Because they use them as mud flaps!"

To Roy's surprise, the room went quiet. Some of his family seemed to pretend they hadn't heard the joke. Janet gave a half laugh. Nicholas shrugged and weirdly mouthed, "Sorry." Aunt Audrey did what she always did—ignored her husband and got up to start laying out the food.

"You don't have to do that," Mom said and went to help.

"Oh, come on everybody. It's funny!"

"*I* thought it was funny, Daddy," Janet said, sucking up.

It hurt Roy. And he didn't know why.

"Okay, then," Uncle Donald said. "How about this one? What's the difference between a homo and a refrigerator?" And once more, before anyone could hope to answer: "The fridge doesn't fart when you pull the meat out!"

Pull the meat out. Roy stiffened. *There was meat in me.*

"That's disgusting, Donald," Mom said while pulling paper plates from a corner kitchen cabinet. "And not proper conversation for a birthday party."

"I don't even *get* it," said Granny. "*Stupid* joke." She picked up Mrs. Kelly's present and shook it.

"*Fine!*" Uncle Donald cried. "Fine. How about this one? What are the two great Polish lies?" Five seconds later: "The check is in your mouth, and I won't come in the mail."

Granny *tsk*ed. Looked around. Started to pick at the tape on her gift. Audrey and Mom started loudly putting things on the table. Nicholas left the room, and a television came on.

"Two blondes fell down a hole. One of 'em says, 'It sure is dark down here, isn't it?' And the other one says, 'I don't know! I can't see!'"

Mom crossed her arms. "Are you forgetting your sister and mother are blonde?" she asked.

Jesus! Roy thought. Told himself he needed to say something. To speak up. His mom was defending blondes. And he was just standing here. But what was he supposed to do? Defend homosexuals?

I'm not a homosexual. But Frank was. And those ugly fag jokes were being told about *him*.

God!

Last week his uncle could have told these jokes and he would have laughed along. For show, even though he hadn't liked them then either. It was a way to keep the jokes quick and short and done with. But now? Things were somehow different.

Nothing is different.

And then his uncle told a joke about black people. Why are so many African Americans being killed in Iraq? Because when they are ordered to get down, they all get up and start dancing! But of course he didn't use the words "African Americans," did he? Roy's teeth came together in a clink, and he closed his eyes. A clear picture of a man who had helped keep him safe for six months leapt to mind. What would Demaine Lewis think of him standing here letting his uncle tell such ugly jokes? God. And the man hadn't been here ten minutes. Did he really think he was funny?

But hey, whose fault was it that he was telling such jokes? Uncle Donald's? Or everyone who had sat around this very kitchen table and let him tell such jokes in the first place?

He thought about Demaine, how the guy had helped watch out for him and made sure a group of four men hadn't taken his virgin ass before he'd offered it up to Frank. Somehow he thought they wouldn't have been as careful as Frank had been. Wouldn't have asked him if he was sure he wanted to be fucked. Made sure he enjoyed it.

Demaine was black. Demaine was that word Uncle Donald had used. What would he think if he overheard this conversation?

Roy could see Demaine in that eternal moment. Could see his dark eyes in that handsome dark face, and he was ashamed. And finally he opened his mouth to say something, say, "Please, Uncle Donald." But before he could....

"Donald," Granny said, not looking at her son and setting her present on the table before her. "I think you need to go out back for a soothing smoke, don't you?"

Once more the room went silent. Except for a little gasp from Janet. Everyone was frozen. And Granny? Her eyes were intense. Clear. Totally aware. Lucid.

Donald opened his mouth.

"Donald," she repeated. Voice cold. Steel.

He closed it with a snap. Looked down. And then strode out of the kitchen.

There was another long silence, in which Roy was ashamed. *An eighty-year-old woman stopped the ugliness. And I just stood here.*

The silence was broken by the doorbell. Roy practically fled the room, only to find Nicholas already opening the front door. More guests, of course.

Things got better then. Food was eaten. There was laughter. Beers were opened and freely drunk. Granny had a couple herself. Presents were opened. It was nice. Roy thought of Frank. He smiled.

Finally, people began to leave.

Granny said she was tired, and Donald and company said they would take her home. On her way out, she reached up and patted Roy's cheek again and leaned in close to press her forehead against his. Whispered, "I am so happy you were home in time for my party. You're my favorite. You know that, don't you?"

The words shocked him, even though they had always been close.

"And I like seeing you smile. I haven't seen you smile so much in a long time."

Roy gave a little gasp of surprise, and before he knew it, she was hugging him tight. It was *so* tight it was like she was pressing her heart to his. A strange weight lifted off his shoulders, and the kinks in his stomach smoothed out. He hugged her back, and then, for some strange reason, everything was wonderful.

When the hug was over, after much clearing of throats and a long sigh and a moan from Uncle Donald, Granny pulled back and told him she loved him.

"Love you too, Granny."

"Glowing," she said. "You're different. Glowing. Have you met someone? Are you in love?"

Roy gasped. Because of course he wasn't. There was no way he could be. But God, she saw something different. Did anyone else see it? His mother had said something when he first arrived.

I need to forget what happened!

Because he *wasn't* different, dammit! And he certainly wasn't glowing.

Once everyone was gone, he helped his mother clean up, and then he went to his room. Decided to go to bed early. He hadn't found a new place yet. It was another of the things he couldn't tell Frank. That he lived at home. Somehow it would make him feel less like a man. Twenty-six and living at home, for God's sake.

But he would get an apartment when he saved up a little money. Soon everything would be back to normal. All he had to do was wait.

Sleep was a long time arriving, though. In the end, he had to masturbate so he could sleep. And try as he might, he couldn't help it when his mind's eye brought Frank to his bed.

CHAPTER SIX

FRANK BROUGHT potato salad to Cody and Harry's place that evening. The aroma of the cooking dinner filled the room. It smelled wonderful.

"Oh good, it's the red-skin kind," Cody said, taking it from Frank and heading to the kitchen. He was a slim man but fit, although he hated working out. Mostly because he hated gyms and exercising in public. But he and his lover did yoga, or he did, mostly, as well as some home exercises. "Gotta keep up my butt for Harry," he had told Frank one night after too many cosmopolitans, and he'd blushed a brilliant crimson. His face was a strange amalgamation of mismatching features and angles that somehow worked in combination.

"We're having cosmos on the balcony. I hope that's okay."

Of course they were. That was pretty damned standard. And okay. He didn't like to drink them at a bar—they were overpriced and sort of silly—but here? In this sanctuary? Fine. Fine as paint.

He looked around the living room and didn't see Harry, so he took a wild guess and walked through the double glass doors. Indeed, there he was, sitting on a deck chair, feet clad in beat-up old Dockers propped on the black metal patio table, looking all cute and bearish.

"Hey, Harry," Frank said and leaned over and gave his bearish friend a kiss. There was pink sugar in his barely-a-mustache. An all-but-empty martini glass with a mouth-sized swatch of pink sugar missing from its edge sat on the table.

"Hey, Frank," Harry said, and Frank noticed his new glasses.

"*Hey*," Cody bitched, sweeping out onto the brick balcony with a fresh tray of pink cosmopolitans, complete with lemon peel and pink sugar. "I didn't get a kiss."

Frank laughed and grabbed Cody's face and, careful not to upend the tray, gave him a big smack of a kiss.

"Harry," Cody said after the kiss, "get your feet off the table. People *eat* off the table."

Harry sighed. "They don't eat *off* the table. There are plates in between. Do you think that the dirt on my shoes is going to crawl up the underside of the plates and then onto the top and get—"

"Harry! Feet. *Off* table."

Harry shook his head and sat up, moving his feet.

Cody carefully picked up a glass filled to the very brim and handed it to Frank. "Your cocktail, *mon-shur*," he said with a hideous French accent. "You might want to sip it before trying to sit down."

"Of course," Frank said and sipped. When it seemed safe, he started to sit.

"Wait," said Cody. "What shall we drink to?"

"The fact that this afternoon I fucked about the hottest guy I've fucked in years," Frank wanted to say, but then didn't. At least not yet. "To friends?" he offered instead.

"No." Harry sat up and held out his new glass, apparently not caring how precariously filled it was. "To the people of Bolivia!"

Cody grinned a very happy grin, and Frank shook his head and toasted. The toast didn't make a lick of sense. But that was an evening with Harry and Cody.

At least he could sit down now. He could still smell whatever was cooking, even out here with the nice breeze. A set of wind chimes he'd bought them made music on the air. "What are we having for dinner?"

"Meat loaf," said Harry.

Meat loaf?

"You said your dad never made it," Cody said.

Because Frank's father never cooked things like that. Rarely cooked at all. And even though there had been a plethora of women—and assorted wives—who had moved through their homes and lives, he couldn't remember one of them ever making meat loaf.

"I thought that was a terrible shame," Cody added. "So that's what we're having."

In fact, curious, Frank had bought a Swanson's meat loaf once and wished he hadn't by the first bite—third for certain. Way too sweet. Not that he didn't like sweet, but it was meat, after all. Or at least partially.

And meat shouldn't be sweet. He hoped whatever Cody was serving was better.

"And he's making his macaroni and cheese, and that's a religious experience," Harry said. "The best I've ever had. And I've had the mac and cheese at Peachtree!"

Frank wasn't sure what that meant. But then, there were lots of things these two said that didn't make much sense to him. It was like he was hearing the beginnings of stories but not always their ends. Although he had heard lots of stories in the year or two they'd been friends.

At least he liked macaroni and cheese. There had been about a zillion boxes of Kraft macaroni and cheese made in his lifetime. He made it pretty often since he'd moved out on his own. Boy, that had surprised his old man, hadn't it? That he had tired of living the gypsy life. That he wanted to settle. Put down some kind of roots.

"But why here?" his father had said. "I mean, Kansas City? Why not San Francisco? Or New York? What are some of those other gay places? Key West? Provincetown?" His father hadn't gotten the least bit upset the day Frank had flung his being gay in his face, and that had been a shock, what with the way the man loved women. Waxed poetic about them. Praised their line and form. Insisted the best classical Greek sculptor could never match their beauty. Or how he would go on about their scent. Their hair. Their skin. Their privy council—one of his words for vagina. And the words he had! Altar of Venus. Phoenix nest. Nature's treasury. Kitty *royale*. Flower. Mound of heaven. And about how he could simply look at them all day. How the only thing that bothered him about Frank being gay was that his son couldn't see the poetic beauty of a woman.

Frank told his old man that Greek statues were fine. Sure. Beautiful. But he'd much rather look at Hercules than Venus. And that he liked Kansas City. A lot. And that it was blooming. Getting more cultured. It was fertile ground waiting for what he could do to help make it even better.

"You mean what I taught you," his father said.

"Of course, Glen," he'd replied. He hadn't called the man Father or Dad since he was maybe sixteen. Which had been his father's idea. He'd insisted. And Frank hadn't minded because by then he'd realized just how much of a father Glen wasn't. Provider? Sure. Frank had wanted for almost nothing. Teacher? That too. He had taught his son a craft that would keep him comfortable well into his old age.

But not much of a dad. No picnics or games of catch, throwing a baseball, or even mowing the lawn. All those things a father and son did. They'd never even owned a house but rented instead. It made no sense when they never stayed in one place more than a couple of years—and that was only because several projects had conveniently lined up (once, magically, it had actually allowed him to sort of have a boyfriend for over a year when he was fifteen and sixteen).

Of course, there were worse fathers. He knew that. All he had to do was talk to a trick after sex, when there *was* talk, to know that. Lying there in the sticky, sweaty, sometimes wonderful afterglow, listening to stories of men who weren't ready to go and needed to talk to someone— anyone—as they told him things that made him cringe and want them to shut up and leave.

"You okay?" Harry asked, startling him back to reality, the porch, cosmos with pink sugar on the rims and in mustaches, and friends.

"I'm okay," he said. And then to prove it, he did something he actually hadn't intended to do. Had planned to keep to himself.

But why the hell should he do that?

"I fucked this hot dude today," he said. *Roy. His name is Roy.*

Cody rolled his eyes dramatically, and Harry grinned and leaned forward, resting his elbow on the black wire-mesh top of the table, his chin in his upturned palm. "Of course you did."

Frank drank down half his cosmopolitan and leaned back in his chair. "And God, he was hot. About the hottest fuck I've had in forever."

For some reason, the word "fuck" sounded a little... harsh. Which was stupid. He loved the word "fuck." He proselytized about how men should use the word. That it wasn't dirty. Neither was the word "asshole." Christ, the words men used for their assholes! Starfish. Back door. Pucker. Rosebud. Entrance. Love hole. Pleasure zone. And best yet, flowerpot! Like something his father would come up with.

But Harry was looking at him in eager anticipation, and Cody was pretending not to, but Frank knew him well enough by now to know he was. The words came out, but surprisingly edited.

"And you're never going to believe it. Remember when I told you about that guy in the orange jumpsuit I saw a month or so ago?"

"The one where I told you to buy a costume online," Harry asked, "and get someone to wear it for you so—"

"I saw him at a gas station," Frank said, cutting him off. "And he was wearing these *very* tight biker shorts that left *nothing* to the imagination. I mean, you could see"—Frank pointed at his own thigh with one finger to demonstrate—"him hanging all the way down to here. So I asked if he wanted to be… serviced."

"Serviced?" Cody asked, a little sarcastically but proving he had been listening.

"You know… because I saw him at a *service* station," Frank lied. "And he said okay, and while I was blowing him, I took a chance and rimmed him—"

Cody looked up from the fingernails he'd been pretending to examine and said, "Took a chance? Like on a new brand of toothpaste?"

"—and I did such a good job that he let me—"

"Yes?" exclaimed Harry, "He let you what?"

Let me fuck him, Frank thought.

"Fuck me. Fuck me, Frank. Oh Christ! So good. So much… better *than I ever thought.* God*!"*

But then quite suddenly, for some reason he didn't entirely understand, Frank didn't want to share what had happened. He saw Roy's blue eyes looking up at him with desire and complete trust, and he couldn't finish the story.

"I should tell you a different story instead."

"*Aww…,*" Harry whined.

"No, really. You'll like it."

Cody reached out and casually picked up his pink drink from the black metal table and began to swirl the half cosmo around in the glass. He gave Frank a funny, piercing look that made him uncomfortable, but then as quickly looked away, as if bored.

"It was Thanksgiving last year," Frank replied, pulling the story out like a file from his brain. "I was horny."

"Which so rarely happens," Cody said, raising an eyebrow, a flicker of a smile at the corner of his mouth.

"I got on E-MaleConnect and in no time found this guy who wanted to come over, as long as his lover could watch."

Harry's eyebrows shot up.

"The picture is of this really pretty guy, and while I'm usually more into butch guys—"

"Frank," said Harry, rolling his eyes—but not nearly as flamboyantly as Cody might, "are there any men who aren't your type?"

"—I told him to come over." He shrugged. "I have no trouble with an audience. And this means the lover knows, and the one thing I don't do is help someone cheat. I've let ladies watch me with their husbands."

Up went Harry's eyebrows while Cody looked on in mock horror.

"The guy gets there, and damn, pretty isn't the word. He is *beautiful*. He's got long blond hair and this nice Tony Stark–like scruffiness on his jaw, really blue eyes—a kind of blond Jesus, you know?"

"Like Jesus hasn't been painted with blond hair and blue eyes since forever," Cody said with a laugh.

"His left eyebrow was pierced out to the side"—Frank pinched his brow to show where—"and the whole look is really working for him. He introduces me to this older guy, reminded me a bit of Christopher Walken—"

"Younger, almost-sexy *Dogs of War* or *The Deer Hunter* Christopher Walken?" Harry butted in again, "or older, creepier Christopher Walken in *Seven Psychopaths* or *Nine Lives*?"

"Older." Geez! "They've brought a bottle of whisky and ask if I have ice, and I'm not usually a 'sit around and have a few drinks first' kind of guy, but what the hell, this was Balblair Single Malt Scotch Whisky. I find out while we're 'getting to know each other' that my trick is some kind of big-deal-and-getting-bigger model. Like in Barcelona and Paris and shit. Runway model, and he's getting his pictures in *Vogue* and stuff like that, and the whole time I'm wondering why they're telling me all this. Like, aren't they worried I'll talk and it will hurt his career?" He shrugged at the strange memory of it. "Anyway, we finished up our drinks and then blondie stands up and says, 'Why don't we get this show on the road?'

"I point down the hall, and he turns around and starts in that direction, and I get my first good look at his ass, and I am wowed. I mean this kid's ass is to fucking die for, and I make up my mind right then and there that I've got to have it, even though they've come over so he can fuck *me*."

"Ohh…," Harry whispered.

Cody stood up and in a quiet voice said, "Wait," and dashed from the room. He was back a few minutes later with a simply enormous cocktail shaker, and he refilled their glasses while nodding and gesturing for Frank to continue.

Do they really think this story is hot with all the interruptions?

"So we get to the bedroom and start making out and tearing each other's clothes off, and then he climbs onto the bed, and I jump on him. I spread those legs and grab that firm perfect ass—"

And for some reason it was Roy's ass Frank saw in his mind's eye then, and while not as small and round, it was still damned sexy. He continued his story, hoping they hadn't noticed.

"—and I spread those cheeks and dive in. He's got this perfect little pink puckered asshole, and I just start, like, *making* out with it."

Cody and Harry sighed. They always liked stories with rimming.

"Blondie tells me to wait, wait, that's not why I'm here," Frank said, and then in a mocking, almost-effeminate voice finished with "'*I'm* here to top *you*, and I don't *like* having my ass eaten, and *oh oh oh oh…!*'" Frank grinned and wiggled his own ass. "He keeps trying to tell me to stop, but he can't because he keeps making those '*oh oh oh*!' noises, and then he stops fighting me and just collapses, moaning like a Siamese cat in heat, and then he's thrusting his ass back in my face, and I am in *heaven.*"

"Frank conquers again," Harry said in a worshipful tone.

"Then I flip him over like a ragdoll, and I see this big ankh tattoo right about here—" Frank slapped himself between his cock and his hip. "—way down low, and I bend him over in half so far he could have sucked his own dick—he did have a pretty big dick, nice one too—and I am tongue fucking him by now. He's totally open to me, and his eyes are rolling back in their sockets, and I have no damned idea what Christopher Walken is doing all this time, but I know now is when I am going to fuck blondie."

Harry and Cody both slammed their drinks, and Cody reached for the shaker.

"I tell him too. I say, 'I'm going to fuck you silly now,' and suddenly he's all, 'No! Wait! I'm supposed to fuck you!' and I am getting out a condom and tearing it open and sliding it down my cock." Once more Frank sort of demonstrated, and he was loving the fact that his two friends were going to have some wild sex after he left.

"Blondie is still saying no, and I reach down with a finger and hush him. I said, 'You know how fucking fantastic my tongue felt up your love hole? Well I promise you're going to love my dick even more.'

"He just hushes up then, and I take aim, and I'm telling you I slid into him like a hot knife into butter. Top? Right! *Sure* he was."

Then once more he thought of Roy and how relatively easily he'd slid into him. He had been thinking about it for days, and he'd decided that if Roy had a girlfriend, then he was sneaking her dildos when she wasn't around.

Frank cleared his throat. "I start slow, but soon I am banging the living Jesus out of him. He's shouting out and *begging* me to fuck him. 'Fuck me! Harder, goddammit, harder!'"

"And you still don't know what Christopher Walken is doing?" Harry asked with a groan.

"Nope. And I didn't care. All I cared about was getting my nut off, and I'm getting closer and closer, and I tell him and he goes all wide-eyed and tells me he wants to see. 'Take it off! Shoot on me!'

"I mean, it was like something out of a porn movie, and I pull out of him and drop his legs to either side of me and yank off my condom, and by this time he's jacking, and I fist myself a couple of times, and then I cum like I haven't since I was about fifteen. Between the kid and me, we drench him!"

"Fuck me," said Harry.

"*Later*!" said Cody.

"So I roll off of him, and we lay there panting like dogs on a hot day, and finally he rolls half on me and gives me the sweetest kiss and thanks me. All that business tone is gone. For just a minute, the kid seemed like he was just that—a kid. Although I know he was eighteen. He was twenty-two, in fact. I checked his ID, believe-you-fucking-me!"

Frank smiled at that and remembered it, remembered thinking since then how nice that sweetness at the end had been. He recalled Roy again and how sweet the cuddling after had been, and—

No! Don't go there.

Frank reached for the shaker, but Cody held out a hand. "It's empty. Let me get another round." He stood, reached for the cocktail mixer, and left.

"Wow," Harry sighed, apparently liking this story, and Frank was glad because it had come easier than the one he had started to tell about Roy, and it had come with no funny feelings in his tummy. He thought that yes, Harry and Cody were going to have fun tonight, and that made him happy.

After Cody brought the next round of drinks, the conversation went to regular things, although Frank thought the electricity never quite left the air. They chatted a bit about the most recent Melissa McCarthy movie and whether it was worth seeing or not. Harry said he thought he could wait until it was available at the local Redbox; Cody thought it would be fun to see at the Cinemark at the Plaza in their VIP section and have a few cocktails. Harry thought it was too much to spend when Cody made better cocktails than anyone he knew. Frank just watched them go back and forth on it as if it were a Ping-Pong game and supposed this was part of what made them a couple. He told them that too.

But it seemed Cody hadn't forgotten story time entirely. "This guy with the orange jumpsuit…," he began.

"He didn't have it on," Frank said.

"Yes. I know. You told us about his biker shorts." Cody touched his inner thigh with a fingertip.

Frank laughed.

"But what I thought was interesting was that you quickly changed the story."

Frank stiffened ever so slightly and hoped Cody didn't notice. From the sharp look in his eyes, he thought maybe Cody had. "Oh?" Frank said.

Cody nodded. "I think there was something different about this one."

"They're all different," Frank said. "Which is why you'll never catch me asking someone to move in with me. I like all those differences."

Cody gave a very slight shrug. Then he leaned in. "But you didn't want to tell his story. Either the guy was terrible in bed and it was a bust. Or you're keeping this story for your lonesome."

Frank caught the twinkle that was now in those eyes. "Is that what you think?"

Cody nodded. "You going to deny it?"

Frank sat there for what felt like a long time but was probably only seconds. Then he shrugged and said, "You know what? I think I'm going to plead the fifth on this one."

Because he and Harry didn't need to know everything, now did they?

CHAPTER SEVEN

HARRY HAD told Frank a surprising story a few months back while Cody was at his salon, Shear Fantasies. The two of them were just about as madly in love as two men could get, and they had been together for seven years now—Frank could hardly imagine seven weeks, seven months if the guy was a stud supreme—and they fully intended on going for the whole forever thing.

But then a year or so ago, as in love as they were, things had begun to, well, stagnate a bit. Games like the UPS thing had spiced things up, Harry told him one night after way too many cosmopolitans. But then that stopped working. Their sex life started to decline, and it worried the both of them. So they got to talking. A healthy sex life was important, especially for men as young as they were. Both of them were just a few years older than Frank was.

The idea of an open relationship wasn't good for either of them. At the very mention of it, both struck it down.

Yet… there was another way. They began to whisper aloud thoughts of a three-way. But how to go about it? Craigslist seemed risky and gross. The meet-up websites caused them both more anxiety than anticipation. The whole thing was resolved one night at Hamburger Mary's during last year's Pride weekend.

Seems this guy, thick and hairy enough for Cody to find attractive and fit enough that he tripped Harry's trigger, started coming on to them, buying them drinks, instinctively finding the fine line between teasing and going too far. After a few rounds, he was cuddling with both of them, touching them, telling them how hot they looked, how much he would love to see them together naked. It was the word "together" that made them comfortable. And the beer bust.

By the end of the evening, Cody and Harry began glancing at each other and sending "is this okay?" messages with their eyes. Harry was hard. He had no trouble seeing that Cody was as well. Not through those slacks he liked to wear at the salon.

When the guy asked them if they wanted to go home with him, they said yes.

But once they got there, things changed pretty fast. For one thing, the dude had gone from Impulse Speed to about Warp Factor Ten. And second, the kisses that had been kinda hot and sexy at Hamburger Mary's beer bust, now that there was a bed only a few feet away, suddenly seemed… wrong.

Really wrong.

Harry found he didn't like seeing someone kiss Cody anymore. He wanted to rip the guy off of Cody and fling him across the room!

And the look on Cody's face.

"Thank God," Harry said. "I could see he felt the same way."

"What did you do?" Frank asked, not understanding in the least. The story had been getting *him* hard.

"I pretended to get sick," Harry said. Went to the bathroom and filled the glass he found there with water and splashed it… "as noisily as I could into his toilet and pretended I was throwing up and asked Cody to take me home."

"Poor guy," Frank muttered, thinking about the man who had spent all evening seducing them into going home with him only to get a pair of royally blue balls for his trouble.

"No, Cody *wanted* to leave."

Frank didn't explain that he hadn't been talking about Cody.

"After that, we knew all that wasn't for us. I only wanted Cody. And he wanted only me."

Frank tried to pretend he got it, but he just didn't. In fact, he also wondered why the whole tale Harry had shared surprised him. Good God, seven years?

He smiled and nodded and gave Harry a fist bump and knew then and there he would never be rolling in the hay with the bear.

Because after their experience with the guy on Pride weekend, Harry and Cody had decided what they already knew. They were monogamous.

However, they liked reading sexual stories. It turned out to be the spice they were looking for. They would find ones they liked online and then read them to each other, and "Bang each other's brains out!" Harry said with a grin.

They liked Frank's stories. And it tickled him to know they were living vicariously through him.

"SO, DOES my model story earn me my meal tonight?"

"Heavens yes," cried Cody. "My God!" He looked at Harry, said, "I've changed my mind," and then mouthed, "I'm going to be the model."

Frank burst into laughter, and Cody and Harry both blushed. Had Cody really thought he hadn't read his lips? Especially considering how dramatic he could be at times?

Weird. It was all so weird.

But then they really didn't get him either. Not in the end. Because even as good friends as they had grown to be, they simply couldn't believe he was happy being single. They were always trying to hook him up with eligible bachelors. They just *knew* if he met the right guy, he'd find out they were right, and he'd settle down and live happily ever after.

"Then who would tell you stories?" he would ask.

And when the apartment buzzer went off and Cody jumped out of his chair and ran off to answer it at about the speed of the Flash, Frank got an awful feeling.

Sure enough, a few minutes later a handsome blond guy, carrying two bottles of wine, came in through the front door.

"I brought red and white," Frank heard him say in a nice deep voice. "I didn't know what you were having."

"Meat loaf," Harry said as Frank reluctantly followed him off the balcony and into the living room.

"Meat loaf?" the guy said, eyebrows raised, obviously surprised.

"You *did* say you missed home-cooked meals," Harry replied.

"I wasn't complaining!" the handsome man said, and his cheeks went pink.

"Frank has never had meat loaf," Cody said, gesturing with a magician-like wave of his hand.

"You've never had meat loaf?" the man asked.

"Only Swanson's," Frank said.

The man grimaced.

God, what if Cody is making a Swanson's meat loaf? Frank wondered with horror. And as if realizing the same thing, the man quickly said, "Not that there's anything *wrong* with Swanson's...."

Cody made a pretend barfing face. "Are you out of your mind? *Blech*! Too sweet! Not that I have anything against sweet, but meat isn't supposed to be sweet!"

"Yes!" Frank cried. "That's exactly what I thought."

"So, Harry, are you going to introduce your friend?" Cody asked.

"Oh shit! Yeah!" The friend turned out to be Jim Musgrave, a bartender at the Meridian Hotel, where Harry worked as a front desk clerk.

"And this is Frank Sinclair," Harry told Jim and pointed to Frank.

Jim held out his hand, and Frank couldn't help but flash on Roy. He made up his mind then and there he was taking Jim Musgrave back to his place. He had been thinking about Roy all day, and it was ridiculous. He even flirted with Jim. Let him know through casual comments how attractive he found him.

But as they sat and had another round of cosmopolitans, which Jim the bartender declared were some of the best he'd ever had (Cody beamed) and then dinner—the meat loaf turned out to be pretty fantastic and actually went wonderfully with the pinot noir—Frank found his thoughts returning over and over again to Roy. He kept thinking Roy might really have enjoyed this evening. Seeing the range of gay men from slightly flamboyant Cody to the pretending-to-be-lecherous Harry to the very-straight-acting Jim to Frank himself, who he hoped defied categories or labels, Roy might realize there were all kinds of gay men, and he didn't need to be afraid of the whole gay thing. As it was, Frank suspected Roy was gay but was either in denial or simply didn't know.

Soon the wine was gone, and Frank told them not to worry. He had another bottle at home, and since his apartment was only at the end of the hall, he would go fetch it. Cody and Harry knew where Frank lived, of course, but he mentioned it for Jim's benefit. If he had anything to say about it, Jim wouldn't have to worry about driving home tonight. He had to get Roy out of his mind, and a good roll in the sheets with masculine Jim would *just* do the trick.

But when he got there, when he went to his bedroom to straighten up so it didn't look so I-fucked-somebody-else-earlier-today, something happened. He stood there looking at his bed, and he could *see* Roy. He could see Roy *under* him, looking up at him with those swimming-pool-blue eyes that started out filled with both desire and trust and then rolled back with pleasure bordering on ecstasy at having Frank inside him.

He bent over, brought Roy's pillow to his nose, and thought maybe, just maybe, he could still smell Roy on it.

Frank stood. Shook himself. "I'm going nuts!"

He found the bottle of wine, a merlot that he hoped wouldn't be too dry after the cosmos and the sweeter wines they'd just finished, and went back to Harry and Cody's determined to get Jim home with him before the hour was out.

When he let himself in, he went into the kitchen for the bottle opener before remembering it was out on the balcony. He joined his friends just in time to hear Jim say, "God, I look at the two of you and I am so damned envious. I want what you have. I'm tired of one-night stands, you know? Tired of slinking home in the walk of shame. I want to be with someone. Forever."

And then Frank knew. He wasn't taking Jim home.

He held up the bottle and then opened it, but Jim didn't want any because he said he had to drive home soon. Of course he did.

Harry put an arm around Cody's shoulder, pulled him even closer, and kissed the top of his head. Frank didn't know how they could be comfortable with those black metal armrests between them.

And Jim wanted that?

Stupid!

Frank knew the truth. He'd seen it with his father all his life: an endless parade of women who came in and out of their lives like… why, like floats in a parade. Usually they lasted only a season at most, or as long as it took his old man to finish a job somewhere in the big wide world. Germany. France. Austria. Greece. Italy. Frank had never really known a home until he settled in Kansas City.

But hell, Glen was right—Frank had *seen* the world. What other kid could say that?

Sometimes his father would say, "I really like this one," after introducing her—Gerda, Angélique, Liesl, Toula, Caterina—and, "You know, this one just might turn out to be your new mama!"

The first few times Glen had made such claims, Frank—that boy Frank once was—had gotten excited. A mother! Someone to kiss his forehead and make him a birthday cake and tuck him in at night. Someone to love. Someone to love *him*.

But, after a few of those had come and gone, he began to give up hope.

In fact, Frank warned one of those women he really liked—Caterina, who would have made a wonderful mother—because by then he was getting way too old to ever think he could have a mother.

"Look, lady," he said that bright afternoon with the Tuscan sun streaming through the window, just after his tutor had left for that day, "you don't want nothing to do with my dad."

"*Anything*," she said, and he was confused for a moment until he realized that *she* had corrected *his* English.

Then she asked him if he wanted some gelato, which he found out was an Italian ice cream, and they got on bikes and rode a few blocks away to a little shop for some. She told him to get what he wanted, but when he asked for the chocolate, she talked him into *pistacchio*, and he was glad she did. He was surprised when it wasn't green like the pistachio ice cream from the United States but closer to an off-white. It was utterly delicious. He couldn't remember what flavor she had, but he would forever remember what he had, and sometimes—now—he could still taste it.

And he would forever remember when she looked at him through a fall of dark hair and said, "You think I don't know about your father? I *know* about your father. I know just what kind of man he is. *Lo so*. And that is okay. That is fine. *Tuo padre?* Your father? He is a man who loves the women, and I don't see that any woman will ever tie him down. Make him their own. *Va bene così*—I am fine with that. I don't think I will ever find the man who wants me *per sempre*—forever."

"*I* do," Frank blurted, and she told him he was *adorabile*.

She ruffled his hair and offered him a bit of her gelato—*limone*; he very suddenly remembered it was lemon—and then she told him she would stay as long as it was good for all of them.

Then, at just a year—she even went with them to France—when he thought he might have a forever mother, she left. She was just gone. No note. Nothing.

That was when he knew. There wasn't *per sempre*. Nothing was forever. They all left him. Even his own mother had left him.

His heart hardened that day. He actually felt it happen, deep in his chest.

But not long after that, he discovered the joy of sex with a Greek boy named Kostas and he knew, knew, *knew* what *did* exist. A boy named Kostas and that marvelous summer were forever. *Gia pánta.*

Blowjobs.

Fucking.

That lasted. Or at least when you were young enough to get it. And he planned on having enough money that he would be able to afford it when he was a dirty old man.

And now he looked at Harry and Cody and felt sorry for them. They didn't know what he did. He gave them six more months. Then they would be over. His stories wouldn't keep them together any longer than that.

But the thought was actually like a little spike in his heart, and....

"Frank?" Cody asked. "You okay?"

He'd done it again. Gone away. "I'm fine. Too much wine. I need to go home."

"I know," said Jim. "Me too."

Frank looked at the handsome man who was envious of Harry and Cody's relationship and was tired of one-night stands and wanted to be with someone forever. Sad. So sad.

He told them then that he had an appointment with a client in the morning, and he really needed to be going. Which was only a half lie because he did have an appointment, although it wasn't until one in the afternoon.

Harry and Cody made sure he and Jim exchanged phone numbers. He even took a picture of Jim so he could link it with the number and know for sure which calls not to answer.

"Did we do something wrong?" Harry asked him in the hall, obviously not wanting Jim to hear. "We know you say you don't like us setting you up, but Jim is such a nice guy. And he's lonely. And a horndog. So I thought he might be the exception to your rule. He's told me he's so tired of being single and...."

God. You're just making it worse and worse, Harry! Shut up.

Frank didn't say that out loud, of course. "You didn't do anything wrong," he assured his friend.

"Okay," said Harry and hugged him tight. He stood back. Then his eyes went wide. "Oh! Whatever happened to Christopher Walken?"

"He's got a new movie coming out very soon," Frank replied.

"Huh?" Harry laughed. "No…. The one with the model? The one…."

"I don't know. He stayed in the shadows, and when blondie got dressed I saw his… friend never got *un*dressed. They insisted that I have another whisky, and all I wanted them to do was leave, but Christ, it was Balblair. And then they left, and I never saw them again."

Which was mostly true.

The next night they contacted him and asked for a repeat before they went home to France, or wherever it was, and he told them no. They tried to talk him into it. He said he was coming down with something and couldn't. But the truth was that he didn't want a repeat. Not even with a runway model. There was something creepy about the whole thing once he could think about it with a mind that wasn't horny.

Impulsively, he hugged Harry again, and then he went back to his apartment, showered, brushed his teeth, and crawled into bed.

He didn't know exactly when it was that he took Roy's pillow and hugged it tight.

CHAPTER EIGHT

ROY TRIED to stay away. He tried. But after five days, as if he had no control, he returned to the scene of the crime.

Not the gas station of course, where it all began. And certainly not Frank's bed, where it all ended. But the building where it all took place.

He wasn't able to park in front. Those spaces, bumper to bumper, were taken. But there was a place across the street, and he sat there now in his electric-blue Jeep, top down, and looked up at the old redbrick building.

It was really rather nice. Nine or ten stories. It was hard to tell because the top floor was different, with white marble or something, and cornices, and impressions of old-fashioned faces carved deep into the surface.

There were balconies of the same redbrick as most of the building, and thinking about it, he couldn't remember seeing balconies like that on any buildings over three stories high. The more common wrought iron balconies had always made him nervous. He supposed he had a bit of a fear of heights. Or at least of falling. The brick balconies must be nice, especially for the upper residents.

Like Frank. His apartment was on the sixth floor.

There were columns in front of the building and a protected porch with at least one swing he could see. An awning in front of the foyer doors bore the name Oscar Wilde Apartments in fancy lettering. The words were repeated—Oscar Wilde—in the stonework over the porch.

He sat there for a good ten minutes before asking himself what the hell he was doing. Did he think if he waited long enough, he'd see Frank stroll through the front door? Frank had made a comment the day they'd met about how lucky he'd been to get a space to park out front. Roy'd had to park nearly a block away.

No. More likely Frank was parked in the resident lot in the back. Roy had seen it when he was driving around the building and…

Jesus, he thought. *It's like I'm casing the joint. I'm a fucking stalker.*

He needed to leave. He needed to get the hell out of here. He should never have come.

But, oh God. He couldn't *stop* thinking about Frank. His movie-star looks, his touch, his kiss, his cock. He found he was *hungering* for the man. He'd heard about that. "Hungering" for someone. But it had always sounded silly to him. Like something you would read on the back of one of the Harlequin romances his mother had always read when he was growing up. Or the bigger, thicker books that Ramona loved so much. Covers with hugely muscled men without any shirts on, their long hair blowing in the wind, and women with "heaving bosoms"—that's what Ramona called them—clutching at their hero's bulging arm or thigh.

But as the days passed after that afternoon in Frank's apartment, Roy had come to see what this "hunger" was all about. Because what he was feeling… that was what it truly felt like. Like a *hunger*. A hunger that wouldn't go away even if he jerked off. No matter how many times he jerked off.

If I could just see him. From a distance. That would be enough. To know Frank was real.

Oh, he's real.

I just want to see him. Because masturbating wasn't enough to help him forget Frank. Not imagining some sexy actress or model or singer. Not Gal Gadot—and the new Wonder Woman was sexy as hell—or Scarlett Johansson. Or even goddamn Emilia Clarke stepping naked out of the fire with baby dragons hanging on her!

Not Ramona either. And he'd nearly called her. Knew he could. He could go and fuck the hell out of her, and then maybe this craziness would be *over*. Then he could stop thinking about *Frank*.

About *men*.

Men.

Not that Frank had started those thoughts. They'd been there before, once in a while, for as long as he could remember. But when Ramona had started her games, those thoughts had kicked into high gear.

When he would get "that" hankering, he would go to one of the websites like Nifty or Literotica or Men on the Net, and he'd find a story about some bicurious man's first time with gay sex. They almost always started off by telling the reader how much the guy— the one telling the story—loved his sexy wife. And then some wild circumstance would happen, and he'd find himself having sex with a man. But that didn't mean he didn't still love his wife, and as a matter of fact, when he got home that night (from his wild circumstance), he fucked his wife.

That was the porn Roy liked to read, and he'd cum *hard*, and then reassured that having sex with a man was only a "wild circumstance" and that he was still straight, still loved women, he would slip comfortably off to sleep.

But that wasn't what was happening in real life.

As much as the sex he'd had with Frank had indeed been a wild circumstance—

"Hey…. you want a blowjob?"

—he'd had no sudden desire to have sex with a woman after he'd left Frank's apartment. Certainly, *no* desire to call Ramona—especially since she'd so surely led him to the worst year of his life. Not that he could blame her entirely. She hadn't forced him. Not really. She hadn't held him at gunpoint, at least. He had to take responsibility for what he'd done.

Of course, even if he'd been willing to hook up with her, his mother would never have allowed her in the house. He would have had to go to her place. But that hadn't interested him in the least. The very idea, in fact, turned his stomach into knots. She was living with someone now— her life had certainly gone on—but she made it clear she and her toys were waiting.

The thing was, though, he didn't want to have sex with Ramona. And not only had any desire for his ex gone away, but any ability to get it up for Scarlett Johansson, Kate Upton, or Taylor Swift. No matter what fantasy he brought to mind, what scenario he created for his mind's eye, no matter how much it featured him as the straight man who went through a wild circumstance and was now ready for his hot wife, the result was the same.

Limp dick.

But if he thought of Frank?

Dick of granite.

Finally, he would stop fighting it, let those women slip away, and let Frank fill his mind. He'd remember as many details about Frank as he could. His face, his incredibly muscular body, his big cock. And each time he jerked off, because he was hornier in the past few days than he'd been since he was fourteen or so, he swore it would be the last time.

It must be.

Had to be....

And yet he was masturbating more than he had in a decade, rubbing out one load after another. Sometimes he'd start jerking off before he'd really gotten soft from his last ejaculation.

I've got to do something. This is just crazy.

And then something occurred to Roy.

He had told Frank he wanted it all, right? To try everything? But he hadn't. *He* hadn't fucked Frank. And Frank *had* offered.

And hey! Fucking Frank could prove something. It could show that fucking the man's ass was no different in the long run from fucking Ramona. Right? Or any other girl? Surely when it came to fucking, a hole was a hole?

The things he'd done already? They were the things he couldn't do with a girl—besides getting his cock sucked, of course. That was no different.

Except that it was....

No one had ever sucked him like Frank. He'd wondered—*marveled*—about that for days. Until it finally hit him. The reason Frank was such a good cocksucker—and the word gave Roy a secret *thrill* it never had before—was that Frank *loved* to suck cock. He didn't suck cock because it was your birthday. He didn't do it because he loved you. No. He did it because he *loved* to do it.

Roy shook himself. Tried to remember where his train of thought had been going. Oh yes. That the things he had done with Frank that he couldn't do with a girl. He couldn't suck cock because girls didn't have one. Now he knew what that was like.

And sitting there in his electric-blue Jeep thinking about that, he began to get hard. Thinking of sucking Frank's cock was making him hard. God.... Sucking cock had been so.... So... *real*. When he went down on Ramona, it was really just sticking your tongue in there and moving it around. But taking a cock in your mouth? That was different!

Oh, *way* different. A cock, especially a hard one, was warm—even hot—and it was flesh and smooth skin and salty sweet and hard, *so* hard. It throbbed. It was alive. It reacted to what you did. The leakings were salt and sweet as well....

Stop! There you go again, off point.

And he had a point. Hadn't he?

Oh! Things he couldn't do with a girl. He couldn't suck cock because she didn't have a cock. And a woman couldn't fuck him.

Except Ramona *had* done that, hadn't she? She had played with his ass for a couple of weeks. His hole. First just touching it, which he had found very disconcerting because no one had ever done that to him, not even a doctor, and he'd heard doctors might do such a thing. He'd sort of grunted and the next time asked her, "What the hell are you doing?"

"Relax, Sweet Cheeks," she had said. She'd been calling him that more and more lately. And although Ramona Moore was a little thing, with a waist so small he could put his hands around her middle and almost have his fingers touch, she had a way of taking complete control of him. For some reason, that had excited him. Excited him more than probably any girl he had ever been with.

He had been with quite a few.

Roy had discovered that, no matter what he thought he saw in the mirror, girls thought he was cute. Why, he'd lost his virginity to a girl at fourteen when he was supposed to be getting help with his math homework. They'd gone to her room with strict instructions not to close her bedroom door. She had promptly closed and locked it, and minutes later she was out of her dress, holding something very different than a pencil or a math book.

Since then? He wasn't sure. At least a couple dozen women had gone to his bed or he to theirs. Maybe twice that. He'd made no notches on his headboard.

"Trust me," Ramona had said, and as it turned out, what she was introducing him to was about the only thing where trusting her hadn't wound up near ruining his life.

The next time she'd poked at the puckered entrance to his ass, she had practically commanded him to relax, her eyes flashing. That order had for some reason excited him.

"Just wait until we reach the day where I'm touching your sweet spot," she said with an almost growl.

"M-my what?" he asked.

"It's kind of like your man-clit," she whispered. "And you're going to love it when I flick it!"

And when that day came, when she had a finger deep inside him and found his secret spot, he'd let out a "*Whoa!*" and an "*Oh!*" and an "*Oh my God!*" That was when she really took control of him.

"Yeah, Sweet Cheeks. You're lovin' that, ain'tcha?"

He'd been a foolish idiot, letting someone own him because of what she could, and would, do to him in bed. But he'd never felt so alive. And so close to… right. *So* close.

One night he'd graduated to the point where she had three fingers inside him, and she was wriggling them like crazy, and he thought he would about die.

That's when she convinced him to go with her and some friends to Hawaii, even though there was no way he could afford it. She even showed him how he could pay his part of the expenses and buy her some things as well.

"You can always fix it later," she said.

It was while they were in their room at the Ala Moana Hotel that Ramona fucked him the first time. She called it "pegging." What it meant was she had put on a strap-on dildo and told him what she was going to do, and he'd been thunderstruck with fear and anticipation.

"Going to make you my bitch," she said, kneeling between his wide-spread legs, looking down at him, in complete control, red hair hanging down around her face. And make him her bitch is exactly what she had done, wasn't it?

"I'm not sh-sure," he had said.

"*I'm* sure," she replied, voice like steel.

At least she was gentle "taking his cherry," as she called it, and she'd actually had her first orgasm when she bottomed out in him the first time.

He had to admit he'd liked it. Liked it better than any sex he had ever had. And in the over ten years since that girl introduced him to sex when she was supposed to tutoring him in math, he'd had a *lot* of sex.

In fact, that night he'd enjoyed it so much, made so much noise, that her friends from the adjoining rooms had teased him unmercifully the next day and the entire vacation.

That he *hadn't* liked. Especially when they all started calling him Sweet Cheeks.

"We wondered why she called you that," Milo, one of the leaders of the group, had said.

"Now we know!" said another, and then they had all roared with laughter.

"Gonna make you my bitch!" Milo cried and began to slap his ass.

The thrill of her taking control began to melt away quickly after that, and any worries that he might have a submissive nature melted away at the same time. In the end the only reason he let her continue to talk to him that way—calling him her bitch and faggot and whatever else she wanted—was because he wanted her to use that dildo on him. It felt so goddamned wonderful.

But not nearly as wonderful as Frank.

The thought brought him up short. He gasped thinking it. But it was true.

Please, I don't want to be gay!

A cock had felt better than what Ramona had fucked him with. It was rubber. Or was it latex? He was never sure of the difference. But it didn't matter. Whatever it was, whatever they were made of—and she'd shown him she had quite a variety of sizes and colors and materials—they weren't *human*. She'd tried a few on him, but they weren't warm. Weren't alive.

He'd had that now.

And wasn't sex about life? Wasn't it about human touch?

God....

That's why the toy he'd bought and used on himself hadn't done it. *I'm not ever going to like that with anything but the real thing again.... Am I?*

He looked at that big redbrick apartment building, and he knew having sex with Frank again would be a mistake. If he did, he wasn't sure he'd be able to stop.

I've got to leave. I've got to get the hell out of here!

He started the Jeep up, looked for a clear spot in the traffic, and pulled out and....

To his astonishment, he saw Frank in his red Mazda, top down, pulling into the gas station where they had met.

Run! Get out of here! That's what his mind screamed. However, his body had a mind of its own, and he pulled into the station and drove right up to Frank, who was just getting out of the car.

After all, he hadn't done it all, right? He hadn't fucked Frank. And Frank had offered.

"Hey, Frank," he said.

The man Roy had not been able to stop thinking about was wearing extremely revealing jeans shorts and a sleeveless T-shirt that said I Can't Even Keep a Straight Face and showed off his biceps and deltoids and triceps to erection-inducing perfection. He was wearing flip-flops that exposed his big, strong-looking feet.

Even his goddamned feet were sexy.

Frank lifted expensive-looking sunglasses and stared at him in surprise.

He is so goddamned good-looking. Christ! I had sex with him? He even noticed I was alive?

"Roy! What are you doing here?"

The words were out of his mouth before he could stop them.

"Hey," Roy Ingalls said. "You want a blowjob?"

CHAPTER NINE

FRANK THREW himself into his work that week.

The kitchen in Central Hyde Park would be a showplace when he was done with it. The wood… it was wonderful, although most of it had been buried under layers of paint. He was sure when the owner showed it to him he was going to be asked to rip it out—how many times had that happened?—and replace it with composite wood from Home Depot or Lowe's. But to his surprise, that wasn't what he wanted at all.

It turned out the owner knew Peter Wagner, only one of the wealthiest men in the country, and he'd seen what Frank had done to Mr. Wagner's kitchen. "I know I probably can't afford you, but I was hoping for some kind of phoenix from the ashes. Would it be impossible to bring back the past with a little bit of today mixed in?"

He wanted the cabinets restored so they would be as close to their original appearance as possible. The new he was hoping for was touch lighting, where all he had to do was tap the glass that fronted the cabinets and subdued lighting would come on. All so if he came down in the middle of the night for a drink of water, he wouldn't have to turn on lights to blaze his eyes out.

God, was that doable?

Fuck yes, it was doable. *So* doable! Frank even suggested heating under the flooring.

"You can do that?" Mr. Beauchamp said, staring down at their feet.

"You've actually got marble tiling here, and it is in pretty good condition. I have men that can lift it, and we can put heat coiling underneath, refurbish the tiles, and replace them. I mean, it won't be cheap, but…."

"Round-about numbers?" Mr. Beauchamp asked. "Let's cut to the chase, Mr. Sinclair, because I like your work, and I think I like you. I'm no Peter Wagner, but I'm not a pauper either."

So Frank had given him numbers—round-about—and Mr. Beauchamp had liked them and hadn't even hinted at negotiating. It had sent the blood zinging through Frank's veins. He thought this was something he was even going to get his hands dirty with. And that could be better than sex. It lasted. Forever. Or at least as long as he would be around.

And then had come an even bigger jackpot. On his way out, as he was being led through the living room to the foyer, he stopped and eyed the threshold between the two.

"Mr. Sinclair?" Mr. Beauchamp had asked.

"Frank. If I am going to touch your wood, then I'm Frank," he said, so engrossed with possibilities that he hadn't even noticed the sexual innuendo in his words.

"All right, then. Frank. But what are you looking at?"

Frank *had* touched the wood then. Stroked the wood of the doorway and said, "This isn't right."

Mr. Beauchamp nodded and said, "Yeah. It was all tore up, nasty, and I had them throw up some boards and—"

"Do you trust me? I'm having a feeling…."

"A feeling?"

"Will you let me pull this out? If I'm wrong, I'll replace it all, and with better wood, for nothing. My cost."

After a pause, Beauchamp said, "Go for it."

So Frank took a crowbar, tore the shittily applied board off, and found just what his secret heart was hoping for. Something that made the zing he'd gotten so far seem like coitus interrupted.

The original pocket doors were actually *there*! Some asshole had closed them into their slots in the wall and sealed them up. All, apparently, because a few panes had been broken. Because the runner was bent.

Mr. Beauchamp was ecstatic. He had practically done the Snoopy dance. In fact, he suddenly seemed to be coming on to Frank. But Frank knew what he was seeing: one of those married men who spent secret nights on Nifty with his dick in his hand, pretending he had the courage to have sex with a man. And Frank didn't do married men. He'd seen far too many of his father's women deeply hurt when they found out that Glen wasn't keeping his dick in his pants.

Nope. The cabinets and the marble floors and the pocket doors would be the only sex had here. Because *it* was forever.

Then, just yesterday, he'd been called to a house in Brookside. Twice in one week because of the work he'd done for Peter Wagner. After barely seeing what he had to do, he was being offered three bathrooms. They wanted original and New Age. Could he do both?

"How about restoring the wood but using some new varnishes?" he asked. "Strawberry? Peach?"

And just like that he had the job.

Between the two, he'd have enough to pay any expenses the business and he had for six months at least. Maybe a year.

All of which made him decide it was okay to spend a day out at Camp Sanctuary, the clothing-optional retreat center where he could go and lie out naked in the sun, work on his tan, skinny-dip, and maybe get laid. There was this little area off the beach where men went to cruise for sex. Who knew? Maybe he could get a blowjob. He needed something to get his mind off the Man in Orange.

So what a surprise it was when, stopping for gas at the station across from the Wilde, occupied with wondering if he'd forgotten anything—quilt for the beach, suntan lotion, cooler, six-pack of Blue Moon—someone said, "Hey, Frank."

The sun was coming from the wrong direction, and when he looked up he couldn't see who was talking to him from the Jeep that was mere feet away from him. He lifted his Ray-Bans, and to his surprise, it was Roy—Mr. Orange—so close he could almost reach out and touch him.

Holy shit!

"Roy!" he said. "What are you doing here?"

The answer was not exactly what he expected.

"Hey," Roy Ingalls said. "You want a blowjob?"

His dick instantly began to get hard. He wanted to say no. He needed to say no. But that wasn't what he said.

"Yes, Roy. I'd love one." Because of course he would. He had made a vow never to turn down a blowjob. There really was very little in this life better than a blowjob. If the person giving it loved giving them. Why, it was just about as close to paradise as Frank believed existed. He figured most men felt the same way. Why else would so many men be happy if that was their birthday present once a year from their wives?

I was going to Camp Sanctuary. I had plans. I had the whole day planned.

And he still could. How long would this take? An hour?

Hard to believe it was little more than an hour that he'd spent with Roy less than a week ago. An hour that had brought itself to his mind again and again. He'd masturbated at least a half-dozen times thinking about it.

There was a loud *click!* as his gas tank finished filling, and he put the nozzle back and nodded at Roy and said, "See you out front?"

This is a mistake, Frank thought. He knew it instinctively. Like he knew there were pocket doors in Mr. Beauchamp's walls. *If I take this man to my place, he will be back.*

And so what? Was there anything wrong with that?

Just because he rarely did a man more than once didn't mean he never did. He'd had his fair share of guys he saw for a while. Not three or four years—which was Glen's record—but three or four months had been all right. As long as the dude knew he wasn't going to get to the going steady stage. There had been many a time when a guy he was getting regular with left first. And that was a good thing.

Frank parked in his space behind the building and went into the Oscar Wilde through the back door, down a hall, and into the lobby. Roy was waiting by the glass doors leading into the foyer. He was looking around as if he were afraid someone was coming for him—and not in a good way. Frank froze watching him. Saw how nervous he was. Smiled in amusement when he read what Roy's T-shirt said: Doing My Part to Keep the Beard Fashionable. But then he saw the bulge in his jeans, and although they weren't as religiously revealing as the biker shorts he'd worn that first day, or as fantasy inducing as that orange jumpsuit, what he saw was still sexy as hell. Roy had a *very* nice cock. One that Frank wanted to suck. Now.

He wondered briefly if maybe he should tell Roy that he'd seen him in that orange jumpsuit along I-70, but in the elevator, Roy was doing that puffing sound again, and his eyes were so wide Frank could tell how nervous he was and figured that revelation very well might freak him the fuck out.

God, his eyes were *so* fucking blue, so intense, and then again, with no warning, Roy kissed him. Such a good kisser for a straight man. Most straight me were so gentle—*too* gentle—and had no idea how to hold their mouth or what to do with their tongues. But someone had taught Roy well, and considering how hot he was, Frank supposed there could have been a lot of someones.

Thank you, he prayed to *all* of them.

Not that Roy started out rough. No. Two or three sweet kisses came first. But soon he had Frank against the wall of the elevator, and his mouth took Frank's, forcing it open, tongue demanding, teeth clashing. Fuck, it was hot. Frank was leaking already.

Roy's hands were up under Frank's shirt and touching, rubbing his skin, stroking, *massaging* his torso, finding his nipples and not being afraid to squeeze them. *Delicious.*

The doors opened to an "Oh my!" Roy leapt back and blushed that furious red of his. The guy standing there—a big black bear; Frank didn't know his name—was grinning. "All right!" he said.

Frank grinned back and grabbed Roy's hand, held it up with their fingers entwined, and yanked him off the elevator and down the hall to the end. He got his key in the door somehow, shaking with need and want, and flung it open. It took all his control not to throw Roy to the floor right there, leaving the door open.

But he did close it, and then he shoved Roy up against the door and kissed him back. Roy's thick beard felt so hot against his face, and he hoped he could convince Roy to do some other things with it he knew would feel good.

Frank slid his hands up under Roy's T-shirt and marveled at those muscles, ran his hands all over that body and paid particular attention to that amazing back and those awesome pectorals.

He's bigger there than me. Frank worked out in the building's basement "gym" nearly every day and knew Roy had worked hard on his body. It wasn't simply a product of some push-ups and sit-ups and wasn't fueled by Cinnabon cinnamon rolls and McDonald's Big Macs. *So now* I'll *work hard on his body.*

Frank pulled Roy's T-shirt off over his head, and before Roy's arms could fall, he buried his face in his armpit and *sucked*. Drew in a deep breath while he was at it. *Tasted* Roy and *breathed* him in, and it was perfect. All pheromones and sweat but clean too—just the right amount. *Man.* He pulled at the hair with his teeth and then went to the other arm, and how nice and gentlemanly that Roy was still holding it up for him. He moaned and hissed delightfully over Frank's ministrations, and then Frank *kissed* him, letting Roy taste himself on Frank's face and tongue.

"I want to taste *you*," Roy gasped, and how fucking hot was that? Straight Boy wanted to stick that bearded face in *man*. Gotta fucking love that. So together they got Frank's shirt off, and then Roy did a good job imitating what Frank had done to him, moaning while he did it, and then kissed Frank—letting Frank taste himself on Roy.

Next they rubbed their chests together, sort of rocking and shifting, letting pecs discover different ways to fit together, letting pebble-hard nipples clash.

"*God*," Roy said, drawing the word out in an almost sob. "The way we fit!"

They grabbed each other's asses simultaneously and crushed, fucked, their hard cocks against together.

"Gotta have it," Frank said through the kiss and then dropped to his knees and yanked Roy's jeans down. Out popped Roy's throbbing erection, the foreskin half rolled back, the head glistening with wet need. The scent of man hit Frank, and he moaned and took the top of the shaft in his left hand and those low-hanging balls in his right and that wet cockhead in his mouth. The taste was sharp and salt and under it all *so* remarkably sweet, and Frank salivated for what Roy had to offer. He wanted that. God! He wanted to hear that man-grunt and then feel the cum pump into his mouth in those same jets he'd seen Roy shoot. He bobbed and twisted, bathed Roy's cock with saliva, massaged under the shaft with his tongue, and Roy made luscious barking sounds and gripped Frank's tight curls in his fingers.

"Oh God!" Roy cried. "Oh God! You... gotta... stop! Please, Frank. I-I'm gonna... cum if you... don't.... *Stop*!"

But Frank didn't stop, and damn the consequences—the possibility that Roy would dash straight-boy quick out of the apartment as soon as he finished his orgasm. Frank had a deep and abiding need to *taste* all of Roy. To *feel* Roy spew into his mouth.

Then Roy's fingers went almost painfully tight, and he thrust his hips forward, and he did cum. He gushed across Frank's tongue in great tidal waves, and it was all Frank could do to keep swallowing.

But he did. *God*, he did. Swallowed hungrily, as if he were a man starving. It was so sweet. Gamey and sweet and thick. Frank shuddered in pleasure, thought he would cum himself, but somehow—*thank God!*—he didn't.

He took it all and milked out the last drops and made sure he cleaned even under the foreskin until Roy begged him to stop from the sensitivity of it. So he did, finally, and withdrew the glistening shaft from his mouth and then pressed his mouth to it. Kissed it. And looked up at the hot man who had that cock pressed against Frank's face.

Roy was looking down at him in a kind of shocked wonder and said in a raspy voice, "God…. You wanted that…. You wanted me to cum in your mouth."

Frank nodded, and Roy gave a shudder of pleasure from the motion. "You swallowed it."

Frank nodded again and said, "That's why you suck a cock. To swallow. What's the point otherwise? Unless you're just leading to something else." He sat back on his heels, knowing his face was wet with his saliva and maybe some of Roy as well. "Can this still lead to something else?"

Roy looked at him with those strange blue eyes. Such big eyes. Elfin eyes. Stared at him.

"Can we still fuck?" Frank asked.

Roy trembled and then trembled again and finally nodded. "Yes," he said. "Yes, *please*."

Yes, please.

Christ.

What could be hotter than that?

CHAPTER TEN

FRANK STOOD and took Roy's hand again, but this time it was… gentler. He led him down the hall, Roy's heart pounding the whole way, and it was less urgent than when he'd practically yanked him out of the elevator. That had been hot. The need. He had been so fucking damned much in need, and so apparently had Frank, and how amazing was it was that the need had been to suck his cock. That had been what Frank wanted. *Wanted.* Roy had never experienced anything close to it—except five days ago, that was.

Frank's fingers intertwined with Roy's once more, and they walked down the hall past another room and a bathroom, and then they were there. Frank's bedroom. Where he had lost his virginity. To a man.

Roy trembled, and something happened deep inside him that he couldn't describe, but it made him want to cry—only not in a sad or frightened or sorrowful way. It was something else. Something that felt like… what?

Like breathing the air outside the doors where he had been imprisoned for what felt like forever. Like the cool mountain air from the one time the whole family had gone camping together when he was a kid—even Granny. He'd never smelled anything so wonderful that long-ago day until the day he'd walked out that horrid gate and seen his mother waiting for him in his Jeep.

They stood there in the shadows of the room, the ceiling fan making quiet whispering noises, and Frank seemed to be looking into his soul. He remembered the eyes that had locked with his on the side of the highway that day, and he shivered, and Frank pulled him close. His body, God, felt so good against him. So solid. Strong. Real. Arms pulled him closer, not roughly, but securely, and Frank rocked him ever so gently as he rested his chin on Frank's shoulder and looked at the big bed where Frank had showed him how men had sex.

Something powerful swept over him then. Something he had no idea how to describe. No words to use. Only that it was huge. Immense.

And terrifying.

Frank pulled back, sat on the bed, and gave him a gentle tug to join him. Roy went into Frank's arms—so strong—then Frank scooched back, rolled onto his side, and tugged gently at Roy's hand again, drawing him into the bed. That big bed. He shivered again. Let himself be pulled in. Beside this handsome, sexy *gay* man.

I shouldn't be here. Once was one thing. That could be explained. A lot of men were curious, right? Curious what it was like to be with another man? He'd looked it up of course, and he'd discovered that 6.9 percent of men tried sex with another man at least once.

This was more than once, though.

But I'm here to fuck Frank. Then I will have done it all.

Well…. Not *all.*

He hadn't gotten Frank off with his mouth. Hadn't let Frank… cum in his mouth. And the idea was crazy scary and hot at the same time. Could he do that? Would it be disgusting? Even Ramona wouldn't swallow. Frank sure hadn't seemed to think it was gross. In fact, he seemed to love it. The way he'd been sort of… shuddering, Roy had wondered if he'd almost cum in his pants. God!

And he hadn't licked Frank's… asshole. Even the word made him anxious. Talk about scary. Was there any way he could do that? It was one thing to fuck someone… there. But to put your mouth in that place?

But geez, Frank had sure seemed to like that too. And he seemed, well, clean. He was clean. His apartment was spotless. Wouldn't he be clean *there* too?

Roy thought of climbing on top of Frank and kissing his way down that masculine muscular back, down to that round ass, and spreading his cheeks as Frank had done to him. Would he be smooth there? Hairy. And his hole—what would it be like? Could he kiss Frank there? *Lick* him there?

A delicious little thrill shot through him. Carnal. Lecherous. Indecent! He realized he was getting hard again. Maybe he *could* do it.

"God, you have a beautiful cock," Frank said.

Roy started. Looked at him in surprise. "Beautiful?"

Frank smiled—and *that* was beautiful!

"Haven't you ever thought of a cock as beautiful before? Well, no…." He sighed. "Maybe you wouldn't." He smiled again. "Rest assured your penis is *handsome*."

Roy blinked. "I guess I've thought of them as sexy."

But then he thought about it all of a few seconds, and his face heated as he realized there was no guessing about it. He *did* think they were sexy. Hot. Soft. Hard. It didn't matter. It mystified him that so many girls thought penises were ugly or funny-looking! God, the pictures he'd looked at online. So many sizes and colors and, yes, even shapes. Thick at the top or bigger at the bottom. Long and thin. Short and broad. Some curved straight up, some bent to the side. Blunt-headed. Mushroom-headed. Some almost pointed. Cut. Uncut. All kinds of foreskins from thin and tight to thick and overhanging.

A stretch and a throb caught Roy's attention. He was completely hard now. Thinking of cock.

God! I should go!

But of course he wasn't going anywhere. Except into Frank's arms. To be kissed. And to kiss back. He pressed his erection against Frank only to feel the fabric of Frank's shorts, and he grunted with frustration. He wanted to press his bare cock against Frank's, and he pulled away, sat up, and grabbed at the front of Frank's tiny jeans shorts, popped the button, and tugged the zipper down with ease. Another yank had Frank lifting his ass off the bed, and Roy pulled the shorts down to Frank's knees, revealing Frank's erection—his big, sexy erection.

I'm sucking that!

All Roy had to do then was scoot down and there it was, inches from his face, and an instant after that, he had it in his mouth. A shock passed through him—wonderful and voluptuous—and he knew this was what he *wanted*. He'd never enjoyed oral sex with girls—women—and when he listened to his friends go on and on about how much they *loved* it, he nodded as if he agreed and wondered what was wrong with him. Why didn't he like it? Why did it kind of… well, gross him out? He knew, could tell, his friends weren't lying. Weren't just being all macho and braggy. They clearly meant what they said. But nothing at all appealed to him about it. He didn't think vaginas were sexy, but his friends *did*. It was so tempting to think their talk really was all masculine bravado. He wanted that to be true. Wanted to believe they were spinning tales to impress each other and prove that they loved "pussy" more than the other man.

But now, quite clearly, everything clicked—powerful and suddenly—into place. What he was feeling rushed through him as he took Frank deep into his mouth—the *aliveness* of it, the velvet over iron of it, the way it leaped, the heat of it, the sweet-salty flavor of it, the almost-intoxicating musky scent of it—and made him see his friends weren't lying. Because now he was feeling exactly what they had described so poetically, so wantonly, so happily.

He froze. Let the erection slip from his mouth, if not his grip, and looked at it. Beautiful. Among so many other words he could use—sexy, erotic, sensual, *hot*—he realized Frank was right. The word "beautiful" was exactly right. At least, this one was.

Oh my God!

In the next second Roy growled and cast aside any fear—fuck it, he would worry about it later—grabbed the erection in both hands, and shamelessly fell upon it and took it as deeply as he could. He sucked as if his life depended on it, almost felt that it did. Tried to imitate everything Frank had done to him while he was pushed up against the door to the apartment. A slickness was forming in his mouth; it was Frank's precum, and he tingled all over thinking what that meant.

I'm a cocksucker. Good Christ! I'm a cocksucker. And instead of denying it or hating himself, he decided not to worry about it. Not now. He decided to glory in it. Let himself be electrified by it.

Gonna do it. Gonna let you cum in my mouth. I don't care. Gonna do it!

Meanwhile Frank was making the most wonderful sounds: grunting, crying out, moaning, begging. All of it inspired Roy to go on.

"R-Roy! You better stop man. If you don't…. Roy! Are you sure you're ready for…? *Roy!*"

It was a bit of a shock when despite every warning—the freely flowing precum, the balls tightening in their silky sack, Frank's body tensing like a violin string—Frank let out a shout and began to cum. Roy almost pulled away, but then exultation hit him—*I did it, I did it!*—and he hung on as Frank pumped thickly, blast after blast, into his mouth.

Hey, you want a blowjob?

For a second he didn't know what to do as his mouth filled, and then instinct took over and he swallowed, swallowed again, swallowed a third time. It wasn't awful, either. Salty. Sweet. Something else familiar that he couldn't quite put his finger on. There was nothing gross about it at all. In fact, it felt… *right*.

"That's why you suck a cock," Frank had said. *"To swallow. What's the point otherwise?"*

Indeed. A surprising sense of pride swept through him as he finished nursing the softening erection. As he licked it. Kissed it. Saw the pearl of remaining semen and licked it up too, gazing at Frank when he did it and hoping it turned him on.

"Jesus Christ," Frank said with a sigh, his eyes shining. "You're a real champ, aren't you?"

A champ? Was that good?

"Come here, you fucking stud, you," Frank said and pulled him up into his arms and kissed him. Kissed him sweet and long and oh so nice. Soft and yielding and giving, not demanding at all. Just a bit of tongue but mostly slightly open mouth, breathing into Roy's. It was like they were sharing breath.

He quite suddenly wanted to cry, and he didn't know why. Because he felt wonderful? Felt better than he had in as long as he could remember?

"Oh, Roy," Frank whispered, relinquishing his mouth. "You sweet, sweet man. I can't believe you did that. You didn't have to do that."

"But you said that was the only reason to… to suck cock. You said there was no point if I didn't swallow."

"I meant me, slugger."

Slugger. For some reason the word delighted him.

Frank kissed his forehead, his nose, his mouth. So precious.

"I didn't mean *you* had to."

"I wanted to do it right," Roy said. "I-I wanted to. And God, Frank. It was hot." Did this mean…? With a slight sinking feeling, Roy trembled. *Am I gay? I must be.* He looked back at Frank. "Does this mean I'm gay?"

Frank started to shake his head but slowed. He looked deeply into Roy's eyes. "Would that be bad?"

Roy shivered. "I… I always thought it would be." But right now he didn't know. He was in a strange mental place. Here in Frank's bed? In Frank's arms? With Frank looking at him the way he was? It didn't seem bad at all.

But in a few hours? Tomorrow? When he had to face the world? When he had to face his family? When Uncle Donald told a fag joke? *Why, then he might be talking about me.*

"You might be bisexual," Frank said, and somehow it felt as if he were throwing out a life preserver. "A lot of men like both."

Two percent. That was the figure that snapped to mind, the one he had read so recently. Two percent. With 1.9 percent identifying as gay.

What happened to that 10 percent gay he'd heard so many times? And what would that have done to the number of bisexuals?

"Or, you know," Frank said, "you could not fucking worry about it. Say we had a great afternoon and don't. Worry. About. It."

He looked into Frank's eyes and decided that sounded good. It sounded like what he'd decided a little while before. While he was sucking Frank's dick. *Fuck it.* For now—while he was in Frank's arms, in Frank's bed, the taste of the man in his mouth—Roy would ignore his fears. Not worry. Because now he felt extraordinary. As if he were on the threshold of a new and wondrous and exciting world—rife and full of possibilities. And on the heels of that he decided—*Fuck it!*—he wasn't going to think about being gay at all, or what that meant.

Right now he was just going to *be*.

And that was good.

CHAPTER ELEVEN

FRANK FIGURED the best thing to do was tell Roy to leave.

But good Christ, how often did he do the best thing? At least when it came to his personal life? The truth was he actually didn't want Roy to leave. Not yet. Later.

Right now he was hungry. He told Roy that too. "Want to go get something?" he asked, surprising himself. This was usually when he gave his tricks the bum's rush.

Roy propped himself up on one elbow, clearly surprised. "You don't mind if I go with you?"

Looking at him lying there all fucking hot, Frank almost lost interest in eating. But then his stomach growled and his eyes went wide, and Roy started laughing, and Frank couldn't help but join him.

They got dressed, which was almost a shame. Roy looked so good naked. Of course, Frank really wanted to see him in orange. God! And he began to wonder if Roy could get one of those jumpsuits. But how would he ask? He'd have to tell him where he first saw him, and he didn't want to humiliate the kid. That got him to wondering, though. What had he done to be wearing it in the first place? Hopefully not burglary. And surely if it was something violent, he wouldn't have been on an out-of-prison work detail.

"Are you *hungry* hungry? Like a big dinner? Or would sandwiches be enough? Because I know this nice little place—"

"Sounds like you want sandwiches," Roy said. "That sounds fine to me."

Frank smiled, opened the door, and started to walk into the hall when he noticed Roy hesitating. "You okay?"

Roy stood there, clenching and unclenching his hands. He grimaced. Looked away. Looked back. But not at Frank's face. "Roy?"

Still Roy looked away, not answering him. Then back again.

But not at his face. At his chest.

Frank looked down. And finally it hit him. His T-shirt. Which in rainbow colors informed all who read it that I Can't Even Keep a Straight Face. Ah.

"You don't like my shirt?" he asked.

Roy looked away again. Sighed. "I'm sorry, Frank."

Frank just stared at him, surprised. And then wondered why he was surprised. The kid was just beginning to wonder if he might be gay. He wasn't going to want to be seen in public with a man who was advertising it. He'd be scared that he would see someone he knew. It put Frank into a momentary dilemma. Did he stand for his ideals? He'd never been ashamed of or felt the need to hide who and what he was; the very idea made him sick to his stomach. But should he put his pride aside for Roy's feelings? Fuck. If only Roy hadn't asked! If only he'd thought about it himself so he could have made up his mind.

Then he realized he could make up his own mind. And not wearing a shirt didn't mean he was denying who he was. He opened his mouth to tell Roy, but before he could, Roy spoke instead.

"Fuck!" His eyes were wide again, and he was making a sound like that puffing he sometimes did. "I'm sorry. I shouldn't have asked you that. I should leave—"

"I'll change my shirt, Roy," Frank said quickly and turned back inside, already taking the shirt off.

"No!" Roy said. "Wear it. Just because I'm afrai—"

"I'm changing, Roy. And don't *you* go *any*where. Except to have lunch with *me*." Then he went back to his bedroom, opened a dresser drawer, leafed quickly through T-shirts carefully folded so the art clearly showed, and picked one out with a smile. This one couldn't bother Roy.

He pulled it over his head and…

Remembered the beers and the two sandwiches in the cooler in his trunk. They could have them on the balcony. They could have them on the balcony naked. He'd been wanting to be naked outside, which is why he'd been heading to Camp Sanctuary when he fortuitously met up with Roy at the gas station (that made twice!) in the first place. But then he thought about it and thought that having lunch together would be a good step for Roy—even with a tamer shirt. Maybe next time Roy wouldn't care what he wore.

Frank laughed. Next time. Right!

He went back to the living room, and Roy's eyes lit on his shirt. A picture of a taco. And below that: I Hate Tacos Said No Juan Ever.

Roy burst into laughter.

"Okay?" Frank asked.

"Okay," Roy answered.

And then they were out the door.

THEY WENT to a little sandwich shop called Lovin' Oven, which was far smaller than Roy had pictured and more delicious than he'd imagined.

It was just sandwiches! How could they be all that different?

But they were.

The bread was fresher, even though he knew Subway baked theirs fresh every day. There was more of a… yeast taste. And the meats didn't *taste* like meat sliced from some big loaf at the deli at the local Sunfresh Market. Meat he'd *watched* them slice so he knew it was fresh. He didn't see this meat sliced. But still it was somehow different. Fuller. Less salty.

"Organic when it can be," Frank explained. "Local when it can be. Grass-fed and no antibiotics. It doesn't taste at all like what you're used to, does it? I hope that's okay."

Roy nodded. It was fine. Very enjoyable in fact. The truth was he was so damned nervous and anxious at the same time sitting here with Frank that he could hardly eat. What if someone saw him? Asked him who Frank was? He hated himself for asking Frank to change his shirt, but damn. He didn't want the rumors to fly around that he was a fag.

But God! I am one? *A fag?* Why, this sandwich was joining a big load of cum in his stomach. A load that he'd swallowed. And he had been turned on when he did it.

"I sucked a man off," he said very quietly and then colored when he realized he'd said it out loud.

"The vegetables are fresher too," Frank went on. Roy must not have said those words loud enough for Frank to hear. "In season, all their vegetables are locally farmed—whenever possible. Even the mayo is made here in the shop. The sandwiches are a *little* more expensive, but God, they are so much better!"

More than a little more, thought Roy.

Two women came in. A large older lady with streaks of gray in her long brown hair and a shorter younger one with big round plastic glasses and hair almost as long as her companion's, but dark brown.

They're together. They're a couple. They look so happy. Roy looked around him. No one seemed to be paying them any attention other than the deli guy at the counter who was taking their orders.

Damn, he thought, and his stomach settled a bit more. He trembled but caught it and hoped Frank didn't see. Roy shook himself. Drank from the big paper cup of cola. He was feeling so… strange. Not bad strange, just different. It was like the air had changed. The light. Almost that Adderall feeling again, but not.

Or it was like something out of a Stephen King book. Except not as scary. Like the one where the tourists got caught up in some strange area of London where there were streets with names like Slaughter Towen and Crouch Lane and Yog-Soggoth. It had given him bad dreams. Or the one where the couple wound up in a town where rock stars like Janis Joplin and Freddie Mercury and Patsy Cline and Kurt Cobain went after they died and had to play concerts all night until the end of time.

He'd read a lot of those, sitting around with nothing to do. God, he'd been so grateful to have the chance to get out, even if it was to pick up garbage on the side of the road, wearing one of those bright orange jumpsuits that had been like giant flashing arrows telling people to look. Look! It's Roy Ingalls, and look what he's wearing! You know what that means, right?

Then of course there was the story *Children of the Corn*. It seemed it was always a couple, wasn't it? And while he was definitely not part of a couple and while this little shop with its organic nonantibiotic meat wasn't nightmare inducing—at least not yet—he still felt as if he were somewhere… *else*. A world from *The Twilight Zone* where there was a man's semen in his stomach and a lesbian couple was totally normal. It was scary and somehow exhilarating at the same time.

He was sitting here with a totally out gay man. They were eating together. What he would have done for such simple food as sandwiches *this* good during the dark time.

But part of it—he didn't understand why—was sitting here in *this* place, this very *public* place, with Frank. He found himself almost hoping that Frank *would* do something, *anything*, to place some kind of public claim on him. It wasn't like this was Overland Park. What were the chances, really, of anyone he knew or who knew him showing up in this place?

What would happen if they did? It wasn't like he had to say, "This is my *gay* friend Frank," right? Certainly no one would guess looking at him. He was so… gorgeous! That was the word that kept popping up in his head. Gorgeous. Ramona's word, but it wasn't like she'd fucking made it up.

But just because a man was gorgeous didn't mean he was straight, did it? Look at all those good-looking actors coming out of the closet. He didn't know why each name that hit the news had made him sit up and take notice, like a cat hearing you running the can opener, its ears up and twitching. But it had.

Matt Bomer and Cheyenne Jackson from frigging *American Horror Story* of all things, both of them with *killer* bodies. Sean Maher from *Firefly*, and Jesus, did he look great without a shirt. He was like *married* to a guy. Luke-fucking-Evans. *Dracula Untold*! Gaston from goddamned *Beauty and the Beast*! Gay. Charlie Carver from that wild show *The Leftovers*. He'd had this nude scene and showed everything. That had been crazy. And sexy. Ricky Martin. Of course, that had been no big fucking surprise. Everyone had known that forever. In the last year or so, there had been pictures aplenty on the internet of him and his boyfriend, or whatever he was, and they were wearying tiny little bathing suits. All of these men were incredible-looking, and all of them were out there making love to other men when they could have any woman they wanted.

But they didn't want women.

"Roy. I don't want women that way. You know that, right?"

"You okay there, Roy?"

Roy started, looked at Frank, and realized he had taken a big bite of roast beef and his mouth was hanging open. He flushed and chewed and swallowed hard.

"Lost in thought," he managed, barely, and took another big drink of his cola.

"Did you want to share?" Frank asked, and he actually seemed interested. Roy couldn't remember when someone besides his mother or granny was interested in anything he had to say.

"The whole… gay thing," he said, whispering the word "gay."

Frank's eyebrows shot up. "*Gay* thing?"

Roy closed his eyes. Took a deep breath. Opened them again. "Don't you worry what people will think? What they'll say? That T-shirt you were wearing…. What if someone started something?"

Frank put an elbow on the table and popped his bicep. Which caused Roy to suck in a deep breath. Fuck, that was hot.

"I think I can take care of myself," Frank said. "And the times, Roy, they're changing. Most people don't care anymore. I'm lucky. The only family I have is my old man, and he's cool with it."

"Really?" Roy was astonished. "I can't imagine what my family would think."

"Well, Roy," Frank said and dropped a big rough man's hand on Roy's own. "You don't know what you are, do you? Gay? Or just testing the waters? A lot of straight men like to fuck guys once in a while."

Roy stared at Frank's hand on his. Before was one thing. But if anyone walked in now, there was no doubt what they would think. And as much as what Frank had said out loud—*"You don't know what you are, do you? Gay? Or just testing the waters? A lot of straight men like to fuck guys once in a while"*—had made him cringe, he found he didn't want Frank to move his hand.

Goose bumps rushed up his arm.

God….

He looked up and caught what looked like an amused expression on Frank's face.

"What?" he asked.

"You tell me," Frank said and took a huge bite of what was left of his sandwich. Another bite half that size and he'd be done.

"But don't you want to be like everybody else?" Roy cried, and to his surprise tears came to his eyes. He trembled. Still not sure what to do. Looked at their hands. Looked at Frank. Whose hand was on his. Where anyone could see.

"Hey" came a woman's voice, and Roy jerked and half tried to pull his hand away. Not quite, though. Frank held on. Strong, but not too strong. Roy could pull it away if he tried.

"Hey," Frank said. He wasn't looking at Roy. He was looking at….

Roy turned his head. It was the ladies he'd seen ordering at the counter. Or the one in the big black round glasses. They kind of reminded him of Mrs. Kelly's.

She smiled and reached out to point at Frank's coffee. "Excellent choice." She was beaming. "I mean, you *did* order The Shepherd's Bean coffee, right?"

"I did," Frank replied. He smiled at Roy. "She works at The Shepherd's Bean. They trade coffee for sandwiches. It's a good deal for both."

She nodded. "It is."

"Honey," said the big woman with the hair that was beginning to go gray, as she came up to them. She had to be at least ten years older, maybe more. "We need to get going."

"Sure thing, babe."

The girl in glasses nodded at Roy. "Woof."

Frank laughed. "Indeed."

"You haven't been around in a while, Prefers Yirgacheffe."

"You haven't had Yirgacheffe in a while."

Yur-go-who? Roy wondered.

"I'll talk to Bean," she said.

Frank smiled. "See you soon, then."

Glasses Lady took Older Lady's hand, and they left.

Roy began to shake again. He didn't like it. He pulled his hand away and immediately regretted it. "You know them?"

"Sorta," Frank said. "The one with the glasses is a barista at The Shepherd's Bean, this coffee shop I go to every now and then. She called me Mr. Prefers Yirgacheffe the same way a bartender knows you by your drink. You think a bartender knows you. But they don't. They know your drink. That makes you feel good, so you tip."

"I see." But he didn't. Not really.

Frank sighed. It was a long sigh. "I'm *gay*, Roy. Always have been. A hot boy taught me that on a beach a long time ago. I don't care what other people think. It's who I am. And it's not about parades or rainbow flags or gay marriage—which I am not interested in, by the way. I have a *right* to be who I am. I like men, Roy. I *fucking* love men. In all their shapes and sizes and ages. I *love* them. I love being me."

"But what about me?" Roy asked and brushed at his face. *Shit. Please don't ask me if I love you.*

But Frank didn't say it that way. "What about you, baby?"

Baby? The word made his heart skip a beat. *Fuck!* "I don't know what I am!" He wiped at his face again. He was not going to fucking cry. *No* fucking way.

"Only you can tell that, hot stuff."

Hot stuff?

"But I really don't think you have to decide today, do you? Like I said. Lots of men experiment."

Six point nine percent....

"Right now I would like to take you back to my place and sit on your cock. What do you say? Interested?"

Interested? Suddenly worries about whether he was gay or not vanished as fast as ice cubes in a furnace. Because wasn't that why he came here? To fuck Frank?

He began to get hard in that instant. Shivered in delight. Pictured Frank with his legs spread wide.

I want to see your asshole. God, did he!

"Yeah," he gasped. "Fuck yeah."

Frank stood up. "Let's do it."

Then he did something Roy wasn't expecting. He held out his hand.

For a second the world seemed to freeze. Frank's hand… it was as if it were *huge*. It was that Adderall thing again. He could see the hairs on the back of Frank's hand. How fucking clean his fingernails were. But how rough the undersides were.

He had a decision to make.

Somehow it was a big one, even if Frank said he didn't have to choose right now. He did.

Roy sucked in a deep breath. He looked up at Frank's face. That movie-star face.

He took Frank's hand.

CHAPTER TWELVE

IT WASN'T like they were *really* holding hands.

That was for elementary-school girls. Girls holding hands and linking arms and skipping through fields like in *Anne of Green Gables*. That was for Cody and Harry, strolling through the Plaza Art Fair or the one they had at least once a year in Westport (although it seemed liked they blocked off Westport Road from Broadway to Mill Street two dozen times a year). Or those kids that looked like they could be maybe fourteen or so that he was seeing at the last few Pride Festivals. It seemed they were getting younger and younger each year, and he supposed that was a good thing. Not everyone had the whole coming-out thing as easy as he had. If those kids wanted to walk around holding hands, cool.

But what he was doing with Roy? That wasn't holding hands. That was him pulling Roy along with him. Pulling him to his car, where he let go and they climbed in and....

Roy took his hand. His blue eyes were wide, his nostrils flared a time or two, his cheeks were pink, and right then he seemed to be some strange combination of man and child, and despite himself, Frank was enchanted.

You need to run. You need to be done with this. You could be taking on something here that could have big *consequences.*

Did he really want to help this man through a coming-out process? Fuck no!

I don't have to help him with that. I give him some fucking awesome sex. Give him something to think about. I don't have to hold his hand while he works through who the hell *he is.*

But he still didn't let go of Roy's hand. For some reason, holding this terrified young man's hand was turning him on.

No....

That wasn't it.

Well, it *was*. But there was something else.

He was enjoying holding Roy's hand. He felt, well, out of control. But in a nice way. Like he was in unfamiliar territory. It was kind of exciting and sweet at the same time. It had been a long time since he'd felt… sweet.

It was a short drive back to the Wilde, and as soon as he parked, he pulled Roy to him and kissed him. Roy fought him all of a few seconds or so and then gave up. Kissed back. Fuck, could he kiss. And not just one kind of kiss. That was what most men did. They had one kind of kiss. Slow. Sloppy. Too much tongue. Too little tongue. *No* tongue. Crazy wild. Damn the torpedoes, full speed ahead. That was the problem. Didn't they know there were different kinds of kisses and that one can lead to another, and the combinations were the spice of life?

Roy here seemed to know that! A straight man. A straight man who must have had some good teachers. And the kisses right here in the front of his Miata were *so* good. Sugar good. He found himself moaning and getting hard and wanting to hold Roy's hand again—of all things!

Crazy.

What I need is cock up my ass. Deep up my ass. And you, Roy, have just the right equipment. He groped at Roy, who jumped and then moaned back and turned the notches up on his kisses. And God, now shy Roy was groping *him*!

"Let's take this inside," Frank said, breaking the kiss, gasping.

"O-okay."

Now Roy was shy again, looking around him as if they'd been making out on some high school's lover's lane instead of the Wilde's parking lot, and cops had shone their light through the window.

"It's okay," Frank said. "Really. The building is almost all GLBT."

"Huh?" Roy said, wide-eyed once more. His nostrils flared. "GLB…. *Oh*!" Now he sat up in obvious surprise. "Really?" He looked up at the building. "Really…? Wow."

"We started slowly taking over in the seventies and eighties. Some renovating their places. Making the Grand Old Dame beautiful again. It's what we do?"

"We?" Roy asked.

"The *gays*," Frank said and gently bumped foreheads with him. "Let's go."

There was no holding hands this time, but as soon as they were in the elevator, Roy blushed and slowly moved closer, then touched one of Frank's hips and then the other, and pressed his chest up against Frank's. Then… *ah…* sugar kisses.

Just as Roy started to nibble at Frank's lips, the elevator doors slid open, and they did take hands and, laughing, all but ran to Frank's apartment. The minute they were inside they were kissing once again. Dancing. Tearing off their clothes and kicking off their shoes, half tripping, banging into the walls of the hallway as they took turns taking lead.

They fell on the bed, and by this time they were already naked, already hard, already dripping. Somehow, through some kind of psychic consent, found themselves in a sixty-nine position, and they hungrily went for each other's cocks. Kissing, licking, sucking. Frank found desperation taking over, urging him to make Roy cum, desiring to cum himself, to see how close they could time it—even though there was really something he wanted more.

And then, as Frank approached the moment of no return—and by the way Roy's balls were tightening in their sack and his amazing abs were tensing, knew Roy was too—an unspoken message seemed to pass between them again, and they separated at the last possible moment, falling back, panting, gasping. Why, Frank had come so close his balls ached. They lay there a long moment, and then it was Roy who propped himself up on one elbow and looked at Frank, almost crazily, and gasped out, "I want to fuck—" He gulped. "—you."

Frank nodded and sat up, swung his legs out of the bed, said, "Wait a moment, sweet prince"—now what had made him say that?—and hustled to the bathroom. As crazy as the words were, he was grinning.

With practiced ease, he cleaned himself, making himself presentable in every way. For one thing, he hoped Roy would at least run that beard up and down his crack, even if rimming was a lot to ask such a new initiate to gay sex.

He practically ran back, checked himself at the last second, slowed down, walked in, shoulders high and back and half-hard cock before him, hoping it would all turn the heat up again, hoping he hadn't taken too long.

Roy, sitting on the edge of the bed, gave a deep moan filled with desire, and Frank had to fight to keep from chuckling. He pushed Roy onto the mattress, half climbed on him, kissed him passionately, and then urged him to scooch back onto the bed. He rode Roy for a moment, running his crack along the length of that big hard dick, listening to more moans and loving it. Delighted by the expression on Roy's face. The almost wonderment.

I'm doing that. It filled him with joy. No matter what route Roy chose for his life, he wouldn't forget their sex ever.

I don't know that I will either.

"Oh God, Frank, please."

"Please?" he asked.

"Don't make me cum this way. I want to be in *you*. I want to see what it's like to…."

"Assfuck someone?" Frank offered.

"Yes." Roy was panting. "Yes. God, I want it to be you."

This was wonderful. Roy's words alone put Frank on the edge of an orgasm.

"Would you do something for me first?" Frank asked.

"Anything!" Roy cried. And then, "If… if I can." The caveat.

"I want to feel your beard—" He reached out and stroked it, again, again. So full and so damned *soft*. "—on my ass."

Roy's eyes narrowed ever so little.

"All over it. Do that for me?"

ALL OVER his ass….

He wants me to rub my beard all over his ass. What did he say to that?

"O-okay," he managed, and the look on Frank's face at his words made him almost ashamed of his hesitation. Delighted. Thrilled. Overjoyed. And suddenly he wanted to do it.

Frank climbed off him and lay down on his stomach, and Roy pushed himself up high, now on a hand instead of his elbow. He looked down the expanse of that muscular back, and up those slim, fit legs. At that round smooth butt. Why wouldn't he want to touch it? He already had. And if Frank could lick his asshole, surely he could rub his beard across the beautiful skin.

Roy sat up completely, rolled over, crawled down the length of his lover, looked down, and was so struck with the beauty of those rounded glutes, he couldn't understand why he'd hesitated. He straddled Frank and went down on his forearms between those wonderful hairy legs, marveled at those legs and the narrow hips. There was no mistaking this body as belonging to anyone but a man, and his cock got even harder. He rested his chin on the pillow of those cheeks and moved his head from side to side, and the *ooh*s and *aah*s he got made him even harder. Now he moved his face, his soft beard, up and down, and Frank tensed and then moaned and pushed his ass up to meet Roy. His cheeks spread a bit, and Roy wanted to see more.

See his hole.

He took Frank's cheeks in his hand and spread them, spread them a little more to create a smooth, smooth valley, ran his beard up and down it, and almost laughed in delight at Frank's mewing response. Then… he spread those cheeks a little bit more.

And there it was. A perfect little knot of flesh, with only a little hair around it. It was…. He didn't know what word to use, but he could hardly stop looking. Certainly nothing to be afraid of.

It flexed the tiniest little bit, and it was as if it were drawing him in.

Frank's most private place.

Roy brought his face closer, pushed Frank's legs a little farther apart, rested his chin right at the spot, then ran his face up, brushing his beard up the crack and over Frank's asshole. That was what it was. *His asshole.*

Roy's cock began to throb when Frank let out a little cry. It only made Roy harder.

He ran his chin down. Up. Down again. And each time, he dared himself. *Do it. He did it to you. And it felt so good. You say you want to do it all. So do it, goddammit! At least let your….* And even though he couldn't even think the words, at last he let his lips skim over that little pucker and—whoa—a little shock went through him. *My lips touched his asshole!* The next time he grazed it, his lips touched Frank *there* again. No doubt about it. There! Roy's heart was pounding, and he paused and looked and the wrinkles flexed again. It almost seemed to wink, and before he could stop himself, he ran kisses down that deep trench right over Frank's entrance. Or at least that was what it was going to be today.

He paused again to contemplate and wondered how that tiny pucker would take his cock. But surely it was no smaller than his own, and he had taken Frank's cock.

Well, you had a little experience with Ramona's toys....

And Frank, of course, had experience with something besides that.

Roy trembled at that, and his cock leapt. A runner of precum slid slowly down his length. Thrilled, he kissed all up and down that living valley, and Frank cried out in delight, moaning, groaning, gasping, begging. Begging. *Begging for me! Oh the hell with it.* And Roy stuck out his tongue and licked. One long, big, wide, wet lick from Frank's balls to his tailbone, and Frank let out a shout that only intensified Roy's excitement.

Okay, now. You've done it. It's already been done. So do it! Do it again. Why not? He did. Ran his tongue all up and down that private valley and was surprised at the taste. Skin. It was just like skin. But it was more. It was smooth, and it was salty flesh, and the musk of Frank was growing stronger, and—*just do it!*—he licked just *there*!

Frank was shouting and crying out, and the noises urged Roy on. He wanted to prove himself. He licked and flicked and curled his tongue and drilled, and oh, oh, oh, the folds were smoothing out and… opening! The hole was peeking open, flexing, closing tight… loosening. The taste wasn't gross. It reminded him of a tang of metal. Like licking a coin. Like copper. Hot. Doing this crazy thing, this so totally taboo thing, it was…. So. Fucking. Exciting!

"Enough," Frank suddenly shouted and pulled himself up, got up on knees and—

He wants me to fuck him now! Like this.

—then to Roy's surprise, turned, pulled out of his hold, and sat down.

"Lay down on your back," Frank commanded.

Roy looked at him, confused. "But…."

"It's my way. I don't care what you do after. But this is what I need, so lay on your back."

Still confused, he did as he was told, and then Frank reached into the drawer of his bedside table, pulled out a square of foil packaging, tore it open with his teeth, and extracted the condom. He wagged his eyebrows at Roy and then got out the lube and fixed everything up nice and neat, all ready for fucking. He straddled Roy, spread his big hands on Roy's chest, reached back with one of those hands, and grabbed Roy's length.

"*...don't you* ever *let a man fuck you without one,*" Frank had told him, and he meant fucking, *period*. No fucking without a condom.

Roy hated it. He understood it, but he fucking hated it. He wanted to feel this. Feel everything. He had wanted Frank to cum inside him. He'd read a hundred stories, and one of the hottest parts was where one man came in another and they felt it happen, and they felt the cum inside them.

Was there no way he would ever feel that? Know that?

But then, oh God, then Frank was doing it, taking him… *God…* taking Roy inside him and… *goddamn…* had anything ever felt like this?

"*God!*" he yelled.

Frank slowly sat, no real hesitation, just one long, *slow* movement, and then it was done. Frank had taken all of Roy's cock to the root, asshole against pubic hair, and it was so tight, so hot, so deep, it was all he could do not to cum on the spot.

"Nothing," he muttered.

"What?" Frank asked.

Roy shook his head. Later.

"Ready, then?" Frank asked.

"God yes," Roy said.

Frank put his hands back on Roy's chest, adjusted his legs—he was squatting on Roy's cock—and began fucking himself up and down Roy's length and… there… had… never… been… anything… like… it!

He was looking up into Frank's incredibly handsome face, and his cock was inside him! Inside this gorgeous man. It seemed impossible. Roy glanced down and froze, because the way Frank had chosen to do this, he had a perfect view. Could see what was happening—to *him*, to *them*—better than *any* porn movie he had ever seen.

Roy looked back up into Frank's face, his eyes, then back down to where they connected, watched his cock disappear, reappear, disappear, reappear, and God, it was the most mind-blowing thing he had ever experienced in his life.

They were two men!

And they were one. Taking pleasure with and through each other, and they were one. Equal. Any fear he'd had that he might be submissive—it was something *he* didn't want to be, he wanted to be an equal—vanished in an instant. In less than that.

Today he was fucking a man.

Days ago, this selfsame man had fucked *him*.

Equals.

He had no idea why *that* was what was striking him so deeply and completely—more than the fact that they were *fucking* and *damn*, it was so *frigging* hot—but it was the glorious feeling of equality that was overwhelming him with its beauty.

Oneness.

Because how more equal and right could you be than when you were making love with someone of your own sex?

It was glorious, and the sex had never been so good, nothing had ever felt like this, but…. He was struck by….

"A-are you close, babe?" Frank asked, panted.

"N-no," Roy cried.

Frank slowed. "What's wrong, Roy? You okay?"

He wasn't going to be able to cum in this position. "I'm not going…. I'm sorry…. I'm not going to be able to cum this way."

"Oh." Frank smiled. "That's okay. Do you need to be on top?"

Roy nodded his head, embarrassed.

"That's normal, babe."

That word again. Babe. Or baby. It made him all melty and wonderfully gooey inside, and… wait… did he say normal? "Normal?" he asked.

"Sure."

Then Frank did something glorious. Without disconnecting them, he moved, got on his knees, clamped down with his thighs, pushed down with his right hand on the mattress, and slowly—oh, he saw what Frank was doing—rolled them together so Roy was on top. They never lost their union!

Now Frank was on his back with Roy between his widely spread legs, which were soon wrapped around him, and then Frank said, "Fuck me, Roy. *Fuck* me."

For a moment he couldn't do it. Roy was so astonished at Frank's beauty, so amazed at what was being offered to him, stunned that he was inside of Frank, that he couldn't do anything. But then Frank began to urge him on, fisting his own erection, and Roy's hips began moving as if they had a mind of their own. Soon he was doing what he was compelled to do. Thrusting. Fucking. Caught up in something so powerful and beyond belief that he couldn't stop. Faster and deeper, sweat pouring off him, muscles tensing, until finally he could not hold back a moment longer.

"My God," he shouted, and a tidal wave of pleasure slammed through and out of him. Frank's locked legs pulled him even deeper, and he came in one of the most powerful orgasms of his life. Dimly, he was aware of splashing across his torso and belly and Frank shouting with him, and the world went all dark and light and night and stars, and then he fell upon Frank, all but blacked out, panting for breath.

He had never felt this way in his life.

Finally, he whispered, "Wow," in Frank's ear with the only voice he could find. Frank helped him roll off, and it was with a whimper that he slipped from Frank's body. He lay there stunned.

I've done. I've done it all. I could die now and I would be happy.

"Wow," he said again.

He wondered how he could ever leave this bed.

And he knew if he had a choice, he never would.

CHAPTER THIRTEEN

AFTER, WHEN Frank pushed up onto his side to help Roy roll off of him, Roy said it again.

"Wow." Roy was on his back now, and his hands were resting on his (*big*) chest.

Wow. Frank got a little thrill out of that. He couldn't help it. Male ego? Probably. But who gave a shit? How nice to have someone *love* sex so much. He propped himself up and looked down at Roy's sexy face. His elfin eyes were wide and filled with, yes, wonder.

My God, he thought and remembered a boy named Kostas.

"That look on your face," the Greek boy had said, staring down at Frank.

Kostas had taken him to a little pocket of beach mostly hidden from the sight of anyone who wasn't specifically looking for them. For them *there*. They'd made love on a blanket in the growing shadows on the beach. The sun was sitting on the rocks like a cherry on top of a sundae.

The memory was so sharp! Of that sun and Kostas's dark beautiful face, black hair, blacker eyes, and his expression.

"What?" Frank had asked, thinking that he'd done something wrong, that Kostas was teasing him.

"You make me so happy," Kostas replied, and then Frank realized that wasn't amusement on Kostas's face. At least not the making fun kind. And that if Kostas did start laughing—and it looked as if he might—it would be from delight.

"I do?" he asked. His smile was almost involuntary.

"Frank. Yes! Of course. Because I made you *so* happy. I was good? *This*...." He laid his hand on Frank's chest, then took a finger and ran it through the wetness of his tummy. "This was good?"

"Oh my God!" Frank had gasped. "Good doesn't begin to cover it."

"I did not hurt you?" Kostas asked.

"No...." Then he quirked his lip. "Well. A little." He struggled onto his side, facing Kostas, and touched Kostas's softening erection. "I mean... this is *huge*."

Kostas grinned *enormously*. "So are *you*!" he said, and he grabbed Frank's as well.

His mind had been awhirl. In a world of uncertainty and constant change, of feeling somewhat lost, anchorless, Kostas had given him something unbelievable. Something *real*. Something to believe in. He felt totally alive. Completely different. *He* felt real. He wanted to go rushing up the hill, past the white houses with their blue roofs, and he wanted to shout, "I'm a man! I'm a man now!"

Instead he asked, "C-can I do that to you?"

Kostas looked at him in shock. "No. *Oh* no. That cannot be. I must be the man."

The disappointment hit him like a slap. He couldn't understand.

Man? What the hell did he mean by that? Kostas had to be the man?

"Oh no," Kostas said and looked so sad. "Your joy is gone."

"You're holding my 'huge' dick. You think I'm a woman?"

"What I think is that I want you to smile again." Kostas stroked Frank's cheek. "And so maybe—" He looked around him in mock surveillance, then back at Frank. "—maybe if you do not tell *any*one, I will let you."

Frank's heart had surged with the news, and he smiled so big it almost hurt.

"Now!" Kostas grinned. "There it is. The joy! That is what I wanted to see. Yes, you may do *that* to me."

Quite suddenly, Frank knew. Looking down at Roy's face. The look on his face. *Joy.* This must be a lot how he had looked to Kostas.

His heart surged exactly like it had that late afternoon on the beach beneath a sun like a maraschino cherry.

The look on Roy's face! Wonder.

No. Frank wasn't feeling male ego. This tingling through him, like a low-current electric charge, was born of the fact that he'd taken this man by the hand—literally—and shown him joy he hadn't imagined. Was it letting Roy fuck him that had done it? Or...?

"So good," whispered Roy. He looked at Frank. "It's like… I don't know how to say it, Frank. I…. Fuck…." He shook his head, clearly frustrated.

Frank laid a hand on his chest. Then he ran a finger through the wetness he had splashed there.

"Shh…," he said. "I get it."

Those swimming-pool-blue eyes went wide. "*Do* you, Frank? Do you? I mean, my whole world…."

Frank smiled. Nodded. "That's the way it was for me. Like I woke up in the Twilight Zone."

Roy's eyes went even wider. "No. That's not what I mean. I-I felt that at the sandwich shop. What I'm feeling now?" He shook his head in frustration, brows furrowed together in a knot.

"Relax, baby," Frank said. "It's okay—"

"I *need* to find the words," Roy said, cutting him off. "*Now*." He stopped and swallowed hard, and the focus in his eyes went away, went blank for a moment, and then, "It's all the fucking *possibilities*. So much I can do now. There's this… equality."

Equality?

"No need for roles, I guess. Part of it's the sex." He blushed. "A *lot* of it is the sex. I mean, we both have dicks. We both can suck. We *both* can fuck. We both can *be* sucked or *be* fucked. But I'm lying here now, and it's really like I'm standing at this doorway. I've felt it before since I met you, but *now* it's like… *pow*! Like I can walk through and nothing will ever be the fucking same again. Or… I can close it."

Sad, but true. Frank nodded again. "Yes, you can. But you've seen what's on the other side of the door. You're always going to know it's there. You can't unknow it."

ROY'S HEART was almost slamming in his chest. It was like he was on a roller coaster, with the slow parts and the crazy racing-out-of-control parts. One minute he wanted to cry with utter joy, and the next he was near panic.

That door. If he walked through it, nothing would ever be the same.

It was *huge*. He looked at Frank. Thought what life could be like at his side, as his partner. His heart swelled thinking about it.

Living his life with a man. How it would be totally different from anything he had ever imagined for himself. Anything expected. He was supposed to get married, have kids, raise them, get old, watch *them* get married and give him grandchildren. A life with Frank would be totally different. Anything could happen. There was a sense of… yes, equality there he'd never imagined possible. Along with the complete unknown.

But then he thought of his Uncle Donald and his fag jokes. He thought of his mother, who had put up with so much from him. Of Granny and what she might think of him. That was too horrible to think of.

On the other hand, there was Frank. Frank and all he represented. All those new possibilities. It was more than the sex. The sex had simply made him aware of so much he should have already been aware of.

He had never felt like this before. Suddenly, there *were* possibilities. Lots of them. That imagined life—wife, kids, graduations, marriages, grandkids—wasn't his only choice, predetermined.

Oh God.

He began to shiver. All that was a life he'd never really chosen. Just a life he'd expected. And now he was not so sure he had *ever* wanted it.

"Roy?" Frank…. Frank was pulling a blanket up over him. Over them. He pulled Roy close. "You okay?"

"I don't know," he answered truthfully.

"You don't have to make any kind of decision right now. In fact, I think it's the wrong time—lying there covered in cum…."

Roy cheeks heated.

"You've got your whole life ahead of you. It's something you owe yourself to think about."

For some reason, the words, said so calmly, allowed his racing heart to begin to slow down.

"You don't have to make any kind of decision right now," Frank had just said. But he also said that Roy was always going to know a whole different life was there, on the other side of some door. That he had seen it. And he could never unknow it.

"Shush your mind," Frank said. "Let it go right now. You just fucked a man up the ass. It's a big deal. Gives you a lot to think about. But you don't have to think about it *now*."

Roy sighed. Frank pulled him close, and he found himself in the crook of Frank's arm, cheek resting on his big hairy chest. The hair was so full across his pecs, and then it stopped, his belly smooth as could be, until the little trail began from his belly button and down. Roy liked it. A lot. Wished *his* was a little more like Frank's. He laid a hand on those pecs, where most of the hair grew. Touched it. Fingered it. It was very soft. Frank was casually rubbing his upper back and that… that felt nice. Really nice. Who knew this could be so nice?

So nice.

He tangled his fingers gently in Frank's chest hair. Then he let his hand slide slowly down, over Frank's tummy and then into the patch of pubic hair above the root of his soft penis. *That's been inside me*, he thought and trembled… and found he wanted it again.

But incredibly, he was yawning, and his eyelids felt *so* heavy. All that fucking. All that thinking. Tired.

And then he drifted right off to sleep.

FRANK WAS a little surprised at Roy's snore, and then not. The kid had been going through a lot. Sexually. Mentally. He was probably exhausted. Part of him wanted to rouse him and send him off. But another part—a "well, I'll be damned" part—didn't want Roy to go. That part kind of liked this. Liked it fine.

After all, what else was he doing? A good beer was starting to call his name. Did he want to drink alone? He'd been going to Harry and Cody's way too much. He didn't want to wear out his welcome. What was wrong with a little company?

He supposed he should probably be careful. He could be treading on dangerous ground. Three times now they'd had *participatory* sex. Roy wasn't just lying back, closing his eyes, and pretending Frank was a girl. Roy was sucking back. Swallowing. Fucking. *Getting*—the ultimate undeniability—fucked.

And it was getting pretty damned clear the kid was starting to suspect he was gay. Or beginning to *stop* denying it.

Frank also needed to stop thinking of Roy as a kid. He was *no* kid. He was a man. Twenty-five, twenty-six, maybe. But a man.

All man, as the pleasant soreness of his ass testified. Roy had done a good job at banging his box. Done a mighty good job of fucking him.

He looked down at Roy. *God, I hope I haven't stepped right into something.*

Frank had done his fair share of virgins. He had to admit, he liked knowing he'd live on in their memories. Now *that* was an ego thing, he fully admitted.

But they could also be a major problem. Virgins could fall in love—or at least think they had. Virgins could be found outside your bedroom window in the rain, boom box on their shoulder, playing Peter Gabriel's "In Your Eyes." Virgins could be barnacles, near impossible to scrape off.

And if you let them stick around, virgins sometimes needed to have their hands held and be walked carefully—like a toddler taking its first steps—through the beginnings of gay life. Frank *maybe* had time to give Roy another week or so test flight. But he didn't have time to walk a new gay through the joys and pitfalls of coming out. If he was going to let Roy hang with him for a while, he better make sure Roy knew this wasn't going to be a love affair.

And they'd already held hands, hadn't they?

He closed his eyes. *Oh fuck.... What have I done?*

He lay there for a while, not sure what to do. He liked Roy. Despite himself, he did. The kid… the *man*, was fun. Sweet. A hell of a kisser—*goddamn!*—and fucking fun in bed. And Jesus, he was a beginner. What would he be like with some experience?

Would giving him a little longer be so bad? What was the harm of getting to know him a little bit?

How about the whole barnacle thing, Frank?

And hot damn, he still didn't know why Roy had been standing there on the side of the road wearing orange, did he? Roy could be a bank robber. A mugger. A rapist.

Frank shook his head. Looked at his sweet face. Thought of how sweet he *was*. And naïve. Somehow doubted Roy was dangerous.

In his mind's eye, Frank saw him again, standing there, the zipper of his orange jumpsuit pulled down low enough to show off his tight little navel. Taking that bottle of water from the cop, drinking from it, Adam's apple working as he swallowed, then pouring the rest over himself, tossing his head to either side, water droplets flying and catching the sun, the rest running down his muscled chest and torso....

His cock gave a little twitch. He laughed. "Whoa, boy," he said. *Haven't you had enough for one day?*

It shifted, as if listening to what Frank had said and giving its answer. *Never enough.* And Frank chuckled again.

His arm began to tingle. Roy had shifted a bit and was cutting off the circulation, so he carefully pulled it out from under Roy and thought, *Might as well get up and take a piss.*

He padded naked to the bathroom and leaned against the wall as he peed *forever*, scratched his ass, his balls. Then he washed up and went back to the bedroom.

Frank went to the bed, looked down at Roy, sprawled there on his stomach, one knee drawn up, smooth ass—even his crack was totally smooth—on display. Yes, there was his asshole. How good it had been to be inside there. Inside Roy.

He wondered again at how relatively easily Roy had taken a cock for the first time. Frank knew himself to be an ass-eater *par excellence*, but still. That didn't account for the fact that Roy took Frank's not inconsiderable length and thickness with no apparent distress. About the only sign that he'd had any trouble at all was when his eyes popped wide, and then he had locked his ankles around Frank and pulled him in.

"Fuck me. Fuck me, Frank. Oh Christ! So good. So much... better *than I ever thought.* God!*"* Frank's ass had hurt for hours, even the next morning, after losing *his* cherry. So maybe Roy was lying and *had* been fucked before. But somehow, Frank didn't think that was the case. He knew so little about this man, but Roy had not struck him as a liar.

Or, and Frank thought this was closer to the truth, Roy had played with a sex toy or two. Had been headed, one way or another, toward a man's bed for a while, even if he didn't know it.

Shit. Frank didn't know either.

And he certainly didn't know the answer to one of the biggest mysteries concerning Mr. Roy Ingalls. What was Roy doing on the side of I-70? And just what was it he did to be wearing orange?

"Those are bad boys."

Frank realized something. He wanted to know. Surely it wouldn't be anything too serious. The young man wasn't a murderer. Probably not a robber. He didn't seem like he could possibly be a molester or rapist.

Yeah, okay. Let him hang around long enough for Frank to find out.

And maybe, just maybe, he'd wear an orange jumpsuit for Frank.

CHAPTER FOURTEEN

ROY AWOKE to an empty bed. Frank's bed. Shit. He'd fallen asleep.

He sat up and wiped his eyes. He heard music coming from another room—a radio or stereo or movie perhaps—and tried to decide what to do.

He looked down at the floor and saw clothes here and there. Whatever Frank was wearing, it wasn't what he'd been wearing when Roy met him at the gas station. Neither the shirt that let the world know I Can't Even Keep a Straight Face nor the one that read I Hate Tacos Said No Juan Ever.

He swung out of bed and got his jeans, slipped into them, remembered the rest of his clothes—their clothes—were scattered from here to the front door, grinned, felt a delightful warmth spread across his face knowing how those clothes got there, and *then* remembered, *saw* Frank—crystal clear and in Cinemark XD and IMAX—naked beneath him, taking Roy's cock inside him.

My God. I fucked a man. I fucked Frank.

And it had been incredible.

The thought, the memory, almost made him light-headed. But in a glorious way.

I was inside *Frank!*

He went down the hall, into the living room, found his shirt, slipped it on. Glanced around. Realized he hadn't really *looked* at Frank's place before. It was nice. Nicer than any place he'd ever lived. Nicer than his mother's house, or his granny's, and certainly nicer than Uncle Donald's trailer.

"Frank?" he called over the stereo, and surely that's what it was. Weird music. But good weird. Moody. Mysterious. The singers were saying something about crazy diamonds and how they should shine on. Roy didn't know who they were, but he made an immediate decision.

He liked them. They reminded him of a group he'd heard before; he just could remember which one.

He went into the kitchen and...

Whoa. Was taken aback at how beautiful it was. The granite countertops, the new appliances, the cabinets that shone with a sure, deep walnut gloss that he could almost see his reflection in. And the floor too. Gorgeous—*that word again*—wood with Roy had no idea *how* many layers of varnish.

But the kitchen was empty, no Frank, so he went back to the living room and called out his name again, "Frank!" a third time.

"Out here!" came Frank's voice. "On the balcony."

Roy went to two big glass doors, one wide open, and stepped out to find Frank lying back on a futon, of all things, and—*and*—he was naked.

Completely naked. One big foot (God what feet) was crossed over the other on a dark wicker coffee table, and his arms were spread out across the back of the futon, and he was bare to the world. Roy actually took a step back in surprise.

"Hey, handsome man," Frank said. He lowered his feet to the ground, leaned forward, picked up a bottle of beer, and took a drink. "Thirsty?"

Roy swallowed hard. "You're naked," he managed.

Frank nodded. "I am. Good catch."

"Aren't you afraid somebody will see you?"

Frank gave him a look that *clearly* said, "Really? Do you think I care?" and then he chuckled and said, "No one's going to see me. The other balcony"—he pointed—"is mine, off the bedroom, and there's nobody else on this end of the building. The people on the seventh floor would have to hang off theirs to see me, and—" He stood and did a little bounce on the balls of his feet, arms at his side, cock giving a little bounce of its own. "—the ledge of the balcony keeps anyone from seeing my ding-dong!"

Roy burst out laughing. "Ding-dong."

"You would prefer pecker?" Frank asked, grinning his incredible smile.

Gorgeous.

"Dick? Peter? John Thomas? Tonsil tickler?"

Roy was giggling now. *You've tickled* my *tonsils.*

"Disco stick? Schlong? Tube steak? Skin flute?"

"Stop!" Roy said, gasping.

"Purple-headed warrior? Pocket rocket? One-eyed trouser snake?"

"Oh my God," Roy cried, tears forming, laughing. "Oh stop!"

"Master of cherrimonies? *Man*hood? Meat thermometer…?"

Then, giving up, Roy joined in, "Dingus? Love muscle?"

"Anal invader?"

Oh! Good one. Thinking of how Frank's had anally invaded *him*. Roy's face heated at the memory. "Anaconda," he offered, thinking of how big Frank was.

"Bologna pony?"

"Meat popsicle?"

"Tallywhacker?" And now Frank was laughing, and Roy was having trouble catching his breath. Frank leapt forward, swept Roy into his arms, and kissed him.

It was a quick one, but it surprised Roy more than his finding Frank naked out in the open. Before he could make sense of it or ask about it, and just as it occurred to him how *much* he liked it, Frank said, "You going to get a beer? Because if you are, I want one."

"Sh-sure," Roy said and went back in the apartment, smiling. He stopped at the kitchen counter, reached out and rested his hand there, and thought about how much he smiled around Frank.

He shook himself and went to the refrigerator, stopped in surprise when he realized the facing of the door was wood as well and matched the cabinets, and then opened it. He found the beers easily enough, something called Sixth Glass Quadrupel Ale from Boulevard, a definite step above the PBR *he* could afford, especially when he hadn't found anyone who would hire him yet. He grabbed two bottles, found the bottle opener on the counter—no magnet; there was nothing to stick it to. He'd never seen a refrigerator without at least *one* magnet—opened the bottles, and went to rejoin Frank.

Naked Frank.

And damn, sitting there, he took Roy's breath away.

Jesus. I… I might be… God, I….

He couldn't say it, even to himself.

Roy handed Frank a beer, and Frank raised his, and Roy realized he wanted to clink them—so he did.

Frank drank and then Roy did, and wow, the beer tasted nothing—
nothing—like any beer he had ever had before. It seemed… thicker.
Heavier. Richer somehow. With an almost-sweet aftertaste.

"You like?" Frank asked.

"It's different," Roy said.

"Uh-oh," Frank replied.

"No," Roy said quietly. "It's… it's just nothing like I've ever had
before." He raised it, took another drink, and it actually tasted different
as it hit the tongue, rushed over it, held there a moment, and then went
down. Sort of strong at first, like coffee. Then came the richness. Then
the sweet aftertaste.

"I… I think I could learn to like this," Roy whispered.

"You'll like it," Frank said, a *little* louder. "It's one of the finer
things in life."

"I…." Roy struggled to find the words.

"I promise you will," Frank assured him. "Like the finer things
in life."

"I…."

"And if you don't, then okay."

"I…."

"It's just so weird," Frank said, "you wearing clothes while I'm
naked."

"What's weird," Roy said, finally finding his voice, "is you being
naked while I'm wearing clothes."

"Then take them off."

"You could put yours *on*," Roy countered.

Frank reached out a finger, lifted Roy's chin, looked at him. "Do
you really want me to?"

Roy sucked in a deep breath and let it slowly out. No. No he didn't.
He liked Frank naked.

"Please?" Frank asked.

How could he say no to that? After looking around once more, he
pulled off his shirt and started to undo his pants, and Frank said, "No,
no! Me! Come here."

Roy did, and Frank popped open the button and pulled down the
zipper, and then Roy's jeans fell in a puddle around his feet. Frank
leaned in and kissed him right above his cock, pressing his face into

his pubic hair and breathing in deep. "You really do have a beautiful cock, Roy—"

That word again, beautiful, to describe his penis. His cheeks burned, and knew he was blushing once again.

"—and you smell *so* good. *So* sexy."

Roy's penis immediately began to stir, and Frank said it again, "No, no!" and, "That can wait a *little* bit, can't it?" He patted the futon cushion next to him. "Sit."

"You don't mind me sitting naked on your cushion?" Roy asked, and then realized that was probably a stupid question.

Frank's raised eyebrows seemed to indicate he felt the same way. "I've eaten your ass, Roy. And you seem pretty clean to me. *Down there.*"

Well…. He *could* say that about himself. There were times Roy wondered if maybe he was a little obsessed with being clean… down there. Down there *any*where.

He sat. And while he wondered briefly how many other men had sat here naked with Frank, he pushed it out of his mind. It felt a little too much like jealousy. And why would he be jealous about who Frank was with?

It's not like I want to marry him. Why should I care who he's been with? None of my concern.

Roy never forgot he was naked. Naked outside. How could he when Frank was so wonderfully sprawled out that way? But it did start to feel kind of nice. Kind of sexy.

He still caught himself glancing over at the other balcony once or twice. Or thrice. He looked around and saw that any buildings tall enough to look out at the sixth floor of the Oscar Wilde were too far away to see anything without binoculars. But hey, some people owned telescopes, and some of them didn't use them to look at the stars.

"Hey!"

Roy jumped in surprise at the sudden shout and looked around him and saw Frank on the other balcony. He was waving. Somehow, he had gotten up and left without Roy noticing, and now he was…. Shit! He was doing jumping jacks.

"Look!" Frank cried. "Look at me."

And sure enough, the ledge of the balcony pretty much kept his privates… private. If he hadn't been doing calisthenics and he hadn't had such a big dick that the head of it flopped up into view for an instant once or twice, Roy really wouldn't have known if Frank was naked or merely shirtless.

Roy shook his head. Smiled. Flushed. Waved back.

"Okay! Okay," he yelled back. "I *get* it!"

Frank stopped the jumping jacks and disappeared into the apartment. A moment later, he rejoined Roy and handed him one of the two beers he was carrying.

Things were better after that. The sexy came back. A little thrill of, well, freedom. Yes. That was it. Freedom after *not* being free was a very good feeling.

Soon they began to talk, which in reality, they *hadn't* done a lot of.

Roy mentioned the kitchen and how beautiful it was. Even the floor. "You're so lucky to have this place."

"I *made* this place," Frank said, grinning, and he jumped up and grabbed Roy's hand. "Let me show you."

Frank gave him the most amazing tour as he proudly showed off his apartment. The floors in the living room—"You should have seen them when I moved in. The previous tenants must have raced horses in here!"—the fireplace mantel—"I had to sand off about 317 layers of paint," he said with an eye roll and a laugh—the bathroom—"Someone actually painted over the tile, and I was shocked to find out there was this wonderful Greek key pattern that must be original. I was even able to find a few replacement pieces at Architectural Salvage downtown."—and yes, he had done the refrigerator door.

"It was a bitch, I tell you. I mean obviously, the refrigerator isn't from the 1920s when the building was built. I went for a fun old-meets-new in here." He waved dramatically all around him, and Roy almost laughed. It was cute. So *not* the sexy-but-silent image Frank was always projecting. "But when I finally figured out how to make this work"—now he was pointing at the refrigerator door—"then I knew I had something special. I think when I move I might have to take it with me, even though that means doing two kitchens in the same color wood."

Wait. Move? "You're moving?" Roy asked.

Frank nodded. Then opened the refrigerator and ducked inside. "I have two more bottles of the Sixth Glass," he said from its depths. "Want one?" He reappeared and handed a bottle to Roy without waiting for an answer.

"When?" Roy asked, inexplicably desperate.

"When what?" Frank asked.

"When are you moving?"

"When I'm all done, like I said. I mean, I'll stick around a year after, maybe, and then the craving will come to take a plain caterpillar and turn it into a butterfly. This is my third here in the Wilde."

A relief so gigantic and unexplainable it was almost palpable hit Roy and practically knocked him back on his heels. "Oh!"

"And the owners love me. They practically let me live in apartments for free because they know when I'm done they're going to be able to ask a fortune for the place. And after all, I only move into one of the two end units."

"End units?" Roy asked, beginning to feel like a mynah bird.

"Each floor has two bigger apartments on either end of the building. They're larger, have three bedrooms, fireplaces, et cetera. They're where the more affluent tenants would have lived back in the twenties and thirties. Whenever I feel guilty that I am pricing my GLBT brothers and sisters out of apartments, I remember that there are plenty of units that are quite affordable." He popped open his beer and handed the opener to Roy. "It's all my father's fault. It's what he does. Restores beautiful places all over the world. Chalets in Austria, châteaus in France, a haveli in India, palazzos in Italy, villas in Greece. Some huge, palatial places—those were in the cities where we'd live for a year or more—and some a lot smaller. Mostly restoring them to look as close to the original as possible. He'd research for weeks, months sometimes. That was where he started me, reading and finding and researching. But soon I fell in love with the wood. And not this kind." Frank groped him, and Roy jumped back and then wondered why. He liked Frank's hands on him after all. A lot.

Frank grinned. "I loved the sanding. Sanding, sanding, sanding. Starting with the coarse papers and getting finer and finer as I went. I love the sawdust. Getting finer and finer. Powder. The *dust* on my hands. It *feels* so good. And the smell of it all. I *love* the smell of the wood."

He closed his eyes and breathed deep, nostrils flaring, and a smile that looked something like love spread across his face.

Roy's heart jumped. He was seeing something deep and personal here. He was seeing *Frank*. It was something he hadn't seen before, something he hadn't been allowed to see. This wood, this kitchen, this apartment, all that went with it, was *Frank*.

And for one incredible instant, Roy *experienced* something deep and personal. It felt like love.

He shook himself just in time to hear Frank say, "The only smell I like as much"—his eyes popped wide and wild—"is the smell of a man's balls."

Now Roy grinned. He grinned big and happy and wild. And it felt deliciously naughty. Quite suddenly, Roy wanted sex. Again. How many times would that make?

"And I love the smell of the varnishes. I smell varnish, and I am transported all over the world."

"You've really lived all those places?" Roy asked and was struck by something akin to awe.

Frank nodded and looked strangely exultant and sad at the same time. "I never got to grow up anywhere. I don't have any lifelong friends like so many people I've met since moving to Kansas City. My old man was my only constant. But hey, I *did* see the world. And I have some pretty magical memories." He took a very deep breath and let it out slowly and then nodded his head to the side. "Let's sit down." In the background musicians were wishing "you were here."

"Who is this?" Roy asked.

"Pink Floyd," Frank replied.

"I don't think I've heard of him," Roy said. "Is he new?"

Frank chuckled. "Pink Floyd isn't a he. It's a group. And no, they're not new. They've been around a lot longer than you or me. Ever heard of the song 'The Wall'?"

"The... wall?"

"The kids singing about how they don't need no education?"

Just like that Roy remembered. "They don't need thought control?"

"That's the one. But I like *this* album best. And then *Dark Side of the Moon*."

Roy listened for a moment. "I really like it," he said quietly.

"You have good taste," Frank said. "It is one thing I can say about my old man. He taught me good taste in music." And then he turned and headed out onto the balcony. Roy followed, looking at Frank's ass. God, it was a nice ass. And there was no mistaking it for a woman's, what with those narrow hips. The very shape of it was man.

I fucked that, he thought in awe.

CHAPTER FIFTEEN

BACK ON the balcony Frank asked, "What do you do?"

"Oh... a little of this, a little of that," Roy answered. He hated that he was evading the question. But he wasn't sure he was ready to tell Frank the truth. He didn't know if Frank wanted to know. It just might end everything, here and now. Roy was enjoying the here and now. He wasn't quite ready for it to end.

Because who wanted a jailbird in their home?

Frank asked him where he lived and he almost said Roeland Park and left it at that, but then it felt dishonest. Like a sin of omission. And he didn't want to be dishonest with Frank. Frank had shown Roy his home. Frank had shown him a little bit of Frank. And being anything other than honest would be somehow wrong. Totally disrespectful.

So he told Frank that he was living with his mom. "I had a place before but... well, there was a...." He stopped, not knowing what to say. Saying it all seemed a lot like vomiting right here on the balcony. "There was a...."

"Bad time," Frank said. "We all have at least one." He was looking at Roy, eyes locked with his, and it was as if he were looking *into* his brain. His memories. Roy shivered.

"We're lucky if there's only one," Frank continued. "But we pick ourselves up. Dust ourselves off. We go on. And things *do* get better."

Frank said it with such understanding, such assurance, as if there were *no* room for doubt, it was all Roy could do not to gasp.

"Do they, Frank? Get better?"

"They do, Roy. I believe that. They have to get better. I think I'd go crazy if I didn't believe it was true."

Roy wasn't sure what to say.

Frank rescued him by saying, "So you're living with your mom. Is that okay? Is she cool or is she giving you a hard time?"

The words "hard time" gave Roy a little shock, but he shook it off. "No. She's awesome. I have a totally awesome mom. I think she was happy to have me move back home."

In fact he knew she was.

"I didn't feel safe when you moved out," she'd told him. She'd told him when he was planning on moving out—that she wouldn't feel safe. But damn, he wasn't a kid anymore, and you move out when you grow up. "When you get married, you do! That's what I did. I lived with my mom and dad until *the* day I got married."

"She actually said that?" Frank said, laughing. But it was clear he wasn't being insulting.

Roy nodded, hardly aware he had even told the story out loud.

"What does she have to be afraid of, living in Roeland Park?"

"I don't know," Roy said with a shrug.

"Well, you're lucky." Then Roy noticed an odd thing. A tightness in Frank's jaw. A narrowing of his eyes. It was very fast, though. Roy's imagination? "I never really knew my mother," Frank continued. "She left us when I was around five years old."

"Oh." God. "That sucks." Roy blushed. *That sucks? Really?* "I mean, that must have been hard."

Frank's faraway look refocused, and then he was back from wherever he'd gone.

"I really don't remember much. I remember one Halloween when she took me around door-to-door. And I think I remember that because in so many places Dad and I lived, they don't do Halloween. At least not like we do it here." He went away again for a second—half a second. "I remember her reading me *How the Grinch Stole Christmas*." He shrugged. "What about your father?"

Roy sighed. "He died when I was in high school. I don't really talk about it."

"Sorry."

"No. It's okay. I just don't like thinking about it."

"So my mom," Frank said, "and your dad. We're a couple, aren't we?"

Roy jolted. Couple?

"Oh!" Frank laughed uncomfortably. "I didn't mean we were a *couple*."

Roy smiled, but it was about the damned fakest thing in the world, and he was sure Frank must see it. Couple. The word had so surprised him. This was all about fucking, right? He didn't want to be with Frank. Not like that. Not set up home with him.

Right?

Then why are you here? Some part of him asked. And for that he had no answer.

Why am I here? You did it. You did it all. You got the best blowjob of your life. *You sucked him off*—and the thought made him blush and his pulse race—*God! Twice! You let him fuck you… and you fucked him.* He came back here to fuck Frank so that he could put all this gay-sex stuff behind him.

He trembled, the images rushing through his head: Frank spread open before him, presenting himself to Roy. *Saw* it happening. The beauty of him offered *for* Roy. It had been glorious. Like something… magic.

Magic? Really?

He trembled again. Oh yes. It had been magic.

He *saw* Frank's cock, all hard, wet, needing him. Thought of sucking him and how truly amazing that had been.

And he *saw* Frank on top of him, felt Frank's cock sliding into him so he knew, finally, what a *real* cock felt like instead of a plastic toy. How unbelievable it had been. Some rolling swirling combination of exhilarating debauchery and the thrill of the taboo, but wildly personal and intimate and beautiful and filled with trust.

The only thing that could have made it better was not having to use that goddamned condom.

He had wanted so much to feel *skin*. Wrapped that way it was too damned close to a dildo. If he was going to have a real cock up inside of him, what an awful thing it was that they had to be separated by that thin layer of latex.

And he hadn't been able to feel Frank cumming inside him. He'd felt Frank's cock jerking, but he hadn't been able to *feel* what those stories on Nifty Archive described. Feel the jets, feel himself filling with the warm fluid that came from Frank. Feel it dripping out of him. He had wanted that *so* much! Had tried to tell Frank he didn't need to wear it because he hadn't *wanted* him to wear it!

"Yes," Frank had told him with such resolve. "Yes, *I* do. *And don't you* ever *let a man fuck you without one.*"

And now he *never* would know what it felt like. It wasn't like he was ever going to do this with another man!

"Well, something is getting you all excited," Frank said with a big naughty grin on his face.

"What?" Roy asked, and when he looked down where Frank was so obviously looking, his cock was getting hard, was halfway there and giving a little leap as it tried to get even harder. "Oh!" He felt the burn spread over his face and sat up and tried to cover himself, but how was he going to do that? There wasn't even a little pillow on the futon to grab as a shield.

"Roy, I've sucked that thing. I've seen you hard. *Felt* it." He wagged his eyebrows playfully. "You don't need to cover it up."

"I...." Well of course that was true. But, "I'm not used to this, Frank!"

"You need a hand with that?" Frank asked. "Want me to slide down to my knees and—" And he already was, but...

"No!" Roy looked around. He hadn't meant to say it so loud. But of course there was no one to hear. And no one could see. "It's just.... I was thinking about something."

"I could tell," Frank said with a pout. "You sure you don't want me to relieve—"

"And that is the other thing I've been wondering!" Roy all but shouted. Because something else had suddenly slammed into the forefront of his thoughts.

Frank slid back into his seat. "What, Roy?"

"I wanted you to fuck me without a condom." And his face heated all the more, dammit. "I wanted to know what that feels like. But you said—"

"I said no, and my answer will be forever no."

Forever?

"I am a gay man, baby. I can't even imagine how many men I've had one kind of sex or another with. Hundreds, Roy."

For some reason that stung. Deep. Stupid, but it did. Like jealousy, and why would he be jealous? He didn't want Frank. Well... not *forever*.

"And I plan to have hundreds more while I'm good-looking enough to get them."

Well, Frank was fucking good-looking.

"In that way I'm like my old man. I don't do relationships. I don't believe in that lovey-dovey shit. Longest I ever knew Glen to be with a woman was a couple years. I've never made it a couple months. Some guy starts getting serious then, and I end it."

God. That hurt. Roy didn't even know why. It wasn't like he wanted Frank to be his boyfriend. But.... Oh, but to wake up to Frank each morning? There were far worse fates.

"Sorry, sweetness, but it's true. I was about fourteen the first time I had sex with a guy, and I knew I had found something brilliantly stupendously fantastic, and I got it whenever I could. Somewhere along the line, two plus two equaled four in my teenage mind, and I realized I could get AIDS. That it was some kind of miracle I never had. Or fuck that, herpes or syph or gonorrhea or genital warts. So as much as I don't like goddamned condoms, I want to live a long life and—"

"So, you don't have it?" Roy blurted and knew in that very second that for some reason, getting a disease had never occurred to him. How pathetically stupid was that?

Frank shook his head. "No. I got hep B once, and the crabs a couple times, but that's it."

"Then why is swallowing okay?" This time Roy was almost shouting because that was on the forefront of what had slammed into his mind. Why could they gulp cum down like it was cream but not the other?

Frank nodded once. Twice. Slowly. He sighed. "Yeah. Well. That's on me and my call, and I should have made sure you understood. You being a virgin and all." He got a funny look on his face at that and Roy's brow came together, wondering why.

"*I* believe it's safe," Frank said. "At least for HIV. There have been about a zillion studies done and opinions waffle back and forth, but I think it's pretty clear that your stomach acids kill it. Your saliva too. Now there is some evidence that if you have some kind of open sore in your mouth or on your dick that the virus can be spread. But—and I don't mean to shock you, sweetie—but I have probably swallowed a kid's pool full of cum in my life, who knows, maybe an Olympic swimming pool's worth, and I am negative. And I gotta have one vice. I should have just made sure you knew that *you* had a choice. It is your decision."

"Swallowing is better," Roy said and then blushed for about the billionth time. Things just seemed to fall right out of his mouth around

Frank. He'd say them before even knowing he was thinking them. Just *bloop*! And there it was.

But it was true. Swallowing was one of the sexiest and most freeing things he'd ever done in his life. Liberating even.

"I think so," Frank said with a laugh, and then his cock gave a little jump and shifted a bit across his muscular thigh. "I fucking love it. But I should have said something. It wasn't… honest."

"Honest?" Roy asked. Why, not giving him the options when it came to swallowing cum hardly seemed dishonest. *He* was the one who hadn't been honest—and then, out of the gate, riding the bull right out of the chute, he did it again.

"I was in jail," he said, shocking himself, spilling his secret without even knowing he was going to do it. "I *went* to jail." And everything in him cringed.

And then Frank said something that shocked him completely and deeply.

"I know," Frank said very softly.

CHAPTER SIXTEEN

FRANK'S WORDS obviously surprised Roy.

But then he'd surprised himself by telling him.

"I know."

I just spat it out there, didn't I?

What must Roy be thinking? It could be anything. *He could be thinking that I stalked him or did some kind of freaking background check on him.* The thought made Frank cringe. *He could think I'm a fucking weirdo.*

But when Roy admitted that he'd gone to jail, the words were out of Frank's mouth before he could stop them.

"I know."

Because he *did* know. Or knew there was *something*. Jail? Was that a softer way of saying prison? A way for Roy to test the waters and see how Frank would react?

Well, from his expression, Roy had clearly not guessed Frank was going to say that he already knew.

But he did. And he'd been struggling with it. He had to let Roy know because it would come out eventually, and that *could* ruin everything.

Ruin what? He's a trick! He's a trick that you're tricking with more than once. So what? What would it fucking ruin?

But then…. He took a deep breath. Roy was a little bit more than a trick, wasn't he? Because a trick was someone he stopped and asked if they wanted a blowjob, they accepted, he gave it to them, and then he kicked their ass out the door.

He and Roy had done a *little* more than that. And even though he had no intention of marrying the guy—Glen had shown him *all* about the institution of marriage and what a joke, a *fiasco*, it was—that didn't mean Frank didn't enjoy occasionally having a fuck buddy. And fuck buddy did mean *buddy*. Someone you might do a little bit more with than just fuck, although he had certainly had his fair share where that was all they did. And then there were his regulars, for whom he was just a phone call away....

"Hey, Frank! Mind if I drop by after work? I have about forty-five minutes and my asshole is twitching to beat the band...."

"Hey, Frank, I got off work early today. I could sure use one of your blowjobs."

"Hey, Frank. I'm having a few friends over to... party tonight. We sure could use a hot, versatile stud. Wanna join us?"

And of course, he'd oblige them whenever he could. He was nothing if not a Good Samaritan.

Yeah, he had a few of those and liked them. Men who wanted no attachments and liked a guy they could count on when Mr. Thumb and His Four Brothers weren't doing it anymore.

But Roy.

Well, what a goddamned surprise. He kinda liked the guy. And he didn't have to worry about Roy getting all romantic. At least, it didn't look like it was going that way—and he hated when it went that way. But Roy still couldn't even make up his mind if he was gay. As someone to fuck and get fucked by—and Roy was pretty good—and listen to Pink Floyd and have a steak with once in a while, Roy fit the fuck-buddy bill pretty well. At least for a *while*. Until they got bored with each other or Roy decided to go back to girls. Which would be a crying shame—Roy could turn out to be a *hell* of a cocksucker! Didn't the world always need a good blowjob?

But then...

Roy was more than that. He was a really sweet man. And that's what the world needed more of.

Well, what do you know? He was starting to think of Roy as a person and not just a way to get off. And he realized he didn't want to hurt Roy's feelings. Frank knew himself. Someday, probably a lot sooner than later, he would accidentally say he'd seen Roy standing along the side of the road in the (fucking hot) orange jumpsuit, and it could potentially really hurt Roy's feelings. That he hadn't said anything.

And goddammit, he didn't want to hurt Roy's feelings. Roy was standing there looking like Bambi, with his big beautiful Disney eyes— well, except that his eyes were blue and Bambi's were brown—and he looked so sweet and boyish and forlorn and innocent—well, except for being naked and having a big cock. That wasn't exactly a standard Disney Studios character now, was it?

Yeah, those eyes made Frank *not* want to hurt him.

He needed to tell Roy. Because he still hadn't told him that those orange jumpsuits were a fetish of his.

Christ....

All this was why he didn't do relationships! Friendships like the one he had with Cody and Harry were hard enough. But at least friendships were a lot more likely to last than "relationships."

"You... you knew?" Roy asked.

It was so *quiet*, but there might as well have been crashing cymbals the way that stopped Frank's thoughts hard and fast.

Frank swallowed. Drew in a long, long breath and let it out very slowly. Was surprised at the shuddering way it exited.

This was *exactly* why he didn't do relationships!

He looked away. Looked back. And took the proverbial bull by the horns.

"I saw you," Frank said. "One day about a month ago. Along I-70. It was a really hot day, and the traffic was moving like molasses in January, and there you were, by the side of the road."

Roy's mouth fell open, and he went a deep red. Frank suspected it was humiliation rather than embarrassment that painted those cheeks.

"And I... well, I...." God! How did he turn this around?

Honesty. Try that.

"Well, you were just about the hottest fucking thing I'd seen in forever. You were hotter than the temperature that fucking day. I saw you, and I wanted you. Bad. You burned yourself into my memory. I... well, let's just say I've thought about you on those nights when I had trouble going to sleep."

Roy turned crimson, but his eyes flashed for a second. Had appealing to his male ego helped?

Then Roy's throat worked, and Frank couldn't help but remember the way it had when he'd drunk from that water bottle on that hot, hot day that now, for some reason, seemed a long time ago. Roy really had burned himself into Frank's mind....

"Wait…. Are you saying you jack—" Roy stopped and turned even redder. Why, it was almost alarming.

Frank smiled. "Yes. I jacked off thinking about you."

Roy's mouth fell open again, did the fish-out-of-water thing, snapped shut. Then, "Is… is that why you offered to give me a—"

"Nope. That was an astoundingly fortuitous coincidence. The luck of the gods or something. I was shocked when I pulled up to you and you turned out to be the hot guy from the side of I-70."

"Wow," Roy said in a voice that was almost too light to be heard. "I remember that day."

"You do?" Frank asked. Why would he remember that day? How could he even know what day in particular Frank was talking about?

"Yeah. And it *was* hot." He got a faraway look on his face. "All those months…. I could have gotten out in four, but…." Roy shook his head. "Well, I was lucky. I was so fucking lucky that day. You know, usually it's only the inmates in the minimum-security facilities that get the outside jobs. And there I was—" He sighed and something happened in his face. It was… beautiful. "—there I was *outside*. I felt so *free*. Freer than I think I had ever felt in my entire life. And I didn't care that it was hot or that I was picking up garbage and that I was wearing that orange suit that told everybody that I was some kind of—"

Bad boy.

"—crook. I am sure everyone who saw me that day thought I was a bank robber or something. Saw me wearing that orange fucking suit."

Fucking hot *orange suit….*

He looked at Frank. "But you know, there *was* this *one* guy. I can remember his eyes, but not him. Just his eyes. It's been bugging me lately. We locked eyes—"

Holy shit, Frank thought, staring into Roy's big eyes. *I don't believe this. He can't be talking about me.*

"—and my heart started pounding, and it was like he was looking *inside* of me. I froze. I couldn't move. I stared into his eyes, and he looked into mine, and—"

Prince Eric. That's whose eyes he has. Not Bambi.

"—I got this incredible rush. Because, and I know this sounds weird, he wasn't judging me."

"No," Frank said. *I was too busy perving on you. Shit. This cannot be happening.*

"OH MY God," Roy said in wide-eyed astonishment. "Oh my God. It… it was you."

It hit Roy like a train. Frank. Frank had been there that day. Frank had seen Roy, had watched him. The man who had locked eyes with him on that hot day in the sun along the side of the highway had been Frank.

That's impossible.

But it had to be true.

Frank was the man who had gazed into his soul that secret day. Or had seemed to. How could Roy now be standing in his apartment? Naked? How could he have had sex with Frank and not even realized it was *that* man?

"I can't believe it," he said. He took a step toward Frank, then one back.

Roy couldn't remember ever feeling such a whirl of conflicting emotions. The strangeness of it all! The impossibility of it. He wanted to run. He wanted to grab up his clothes and run as fast as he could. But he also wanted to grab Frank and kiss him hard enough to take the breath out of him.

Frank made up his mind for him. He closed the distance between them, put his arms gently around Roy, pulled him close, and kissed him. Roy responded—opened his mouth and pushed at Frank's lips. But to his surprise, Frank pulled back. "No," he whispered. "Like this." And then he kissed Roy again. Soft. *So* soft. God…. Soft and sweet and slow. It was maddening. He wanted to take Frank's mouth, but when he tried, Frank pulled away.

Frank's eyes swirled with something mysterious and dark and exciting. Roy's pulse quickened, and he felt all dizzy, and it was crazy and breathtaking. He melted. All Frank would have to do is say, "You are mine," and he would give himself totally and willingly. Forever.

Some tiny voice reminded him that this was what Ramona had done to him. Dominated him. Subjugated him. Made him submissive.

But another part knew this wasn't the same thing. That what was happening with Frank was something else. He simply didn't have the words or the experience to know what it was. But with Frank? He wouldn't care if that meant he was gay or not. He knew he would move in tonight if Frank asked.

"Do what I do," Frank said softly, and Roy was ready to be shown. To be taught.

Frank kissed him again. Ever so lightly; ever so slightly. The barest brushing of lips. Roy gasped. Imitated Frank. Did as Frank instructed. And Frank kissed him *again*. Softly. Gently. And so that was what Roy did. It was maddening. But also—God yes, once again—it was *freeing*. It was like being let out of that facility where he'd been held behind bars. As if he were being let out of a cage.

Now Frank kissed him with a bit more pressure, and Roy returned it. And then longer—only a little—and Roy responded in kind again. Then more. More pressure and longer and oh, oh, oh, it was amazing. He melted against Frank like their bodies were becoming one. He got hard and shifted a hip to free his cock from its confining position so it could rise up between them, and there—yes, it made Roy growl down deep—it joined Frank's hardening length.

Roy had never been kissed like this, and it was like a cool spring. Next—oh now—Frank's tongue touched his lips ever so slightly, and finally Roy was able to let his join Frank's. A little dance. Give and take, and it was like making love somehow.

Finally, Frank's mouth opened to him, and Roy was allowed—no, encouraged—to do the same! Because this wasn't dominance. It might be teaching…. Yes! Frank was teaching him.

But more than anything, it was an equality Roy had never felt in his life.

Then—*no!*—Frank pulled back and—*yes!*—looked into his soul and…

"Damn," Frank whispered.

Damn? Roy felt his heart skip. Damn?

"I'm *hungry*, Roy. I want to swoop you off to bed again, but I am starving!"

To his astonishment, Roy realized he was ravenous too.

So he let Frank step away from him, their cocks almost obscenely hard, and shepherd him to the kitchen.

Frank got a couple of steaks from the refrigerator, and Roy—his stomach growling—was happy to see they were already thawed. To those, Frank added two big potatoes from a bag under the sink, poked them a few times with a fork, and put them in the microwave. Then he put the steaks on a cookie sheet, placed them on a rack that was mere inches from the oven's upper heating element, and then closed the door—but not all the way.

Their cocks went down around the time Frank took a bag of frozen broccoli out of the freezer—apologized that it was frozen!—and put enough for two hungry men in a colander and ran it under hot water in the sink.

Surprisingly soon after that, he flipped the steaks over with tongs—"Never use a fork!" Frank warned. "You don't want the juices to escape."—and the room filled with incredible smells. In what seemed like an impossibly short amount of time, they were sitting back on the balcony, naked of course, and devouring the meal, along with a rich, deep red wine. From the apartment, Pink Floyd serenaded them, promising to meet them on the dark side of the moon. Dessert was some kind of ice cream—but different, richer—called gelato, and it was decadently delicious.

They washed the dishes together, two men, still naked, and Roy had never felt so close to another human being in his life.

"Shower?" Frank asked when they were done, and Roy nodded and did something else he had never done before. Well, of course he had showered with other men before. But when he and Frank showered together, it was worlds different from the shower room in high school, or in jail. They soaped each other up, everywhere, touching each other in places that Roy hadn't really touched before. Certainly not on another man. God, it was so sensuous to run his soapy hand up and down the cleavage of Frank's ass, touch his hole as Frank was doing to him. Soaping a hairy chest was fucking sexy too, as well as testicles, which hung low because of the heat of the water, and the length of Frank's hard cock.

Before he could make Frank cum again, Frank stopped him—to his frustration—but then rewarded him by drying him off with a big, thick, warm towel. He'd returned that favor (God, that had been exciting!). Afterward, Frank dug out a toothbrush, still wrapped in plastic, and gave it to Roy, and they shared the sink and brushed their teeth, and even that was intimate.

When they were done and had wiped off their mouths with a warm wet washcloth, Frank looked into his eyes and said, "*Now* I can make love to you."

Roy's heart raced at the words, and Frank took his hand—Roy loved it when Frank did that—and led him to his bed. They tumbled onto it, and then Frank showed him wonderful things. Showed him they didn't have to rush. They could take their time. Slow and easy, touching everywhere. Kissing. Caressing. Sucking here and there. Nibbling Roy's collarbone. Sucking his nipples soft and hard and soft again.

At the end, Frank sucked at Roy's cock, but only that spot right below the underside of the head, as if he were trying to give Roy's penis a hickey. But he sucked too softly for that and let his tongue flicker and touch and dance. It was so intense, such tiny caresses with his mouth. Frank's cock was too far away for Roy to reproduce what he was doing, and that nearly drove him crazy. But soon—oh God, soon—in all the world there was only that small section of his cock and Frank's wet mouth, and he rose slowly, exasperatingly slowly, to orgasm, rising and rising and rising and rising, and *finally, dear Christ*, he came.

Nothing. There was nothing, nor had there ever been anything, like that orgasm. It came up from deep inside him, and it was as if he had been plunged under wonderfully warm water. Deep water where he could simply float, lazily, peacefully. After a while he returned to his senses, and he thought that he might have passed out. Frank was close, very close. He opened his eyes to see Frank's face inches away, his eyes closed and his head resting beside Roy's on the same pillow.

My God. I could fall in love with you.

It wouldn't take much. Only the tiniest nudge.

He closed his eyes and wasn't afraid, and he might have drifted off to sleep again because then Frank was pulling him against him, back to chest, and asking him if he wanted to spend the night.

Roy's eyes sprang wide at the suggestion. Spend the night?

He rolled over enough to look at Frank. "You sure? I mean…."

"What?"

"You…. You made it pretty clear that you don't want to get serious with anyone, and in my experience, spending the night is bordering on serious."

"*Really?*"

"Well, when you stay the night at a girl's place, she's making a statement to the neighbors. That's how my ex explained it. She's telling the neighbors she's sleeping with someone. It's a pretty serious thing for a woman."

"Yeah.… Two-sided thing, isn't it? If your car is parked overnight in front of my place, the neighbors say I'm a stud. But if I was a woman, they'd say I was a slut."

Roy nodded.

Frank shrugged. "Well, I can't help that I'm a man. And just because I don't do boyfriends doesn't mean I don't want friends. And friends with benefits are nice."

Friends with benefits? Was Frank suggesting that?

Whew. That was a big thing. Did he want a man as his "friend with benefits"?

Very quickly he realized that, yes, he'd like that a lot.

It was surely better than crawling back to Ramona, wasn't it? And his toy at home really wasn't doing the trick. Frank was nice. He was *so* nice. He knew immediately after that there was nowhere else he wanted to be.

But shit. He would have to call his mother. She would already be wondering where he was.

Roy told Frank what he needed to do, and Frank said, "Of course," and Roy found his cell and prayed to God she wouldn't ask too many questions.

"You're not with Ramona, are you?" she asked, and Roy could hear the dread in her voice.

He laughed and assured her he wasn't.

His heart pounded till he thought it might explode when he thought of where he would be spending his night. But he wasn't afraid. At least in the moment, he didn't care what it might mean. Only that there really was nowhere else he'd rather be.

"You'll tell me later?" she asked, and the dread was gone, but there was something else there. Something that needed assurance.

"If it turns out there's a reason for me to," he said quietly.

Then with a little more warmth, "You sound happy, Roy."

Roy's heart skipped a beat. *God! I am happy!*

He grinned, and the smile seemed to come from the marrow of his bones.

"I… I am, Mom."

"All right, then," she said. "That's what matters."

And then, just as he was telling her he loved her, she said, "Don't forget. You promised to help Granny with her garage sale tomorrow."

Fuck! he thought in surprise. He had totally forgotten.

"You know she's counting on you," Mom said.

He nodded. "Of course. I'll be there."

"Take whoever you're with along with you."

Roy shook his head. He didn't think the family was ready for anything like that! In fact, *he* wasn't.

But after he hung up and joined Frank in bed, was pulled into his man's arms and against his man's body, he wondered if he might be getting ready.

Wouldn't that be something?

CHAPTER SEVENTEEN

THE NEXT morning, Roy woke in a man's bed and arms for the first time in his life. For the barest moment, he was shocked. And in the next his heart… soared. He shifted and rolled so that he was facing Frank. Frank's nose crinkled, his mouth twitched, and then his breathing went steady as he fell back into sleep.

My God he's beautiful. It hit Roy then, deeply and truly, that yes, he thought Frank was beautiful. No fucking around. Roy had never seen a man who was secure enough in his sexuality that he could admit another man was good-looking. Certainly not to anyone else. But it was a lot more than just acknowledging Frank's beauty, the things he was feeling as he gazed on Frank.

I never felt like this about Ramona. Or any girl. And there had been girls. Quite a few of them. He'd liked being with them. *I did.*

The touching and holding. The snuggling. The sex had been good. Who didn't want to be touched? Who didn't want *to* touch? Who didn't want to be held? And he liked waking up with someone. He had liked being with Ramona. Especially once her games started. The sex had been so much better then. He liked her being *in* him.

He liked it more than being in *her.*

But he had to tell the truth. Looking at Frank, he had to.

There had always been something… missing when he was with girls. He kept thinking, *Is this it? Is this all there is?*

Except now, with Frank? It was the best sex he'd ever had in his life.

God. He suddenly felt a little numb. *I'm gay. I've got to be.*

"I'm gay," he whispered, to see how it sounded. To see how he sounded saying it. *Can I say that?* Could he have a life of saying, "I'm gay?"

"I'm gay," he said a little louder.

Suddenly his heart was racing.

Suddenly he was… scared.

"I'm gay," he said louder, and this time his voice trembled.

"You don't know that, do you?" Frank asked and opened his eyes.

Roy didn't answer.

"Just 'cause I gave you the best head you've ever had in your life," Frank pointed out, almost saying aloud what Roy had been thinking, "doesn't make you gay. I've blown a lot of straight men."

"How many blew you back?" he asked.

Now Frank shrugged. "A few."

"And they were straight?" *Really?*

"Maybe a little bi," Frank replied. "I said that before, didn't I? That you might be bisexual? A little bit?"

A *little bit* bisexual? "What does that even mean?" He blinked at Frank. "A little bit bisexual? Aren't you bi or not bi? How could I be a *little bit* bisexual?"

"Well, there are degrees of everything."

Roy found himself wanting to laugh. "Degrees?"

"There's the scale. They call it the Kinsey scale, and on one side of it you're totally gay—that's me. On the other side you're totally straight." He rolled his eyes. "That's my father. *God.*"

"And me?" Heart all over the place now.

"Then there are guys who are only a little bit bi—but mostly gay. And then totally bi. And then a bit, except mostly straight. Maybe that's you."

Somehow the possibility didn't make his heart slow down.

"Maybe," he repeated, whispered. "Maybe." Louder.

It didn't feel like the truth, though.

There was a loud beeping then. His cell phone. Telling him he needed to leave. They looked at each other.

Roy reached out and grabbed it and hit the snooze button.

Then he looked at Frank and wondered what was next.

"Do you have to go?" Frank asked.

Roy nodded. "My granny."

"Sure."

Kiss me, Roy thought. And when Frank didn't kiss him, he was relieved as much as disappointed.

He got out of bed, tried to remember where his clothes were, and then remembered that most of them were on the balcony. Imagine.

Frank got up with him and, while he found his clothes, asked Roy if he wanted something to eat before he left. "I've got eggs and some great sausage I got at City Market. Local meat, organic, grass-fed."

"I'm going to stop and get some doughnuts," Roy said. "Granny loves doughnuts."

"She's pretty special to you, isn't she?"

It was more a statement than a question, but Roy told him that yes, she was. "Really special."

Frank sighed. "You're lucky, you know. To have a grandmother who loves you. I never knew any of my grandparents. And my mom…. Did I tell you she left me?"

"Yes," Roy said, and *now* his heart was breaking. *If I don't get out of here, my heart's just going to stop.*

Then he was dressed, and thank God Frank put something on because if he hadn't, Roy was going to have to have Frank again, and even dressed, Roy wanted him.

At the door, he waited. Waited for Frank to say something. But then he'd already asked him if he had to go, hadn't he? *I don't want to go. Tell me not to go.*

But he had to.

Do I kiss him? Is that what I'm supposed to do? Do I get to see you again?

And then just as he was turning to leave, Frank kissed *him*. Soft and sweet.

So sweet.

"I guess you'll be busy the next couple of days."

"Yes," Roy said.

"Maybe come 'round next week, then? We'll have dinner?"

Yes! "Sounds nice," Roy said. His heart was pounding again.

"All right, then." Frank squinted his eyes. Then he said, "Wednesday?"

That was four, five days away? It seemed like forever.

"O-okay."

"Give you enough time," Frank said.

"Time?"

"To decide if you're bisexual enough to come back."

"Oh." Galloping. Now his heart was galloping! His swallowed hard and nodded and thought, *He's right.*

"You'll either decide this was all a fun experiment but you're that little bit of bi that prefers women—"

Roy trembled. Thought of Ramona. Almost laughed. Thought of the other girls. None of whom had made him feel this way. This crazy. This fulfilled. This wonderful *crazy*-fulfilled.

"—or the little bit of bi that says you like men equally."

"Or…," Roy said, "the kind that…." And couldn't finish.

"That likes men a lot."

Roy swallowed. Hard.

"We could be friends with benefits," Frank said and waggled his eyebrows.

Galloping like it could race off a cliff.

They kissed again, very lightly, and then Roy was in the hall and walking to the elevator and trying not to look back. Just as he reached the elevator doors and pressed the button, Frank called out.

"Roy? Will you at least let me know if you're not coming?"

Roy looked back, and oh, he wanted to race back into Frank's arms. How could he be anything but gay the way he wanted Frank right now?

Frank stood there waiting for an answer. And when the *ping!* of the elevator told Roy it had arrived, he said, "Yes," and then ducked inside.

Roy rode down in silence. He trembled and tried to calm his heart and his breathing, and then he found his Jeep and got in and trembled more. On a whim, made the extra trip to go to Lovin' Oven for the doughnuts. He hoped he would see the lesbian couple, but he didn't.

He wondered if he would ever see them again. Then he realized something. He wanted to. He really wanted to.

And he wanted to see Frank. He would be showing up at his place Wednesday. If only to see if what he was doing was an experiment.

By the time he got to Granny's he was smiling.

"WILL YOU at least tell me if you're not coming?"

Had he really said that? Frank shook his head. *I'm going nuts!*

He laughed. Thought of Roy. *God. He's something else.*

Then it hit him. They hadn't exchanged numbers. How would Roy let him know? He'd have to show up. And if all the second thoughts Frank expected Roy to be hit with happened, he wasn't going to be letting Frank know shit. Which was probably a good thing.

Because Frank didn't do boyfriends.

Work. I've got work to do.

But then he wasn't going to see—or *not* see—Roy until Wednesday. That was five days away. In that time he could get lost in the wood. The sanding of it. The shaping of it.

He took a deep breath. Could almost smell the wood. The sawdust. A guy who used to work at the local Home Depot—great guy who recently passed away—had said he wished he could patent a cologne that smelled like sawdust. He would make a million.

Frank thought he would have bought some.

He went to the kitchen and unplugged his phone, saw he had three hang-up calls, an unknown number, and several messages as well. He deleted the first two before he was more than seconds into them. Crap and crap. The next one was Mr. Beauchamp, who wanted to know if strawberry stain might be a little too effeminate for a man. Maybe. Maybe not. Frank would bring the man some samples. It might help him decide.

The next call shocked him senseless. "Hey boy! It's your old man."

Frank stiffened and gripped the phone as he listened.

"You're never going to believe it! I am in town. I'm staying the Meridian."

Of course, never anything but first-class for you, Glen.

"Hey! You know me! Never second-class." He chuckled. Except it was his fake laugh. His make-the-potential-client-feel-relaxed laugh. It was a good one. But Frank knew it wasn't real. And Glen knew he knew it. So what the fuck was this going to be about?

"Anyway, I'm only going to be in town today. Well, and tonight, of course. I was hoping we could have a few drinks. Maybe dinner. What do you say?"

Glen paused, and Frank squinted his eyes and wished, wished, fucking wished he hadn't called. Because of course, goddammit, he was going to see him.

"Well…. You call me. You should have the number there. Call me. Okay, Frankie?" The call bleeped off and the phone service asked him to hit #7 if he wanted to delete the call, #9 if he wanted to save it.

He sighed. And hit the #9.

CHAPTER EIGHTEEN

ROY LET himself in through the kitchen. It was what he did. Even when it was Granny's place and not his mom's.

The backyard already had several card tables and a plastic dining table set up and was covered in knickknacks and dishes, two lamps (one chipped), some old vases, and a ceramic clock. Most of it had come from Granny's garage, which was small but *full* of stuff and would only have fit one car if she hadn't turned it into a storage unit.

God, he thought, pulling out his cell phone. *Am I that late?* But when he looked at the time, he saw he wasn't late at all. In fact, he was early.

But then, he was talking about Granny, wasn't he? And she was finding it hard to sleep these days. Knowing her, she'd probably been up for hours. Still, it made him feel bad how much she'd had to do on her own.

Roy went into the dining room without calling out, and then at the bend that led into the living room… he froze.

Froze.

His eyes went wide. *Way* wide. He stifled a gasp, fell back, and hoped, *oh my God*, that he hadn't made any noise.

Holy shit!

Granny was sitting on the couch. With Mrs. Kelly.

You didn't see that. You didn't!

But, he found he had to know.

Very, very carefully he leaned forward as far as he could, praying a floorboard wouldn't creak, and peeked, ever so quickly, and… oh my God, yes, he *had* seen what he thought he'd seen.

Granny was sitting on the couch, but she was leaning *against* Mrs. Kelly. Her head was half on her shoulder, half on her chest, and Mrs. Kelly was stroking her hair.

It's not what it looks like. It could be anything! *God*, maybe there was something wrong. *Maybe she's not okay!*

He almost leapt forward to find out, and then it hit him…. What if he saw exactly what he thought he had seen? What if she was fine and dandy? What if he found out she was fine and dandy after he charged in on the two of them? And he surprised them doing… what they were doing? He *had* let himself in without knocking. Without even calling out to her.

Mrs. Kelly is holding my granny! They're snuggling. But…

No. You don't know shit. It could be anything.

He went back to the kitchen, ludicrously walking backward a few steps before realizing what he was doing and turning around to take the last steps. He closed the kitchen door quietly, knocked on it once, twice, three times, loudly, and then opened it as noisily as he could open a well-cared-for door. After all, he'd taken care of it for her. Like he did anything she asked him to do. Which was part of why it had been hell when he couldn't help her all those months.

Maybe she's been playing cuddle-bunnies with Mrs. Kelly while I was gone. It isn't what you think. You just have your mind on sex because of what you've been doing lately.

"Granny?" he shouted. Over-the-top. If he were an actor, he'd have been booed off the stage. "You home?" *Of course she is, you tool! Where else would she be?* Especially with all that shit in the backyard.

"In here!" came the answer, and this time after he made the journey through the house to the living room, Granny was sitting on the couch alone, and Mrs. Kelly had a big cardboard box in her hands.

He gave Mrs. Kelly a long look—he couldn't help it—and hoped it didn't make her suspect anything. Holding out the brown paper bag with the words Lovin' Oven printed on the side, he went to his grandmother. "Look what I brought!"

She smiled, all sunshine and light. "What did you bring?" She held out her hands, as excited as a little girl.

He gave it to her, and she opened it and looked inside and smiled *just* like a little girl. "Oh, look! Kelly, come look. Doughnuts."

Mrs. Kelly handed Roy her box and peeked in the bag. She smiled.

"And what luck! Roy brought your favorite."

Roy wasn't sure what that would be. He'd bought a half dozen, and almost bought twice that, but he knew they'd go to waste.

"Let's sit down in the kitchen and have us one or two," Granny said, standing up. She headed that way. "I've got a fresh pot of coffee."

Roy followed the two of them into the bright pink kitchen. "Will you get some plates, dear?" she asked, but before he could comply, Mrs. Kelly nodded and went to the correct cabinet. She brought out a dinner plate and three smaller ones—"I don't need a plate!" he said, and Mrs. Kelly waved his comment away—and placed them on the table. Then Granny arranged the doughnuts on the single larger plate, but put the white, sugar-glazed cake one on Mrs. Kelly's plate. Mrs. Kelly, meanwhile, poured the coffees and put three sugar cubes and a dab of half-and-half in Granny's, just the way she liked it. She sat next to Granny too, leaving Roy a place to sit across from them.

Are they playing footsie under the table?

Stop! Granny is not *a lesbian! I would know.*

What if she is?

She can't be! She's got kids. She's got grandkids. She's got me*!*

"What's wrong, sugar?" Granny asked, and before today, he would have thought she was talking to him. But now? Sugar? Could it be she was talking to Mrs. Kelly?

Granny reached out and laid a hand on his. "Roy?"

"Nothing," he shot back and hoped it didn't sound weird. He looked at the two of them next to each other and tried to imagine them— *No! Don't go there. Why would you go there?* What purpose was there in going there?

The lesbian couple from Lovin' Oven suddenly leapt to mind. How he'd wondered if he would ever see them again. He'd *hoped* to see them again.

But if he stopped seeing Frank, would he want to hang in that world?

And here was his own grandmother.... And Mrs. Kelly. He looked back and forth between the two of them. *They're so old!*

But then he remembered Ramona's grandfather and how his wife had died, and less than a year later, he was married again.

"He told me," Ramona said, "that when you get to be his age, you don't want to be alone. And you don't know how much time you have left, so why wait?"

Roy thought about that and how Grandpa had died two years ago. And he thought about Mrs. Kelly, who he had known all his life, and how he knew there had been a *Mr.* Kelly once, a long time ago, but Roy had never met him.

Maybe they're both just lonely.

"You're not overthinking things, are you?" Granny asked abruptly.

"Huh?" he replied. "What-what do you mean?"

"You tend to do that, honey. Sometimes it's just not worth all that thinking. Sometimes it is what it is."

The comment seemed to come out of left field, and then it occurred to him that maybe she was trying to tell him something.

Sure. She's saying to stop overthinking things!

Only for some reason, he wasn't sure that was it. But what had he said that motivated her to give such advice?

Unless she really was saying, "Yes, you've figured it out. Stop worrying about it."

Granny can't be a lesbian. She can't.

But then…

Would it be such a bad thing? He looked at the two of them again. Thought of the lesbians from Lovin' Oven and how they seemed to be so in love. Looked at Mrs. Kelly and wondered how long it had been since someone had loved her. Remembered how Granny had told him, and made him promise not to tell anyone, how lonely she was since Milton, her husband—Grandpa—had died. "He was my best friend," she'd said that day, but those words had struck him as strange.

"Really?" he'd asked her.

She had nodded and looked away, *went* away, to some other place.

That was one of those days when he had wondered why, for most of his life, his grandparents had slept in separate bedrooms.

"He snores *so* loud," she would say, and Roy had always taken that as gospel, because, *wow*, Grandpa surely *did* snore loud. Really, *really* loud.

"We sleep together on my birthday," Grandpa told him once while working on some shelves Granny had asked him to make. Then winked.

The memory was *so* crystal clear that, for a moment, he was transported to that day.

He had been helping Grandpa make those shelves—the ones even now in the kitchen filled with knickknacks, cookie jars, and cookbooks.

"Remember always to measure *twice* and cut *once*," Grandpa had said. "Because if you measure wrong and cut wrong, the board is ruined."

With almost-shocking clarity, he remembered that weekend and—

"Roy?" he heard Granny ask, "Are you okay?"

—Grandpa praising him for how well he'd cut one of the boards. Letting him use the belt sander on the ends of the boards but warning him, "Not too much, or it'll be the same as cutting it too short!" and then the sanding…. *God!* How had he forgotten this? He could literally smell the sawdust, and *that* reminded him of Frank, and that made him look at Granny and Mrs. Kelly again. Two women. And him and Frank… two men.

He smiled.

It was like the sun breaking through the clouds on a gray and dreary day, and his heart raced. He wanted to see Frank and hear his voice and feel his touch….

"There we go," Granny said. "That's what I like to see! What a smile. Looked like you were in a bad place there for a minute, son, but now—"

"Now you're glowing," Mrs. Kelly said.

"Yes!" Granny cried. "Glowing like at my birthday party. I thought *maybe* it was because of me that day, but no!" She grinned. "You've found somebody, haven't you?"

God! Had he? Had he really? A *man*?

And the idea sent his heart all over the place again and made the blood roar through his veins.

Me and a man? Really?

"Your mother said something to me. Said you were spending the night at a new friend's place and how… how your friend might come with you today. But I don't see anyone."

Roy shook his head. "Not today." Maybe someday. Would he, could he, introduce Frank to his grandmother? Say, "This is my boyfriend, Frank"?

Now the blood really was tearing through him, like an electric shock, and his face burned, and he felt like he really *was* glowing. Even though he knew that if he did find love with a man, it wouldn't be Frank. He could pretend, though. Why not?

"Oh whee!" Granny said and laughed. "Look at that face!"

"He's in love," Mrs. Kelly said, and Roy thought, *In love? Really? In love with a man?*

Some wild sex was one thing, but love?

Oh, Frank, he thought and *longed* to see him and touch him. Touch him and kiss him. Feel his cock inside him.

"Oh yes," Granny cried. "I know love when I see it. Are we going to meet your *friend* anytime soon?"

Meet Frank?

Whoa!

He didn't know about that. He figured that was a long day coming.

In the meantime, Wednesday seemed forever away. And he didn't know how he was going to wait that long.

CHAPTER NINETEEN

FRANK AGREED to meet Glen at the Meridian. His hotel room and not the Nadir Lounge, which didn't make him happy. The Nadir meant other people and lessened the possibility that his father would start some big Shakespearean scene complete with rising voices, sweeping gestures, and maybe even a thee and a thou or two. Glen's room, on the other hand, meant hugs (more than one), drinks from tiny little bottles, and them getting at least partially drunk before they even sat down to eat.

Frank was nervous. He hated that Glen could still do that to him, still had that power, but he couldn't help it. And something was weird. Glen was only here for one day, for one thing. That meant he didn't have some kind of job here, and that was good, because they'd agreed that Kansas City was Frank's territory. The only way Glen could take a contract here was if Frank was in charge of everything his company did. He didn't want to work with Glen. Not with all the drama that would ensue. *"Frank, have you thought of doing it* this *way...?"*

No! Please have him not *be looking at a job in Kansas City*, Frank prayed.

But he really didn't think that was what it was.

No. The only reason Glen could be here was that he wanted to see Frank. They weren't close. Not anymore. Hadn't been in a long time. This wasn't bosom buddies catching up on old times.

So he wasn't here for a job. And he wasn't here for father-and-son time: shooting a few baskets, punching each other affectionately on the shoulder. So why the fuck was he here, then?

Glen had given him the room number, so Frank went on up but hesitated what felt like an hour before knocking on the door.

"Be right there" came his father's booming, unmistakable voice. Frank's stomach dropped, and then the door was *flung* open, and there he stood. Frank's old man. His father. Glen.

Of course, Glen hugged him.

Hugged him fierce and powerful, but not because that was necessarily the way his old man hugged. No, it was the way Glen hugged *him*. Like the way some macho assholes squeezed your hand while shaking it—not in a firm, gentlemanly way but as if trying to break every bone in your hand. So of course Frank hugged back as hard as Glen, and did he hear Glen's back pop? Hear an "ugh" from the SOB?

It brought a smile to Frank's face, even if it was childish.

Glen let go, stepped back. Smiled and said, "Good one," as if indeed proving that they were participating in some game called "Who's the Bigger Man?".

"Looking good," Glen said, pointing at him. He gestured to take in Frank's entire physique. "*Real* good."

"You too," Frank admitted. Because it was true. Despite a lifetime of drinking like the proverbial fish and sleeping with enough women to make Hugh Hefner smile in approval, his old man looked good. It was one of the only things his father had given him that he was truly grateful for—his physical appearance. Not that Glen really had much more to do with it than making Frank's mother pregnant, of course.

But Frank knew *he* had nothing to do with his own good looks. And while he had certainly used them to his advantage, he had never taken them for granted. He certainly hoped he had never considered himself better than anyone else *because* he was good-looking.

That was something else he had to thank his father for. Glen was the same way. Never conceited about *his* looks. A good lesson.

Although he had used them to *his* advantage!

"Let's have a drink," Glen said.

This is where he'll open the tiny little bottles.

Glen turned, and Frank followed him and was a bit surprised to see he hadn't gotten a suite. Just the one room. One bed. Nothing extra.

And then there was another surprise. No little bottles. Just one bottle. And it was… nice. Lagavulin. A single malt whisky. One of his favorites. Not cheap.

"Rocks or no?" Glen asked.

"Rocks," Frank said. Yes, it would melt a little, but sometimes a little water helped. Lagavulin was very thick and rich, very smoky, and very concentrated. Concentrated enough, in Frank's opinion, to obscure the whisky's more subtle flavors. Water, a sprinkle, mellowed the heat and released its more nuanced notes. And with Lagavulin, he wanted to appreciate those notes. The little bit of ice that melted would make up that sprinkle.

Besides, he preferred the things he drank—no matter what they were—to be cold or hot. Lukewarm was awful.

Glen got the ice, poured a good two fingers, and handed Frank his drink. But as much as he anticipated the peat-and-oak richness, the offer made him even more nervous. Lagavulin wasn't the most expensive whisky around, but his father was usually fine with cheaper. Frank knew his old man. Glen was up to something.

But what?

Glen sat down at the desk and crossed his legs, offered Frank a place to sit. He chose the end of the bed. By not having a place to set his glass, he hoped to broadcast the message that he didn't want to be here long.

Frank waited. Looked around the room. Tried to figure out what was missing.

His phone buzzed in his pocket. He pulled it out. The unknown number again. He should answer it. It could be a new client. Then again, it could be the *Kansas City Chronicle* wanting to know if he wanted a subscription.

He sent it to voicemail.

And waited. Waited to see why he was here. Why Glen was here. While he waited, he sipped his Lagavulin and… ah… closed his eyes and luxuriated in malt and sherry, fruity sweetness, powerful peat and oak, and a wonderful long, spicy finish of figs and dates, smoke and vanilla. *Wondrous.*

He had to hand it to Glen. He had taught Frank to appreciate good whisky. To the uneducated tongue, whisky could be nasty. But with time he had learned to understand, catch, and appreciate the smell of it, the way it lay on the palate, and the finish.

I wonder if Roy would like this. He says he's always drunk crap like PBR. I wonder if I could teach him to be able to enjoy something like this.

Then, on the tail of that thought: *Wow! The little bastard has worked his way into my thoughts, hasn't he? Harry and Cody would have a field day with this.*

I think maybe Harry and Cody don't need to know….

"What?" Glen asked.

Frank looked up from his glass. "Just thinking about how fine this Lagavulin is."

"Sixteen-year-old scotch! It *should* be fine!" Then Glen did something horrible. He tossed his back and poured another.

What a waste.

Frank looked around the room and finally realized what was missing. There was only one suitcase. One jacket that he could see. The closet door was open, revealing nothing inside but empty wooden hangers, attached to a rail to keep people from stealing them. What good was a hanger without hooks?

"So Glen. Where's your lady du jour? You send her shopping? Be careful! There's some expensive shops down there. I saw a leopard-skin-patterned scarf selling for $70 last year, and it was 50 percent off."

Glen laughed. "No lady for me right now, Frank." He held up his glass up as if to toast the idea.

Frank feigned shock. "My God, old man. You must be as horny as a three-balled tomcat."

"Hey," Glen said with a grin. "I didn't say I wasn't getting laid. Just not sponged off of." The look on his face was somehow both lecherous and horrible at the same time.

Really, Glen? Really? Sponged off of you? That's all the ladies in your life wanted from you?

Some, maybe. But he could think of a few who hadn't given a tin shit about his net worth. He thought of Caterina, for one. Saw her looking at him through a fall of dark hair and telling him she would stay as long as it was good for everyone.

Glen must have seen something on Frank's face because after a minute he shrugged and put his glass down on the desk.

"Last one ended bad, my boy."

My boy? Really?

"Her name was Theresa. She somehow got the idea I was marrying her, and I know I told her I was never getting married again. Third time was the anticharm!"

Really? Three times? Were you only legally married three times? I was fucking sure there were at least four Mrs. Sinclairs.

"She went bananas! Screaming and shouting. She threw a brick through a beautiful art deco window I had restored! Can you believe that shit? No respect for art? This wasn't a window from Home-*fucking*-Depot!"

Well, that did suck.

Frank hoped that she hadn't done too much damage to something historical. "There was no need for her to take her beef with you out on something that can't be replaced," he said.

"You saying I *can* be?" Glen replied with that grin of his.

"Never, Glen. No one could ever replace you." And then Frank did it. He swallowed all that remained of his whisky. If it had been just about anything else, what was left wouldn't have been much more than a swallow. But one sipped fine whisky. In this case, though, he already needed some fortifying. What was going on here? He hadn't seen Glen in a year, and they were shooting the shit in his hotel room? Why hadn't they met in the lounge?

His father went to the window and posed. Frank figured he didn't even know he was doing it. Looking at Glen, Frank could see what he might look like in twenty-five years—if he was lucky. He might be. He took better care of himself than Glen ever had.

God, look at him. Does he have a clue how lucky he is?

Glen leaned there against the glass, looking like an ad for men's skin products or maybe some expensive clothing line, and the sun hit him, but not directly, so that it showed off his blue eyes without making him squint. His wavy hair—just a bit less curly than Frank's—his terrific skin, his still-youthful physique. Women fell for him the world over like dominos, and he didn't have to do anything but lean against a window and look off to the horizon. How could a man who spent so much of his life under Tuscan or Santorini or Marseille suns not have at least some deep crow's feet? Portrait in the attic? Except Glen didn't have an attic. At least not one where he'd want to leave something so important. There were a couple of places here and there he rented out to tourists and such for most of the year. Places he could just drop in when he wanted and fuck anyone who had contracted it for a vacation.

That disregard for others was part of why Glen couldn't keep a woman. Not that he wanted to. He liked one, more or less, for a while, and then he was looking over her shoulder to see what else was coming along: something better, prettier, sexier, bigger breasted, narrower of waist, wider of hip. Glen loved women. *All* women.

Frank had been watching stand-up comedian Ron White on Netflix once, and he'd said something like, "Once you've seen one woman naked, well… you pretty much want to see all the rest of 'em naked as well," and Frank immediately thought of his father. It was something that should be engraved on his tombstone.

Playboy. Player. A womanizer. That's exactly what he was.

At least I'm dealing with men. Most men expected a one-night stand to be a one-night stand. They understood that you could have sex without proposing love or marriage. Frank never led a man on. He let him know from the beginning—if it was turning out he'd met someone he wanted to fuck more than once and maybe even get to know—that he wasn't interested in getting married. Especially these days when two men *could* get married.

I'm going to have to tell Roy on Wednesday. He was starting to look like the type to suddenly proclaim undying love. As hot as he was, as sweet as he was, that just wasn't something Frank wanted. He loved men too much. Loved their different shapes and sizes and builds and types. Hairy or smooth, muscular or chunky, all different ages. From a Josh Hutcherson or Tom Holland to a Chris Noth or Sean Connery—all could be hot. He liked them pale or dark, short or tall. Cut or uncut. If he settled down, he would have to give that up. Stick with one flavor of ice cream. How could he do that? Why would he?

And looking at his father, something suddenly occurred to him. That Ron White joke? Why, it applied to him too. Because once he saw one man naked, he pretty much wanted to see all the rest of them naked. Right? He needed to check his disdain at the door, didn't he?

Being with only one man would suck. Right?

Right?

"So, Frankie, what about you?" Glen asked as he stepped away from the window and added whisky to his glass—*no* rocks.

Frank shuddered and then locked on to the fact that he'd been asked a question. "What *about* me?"

"Do you have a man du jour?"

"Maybe," Frank said and was amazed at himself that he'd said it.

"Well, damn. Look at you. He must be good in the sack."

"He is," Frank snapped, feeling defensive for some reason. He took a deep breath.

"How long have you—"

"Not long," Frank said, cutting him off. "And besides, it'll probably blow over in a week." A feeling of betrayal shivered over him. Not an expected feeling. He didn't like it. He liked having such a discussion with Glen even less. It made him feel like he was only a gay chromosome away from being his old man.

Glen smiled and toasted him—again. "A chip off the old block!"

Frank wanted to growl.

"Just be careful, Frankie. Now that it's legal, they'll be trying to put a ring on you too! Stay one step ahead of him. I think the biggest reason I never gave a shit that you like dick instead of pussy is that we are more alike than anyone would guess."

Pussy? Had he *really* said that? At least he hadn't used the C-word.

"*How* are *we* alike, old man?" Frank asked.

"You like Almond Joy, and I like Mounds. You like nuts, I don't. But we both love the beauty of—well—the human body! Yeah. I like that. And it is beautiful. I don't deny that I've met a man or two in my life with an ass so fine I was tempted. But then I thought about those balls hanging down, and…." Glen shuddered.

Frank nodded. "Sure. I guess."

"And those bodies can be fun outside of bed too. But you know what I'm saying! There is always that next body. Not necessarily better, but different. And *vive la différence!*"

Frank had heard it all before. A hundred times. A hundred times a hundred. And while he understood that this was all supposed to be about how they were a grand pair and a famous father-and-son team or something, he'd long ago gotten tired of Glen and his life. It had worn him out. And he was already getting worn out tonight. Yeah. Already he was exhausted. He didn't have the energy to play Glen's game of what a perfectly ordinary—no, *extraordinary*—father and son they were.

"Glen?" Done with it. "What are you doing here?"

"What do you mean, Frankie?"

"Out of the blue, you just show up? Really?"

"Can't I just want to see my son?"

"But that's not you, Glen. So spill it. Tell me."

Glen gave him a look that pretended hurt.

"*Spill it*," Frank repeated.

Glen sighed, then sat on the edge of the desk. He opened his mouth, seemed to freeze, and slowly shut it. Finally: "Fuck."

"Fuck what?" Frank wanted to shout.

Glen sighed. His shoulder slumped in a way Frank had never seen from his father.

He's got cancer, Frank thought. Knew.

"It's your mother," Glen said.

At first Frank didn't catch what Glen had said. It had sounded like "It's your mother," but that made no sense. "What?" he asked. "My *what*?"

"Mother."

Frank stiffened ever so slightly. *Mother?* No. He still wasn't getting it. "What did you say, Glen?" Another? Smother? Smugglers? Had his father gotten involved with smugglers of all things?

"Your *mother*."

Frank put his glass down on the bed. The whisky was gone. There was a ringing in his ears. And cotton. Lots of it.

"Mother?" he asked.

Glen sighed heavily. "Yeah, Frankie. *Mother*."

"Wh-what about her?" he asked through air that had somehow become thicker.

Glen looked away. Squared his shoulders. "She wants to see you."

CHAPTER TWENTY

GRANNY HAD plenty for Roy to do. First and foremost were the signs. She had a half dozen or so of them, with numbers and a map showing where each one was supposed to go and on which side of the street, which corner.

"And on Sunday I want them pulled up at noon. That's when we end things."

"You're going to be open on Sunday?" he asked. *Gosh, did my volunteering mean the entire weekend?* Not that he minded that much. It wasn't like he really had anything to do over the next three days. It would help Wednesday get here faster.

"Yes. And on Sunday you're going to replace them with the 50 percent–off signs. I always make a killing on Sunday. Oh! And pick up a couple bags of ice right before you come back. I am going to sell cans of Sam's Choice for fifty cents apiece. It's going to be hot today."

"You want me to do that first? So they'll get cold?" And then he immediately regretted asking her. Of course she didn't. She knew exactly what she wanted and how and when.

She reached out and patted his cheek. "Baby. No one wants a cold one this early in the morning. At least not a cold soda pop. What they want is directions to garage sales. Lots of people get up really early and start their shopping to avoid the heat and to get the stuff they want before someone else does."

Which made sense. But then almost everything Granny did made sense.

He saw immediately that every sign that he pounded into the ground—no tiny eight-by-tens stapled on telephone poles for her—had their arrows pointed in the correct direction. And the lettering was crisp, the address clearly legible. It made him laugh. Nothing halfway for her. It took him over a half hour to do the work, and none of them were more than five or so blocks away.

When he got back with the ice, there were already some people in the driveway, looking at stuff placed on a table made out of a door laid over two sawhorses. Now how had she done that by herself?

She isn't by herself. She has Mrs. Kelly.

It was just so wild, was all. The lovey-dovey stuff he could see. It was… adorable. Reminded him of that movie where Olympia Du-something played a butch old lesbian. He couldn't remember the name of the movie. Something about clouds? He had seen it accidentally one drunken late night with Ramona, sitting up in her bed after fucking (or him getting fucked, actually). At first he was shocked, but then it turned sort of sweet. Two old ladies loving each other, and Olympia and her lady love running off to get married in Canada. That was before they could get married here in the United States, and wasn't it fucking amazing that had happened? Gay marriage legal from sea to shining sea.

Yeah. The love stuff he thought was kind of nice. Before today he hadn't thought of Granny as a sexual being. Who did? It was weird enough thinking that your parents did it, otherwise how else were you in this world?

But your eighty-year-old grandmother?

And in this instance, your eighty-year-old grandmother carpet munching?

Weird. *Way* too weird.

But then just because they were doing cuddle-bunnies didn't mean they were eating the peach, right?

Stop thinking about it. It's rude. It's none of your business. You want her thinking about you and… well… anyone? Of course not!

After that he did stop thinking about such personal things. Mostly. He saw other things, though. He saw the way they smiled at each other. He saw how their hands touched when they were rearranging things on the tables after stuff sold. The way they called out to each other. Dear and sweetie.

By the time they closed up for the day, it was clear. He knew it. Granny and Mrs. Kelly were together. A pair of Dutch ladies. A real lady couple. Gal pals to the max.

He had to ask. He wasn't sure why, but he had to. Except that was a lie, wasn't it? He knew why. He had to know because the more he thought about it, the more he realized that now, somehow, he had a wonderful connection with them. Something in common.

Which made him realize he was seriously considering the idea that he was gay. All he had to do was think about Frank, and how could he deny it? His heart would speed up, and he would wonder how the hell he was going to wait until Wednesday to see him again. And if he thought of Frank naked, why, he started chubbing up right away. And he daren't think of sucking his cock or fucking him or getting fucked by him—not even for a moment—or not only would he get hard, he'd start leaking, and the last thing he wanted to do was have a big wet spot on the front of his pants for Granny or Mrs. Kelly to see. God! Talk about mortifying.

But what about just the sweet part? The lovey-dovey part?

Lovey-dovey? Really? Now you're thinking....

Love?

God.

To his surprise, he started to get hard.

He sat down at the table just as Mrs. Kelly came into the kitchen and placed a Pizza Hut box down on the table. "I got thin crust, Roy. I hope that's okay."

"Is there anchovies or pineapple on it?" he asked.

"No," she said, turning to pull plates out of the (correct) cabinet.

"Then we are made in the shade," he replied, and everyone laughed.

She got some PBR out of the refrigerator and handed everyone a can, and it was funny to see Mrs. Kelly drinking beer. He knew Granny tipped one back now and again, so that didn't shock him. But seeing Mrs. Kelly drink from a beer can? Why, it was like seeing a purple people eater. She had always seemed like the female version of Mister Rogers. Arriving and smiling and talking all syrupy. You couldn't imagine Mister Rogers went to the bathroom to pee, let alone tipped back a brewski.

But then, she's been going down on Granny. What's a beer between friends?

Stop! None of your business!

God, he wanted Mrs. Kelly to leave. He wanted to ask Granny if it was true.

Of course it's true.

And how long it had been going on and how the hell it had started?

None of your business!

Fuck that shit. He had to know!

Did Mom know? How could she? She with her Brady Bunch outlook on the world?

When he finally realized that Mrs. Kelly wasn't going anywhere (she was probably spending the night K-I-S-S-I-N-G!) he finally decided, fuck being subtle.

"All right," he said, a few chews short of finishing his last bite of pizza. "Spill the beans!"

"About what, dear?" Granny asked.

Mrs. Kelly said, "What do you mean?" and then had the good grace to blush.

"About you two," he asked. "How long?"

Granny blinked at him, all innocence, and then looked at her lover. The way Mrs. Kelly stared back made her sigh and then turn to Roy again. "Is it really any of your business?"

See! None of your business!

"*Yes,*" he cried.

"Oh?" she said, turning on her stern face.

He grinned. "Yes. You gotta tell me!"

"And why is that, dear one?" she asked.

"Because…." His throat froze up. He'd almost said it. Then he saw Frank in his mind, and his heart leapt and the sun came up and the stars came out.

"Because I think I'm gay, Granny. And now I see I might not be the only one."

He shocked all three of them with that. But a few minutes later they all began to talk at once.

CHAPTER TWENTY-ONE

"MY MOTHER wants *what*?" Frank asked, stiffening, jaw clenching.

Glen turned so he was facing Frank again. His brilliant blue eyes—made only the more so by his going-a-lovely-silver hair—seemed suddenly washed out. And something else. Furtive?

"She wants to see you, son."

"See me?" What? Glen might as well have told him that George W. had revealed in a press conference he was trans, or that a spaceship had landed in New York City and Gort the robot had come out of it, or that he, *he himself*, Frank, had carved the roast beast. It made no sense.

Frank's phone buzzed in his pocket again and he yanked it out, hardly glanced at the screen, saw Unknown Caller, and once again sent it to voicemail.

"I told her to stay away from you. Like I've done for years. But she has a lawyer and everything. A good one. And since you've settled down in the United States, I can't keep her away from you."

More nonsense. What he had done for years? Glen had told her to stay away from him for years? "What do you mean you told her to stay away?" For years?

Glen's eyes flashed. "She dumped you, Frank."

No shit, Glen. You've never let me forget it either.

Like picking at a blood scab.

"Now she suddenly wants to see you," Glen went on. "Fuck that! I wasn't going to let her hurt you."

Wasn't going to? Past tense.

Things were coming into focus, but a crazy focus. One that didn't quite make sense. He must not be understanding. Had Glen had too much to drink? *That* made sense. He was tipsy and talking nonsense.

"When did she tell you this? When did she talk to you?"

"Yesterday."

Frank went ramrod straight. *Wait. What?*

"She said she tracked you down and was coming to see you, and that I better not...." His voice suddenly lost its strength and anger and faded off instead.

"You better not *what*?" Frank exclaimed.

Glen looked away.

"You better not what!" Frank asked through grinding teeth.

Glen jumped as if he'd been goosed. He looked back with eyes that seemed to reflect something Frank had never seen before. Was that guilt? No. Fear? It seemed impossible.

"I better not get in the way."

Then, like some morphing special effect, scared/guilty/weird/other Glen transmuted into the Glen that Frank had always known.

"She's a bitch, Frank! And she's going to fill your ears with all kinds of shit to get back at me."

Frank fought off shivers. Something was happening. It was hard to tell what because it was all so surreal. But it was important.

"Back at you for what?"

Glen laughed. Or pretended to. It was his fake laugh. The laugh that only a few people knew was fake. "For what women are always trying to get back at me for. You know. You've seen it over and over. I know it's even happened to you. Guys thinking you were going to give them more than you ever said you would. Manipulating you. And maybe I wasn't always perfect. Promising forever by the fucking dashboard light when all I ever planned on giving them was a night. *Maybe* a month or two. Or not lying, but letting them think they were getting more than I was ever going to give them. Sins of omission or some such fucked-up shit."

"*Glen*," Frank cried. Then he breathed deep. Deeper still. He wasn't going to lose control. He'd long ago learned what a mistake losing control was. It accomplished nothing. Nothing but disaster. Yelling at Glen resulted in nothing except to send him running off into the sunset. "Glen." Calmer. Quieter. "Tell me what's going on."

Glen nodded. Rubbed his face. Poured a half glass of *not*-cheap whisky. Downed half of it. God.

He smiled, nodded again, regained his composure. "Your mama left you, left us, when you were five, going on six. She wanted to be a nurse or some *fucking* thing. She said she would come back, and she never did. Then several years later she started contacting me, telling me she wanted to see you. After she *dumped* you! Well, I told her to fuck off. She didn't deserve to have you in her life. And since I lived all over the world, since we did, she couldn't nail me down, couldn't get lawyers or anyone to stick to me. I kept us safe. I kept *you* safe!"

"So you're telling me she's tried to contact me before?" Keep calm. Very calm. Frank had the idea this might be one of the most important things he had ever done in his life.

"Yes!" Glen all but shouted. "But I was your *legal* guardian, and I wasn't going to let her swoop in and *take* you. And here in this country, that is exactly what some lame bleeding-heart judge would have done. Oh! The *mama* is *so* important for a child. And the dad is *shit*!"

Frank said his father's name. Or tried to. It garbled and stuck like phlegm in his throat. He coughed. Cleared his throat. "Glen." Successful this time. "You're saying my mother… my mother has tried to make contact with me?" he asked again.

"I told you that already! But I stopped her. You can't ditch your own child and then come back when it's convenient—or guilt compels you to."

The world was a little wobbly suddenly. He couldn't believe what he was hearing. His father had told him—for years—that his mother had left them both and had no interest in having Frank in her life. But now Glen was admitting that wasn't the truth.

"You-you *lied* to me, Glen?" And now more than ever he was "Glen" and certainly not "Father."

"Not *lied*," Glen replied, waving his hands around him. "Stretched the truth a little, maybe. But I was doing it to protect you. Can you imagine how much it would have confused you when she showed up out of the blue after leaving you without a thought?"

The words hit Frank like a punch in the stomach, and as the air left him, Frank saw a dim vision of a memory. A smiling face. Dark hair falling past tan shoulders. Dark eyes. And a smile so beautiful…. The faint vision focused into crystal clarity—if only for an instant.

My mother tried to get into contact with me?

"What did she want?" Frank snapped.

Glen didn't answer. And God, look at him. Why, he looked a hundred years old. How could that be? Not around the eyes or the mouth, but *in* the eyes and mouth. His blue eyes were darting back and forth, and his mouth was pressed in a straight line. His Adam's apple bobbed. He was rubbing his hands together as if he were trying to knead away arthritis.

"Glen," Frank said, another wave of shock settling over him. "What did she want?"

Silence.

"*Glen*," he said so loud the shock went away for a second, and his father jumped.

"To see you." Glen rubbed one hand roughly with the other, then reversed it. "She said she just wanted to see you."

"And you didn't tell me?"

"I did what I felt was best," he muttered.

"You should have given me a choice!" Frank cried.

"I was protecting you," Glen said, his voice now a whisper, and he stared at Frank with eyes that seemed to quiver in their sockets.

"I am thirty years old, Glen. I don't need protecting."

His father—no, *Glen*—sighed a sigh so long Frank thought he might collapse on the floor with it. His whole body seemed to melt. "That's why I'm here. To tell you."

No, you're not. You're here because you were hoping you could convince me not to see her.

Frank shivered. Something felt really… wrong.

He's scared.

Of course he is. It's normal. He spent most of his life raising me. And now this woman pops up and wants to be a part of my life.

But….

But nothing. To hell with her.

Where was she when the man she left—her husband—was raising a son while working all over the planet to support and take care of him? Who knew and who cared? What kind of woman abandons her own child? Not a mother for sure. Yes. To hell with her. And the idea that Frank would forgive and forget what she had done? Why, of course, it would justifiably scare Glen. Who *had* been there Frank's whole life.

But then that image of his mother, which may or may not have been her or anything like what she looked like—and God, it could have been a memory of any one of his father's many women from when Frank was a kid—came back fully clear.

The dark hair falling to her shoulders, the dark flashing eyes, the huge warm smile....

Frank shook it away. No. Why should he let her come back now? Surely all she wanted to do was alleviate some kind of guilt.

Had his father been so bad? Of course, the answer was no. The things Frank had seen! In Tuscany he'd stood right before the Leaning Tower of Pisa and Michelangelo's *David*. In Berlin he'd seen the Brandenburg Gate and the East Side Gallery, a remnant of the Berlin Wall that was painted by artists from around the world. He'd spent over a year and a half on the gorgeous island of Santorini (where he met Kostas), with its white buildings and blue roofs, as well as getting to travel to Rome to see the Colosseum. And of course there had been the ancient city of Chhatarpur in India, famous for its erotic sculptures and carvings. Frank had been thrilled to find, while looking very carefully among all the hetero and even bestial couplings—as well as orgies—to find a few gay ones as well. There was verification there....

And there had been more.

"It really wasn't so bad, was it?" Glen said then, as if reading Frank's mind. "Not having a mother? Growing up with me? We had adventures, didn't we?"

Frank nodded absently. Then turned to Glen and nodded again, this time more strongly.

"I know our life cheated you of lifelong friends," Glen went on. "But you *had* friends, right? All over the world?"

Friends? Some.

Now and then. One did that. Found friends. And boys found ways to cross language barriers. Games were games. Playing was playing. Swimming was swimming. And climbing trees, hiking, football—what most of the *rest* of the world called football. You didn't need to speak the same words to do any of that. Boys found a way. And then as boys got older, they found other things to do. You didn't need to speak the same language to do those things either.

Not speaking the same language came in handy in other important ways as well. It helped Frank avoid getting *too* close. Helped him keep his distance. Which made it easier to leave and go somewhere else.

"Frank?"

"It wasn't bad," Frank lied, to his father and himself.

Because in the first years, he had longed for friendships that would last. But after a while, he'd learned to distance himself. That was good. To *not* need something that lasted any longer than a season, a year or so at best. Because in the end, those friendships wouldn't have lasted anyway, would they?

Would they?

It saved him a lifetime of hurt. He'd seen what love—no, the *loss* of love—could do to people. Turned them into heartsick fools. Whining, crying, disgusting fools.

He would never let a man do that to him.

So even as an adult, when he found himself getting a little too close to a man who had become more than a one-night or one-weekend stand, he ended things.

If that hurt anyone, well, he was sorry. But wasn't it better that he ended things *before* they got too serious? If he and a man reached a point where if they stopped seeing each other it could be called "breaking up," that was the instant he *did* end whatever was happening between them.

Because he didn't want to hurt anyone. Never. He wanted laughs. And some bit of joy. And great sex. *Never* pain.

Not for anyone.

Not for me.

Love, whatever *that* was—that gooey, giddy, light-headed feeling— did not last.

He thought of Cody and Harry and his prediction that *their* love was doomed, had at most one year left. It made him feel sad.

It's not even my fucking relationship and I feel sad!

He thought then of Roy.

God. He's just the type to fall head over heels, isn't he? Despite the fact that Roy's orange suit had made Frank think of him as—

A bad boy.

—someone who was rough and tough, he'd learned instead that Roy was innocent and naïve and very capable of being hurt.

I don't want to hurt him.

He thought of those huge blue anime eyes and that smile and his expression when he rocked with pleasure and his expression simply when he was happy and...

I don't want to hurt him.

But the idea of "breaking up" with Roy hurt *Frank. Oh God!*

"Frank?"

He came back from wherever he'd been going. Looked at Glen. Took him in. Whatever had been happening to Glen—worry? Fear?—was gone, replaced by genuine concern.

"You okay?"

Frank nodded. Then sinned by slugging back his Lagavulin. "You hungry?" he asked.

Glen smiled. "You fucking bet. Want to go up?"

"Up?"

Glen pointed at the ceiling. "Apogee."

"Pricey," Frank said.

"We're celebrating!" Glen exclaimed.

"Celebrating what?"

"You and me, kid!" Glen replied. "The dynamic duo."

Hardly. But good food would help him stop thinking about Roy. And God, his mother too. "Let's do it," he said.

And for a very little while, it worked.

CHAPTER TWENTY-TWO

THEY TALKED over each other, all excited to *be* talking, and listened to each other as best they could.

"Oh, Roy," Mrs. Kelly said, cheeks bright pink. "I've loved your granny forever."

"It feels like Kelly has been my special friend forever," Granny said.

"I fought this for so long," Roy said, heart rushing.

"The first time I laid eyes on her, my heart—" Mrs. Kelly laid a hand on her chest and drummed it with her fingertips. "—started to pound, and I thought I'd never seen anyone so beautiful in my life."

"I think it was two years after we met her that Milton told me how jealous he was of the way I looked at Kelly." Granny smiled like a schoolgirl.

"There was this boy in my gym class named Joey," Roy inserted, "and my heart would race like a runaway horse when I saw him." Especially in his gym uniform. His muscular arms and his hairy legs…. *God!*

"I was so surprised when Milton said that," Granny said. "I had no idea I was looking at her like that!"

"I *hoped*," Mrs. Kelly said. "I would see her gazing at me across a room, and I could barely breathe."

"I couldn't look at Joey when we showered because I might…." Then because Roy couldn't say, "I'd get a hard-on," out loud, he blushed as pink as Mrs. Kelly. And oh, thinking of that boy now! He'd gotten to see Joey without any clothes on a few times when circumstances aligned just right, and it had only been that few times because he tried not to be in the shower at the same time and dared not look except maybe out of the corner of his eyes, because yes, he would start to chub up, and that would be death when everyone saw.

Damn, Joey had looked so *good* naked, and *How am I thinking about this now?*

"I just know I felt… happier when I was around her," Granny said. "I was so naïve, I had no idea *what* I was feeling."

"I knew what *I* was feeling! I'd always known I was different." Mrs. Kelly laughed. "I knew I liked girls when I was in something like fourth grade."

"How did I *not* know I was different?" Roy said. "I look back now, and… geez… Joey wasn't the first boy I liked!"

Then they really did all speak at once.

"I just loved movie stars like Jane Mansfield and Betty Grable…"

"I thought I loved Milton, but…"

"I had sex with a lot of girls, but…"

"…who your Granny looked just like…"

"…I was never that pretty!"

"…and I thought I liked it until…"

"…you were more beautiful than Betty could ever be…"

"…and you were so pretty and so smart and exciting and…"

"…and then this week I met Frank, and everything changed and…"

They all, as if beaming some message to each other, stopped speaking at once. Looked at each other with wide eyes. And then took turns.

"I MARRIED Clarence," Mrs. Kelly said, "because unless you moved to San Francisco or Paris or some such place and joined bohemians, that's what you did. I had no money. And there was my family and my job and…. I was too scared. But I always knew it was girls. *Always.* I didn't know what I was and that I wasn't the only one until I went to college and read about the island of Lesbos and the poetry of Sappho and…." She let out a long sigh and Roy couldn't figure out if it was happiness or sadness or a combination of both.

"She that fain would fly, she shall quickly follow," Mrs. Kelly continued, and Roy realized she was quoting….

She that now rejects, yet with gifts shall woo thee,
She that heeds thee not, soon shall love to madness,
Love thee, the loth one!

Mrs. Kelly sighed again. "I longed for that. For just one of the girls in college I crushed on to turn around and woo me." She blushed fiercely then and gave a little laugh that sounded so like a schoolgirl. Roy thought it was adorable, and he felt a little thrill that she was talking about love she felt for girls and not boys. Not because of the girl-on-girl thing that seemed to thrill so many guys he knew and had never excited him. But because he felt a wonderful kindred spirit with her. *We're the same even though we're different.*

And it hit him again—*whoa!*—that he was doing it. He was accepting it. He was embracing it.

I-I think I might be gay. How did I not know?

"But no," Mrs. Kelly continued. "No girl told me she loved me and begged me to fly away with her to Lesbos or Paris or even San Francisco to find the Gertrude Steins of my time. I was with a girl only once, that last night of school, when I got drunk with a girl on strawberry wine. Sounds like a poem, doesn't it?"

She glanced at them shyly, and for a moment there Roy saw her as she must have looked when she was his age or even younger—a young woman of about twenty-one—and felt a deep sorrow for her that she hadn't found what she wanted and needed. "I met Clarence at a dance between my college and his, and I was a virgin on the night we got married. I told him it was religious reasons, because even in the late fifties, girls rarely waited until they got married. He waited, and I did what I had to do…."

Now she looked even sadder, and Roy's heart actually hurt for her. To know…. To know what she wanted and needed and to have tasted it only once before she had to get married and live a life she didn't want to live.

"I can only blame the world so much," Mrs. Kelly said. "I *could* have been brave. I *could* have! I could have cleared out my bank account—and Clarence let me have my own, which wasn't all that common back then, a wife having her own money—and I could have run away and gone to Paris and found my own Alice B. Toklas. But I didn't. I played it safe. Even when Clarence died just two years after we married. I stayed in our house. The insurance paid for it after he was gone—he'd watched out for me that way. I just stayed and stayed and stayed. I taught school, and I was alone."

Pain. Oh, the pain in her eyes!

"But then I met Billie." She reached out and touched Roy's grandmother's hand, and Granny took it, and the idea of these two senior ladies being "gal pals" seemed wonderful and not weird at all.

How different might things be today had the two of them been able to be together back then?

Well, for one, I wouldn't be alive, he thought and covered a laugh with his hand.

Mrs. Kelly looked at Roy and said, "Your family moved in next door, and I would see your granny now and then. More after you were born. And even more when your father… passed."

Roy caught his breath and let it out. What was there to say about that?

Granny nodded. "Because I would come over every day and be there when you got home from school. And when you got old enough for me to stop"—she smiled at Mrs. Kelly—"well, I didn't. Because Kelly would come over, and we would talk and talk and talk."

Roy remembered, and his eyes went wide at the sudden realization that something different than he'd ever imagined had been going on. Not just cards or Scrabble or reading to each other but…. "Were you two…?"

"Oh no!" Mrs. Kelly said, and Granny shook her head.

"I never cheated on your grandfather." She looked back at Mrs. Kelly and gripped her hand. "At least not physically. I see now of course that she was always the one in my heart. And when Milton died two years ago…."

Mrs. Kelly held up a hand. "I waited another year! It was proper to give her a year to grieve her husband. I waited a lifetime, but I waited another year before—"

"A year and a half," Granny said. "While I held my breath, and wondered and wondered. Wondered if you would…." She turned bright eyes Roy's way. "I finally had to be the first one to kiss *her*."

"You did not!" Mrs. Kelly said, raising her hands. "I kissed *you*!"

Granny shook her head and gazed into Mrs. Kelly face. "No. You almost did. You brought your face so close to mine. But I suddenly realized that if I didn't kiss you, you might never kiss me."

Her voice was thick and sweet and soft and filled with love, and Roy's heart leapt at her words.

"I would have kissed you," Mrs. Kelly said very quietly, and Roy almost felt as if he were intruding and that he should go away. "I would have. I was so scared."

"Me too," Granny said.

For a long moment, no one said a word, and then Granny turned back to Roy.

"I really was naïve. I mean, I heard words like lesbian and then later words I didn't really like. Queer and dyke and lezzo, and then very ugly words that I won't say. I thought, I'm not that. I'm not a *dyke*. Because back then when people used that word, it was with such disgust. Even Milton, who was never an ugly man, would nod at some woman who was heavy or had short hair, a woman who didn't look feminine, and he'd whisper that word. And I realized he used it to mean that there was something wrong with her. Something sickening. Or at least he *did*. He stopped. Without me even having to say anything." She smiled a small smile. "I like to think he figured it all out before I did. That when he was disgusted, he realized he was disgusted with the woman he loved. And he did love me, Roy. He loved me so much."

Roy nodded. He knew that. Always had. Saw it in Grandpa's eyes and in his words and the way, right up until his death, that he always held doors open for her and brought her flowers and took care of her garden and never forgot Valentine's Day or their anniversary or anything.

"But I did know I loved Kelly. I knew it more and more. As the years passed, I would joke with her. Call her my wife—"

"My heart would skip every time." Mrs. Kelly.

"—because I knew what we had was special. And I thought, wouldn't it be crazy if we ever were together? Like me and Milton? And I would think of your mother and your uncle and all of you, and I would worry what you would think. And then…. Then we kissed, and I knew she was my wife from that moment on."

Roy saw both their eyes grow wet and almost whistled in awe. To think. They waited… how long? Longer than he'd been alive. At least twenty-five years! Imagine waiting that long to be with someone. And to have waited because they didn't think there was anything they could do about it. Waited because they thought they never could be together. That the fact that they were both women was only a part of it.

"So we have kept it between the two of us, mostly," Granny said then. "No gay prides or anything like that, but you can know I *didn't* vote for Trump!" She looked at Mrs. Kelly again and squeezed her hand. "I think your mom knows—or suspects at least."

Mom suspected that Granny was gal pals with Mrs. Kelly? He hardly thought so. Mrs. Brady suspecting anything "queer" about the Brady Bunch? Especially with her own mother? He didn't even know if she understood what being gay or lesbian was. Not that he knew either. Only what he was beginning to suspect. To take in. Why, it scared the shit out of him to think of telling her what he suspected about himself!

"She looks at us," Mrs. Kelly said. "We catch her looking at us—"

"After we get caught staring at each other."

It hit him then. "So, you two have only been—"

"Together," Granny said.

"—for six months?"

"We've been together in our hearts for a lifetime," she answered. "But more than that? Yes. Six months. And they've been the happiest of my life."

"Oh yes," Mrs. Kelly replied. "The best of mine."

"Granny…," he said with a sigh. And was happy for them. Astonished how happy he was. "Mrs. Kelly."

"You know," his lifelong neighbor said then, adjusted her big black glasses, smiled. "I think you should call me Kelly now."

His eyes went wide. Call her Kelly? It seemed crazy!

"After all," she said, "you're an adult now. And we are coconspirators. Members of a whole new family."

His mouth dropped open.

She smiled a radiant smile. "Please? Kelly?"

Roy closed his mouth. Looked back and forth between them. Smiled. Granny nodded.

"Okay," he said quietly. And then tried it on for size. "*Kelly.*" He laughed. "It'll take getting used to."

She laughed too. "I love you saying it."

"Me too," Granny said.

"But I am not calling *you* Billie!" he cried, pointing at his grandmother. Her brows came together. "Of course not! That would be disrespectful."

And they all laughed.

"Your turn," Granny said, and he bit his lower lip. Hard.

God!

He waited a moment while they watched him expectantly. Sighed. Drew in a long breath and let it out very slowly.

"It's nothing like you two. Nothing so…." *Romantic.* And seeing those expectant faces, he said aloud, "Nothing so romantic." In fact, he was suddenly embarrassed. *His* experience was *so* sexual.

"Hey" came the echo of Frank Sinclair's voice. *"You want a blowjob?"*

How stunned he'd been. He had done a double take and realized that it *was* a man who had asked him the question. And then he'd seen how fucking gorgeous he was. How movie-star handsome. How muscular, even though all he could see was Frank's arm and neck through the window of his little red car.

How stunned he'd been when he saw the man meant it. This wasn't somebody fucking with him.

He remembered quite suddenly how a friend of his had once said that he would never pass up a blowjob. "I mean, is there anything better in the entire fucking world? Especially if they swallow?" They'd been drinking and he'd gone on to say, "Fuck. I'd let a *dude* do it. Guys are supposed to give better head." And then…

Holy shit! That buddy had given him a long look, hadn't he? Fuck! Had he been telling Roy, "You can suck my cock if you want?"

But when Frank had made his offer, Roy hadn't been thinking about that. Only the idea: never pass up a blowjob. So he didn't. He said okay. By the time they got up to Frank's apartment, he'd decided he was going to go for it. *All* of it. He was shaking and sweating and scared half to fucking death, but he knew he would never, ever, ever have sex with another man again, and it was better to regret what you'd done than what you hadn't done—

Except for what landed him in jail, that is.

—and knew, knew, he wanted to know what it felt like to have a real cock inside him and not something made out of plastic or rubber or whatever the fuck they were made of. Something real. *Alive.*

When Ramona—alive—would crawl on top of him and then put that thing—*not* alive—inside him, *fuck* him with it, he would wonder. Wonder what it would be like to have real flesh taking him and not something so unreal. But he thought that would never happen. How could he let it? He certainly couldn't ask a friend. Couldn't ask the buddy with the philosophy on blowjobs.

"I mean, is there anything better in the entire fucking world?"

He actually got on craigslist once. Well, a few times. Read the ads. They'd made him break out in a sweat and made his stomach twist in knots, and the very idea of letting a complete stranger into his place was impossible.

What if he invited a serial killer over? Hadn't that happened? Even close by? Kansas, maybe? What would be worse? Him vanishing and no one ever knowing what happened to him? Or finding him dead and knowing exactly what he'd done to "earn" death?

Yet there he had been, hadn't he? In a stranger's apartment. Somehow, though, he'd thought he was safe. And he'd done it. He'd asked Frank to fuck him.

"You want me to...?" Frank had looked at him with huge, surprise-filled eyes. *"Are you sure? I mean it can really hurt the first time and...."*

Then he'd said those words. *"Please don't talk me out of it. I want to do it all. I know, but I don't want to regret* not *doing it. Because this is never going to happen again."*

And dear Jesus! Frank had fucked him and nothing, *nothing* had prepared him—not even Ramona's arsenal of sex toys—for the pleasure and intimacy of having a man inside him.

He knew no matter what he told himself—he could see it now in retrospect—that he could not let it be the only time. He had to know it again. Feel it again.

But then Roy saw Granny and Mrs. Kelly—*Kelly*—looking at him and realized he'd gotten lost. He couldn't tell them all of that. And really, were they expecting or wanting him to? They sure hadn't shared whatever they did behind closed doors.

"Honey?" Granny asked.

"It was just sex," he blurted. "I never let a man touch me, not even in jail." Although he'd thought about maybe being with Demaine, hadn't he? Because he thought that was what you were supposed to do. Give yourself to some big bull of a man who would then protect you. He'd half made the offer but only half because he was too shy to say it right out, and to his surprise, Demaine turned him down.

"Ain't gonna take advantage of nobody," he'd said. "Besides, you ain't my type. I dig a brother." It took Roy a minute to realize Demaine didn't mean a relation, but a fellow black man. They'd both realized that at the same time and laughed and laughed.

"It was just sex," he said. But it wasn't. Somehow it felt wrong to put it that way. "It was just supposed to be sex. I was curious. I went home with him and it was—"

"Everything that being with a woman wasn't," said Kelly. She smiled. Winked.

God yes. That was it exactly, wasn't it?

Being with Frank was everything that being with a woman had never been. He'd liked sex with women. Girls. Females. *Whatever!*

But it had never been the raving big huge gigantic deal that his friends had endlessly talked about, had it?

Yet with Frank….

"Yes," he said. "I don't understand it, but yes." He peered at Kelly. "I didn't always know like you did. I didn't always know I was different. Or at least I didn't know *that* was what made me different. I guess I felt—"

Apart from other people.

"—outside," he whispered.

"But with your friend?" Granny asked.

Friend? Was Frank his friend?

He saw Frank in his mind, and he hoped so. Hoped that they were that much, at least. At *least* friends.

"Frank," he said.

"How do you feel with Frank?" she asked.

"A *part* of something," he said before he knew he was saying it, and wondered if they knew the difference. "A part instead of—"

"*Apart*," Kelly said.

He smiled. Yes. Part of something instead of being on the outside. He'd always felt like he was on the outside. That was a big reason Ramona had been able to talk him into the Hawaii trip and what he'd had to do to get them there. To try and be a part of her circle.

Roy shook that away. Returned to happy thoughts.

"I feel like I've found this… this… *brother*hood or something."

They were nodding. Nodding! "Yes," and "Yes," they said, eyes filled to overflowing with understanding. And just like that he felt part of another family he'd just begun to suspect existed. He liked it. A lot.

"Can there be something more?" Granny asked. "With you and Frank?"

"I don't know," he said. "But I hope so."

And wow. He did, didn't he?

He hoped so.

He hoped it very, very much.

CHAPTER TWENTY-THREE

FRANK'S LATE lunch/early dinner was delicious. But then, they were at Apogee. How could it be anything less? Apogee was one of Kansas City's premier restaurants. A dinner salad, which didn't come *with* dinner, had a ridiculously high price. But this was fine dining at a five-star restaurant, and anyone who ate here on a regular basis wouldn't even look at the prices on the menu. He didn't usually do such frivolous spending, although he could certainly afford it now and again.

Besides, he wasn't paying, was he?

Frank skipped the salad and had braised-rabbit-stuffed cappelletti with parmesan and mousseline—a soft, light mousse—for an appetizer. Utterly amazing. He'd heard about their foie gras and decided he wanted it. Remarkable. It was rich, buttery, delicate, unlike regular duck liver. It came with strawberries, walnuts, and black pepper, an odd combination that set it off perfectly.

He split it with the old man because that's what they'd always done, tried different wild foods all over the world together. And too often Glen would say something like, "Isn't this *great*, Frank? Certainly nothing your mother would have ever eaten. Not even *tried*."

Frank did note that Glen didn't say anything like that today.

Smart thinking.

But then dumb was not a word one would use to describe Glen Sinclair, was it?

For his entrée, Frank couldn't decide. He was really tempted by the black-angus ribeye with toasted Italian farro, petite onions, and watercress, but somehow steak made him think of Roy, and he didn't want that… connection. Didn't want to have steak with Glen instead of Roy, and that…? Now *that* was dumb and *not* something Glen would do. Would, in fact, ridicule.

Not that he was planning on telling Glen about Roy. And really, what was there to tell? "I had steaks with this cute, sexy guy out on my balcony. Naked, and now I don't want to have steak with you."

Right!

Dumb.

Then Frank couldn't decide between the scallops and the lamb. They were two of his favorites, and he figured that at Apogee they would be remarkable. He told Glen so, and Glen suggested they get both and share.

"It's what we do, right, Frankie? It's the Dynamic Duo thing, right?"

Somehow, Frank couldn't imagine Batman and Robin splitting the entrées at an expensive restaurant, even *if* they were sautéed scallops in *vadouvan* curry with almonds, carrots, and puffed rice *and* New Zealand lamb with english peas, Niçoise olives, and spring garlic.

But whether the superheroes would split such meals or not, Frank and Glen shared, and the food was indeed very, very good. Try as he might, Frank couldn't stay mad at Glen. His father was simply being… Glen.

And no, Frank's childhood hadn't been bad. How could he complain, really? His father bragged on him wherever they went. "This is Frankie. A chip off the old block. My son is my world, and that's why I show him the whole *wide* world!"

Yes, he'd built up resentment over the fact that they never *stayed* anywhere. That he made friends and had to leave them over and over and over again. He'd cried for weeks when they left Kostas and Santorini behind. It's why he'd finally chosen, some five years back, to get off the Glen & Frank Sinclair World Tour. To finally be able to settle down, for the first time, and put down some roots. To make friends. Memories.

But he hadn't really done that, had he? Except for the most unlikely of friends, Harry and Cody. As different from him as the proverbial night and day. Romantic and believing in impossible stuff.

"*Magic*," Harry had said to him one Sunday afternoon. They were drinking Bloody Marys, which was perfect because he'd had way too much to drink the night before and had a hangover. Whatever he might say about the couple, they *had* perfected the cocktail. Why, they even kept celery in vodka overnight to make the perfect addition for their Bloody Marys.

"Magic?" he'd asked as Cody cleared his throat and the two of them looked at each other, exchanging some kind of couple message.

They'd both turned back to him then, and Cody said, "There are more things in heaven and earth than we can possibly dream of. Don't discount love, Frank."

Yeah. His best friends were two men who believed in both love *and* magic. Two things he'd long stopped believing in.

As it turned out, Glen had, until mere weeks ago, been in Japan, a new country for the old man. He'd been there close to a year restoring a shoin-zukuri—a residential mansion that had been the home of Zen abbots during the Edo period.

"Different world entirely," Glen said. "Real frigging mix of the old and new. The old don't appreciate my charm or sense of humor."

No. I don't suppose they would have, Frank thought. Probably weren't too crazy about the womanizing either.

"And considering the age of that old building, there were some *old* people involved. They wouldn't let me even have an opinion on the gardens. And then there was that whole feng shui thing…."

"Which is Chinese, not Japanese," Frank said.

"I know *that*!" Glen snapped. "But you don't think they have their own version of that? *Very* fucking precise ways of doing things? Colors? Woods? Paper? Stains?"

Then, seeming sorry for his retort—or at least the way it was delivered—he softened his tone. Quickly. "That's a good thing, though, yeah? My reputation is for getting things done *right*. I had to do a ton of research. All I could think of was that I sure wished I'd had you there. You were so good at that. Remember how dependent I was on you?"

Flattery, flattery.

"Remember how good you were at it?"

"Still am, Glen," Frank said. Because it was true. He was. It served him well.

"I suppose you are," Glen said and went silent for a moment. Frank was just opening his mouth to break the silence when Glen abruptly continued. "Thank God the *new*, the people more your age, liked me *a lot*. Hell. I was like a goddamned hero or something." Oh how he laughed at that.

And Frank guessed they probably didn't object to his womanizing. Maybe even admired it.

"Double-edged sword, though. It's one thing to add modern conveniences like central heat and air, modern bathroom facilities, and a kitchen with all the tech. But some of the shit the grandson wanted? Solar panels on the roof? On a traditional, ancient-style roof! No fucking way. We came up with a solution, though…."

Glen faded and then came back and started up with a series of "Do you remember whens?" and "Do you remember hows?".

Frank remembered them all, if not precisely the way Glen did. Glen made every story grand and exciting. That was what he did. It was how he sold himself all over the planet. And Frank knew exactly what the old man was up to today. Fanning the flames of bonding. The "How great we weres" and "How great we *ares*." Designed to get Frank's mind fixed entirely on the "Brotherhood of Glen and Frank Sinclair." How the two of them didn't need *any*one. It was the two of them against the world, so why would Frank waste time thinking about some woman— his mother—who wanted to contact him? Glen was saying, though not in so many words, "Don't think about her. We never needed her. We don't need her now."

Except it was having the opposite effect. Frank *was* thinking about the woman who after *twenty-five years* had suddenly popped up and was trying to… what? Talk to him? *See* him?

As he sat there, only half listening to Glen now, all kinds of emotions began to stir and then stir harder within him, most of them conflicting. Curiosity. Fear. Anger. Resentment. Anxiousness. Excitement. Dread.

His mother!

Imagine!

Why did she want to see him? Was it guilt? Was she wanting forgiveness? Some kind of absolution? A fucking kidney, maybe? Or could it be for a different reason altogether?

And what about dear old pop? Why would he be so against them meeting? Was he watching out for Frank? Saving him from disappointment? Or was there something else going on there as well?

Who knew with Glen?

But come on! Was there a boy alive who had never known his mother who did not wonder what she was like? Or wonder why she had given him up? Who fantasized that maybe she was someone famous: a president's wife, royalty, a movie star? Hoped there was some reason *why* she'd abandoned her boy?

He, Frank, had done it, hadn't he? *Wondered.* Wondered who she might be. Watched television or a movie, stared at *any*one who he resembled, and thought... could it be *her*?

Demi Moore, maybe? He'd wanted that to be true when he was around ten. Or Princess Stephanie of Monaco. Perhaps she couldn't admit she had a son out of wedlock and told Glen to take him. On his sojourns all over the world, mightn't Glen have once gone to the French Riviera? Charmed the princess? Had one of his affairs with her?

A kid wished and hoped all kinds of things, especially when there were important unanswered questions.

The waiter came then and asked them if they wanted dessert. Why not? Do the full treatment. Glen was looking at some kind of banana fritter, but Frank's eyes were drawn to only one item. Something called dark chocolate crémeux. The line under it read only—intriguingly—pistachio, rose, blackberry. Frank loved chocolate. Any kind, but especially dark chocolate. Not surprising, he guessed. He'd read somewhere once, or heard, maybe, that chocolate caused a chemical reaction in the brain that was triggered by only one other thing. Orgasms. And he certainly liked orgasms. Causing them too. Of course, that probably hadn't been part of the research. If there had been any research. He'd never googled or snopesed the story. He didn't want to find out it wasn't true. He loved the idea that chocolate and sex were linked. What could be better? Except maybe sex and an expensive whisky?

Except maybe chocolate and sex with a man in an orange jumpsuit!

When Glen suggested they get both and share, Frank nixed the idea immediately.

"*Mine*," he said. Although he might have been willing to share with Roy.... *Whoa!* Now that was a crazy idea.

His cell phone vibrated in his pocket, and he slipped it out, once more saw Unknown Caller, and once *more* sent it to voicemail. He knew it really was time to check to see who the caller or callers were, but at this point, with his and Glen's time winding down—and it *was* winding down; he needed to get away from Attention Monger Glen so he could fucking *breathe*—Frank figured the calls could wait a little while longer.

But before Frank left, Glen insisted on one final course. A liquid one. It wasn't coffee either. It was Laphroaig Quarter Cask scotch. Glen knew him. Knew him well. In this case it was Glen who had given him a love of fine whiskies.

A relatively young single malt, its maturation had been sped up by aging it in quarter casks. It had a soft sweetness with a wonderful velvety feel when it first hit the tongue, and then an *intense* peatiness, so unique to Laphroaig, came bursting through.

It was exquisite.

"*Ohh…*," Glen said with an appreciative moan. "*Beautiful*, isn't it?"

Frank nodded.

"Almost enough to give up titties for, huh?"

Frank raised an eyebrow.

Glen laughed. "Pectorals?"

Frank smiled. "Not *forever*," he replied.

"But it's like what Ron White said? Once you've seen one lady— ah, *person*?—naked, you pretty much—"

"Want to see them all 'nekkid,'" Frank finished.

And hell. It was true. He did love seeing men naked. Spotting some hot guy and, if things went right, talking to him, hitting on him, getting him somewhere he could get his clothes off. It was like opening a splendidly wrapped present. You knew if the gift was half as good as the way it was wrapped, you were in for something wonderful. And then to find out it was fantastic was even better!

But would you want to stop unwrapping presents, no matter how fantastic the last one had been?

Of course not.

Which was why his old man had trouble settling down. There was another "nekkid" woman out there somewhere—just around the bend, in the next coffee shop, attending the dinner party given by a friend, at the gas station across the street. How could Cody and Harry not see? Not understand? Because after all, they'd been hit by the famous wanderlust like any normal man. They'd gotten the seven-year itch two years early! And maybe they had found that an open relationship wasn't for them—as long as *they* lasted, that is—but they still liked Frank's stories, didn't they?

It was because they were men!

"That Ron White is a wise man," Frank said.

Glen nodded solemnly. "That is Ron White's First Noble Truth. And the second is"—he held up his almost-empty glass—"if life gives you lemons, you should make lemonade… and then find somebody whose life has given them vodka and have a party." He burst into laughter as the waiter arrived again and pointed at Frank. "This is my son," he said, his tone bragging and thick. "He's the best son a man could ask for. A chip off the old block, eh, Frankie?"

Frank shrugged. He wasn't sure what to say. He never was. Especially tonight.

"And you should see what he can do with wood. *Gorgeous*. His hands are magic!"

The waiter smiled politely, feigning interest. "Really, sir? That's excellent."

"*Second* most talented man you'll ever meet, 'cause of course the old block himself is best." Glen laughed again, and then his eyes went wild. His grin turned lecherous. "So if you ever need someone to work on *your* wood, give my son here a call!"

The waiter froze, and so did Frank. Then the poor server cleared his throat and said he would keep that in mind and did they need anything else?

Glen pointed at his glass, and Frank shook his head in a way that he hoped told his father that there was no way in heaven or on earth *that* was happening. Because after his embarrassing comment to the waiter, it was certainly time to go.

More than time.

The scotch and laughter had relaxed Frank enough to settle the whirlwind of emotions that had begun inside his head and heart earlier. Allowed him to *not* be angry with Glen. Because surely it was as Frank had guessed already.

The old man was scared. That was what this was all about.

Glen was scared of this woman—his ex-wife and Frank's "ex-mom"—who had suddenly reappeared from nowhere, wanting who knew what? Glen had raised Frank on his own. It only made sense that he would be apprehensive.

After Glen paid, they made their way to the elevator, where they hugged like "real men," and Frank knew they were still on stage. It was okay. Glen probably wasn't even aware he was doing it. At least that's what Frank hoped.

He also wondered if Glen knew that probably quite a few people who had watched them—and people *had* watched them—assumed they were lovers. Two attractive men having dinner. *Sharing* dinner, for God's sake. Hugging. Their difference in age meant nothing. Why, he could be Glen's kept boy.

Eternally being onstage was who Glen was. His presence and his charm—that the old guard in Japan didn't like but the younger generation considered goddamn heroic—was so much of why he was successful. Selling himself was nearly as important as selling the transformative work he did and was one more thing he had taught Frank. How to sell *himself*. That skill had helped Frank be successful and allowed him to ask the prices he did.

It also helped him sell himself in bed.

Not that he charged.

They went their separate ways on Glen's floor, and this time—for some reason—Frank was hesitant with his second hug. This one was just the two of them. No audience. Was it a real hug that Glen was offering, or was he still onstage, with Frank the only person in the audience? It was hard to tell and a big part of why, even though he loved the man who had sired him, Frank was also... not estranged, exactly... but compelled to get away from him and begin his own life.

In the end he accepted the arms around him and drew Glen close and rocked him from side to side.

Whatever else Glen was, he was a father who loved his son.

They parted with promises to make sure it wasn't a year before they saw each other again, a "Who knows? I might stay another night," and an unspoken desperate plea that Frank not see his mother.

Frank was glad it was unspoken.

Because then he didn't have to answer.

CHAPTER TWENTY-FOUR

WHEN FRANK got to the lobby he realized he was a bit tipsy, maybe a little too much to drive quite yet. There was a small kiosk selling coffee, and he went to it, thanking God it was a Roasterie Kansas City Air Roasted Coffee and not a Starbuck's with their bitter, burned-tasting brew. He got a medium (no silly, pretentious words like grande and venti and trenta), sat down under a huge kinetic sculpture, and sipped and relaxed and closed his eyes.

Jesus what a day.

Glen popping up out of nowhere and telling him his mother was trying to contact him!

His *mother*.

Frank trembled, and it took him by surprise. Trembled again, a little harder. Suddenly his stomach cramped hard, and for a moment he was afraid he'd lose that Apogee dinner and scotch. He was shocked to find tears threatening, and his throat closed, and he couldn't breathe. Where had all that come from?

It passed quickly enough, thankfully, but it left him shaking still. Apparently, the calm in the whirlwind of his emotions had simply been the eye of the storm.

My mom. The eye had passed by.

He looked at his coffee and no longer wanted it, but he had to drive. He couldn't sit here. So he drank half of it as quick as he could, considering it was very hot, and then he stood…

…and got another call.

He snatched it out of his pocket and answered without thinking, "Sinclair Solutions—It's in the Grain! How can I help you?"

"Frank?" came a voice he didn't know. A woman's voice. "Frank Sinclair?"

But then he *did* know who it was.

A chill washed over him, followed by a wave of gooseflesh. Another stomach cramp. He sat back down quickly.

"Yes," he somehow managed without stuttering.

Don't say it. Don't say it. Don't say it.

"Frankie," she said. Paused. "I…. This might be a s-surprise. Or then again your father m-might have w-warned you I would be calling."

Don't say it. Don't say it. Don't say it.

At least she was stuttering!

"I…. There is no easy way to say it. This is your mother."

She said it.

"A-and I was wondering if there was any way I could see you."

Frank knew he should say something. He needed to say something. But his throat seized up, and there seemed no way to get any words to come out.

"Frankie? Are you there?"

Frankie.

"Fran—" Her voice caught, and he thought he heard a sob. There was another voice too, murmuring in the background, and then she said, "*No.* I'm… fine." Not sounding at all fine.

"Son…."

Son? Really?

"I…." Softly.

You what?

"*Frank.*" Stronger now. "Are you there?"

"I'm here," he said and couldn't believe he'd managed to do it. He began to tremble again.

"I know this has to be a shock. I am hoping your father told you I would be calling…."

"Warned me," he somehow said.

"*Warned*…." Another pause. Then, "Okay. That is certainly fair…."

He suddenly noticed that she had a nice voice. Rich, with a slight accent he couldn't quite identify. And with it an echo from long ago. An echo that said that *every Who down in Whoville liked Christmas a lot….*

Goose bumps rushed all over him again.

"Frankie…. I'm in town."

He stiffened ever so slightly. *She is already in town.*

"And I wondered… is there any way I can see you? Would you see *me*?"

God, she said it.

"I know you must be astonished at me being so audacious."

Audacious was right!

"You must be thinking, *How dare she show up after all this time?* But I want to explain. Tell you *why.*"

Like there ever could be an explanation good enough.

"And that I never, ever left you...."

Wait. *What?*

"I've tried to find you for years. I finally all but gave up. Twenty-five years ago, *ten* years ago, there was no Facebook. I would find traces of you, and then, well, your father would.... No. I *won't* say that."

"S-say what?" God! There were tears in his eyes. They stung. When had that happened?

"I won't say anything bad about your father. You don't know me." A sob.

You better not say anything bad about Glen!

There was a long pause.

"Mama? Are you there?" he whispered and then thought, *Oh my God. I called her Mama!*

He heard what he thought might be crying on the other end of the line. "M-my God. I c-can't believe I'm *talking* to you!"

And then he heard her break down for sure. Heard that other voice, even though he couldn't make out what he—and it was a he—was saying.

"No. I can...," she mumbled.

Then...

"Frank?" The man's voice.

"Yes," he said, cautious.

"My name is Theo Gardener. I'm... I'm your mother's husband." He spoke with an English accent, and Frank realized his mother had the same accent. Hers was lighter than her husband's, though. Not as thick.

Husband's. Frank shivered.

"She won't say anything bad about your father. But I will."

What? What? Who the hell do...?

"Your mother has been trying to find you your entire life. And he kept her from doing it."

What? Kept her from.... No! *Glen said she didn't want anything to do with me. That she ran off with some man.* The man he was talking to right now? Anger rose up inside him. How dare this man....

"And I hope you will at least give her a chance to tell her side of the story. She wants to see you. *Desperately.*"

"Why should I see her?"

"Frank. She *loves* you. She's never *stopped* loving you."

He began to shake. Caught up full in the hurricane now.

"I don't know where you are, but we're here in your city. We are staying at the Meridian Hotel and—"

"The *what?*" he cried. *The Meridian? My God!*

"The Meridian Hotel. Do you know it? It's in your... what do they call it? Crown Center?"

Frank croaked. It was the only sound that would come out. They... she... was in the Meridian?

He looked up at the ceiling. Past the moving sculpture. Barely saw it. Up there, above him in a room, was his mother?

"Frank?"

"I know it," he said.

"Good. We will be here a few days. Hell, we will stay as long as you like. Will you please, *please* consider meeting her?" God! Was that a catch in his voice?

It hit Frank then. Hit him hard and horrible and dark and painful. The Meridian. The same hotel his father had chosen. *Why* had Glen chosen it?

He is just trying to protect me.

But that didn't ring true.

Mama?

"Frank?"

"I'm out of town," he said, lying before he knew he was going to do it.

There was sigh from the other end of the line. "I see." A muffled sound, and then Theo continued, his voice softer. "From what her ex-husband said—your father said—we thought you were in town."

My father. He's protecting me.

"N-no. Sorry." Because God, he *couldn't.* He couldn't see her. "Look, I have an incoming call on the other line that I have to take. Later, okay? I'll call you."

And then he hung up.

CHAPTER TWENTY-FIVE

THE DRIVE home from Granny's was especially… weird.

Roy was in another world. A different reality. A fifth dimension, maybe. Beyond that which is known to man. To paraphrase the words he'd heard a million times in his life, between the pit of all of his fears and the total of all of his knowledge. That Adderall feeling again.

He had a lot to think about. A lot was happening, and it was happening fast. A few days ago, he had been plain old Roy. No different, more or less, than he'd ever been. And now he was contemplating the idea that he was gay.

Wow.

Funny how long the drive seemed. It couldn't be more than twenty minutes or so. Felt like forever, though. But he was traveling a road that was between light and shadow, science and superstition. So to speak.

The thought made him laugh. God! The way he was feeling! Exhilarated! And scared. Really scared.

Was he really thinking of doing this? *Coming out?* A little soon, wasn't it? Ridiculously soon? What he'd had with Frank could have been nothing but really good sex, right?

Maybe he was just *bi*sexual.

All that stuff Frank had said about a Kinsy report. Kindsay? He'd have to look it up. Frank had said there were degrees of sexuality. He didn't have to be all one way or the other, right? He liked women. He liked sex with women. Or he had.

Yet why didn't that feel real? Feel true?

"…on one side you're totally gay—that's me," Frank had said. *"On the other side you're totally straight."* And *"Then there are guys who are only a little bit bi—but mostly gay. And then totally bi. And then a bit, except mostly straight. Maybe that's you."*

Maybe.

But Roy suspected something else. He'd liked sex with women. He had. So it wasn't like he had to take on the whole gay label, right? Because there was that whole scale. Although he did think that he might be more than "a little bit bi." That the side of the scale he was falling on might be more on the gay end. Because the best sex he'd ever had with a woman was with Ramona. And that was when she was fucking him with a strap-on.

That was when—in the weirdest *Twilight Zone* addition to the day, even weirder than finding out his granny and Mrs. Kelly were a lady couple—his phone rang.

Mom. Wondering where I am. It worried her when she didn't know where he was. He might be getting into some kind of trouble.

But when he picked up his phone and glanced at the screen, it wasn't Mom's name he saw. It was Ramona's.

He stared, shocked, and almost drove off the road.

Shit! Ramona. Getting him into trouble when he hadn't even answered the call.

Don't answer! He almost didn't. But at the last second, he did.

Stupidly, he did.

"H-hello?"

"Oh my God!" came her familiar voice. A voice he hadn't heard in over seven months. Not once between then and now. It gave him goose bumps. Bad ones.

"Sweet Cheeks! Is that really you?"

Don't say anything. Hang up!

Before it's too late.

"How are you? Are you there?"

Hang up! But instead he said, "Hello."

"Roy! I can't believe it's you."

Dear God. He couldn't talk.

"Say something!" It was more one of her commands than an enthusiastic feminine squeal. Damned if he didn't respond.

"Yes, Ramona. It's me."

He did pull off the road then, into a grocery store parking lot. He was sweating. His stomach felt like there were stones in it. Heavy ones.

"Oh, Sweet Cheeks. It is so good to hear your voice."

Don't call me that. He knew it wasn't for the cheeks on his face that she'd given him the nickname.

"We wondered why she called you that. Now we know!" Then laughter.

"Are you glad to hear from me?" she asked.

No. Not at all. In fact, he wanted to puke.

"Roy?"

Well what was she expecting? Him to say he was happy to hear from her? After all that had happened? She hadn't tried to call him once while he was "away." That's what he had come to call it. "Away."

"What do you want, Ramona?" It was all he could do not to hang up on her.

"Gosh. *Your* voice just turned frosty."

"What did you expect? This is the first time I've heard from you since before—"

"I know," she said, cutting him off. Her voice had gone soft; all the girlish enthusiasm had vanished. "And I don't know what to say."

"How about 'sorry,'" he snapped.

There was a pause so long he wondered if he'd lost her. Was kind of glad.

"I'm sorry, Roy."

Was… was she crying?

"I don't know what to s-say." Her voice caught. "I *should* have c-called." There was a sob then and, holy crap, she *was* crying. No way.

"Ramona…."

"I am so s-sorry." Another sob. "*Sooo* sorry."

He could almost believe she was. "Ramona."

"I've felt so guilty. If it wasn't for me, none of it would have happened. You wouldn't have gone to—"

"You didn't force me to do anything. I'm not a little kid." *I did the stupid things that wound up ruining everything. You only helped.*

"You… you wouldn't have done what you did if I hadn't talked you into it."

No. I wouldn't have. He didn't deny it. But he didn't say that out loud.

"Roy. Come over."

What? "Wh-what?" Thank God he wasn't driving. He would have wrecked the car.

"Come over. Please. *Please*, Roy."

What about Milo Giancarlo? "What about Milo Whatshisname?" he said aloud, mangling the man's name deliberately. "I don't think he'd be too happy about—"

"We aren't together anymore."

Roy stiffened. What? She wasn't seeing Milo, the guy she'd started seeing after he was arrested? The guy who led her friends in calling him Sweet Cheeks? The guy who'd called Roy her bitch?

But wasn't he? Or at least he *had* been.

"Please, Sweet Cheeks?"

She did not just call him that!

"Please?" And was that a growl in her voice?

Oh God....

"Maybe we can comfort each other.... If you know what I mean?"

Did he? He thought maybe he did. *Oh God, God, God....*

He could see her then. On top of him. Looking down at him. Right before she fucked him.

And damn if his cock didn't twitch. Really...? That surprised him. It might mean he was bisexual. Maybe he needed to find out.

"I'll be there in ten minutes."

It wasn't like he could see Frank. Like he even knew how to find him. Frank didn't do relationships.

Do I want a relationship with him?

"Really?" came Ramona's voice.

Maybe he needed another taste of heterosexuality before making such a radical decision. Sounded like a smart idea.

"Ten minutes," he said.

And pulled his Jeep out of the parking lot onto the road.

CHAPTER TWENTY-SIX

FRANK'S FIRST thought as he slammed out of the Meridian Hotel's big, thick glass doors was *How dare he! How-fucking-dare that fucker say anything about Glen! He doesn't know him!*

His second thought was, *Roy...*, and he didn't know why. Roy was a *trick*. A fuck. Nothing more!

Yes... he was hot. Frank thought of that orange jumpsuit undone all scandalously low.

Yes, Roy was fucking adorable. Frank thought of those huge blue eyes and how you could fall into them and—

No!

Hot and adorable didn't make Roy any more than a trick!

Frank reached the garage and veered into the entrance, despite the sign that clearly stated, "No Pedestrians This Way, Vehicles Only, Thank You."

For some reason he thought of Harry and Cody, the only real friends he had, and maybe.... God, maybe he could go to them? Talk to them? Would either of them be home? What day was this?

He could always swing by Shear Fantasies and see if Cody was there. Wait. Would it be closed? What time was it?

Hell, he could *call* them, see what they were up to.

Frank got to his car and unlocked it, got in, started it, and goddamn, pulled out his phone, opened contacts, and...

Saw the Unknown Caller on top and growled and...

Thought of his mother. He wanted to scream. Really, truly *scream*.

How dare she! How dare she just show up! Twenty-five years gone, and she felt like she could just *show up*?

Pop in, like he was a convenience store. "Oh look! There's QuikTrip. Let's 'pop in' and get a Coke."

"Oh look! There's Frank Sinclair. Let's 'pop in' and introduce ourselves after twenty-five fuckin' years and say, 'This is your mother,' and, 'I was wondering if there was any way I could see you.'"

How. Dare. She.

Frank thought of Roy, suddenly, again, and he didn't know why. Thought of grabbing him and kissing him hard and rough and then spinning him around, bending him over, *fucking* him. He could *see* it! See that muscled back in his mind's eye, that incredible ass taking his cock.

Frank got hard.

He saw those big eyes, wide and so blue and full of naïve joy and....

God! Stop it.

He pulled out of the parking space, paid the ridiculous twenty-five-dollar fee because he'd been there over an hour, and merged into traffic.

Harry and Cody. He could talk to them. Yes. They would listen. They always listened. And not just when it was about sex. In fact, the three of them talked about anything and everything. It surprised him the subjects they discussed. Movies, Netflix—ad nauseam, what new show was awesome and which was a waste of time. That time-honored subject, "What would I do if I won the lottery?" Politics—and it wouldn't get ugly or nasty, with no one being Mr. Know-It-All. They could even talk religion, and it was interesting even though Frank had no real beliefs either way. Why, the only thing they wouldn't talk about was how Harry and Cody went from being best friends to lovers. They would get all quiet and look at each other and paraphrase Shakespeare. "There are more things in heaven and earth than we can possibly dream of...."

The only other thing they did that he could do without was their constant assurance that he would be happier if he settled down with a good man. Why couldn't they believe he was happy as he was? He didn't *need* someone to complete him. No one should. You needed to be complete unto yourself! If you needed someone to complete you and if that someone went away—*when* they went away—you were left devastated.

Sure, you could have some warm feelings about a guy. He had them for Harry and Cody. But love?

When a woman could leave her five-year-old son, *how* could there be anything called love?

The thought angered him again, which made him *think* of the woman who called herself his mother. The woman who wanted to see him.

Bitch.

Showing up now? Really? Guilt is what it was.

And that man of hers making accusations. He hadn't been around. He wasn't there while Glen was raising him. Neither of them saw all Glen had done to care for him, raise him, sacrifice for him. How dare they!

Love was a myth created by people too afraid to be alone. Who couldn't be complete all by themselves.

His vision went blurry then, and he wiped at his face and—*fuck!*—found tears in his eyes. *Goddammit!* He was fucking crying? When had he started crying? Crying was weakness. Glen had taught him that. Had taught him the way of the world. Taught him to find joy where he could, *when* he could. To grab pleasure with both hands because pleasure was real, but it was fleeting. If you found someone fun, okay, keep 'em around for a while. Especially if it was good for both of you—

(And couldn't Roy work for that?)

—but end it before it got bad. God yes! Don't let it degenerate and disintegrate and fall apart and turn hurtful or ugly or mean.

Once, while talking to Harry and Cody about some show on Netflix, *Friends* or *Frasier* or maybe *M*A*S*H*, they told him something he didn't really know while living abroad. How a network decided to end a television series while it was *good*. Before it "jumped the shark." Ending it so that years later you only remembered how good the show was instead of how it fell apart and died an ugly, lingering death.

The discussion had set off a lightbulb in Frank's head, and he'd cried, "Yes! Just like in a relationship." End it while it's good so that's what you remembered. Good times and laughter, good beer and steaks made perfectly, wonderful weekend getaways, and great sex. End it before you started noticing the other person farted, drank from the milk carton, and never, *ever* changed the goddamn toilet paper. But worse—far worse—before you realized you weren't really having fun anymore and the sex wasn't as good as it was and—worse yet—you really didn't *like* the other guy.

At least not anymore.

Harry and Cody disagreed, of course; they still believed in love. They'd find out sooner rather than later. They were *just* the kind to let their relationship die. The thought struck him as terribly sad. It was sad that something *so* sweet would fall apart and leave them both with nothing but feelings of hurt and anger and disappointment.

They'll be done. All they'll remember is how their relationship fell apart and died an ugly, lingering death.

And God! That made Frank feel deeply and profoundly lonely.

The tears came back, and his vision went wild, and with a shout he slammed on his brakes and nearly hit the sports car stopped at a red light in front of him. Thank God it was bright canary yellow or he would have, and....

This! Goddammit, *this!*

He wiped fiercely at his face, and bared his teeth, growled. *This! This is what you get for feeling!*

This was what he avoided. So, fuck it all!

Fuck Harry and Cody. He'd warned them.

Fuck his mother and her guilt and inability to give a little boy what he needed. Or *thought* he needed.

Fuck Glen! Yes, fuck him too.

And fuck Roy. Fuck him and his big blue eyes and his innocence, and the expectations he would most likely have for Frank. And his hurt. His hurt, just waiting to happen. His hurting *and* his blaming Frank for it despite the fact that Frank had let Roy know what he could have and what he couldn't.

Fuck *all* of it!

And by God, *that* was what he needed, wasn't it? To *fuck*! He wanted visceral. He wanted *real*. He wanted flesh and bone and cock and ass and fucking and cumming.

But if he did that with Roy? Well, that would only lead the guy down a primrose path of misunderstanding and misplaced expectations. So, *no*! Roy would be a big mistake, even if Frank did have a clue where to find him. He had no idea where Roy was, except possibly Roeland Park, and no way to call him. They hadn't exchanged phone numbers, a habit he'd purposely developed. If you don't give a trick your number, he can't hound you or pester you or beg you for one more chance.

"Please, Frank! If you give me a chance, you'll see!"

God!

No. The best thing to do, the thing that would solve everything, would be to pick up a trick and get lost in the heat of sex with a total fucking stranger.

He wouldn't be lonely. He wouldn't lead Roy on. The heat would pull him out of this whirlwind, would divert his mind to a single purpose, because you couldn't be distracted when you were looking for ass. And *ass* was what he wanted. He only bottomed about 25 percent of the time at most, and nothing was worse than hooking up with a lousy top after you had recently been royally, wonderfully fucked. That was the epitome of the "anti" in anticlimax. And that was something he could say about Roy: Roy had royally and wonderfully fucked him.

Frank knew then where he was going. The Watering Hole. If he remembered correctly, today the Heartland Bear Clan was having its monthly meeting, followed by a beer bust.

What he needed was a big old piece of hairy bear ass.

Grrrrrrreat!

And sure enough, the minute Frank walked in the front door of the bar, he saw he was right. There were two bearish dudes at the bar itself ordering beers, and behind them in the room beyond—normally a dance floor—he could see quite a few men, most of them chunky and bearded. But they were talking, not dancing.

I've caught them during their meeting. Piss.

But as he got closer, he saw it was winding down. A hot bearish guy of about thirty or so—shirt unbuttoned and open over a nice hairy chest and big nipples and a sweet round belly—was standing on a wooden crate with the words Bear Soapbox painted crudely on its side. The hot guy was talking.

"Please remember, guys, please, if your dues are up, see Mr. Tucker here. Keep the Clan alive!"

Frank looked to where Soapbox Guy was pointing at an equally hot bearded otter, slim, hairy, shirtless, and waving his arms high over his head (probably showing off his armpits to the fetishists in the room. There were a lot of dudes that were into pits, especially in the bear crowd).

"And if you don't know when your membership is up," Soapbox Guy continued, "talk to him. He can help you."

"And if you want to show me your dick," Mr. Otter said, grinning widely, "you can *cum* see me for that too. No problem. I don't mind!"

Frank had no doubt Mr. Otter would get at least a few takers on his suggestion. On another night, Frank might oblige him. The guy was quite hot. But bears were what Frank had a taste for right now, and with a room full of them right here in front of him, a bear was what he was going to get.

Soapbox Guy, a bear that Frank certainly had eyes for, turned and looked down at a short man with a thick, full, bright red beard and a T-shirt that said Heartland Bear Clan and asked him, "Is there anything I'm forgetting, Harvey?"

Harvey was looking down at a big open three-ring binder. "Nope. You got it all." He adjusted his wire glasses with one hand and his baseball cap with his other. "Oh! Wait. Did you tell them about next month's meeting…?" Frank wondered if his chest hair was equally red. "Oh yes! You did tell 'em. I've got it right here." He tapped the open notebook. "Sorry."

A few men chuckled, but Soapbox Guy raised a hand. "Yeah. A reminder anyway! Next month we're not meeting here at the Hole. Hey, Wilbur? Will you stand up?"

A guy obliged, but Frank couldn't see his face as he had his back to Frank. He could tell he was big, though. Rubenesque. But tall. He was wearing sweats, and God, he had a wonderful big butt, just what Frank had his heart set on. Or *some*thing set on anyway.

"We're having our Fourth of July meeting at Wilbur's farm," Soapbox Guy announced. "It's a half hour or so north of here. Wilbur has a permit, and we're going to be able to set off all the fireworks we want. We'll have a good show once it gets dark. I think it's going to be a lot of fun. We raised a tidy little sum at the Blow 'Em Up party last month, and from what I've heard, Wilbur knows the guy we're getting our fireworks from *pretty* well! So hopefully that will assure we have a good time!"

He smiled and winked in the face of lots of whoops and hollers, and when the Fourth of July party host turned to face everybody, he was a nice shade of red. It was a sight to see because his skin was creamy pale, and the redder he got, the more he nearly glowed, his green eyes shining.

Frank saw exactly who he was going to go for in that instant.

Round-faced and round*ed*—with orange-red hair cut short and a matching trim beard—he was adorable. His sweatshirt was half-unzipped to show his chest hair, which was only a bit darker. It was hard to tell in the shadowed bar lighting. It could be dirty blond.

God, what he would look like naked!

Frank decided he *would* know what color that hair was.

His skin began to heat up. His eyes narrowed as he studied his prey. The lion inside him shook its mane, flexed its claws, and flared its nostrils, testing the wind. The great hunter took over.

Mr. Soapbox Guy closed the meeting, and it was a good thing that Frank had set his sights on someone else because a hot cub sidled up to the man and hugged him and gave him a kiss. Soapbox Guy wasn't single.

Didn't matter.

Frank watched Wilbur and studied the lay of the land to determine his best approach. No one went up to Wilbur and gave *him* a hug or kiss, and his left hand was ringless. That told Frank the cutie was probably single. He hoped so. The only way his No Married Men rule could be negotiated was if a trick's husband assured him all was well and he didn't mind. And if the husband was cute enough, why not a three-way?

Wilbur hadn't moved and was looking around nervously, biting his upper lip. *Interesting*, Frank thought. No one was talking to him despite the fact that he was hosting this room full of men at his place next month. He wasn't moving. Except for his green eyes. They darted back and forth very rapidly. He looked almost…. What?

Well, like that animal on the edge of the herd and ready to be stalked. And stalking was what Frank was going to do. It was only then that Frank saw a lot of the men who had so hastily left the room were coming back with—of course—food.

It wasn't a potluck. Mostly a huge variety of snacks, chips, and dips. The men were taking them past the dance floor and out to the back patio. It was a Friday night, and the dance floor would be the bar's main draw, especially once its biggest rival in the gay club scene, The Male Box, filled its own dance floor with chairs for its popular drag show, which would be starting soon.

But Frank wasn't paying much attention to the food. His focus was on Wilbur.

Wilbur. He'd never met a Wilbur in real life. If he was as rounded as a kid as he was as an adult, Frank bet he'd been teased by the other children in school.

The redhead suddenly headed to the bar, and Frank followed him. Got there just as the bartender was asking the hottie what he wanted to drink.

"Seven and seven," Wilbur said.

The bartender was a guy named Buck, who had worked at The Watering Hole for at least a decade. Frank knew because he'd tricked with the man once or twice.

"And I'll take one too," Frank said elbowing up next to the redhead. "Minus the 7Up."

Buck eyed him.

"What?" Wilbur asked.

Frank put a twenty-dollar bill on the bar, and Buck nodded and asked him what kind of whiskey he wanted.

"I'll take... do you have Jameson?"

The bartender nodded. "You know that I do."

"That'll work. And this should pay for both of them."

"Um, thank you," said Wilbur.

"You're welcome, Wilbur. I'm Frank." He held out his hand, and when Wilbur shook it, looking like he was about to run for the front door, Frank let his hand linger, stroked Wilbur's palm with his first two fingers.

Wilbur bit his lip again, pulled his hand away, and asked, "How did you know my name?"

"I heard your leader say it," Frank replied, using his practiced warm-honey voice.

"Ron?"

"I don't have a fuckin' clue what his name is," Frank said. "Yours is the only name I'm interested in." Which wasn't exactly true because you didn't need to know a man's name to fuck him, did you?

"*Mine*?" Wilbur said, eyes wide and amazed.

"*God* yes," he said with a growl. "You're the hottest thing in this bar."

"*Me*?" Wilbur blinked at him, eyes so wide, so green, so surprised.

Frank took a step closer. "Yes, *you*." The growl was back. "You see anybody in this place that is as hot as you?"

Wilbur took a step back. He looked terrified. Frank needed to change that. "Most of the guys here are hotter than me," Wilbur said. "Did you see Paddy? Or Jon?"

Frank shrugged. "I don't know who the hell they are."

"Jon's our treasurer. He-he's the one Ron said to go to, to check if your membership was—"

"Mr. Tucker," Frank said.

Wilbur nodded. His eyes, pretty green things—

(although not quite as pretty as Roy's)

—were still wide.

And then for a second, Frank *saw* Roy. Roy looking at him the same way. When Frank had asked him if he wanted a blowjob.

No! He banished the image. What was he doing thinking of Roy? He needed to be thinking of the hot motherfucker in front of him. God, he bet Wilbur had a big smooth white ass! A big smooth white ass that would *swallow* his cock. He shivered with anticipation.

"Did you see Ron's *boy*friend?" Wilbur sighed. There was sadness in that sigh. A longing. A crush on Ron's boyfriend, maybe?

Frank shrugged. "He's okay, I guess." He closed the gap between them again. By *two* steps.

"*God*, you're pretty," he said, turning the subject back to Wilbur and not Jon or whatever the other guy's name was.

Wilbur's Adam's apple bobbed. "*Me?*"

"And God, I would love to see you naked. If you are half as beautiful without your clothes as you are in them, I'll cum before I get mine off."

The drinks arrived. He was so hard his cock hurt just from looking at this guy and the wonder in his eyes. He was going to fuck Wilbur's socks off. He would *never* forget Frank!

"Are you *drunk?*" Wilbur asked him.

"Not yet," Frank said, although he'd had quite a bit to drink today. Tipsy he *might* be. *Would* be after this drink. But no. "I'm not drunk. Why?"

"Because you're *perfect*," Wilbur said, barely above a whisper. Had the bar been blasting music like normal, Frank wouldn't have been able to hear him.

"Shit," Frank said. "I'm not perfect." He leaned in, had intended to give Wilbur a little kiss. And then suddenly… couldn't.

Couldn't.

But now he was all leaned forward and really in Wilbur's space, and he *had* to do something or it would look really weird. Say something.

(Why couldn't he kiss the dude?)

"What do you say we get the hell out of here?" he blurted.

"Wh-where?"

"My place. It's close. It'd take too long to get to your farm—"

"Well, it's not *really* a farm per se—"

"—and I'm so horny for you I could tear your clothes off right *here*!"

Wilbur gave a little gasp. "Oh God." He looked around him. Stared at a couple that were looking at him with raised eyebrows and a "Well, look at *Wilbur*" expression on their faces. Fuckers. Did they think they were better than Wilbur? Frank decided to add to the show. He reached out with both hands and gently took Wilbur's nipples between thumbs and forefingers. "You have great nipples." They were quite small but oh they were getting hard under his ministrations. Dark pink. "I want to suck on them."

"Oh God…," Wilbur whimpered.

"Do you mind if I do?"

"Here?" His voice cracked.

Frank raised and lowered his eyebrows. Leaned in and took one gently between his lips, licked it, sucked it ever so slightly into his mouth.

"Oh my *God*," Wilbur said, voice shaking now.

Frank let go and looked up into those pretty green eyes. "I've heard something, and you make me want to know if it's true."

God! Was he really using this line?

"Wh-what?" Wilbur asked.

"I've heard that a man's nipples and his asshole—"

(He whispered the word asshole, making it naughty/sexy.)

"—are the same color. You can look at a man's nipples and know just what color his most secret place is. I'd love to find out. With you."

"Oh fuck it!" Wilbur cried. "Let's get the hell out of here!"

And fucking it was just what Frank wanted to do.

CHAPTER TWENTY-SEVEN

ROY PULLED up in front of the little white-and-red brick bungalow, and his first thought was, *What the* hell *am I doing here?* He looked at the place he'd spent so many nights. The porch light was off, the windows like dark black eyes. Wrought iron bars striped the windows and the front door—this was not the nicest of neighborhoods—and Roy remembered the doors that had clanged shut each evening on his cell.

His second thought was, *Go! Go home. Now. Before it's too late.*

What would his mother say? The same nothing she said anytime he got home later than he'd said he'd be? That look, eyes dark with wondering and maybe a bit of fear, asking without asking if he'd been with… *her*?

He hadn't. Roy hadn't seen her once. He'd not heard her voice until less than a quarter of an hour before. But if his mother found out he was here tonight, would she stay silent? He doubted it.

"What would make you go there, Roy? Are you crazy? After all she's done?" Those questions his mother voiced in his head were his third thought, of course. Followed by a fourth.

Ramona did do it. It was *her.* Because despite the fact that he'd taken responsibility for what he'd done—after all, she really hadn't put a gun to his head when he'd signed his name on those checks—he knew that *I would never have done it if it hadn't been for her.*

But he'd been led by his dick. Or hers. Her big rubber cock. How many times had he lay on that cot in that cell, stared up into the shadows, and asked himself, *How could I have been so stupid? How?*

Was it really like that old joke? Something about how a man could have money and power and position and all the intelligence in the world, but all a woman needed was what was between her legs and she could get a man to do anything?

But he knew that was a *horrible* thought, and maybe as chauvinistic as something his dad might say. Roy had dated many sweet, unselfish girls. None of them had played head games with him. Not one. Until Ramona. And he had examples of three outstanding women in his life: his mother, Granny, and Mrs. Kelly. What would they think if they knew he'd let such a thought even flit through his brain?

Besides, what had led to his downfall might have been between Ramona's legs, but it wasn't what God had given her. It was what she'd bought from an adult store. And it wasn't just her fucking him that had done it. He'd wanted to go to Hawaii with her and her friends. Friends he knew were a lot more upscale than her. Or him. The kind of friends that wouldn't have had anything to do with either of them while they were in high school. He wanted to know what it was like to hang out with people who would have scoffed at him and Ramona or, worse, walked by and looked right through them. People that Roy had let himself think were better than him.

But they weren't. That was another thing Demaine had done for him. Besides making sure his asshole wasn't so big he could sit on a fire hydrant and make it vanish.

"I ain't here 'cause I'm black and grew up on the wrong side of Troost Avenue. I'm here 'cause I'm a *fool*." He sighed. "And I'm thanking the good Lord I ain't in the big house! It's where they shoulda put me. But God is good—all the time! And I *am* here, and maybe I has finally learned my lesson. You thought your girl's friends was better than you? No way, bro. Ain't nobody better'n nobody else. You remember that, okay, brother?"

Roy hadn't known what to say. He was too surprised.

"I axed you if you'll remember that, brother?"

"I'll remember."

He remembered now, sitting in his Jeep in front of Ramona's house. And he was just reaching for the key to start it up when she called out to him.

"You comin' in?"

Roy jumped and jerked his head to the left, and there she was, standing in the shadows of the porch. He couldn't really see her face, but he knew it was her and not just because it was her voice and her porch. It was her size and her build and her stance.

"I've got beer," she said.

Sixth Glass Quadrupel Ale? he wondered and then laughed at himself for it. He'd be lucky if it was Bud Light. He shuddered.

Thought of Saturdays, drinking Bud or Miller or Coors with all the people he'd had beers with in his life. (Ramona's upscale cronies thought they were classy because they drank Corona with a lime or Blue Moon with a slice of orange.) Then he thought of drinking a couple of Boulevard beers with Frank on his balcony, naked. *God....*

Funny. A few bottles of something tastier and now he was too cool for Bud. Thought his tastes were better? More sophisticated?

Not better. Just different.

Like being in Frank's bed versus being in Ramona's. Better? Or just different?

Ramona took a few steps down from her porch, and he could see her now in the pink-orange light that was left in the sky. "You coming... Sweet Cheeks?" she asked, and there was that faint touch of bad girl in her voice to catch his attention. Or at least his cock's.

So a girl could still get him hard?

Maybe this was a sign. Maybe he should stick with women. It wasn't like Frank was planning on getting down on one knee, right?

I don't even have his fuckin' phone number.

One more step and Ramona had reached the walkway between her house and the sidewalk.

Roy got out of his Jeep.

CHAPTER TWENTY-EIGHT

IN THE car, Frank got cold feet. That was a bit of a shock. He didn't get cold feet. But he'd no sooner started the engine and put the car in gear than he began to have second thoughts. His boner, which had been throbbing up to that point, was deflating like an air mattress with a slow leak.

"Just think of those pretty eyes," he said aloud, urging himself on. Think of how sexy he'll be without those sweats on. His ass is already hot as hell. Big booty!

And it'll be white. Like cream. His pretty eyes will roll back as you fuck him and....

But it was Roy's eyes he saw in his head. Roy's voice he heard. *"Please, Frank. Fuck me. I want to know...."*

Frank forced his imagination back to Wilbur. *It'll be okay once we get back to my place.* That's what he told himself. Kept telling himself. All the way home. Which wasn't that far away. Why did it seem to take forever to get there?

Frank pulled into the tenant's parking lot behind the Oscar Wilde after pointing Wilbur to the street. Once he parked, he got out and waited. When Wilbur came out of the deep shadows of the evening, Frank was relieved. The excitement came back. Wilbur had an expression of both fear and anticipation on his round face, and there was an obvious bulge in the front of his sweats. When was the last time anyone had looked at Frank with such want?

You know when.

"Is everything okay?" Wilbur asked. "You haven't changed your mind, have you?"

What could he say to that? Only one thing really. "Of course not."

But he did take Wilbur in the back way. A separate ugly foyer with junk against one wall—several mop buckets with mops, brooms, a chair without a leg, trash bags, a single blue high-heel shoe. Double doors

opened by the elevator at the back of the lobby. Frank didn't see a soul—
let alone Roy.

What was he doing thinking of him again? Why?

In the elevator, Wilbur tried to kiss him, but he turned his head.
He heard the frustrated little sigh, then let Wilbur kiss his neck and the
hollow of this throat. Wilbur unbuttoned Frank's shirt and kissed his
chest, moaned. "You are so perfect," he said.

Usually that would make him hard as steel.

Not tonight.

With a ping, the doors opened on Frank's floor. He nodded and led
Wilbur down the hall to his apartment. It would be his luck that Harry or
Cody would step out of their apartment right now. He didn't want that.
Not tonight.

I talked to my mother tonight.

That hazy image of her came back, and he wondered if she looked
anything like a child's memory.

That's what was wrong!

An image of Caterina followed. How he'd wanted her to be his
mother. Yet still he'd warned her. "Look, lady, you don't want nothing to
do with my dad." Because he was tired of thinking she might be the one
to hold him and kiss his bloody knee to make it better and read to him at
bedtime. And he'd warned her because he was tired of seeing his father
hurt the women who loved him.

Neither Harry nor Cody stuck their head out their door, so Frank
opened his and they went in. Wilbur was on him the minute he closed it.

He still wouldn't let Wilbur kiss him on the mouth. It was usually
one of his favorite things to do. And it wasn't that Wilbur grossed him
out or anything. Not at all. *God* no. He couldn't understand what was
happening.

You just talked to your mother.

He was only now starting to see that his world had been turned
upside down and topsy-turvy. Maybe this time sex wasn't the answer.

Wilbur went to his knees, kissing and nibbling his way down. He
was a big man, and that meant tall as well as husky. Knee level didn't put
him at Frank's cock, but that didn't stop Wilbur. To be fair, it wouldn't
have stopped Frank in the same situation. Wilbur fumbled with Frank's
belt. Frantically unzipped his pants. Pressed his face against Frank's
cock, which was barely half-hard.

He wanted to tell Wilbur to calm down. *My cock isn't going anywhere!* But there was the whole deflating air mattress thing, which never happened to him.

God. Am I going to do this? Can I do this?

His pants fell down around his ankles, and Wilbur pulled down his underwear and....

"Let's go in the bedroom," Frank said. Delaying things at least for a moment.

Frank looked down. There was lust in Wilbur's eyes, and panting, he said, "O-okay."

Wilbur stood up, and it was only now Frank noticed that Wilbur was actually a little bit taller than him. How had he not seen that before?

Then it hit him. Hard. *Because he was slouching.* Frank shook the thought off.

Wilbur stared at him expectantly, and so he started to take a step, nearly tripped over the tangle of his own pants, toed off his shoes, and stepped out of it all. "This way," he said.

They went to his bedroom and... the bed. It was still a mess. He hadn't made it since... since Roy.

Goddammit!

This thinking. All this thinking! What the hell was wrong with him?

Frank reached out quickly and unzipped Wilbur's sweatshirt, revealing a chest that was hairy across his pecs—dark blond hair, not quite red—and a belly with a wide happy trail. He pushed the shirt off Wilbur's shoulders and—*whoa*—what arms! *Big* arms. Powerful arms. Biceps like cantaloupes. Who knew he was a muscle bear under all that delightful padding? Frank's cock started to get hard again. Thank God.

"Take your clothes off," he ordered.

With a big goofy grin, Wilbur did as he'd been told. Eagerly. Or mostly. He hesitated to take his hands away from his crotch, had even—for a second—tried to cover his belly, but must have realized that was silly. Wilbur needn't have worried. He looked good. *Really* good. Rounded but powerful. Thick and strong. A belly with a big thumbprint of a navel that begged to be kissed and licked. Rubenesque was the perfect word to describe him. And what his cock lacked in length, it more than made up for in girth. Frank pitied the man who got impaled with that thing. Or then again, maybe it would be a blessing.

Frank pulled his shirt off over his head without unbuttoning it the rest of the way and then shoved his underwear down his hips and stepped out of them. He was three-quarters hard now. His cock wasn't going to fail him.

"Get on the bed," Frank said, another order.

Like a happy puppy, Wilbur complied. And yes, when he turned around and crawled onto the mattress, he had a big ol' ass, and it was sexy as could be. Big, but solid. The very color of cream. Frank could see that even though the room was heavy with shadows. God, he would love to fuck that ass!

And then, dammit, Roy was there again, filling his mind's eye. He *saw* Roy under him, taking his cock, eyes rolling back, shouting in pleasure.

I'll make Wilbur's eyes roll back!

He went to the bed and turned on the lamp. He wanted to see this.

Wilbur was staring at his cock. His throat was working. He looked up, lust ablaze in his eyes. And once again there was that other look. Surprise. Awe. Fear?

Jesus, Frank thought. *I'm just me.*

"I can't believe this is happening," Wilbur said. "A guy like you. And me."

What did you say to that?

Fuck. Stop talking. Just suck my cock. Please.

"Can I suck it?" Wilbur asked, and Christ, why was he asking? Why wasn't he sucking already?

"Yes," Frank said. "*Fuck* yes."

Wilbur surged forward and practically attacked Frank's almost-erection.

It was pretty sudden. Like handing a piece of bacon to a puppy. Bite your fingertips along with it. Jesus!

"Easy," he hissed.

Wilbur froze. And then he started doing better.

It made no difference. Frank started losing his hard-on again.

No!

Frank didn't understand it one bit. But he couldn't do it. He kept seeing Roy. It infuriated him. *I never promised you anything. Not one thing!* Roy didn't even fucking know if he was gay or not. *And I don't do lovers. Never have! I told him that.*

Didn't I?

Had he?

Yes. He remembered. Because Roy had asked if it was all right to spend the night when Frank had made it clear he didn't want a lover. He told Roy he did do fuck buddies.

But crap, Roy really *didn't* know if he was gay or not. How stupid of him to even think of seeing someone who didn't know if he was gay.

I am not seeing anyone!

He never "saw" anyone.

Well, he had. Once or twice. He'd had a Caterina or two. Not a yearlong Caterina! No. But a few months here and there. When they both understood what there could be between the two of them. Men like Caterina who knew what kind of man he was.

"I know about your father. I know just what kind of man he is. Lo so. *And that is okay.* Tuo padre? *That is fine."*

If the other guy thought they had a future, he never let it go past the second or third roll in the hay. He made it clear what they could expect from him.

"Your father? He is a man who loves the women, and I don't see that any woman will ever tie him down. Make him their own. Va bene così—*I am fine with that."*

He'd always been honest. He didn't lie. He never broke a woman's heart!

Woman's? Jesus H. Christ. *I'm my old man.*

He wasn't sure he liked that. And he'd totally lost his hard-on.

Wilbur was starting to hurt him. "Wilbur," he said.

Wilbur's sucking grew even more frantic.

"Wilbur.... *Stop.*"

The ginger-bearded bear stopped and looked slowly up at him. There was hurt in his eyes.

"I'm sorry," Wilbur said, "if I'm not doing it good."

"You're doing it fine," Frank said. Because what man, gay man, wanted to hear that he wasn't any good at sucking cock? "Really."

Wilbur's eyes had turned glassy. "It's because I'm *fat*, isn't it?" He said the word "fat" as if he were saying "shit" or "vomit."

God.... Frank's heart lurched. "No, Wilbur," he said.

"You saw my huge fucking fat ass and you changed your mind."

Wilbur's eyes weren't glassy. They were wet.

Frank squatted next to the bed. Looked into Wilbur's pretty green eyes. Not as pretty as Roy's, but pretty all the same. "Wilbur. I saw your *ass*, and I got *hard*."

"Y-you did?"

He reached out to touch Wilbur's round cheek and Wilbur flinched as if he thought he was about to be struck.

Oh dear God, what have I gotten myself into?

He looked in those eyes and... and knew. He wasn't going to be able to have sex with Wilbur. He couldn't stop thinking of Roy. He had to make sure things were clear with Roy.

"I fucked up," Frank said. "It's not you. It's me." And fuck did that sound lame! Pour salt in the wound. All he had to do was look in Wilbur's eyes to see it was true.

"It *is* me." He went to his knees. "I...." Frank looked at Wilbur. "There's this guy...."

"Guy?" Wilbur asked.

And for a second Frank couldn't reply. My God.... He'd stunned himself. Hadn't even known he was going to say it. *There's this guy?* Really? Had he just said that?

Then Roy was there, *again*, in his mind. Refusing to be ignored. Smiling. Looking sweet. Looking hot. Looking naïve. Hell! Pouring water over himself.

Why do I keep thinking of him? Do I have a crush?

It almost made him laugh. The idea was preposterous. But it was certainly something he had to resolve.

Frank turned back to Wilbur. "It really isn't you. I promise. I really *is* me. There's this guy. And I don't know if I like him or not, but I certainly need to talk to him. I think this"—he pointed at the two of them—"would really hurt him, and I don't want to hurt him."

Wilbur nodded, and a tear rolled down his cheek.

"And tonight.... I heard from my mom for the first time in twenty-five years."

Wilbur's eyes flew wide. "*What?*" He sat up.

Frank told him. Couldn't believe even as it happened that the words were spilling out of his mouth. To a stranger. Not to Harry or Cody. He started talking about how she left when he was five—"Only five, and she *dumps* me! Her own child! Who leaves a kid when he is only five?"— and how after all this time she had called today and said that she wanted to see him.

"Did you?" Wilbur was clutching sheets in his lap. His eyes were so big.

"No! No way." How could he even ask?

"You didn't meet your *mother*? My God! If I had ever had the chance to meet my brother…."

Brother?

"He died when I was two. So I guess I met him, but I don't *remember*…. And if I ever had a chance to meet him…."

"Your brother died?" Frank asked.

Wilbur nodded….

Like Roy's.

"I never got to know him. All my life I heard about how great he was and perfect and smart and…." He stopped. "How athletic *he* was. And there *I* was. *Fat.*"

"You're not fat," Frank said. "You're hot. You're really hot."

Wilbur shook his head. "I'm *fat*." Said it again as if he were disgusted. "My ass is *so* fat that—"

Frank hushed him. "You're not fat."

"I *am* fat. I have this huge fat ass, and—"

"You do *not* have a fat ass. It's hot. It almost got me to cheat on Roy."

"You were going to cheat on him with someone like me?" Wilbur asked, clearly astounded.

Cheat? How could it be cheating? They'd only known each other a few days. They weren't "seeing" each other. They'd made no promises. They didn't even have each other's phone numbers. *And*—he reminded himself again—*Roy doesn't even know if he's gay or not.*

Oh, he's gay. Definitely. Certainly. Gay.

Well he doesn't know that.

But somehow, he knew, *knew*, that this—he looked at Wilbur— would hurt him. And Frank saw, clearly saw, he did not want to hurt Roy.

Why do you care? He's a trick! Nothing more.

But he knew, *knew*, that wasn't entirely true either. And whatever Frank was, he was an honest man. So he needed to talk to Roy. Before it got out of hand. Make *sure* he understood what was going on. What they could be and what they couldn't.

He owed Roy that.

And he owed Wilbur that explanation. He told the ginger bear all of it. And only then realized he was doing the talking he had needed to do.

"Yes," Wilbur said when Frank finished. "You *do* need to tell him." Wilbur's eyes were still wet. "It hurts when you think you're something to someone when you're not." He looked away. Wiped his face. With only a bare arm to do it with, he didn't accomplish much. Wet the reddish-blond hair on his arm, perhaps.

Wilbur had obviously been hurt in just such a situation.

"I'm sorry," Frank said. Found he meant it. Completely.

And this is why I don't do romance. The two of us could be fucking so hard right now that the neighbors would be pounding on the wall. All because I didn't kick Roy's ass out the door the minute we were done fucking.

But the stuff after the fucking had been nice. And sweet. And cute. God!

"Do you need to talk about it?" Frank offered.

"Talk about what?" Wilbur snapped, not looking back.

"The guy who hurt you. Who let you think you two were something you weren't."

Wilbur turned back, blinking. "You don't want to hear that. You probably wish I would get the hell out of here." He swung his legs over the side of the bed. "I should get the fuck out of here while I have any dignity left."

Frank placed a hand on Wilbur's knee. "No. Tell me. I'll listen."

Wilbur blinked again. Looked at Frank.

Frank nodded.

Then it all came out, flowing, like when Frank had spilled *his* guts. "It was Paddy," Wilbur said. Paddy, the boyfriend of Ron, the president of the Heartland Bear Clan. Who had taken Wilbur on a date or two, but then it had become clear that they weren't dates at all, but just two people hanging out. Wilbur had thought it was more. And how Paddy had been in love with Ron and Wilbur hadn't had a chance in hell of being anything more than the friend he was. And then when he *did* figure it out, Paddy wouldn't even have sex with him, not even that, though at the time it looked like Ron didn't like Paddy. Not at all. But at least Ron had been a big man too, so Wilbur had known it wasn't because he was *fat*. Then again, that hadn't helped either.

"I'm always left out. Always the fucking bridesmaid and never the bride. I'm going to be alone for the rest of my life!"

"I think you'll find someone," Frank said and meant it. "You really are hot."

Wilbur scoffed at that, shook his head, rolled his eyes.

Frank had to take him by the upper arms and all but shake him. "No. Listen. I mean it. You *are* hot. You are *so* cute. And your arms…." He squeezed them. "Fuck they're hard."

Wilbur gave him a half smile. "I work out four or five times a week."

"And your ass really is to fucking die for. If it weren't for Roy…. If I get this all cleared up with Roy, and he isn't interested in getting with me, then maybe we could get together. 'Cause I really would enjoy fucking you."

Now the smile turned unbelieving. "Yeah. Like I haven't heard *that* before. *More* than once."

Frank felt terrible that he was one of those *mores*.

"I could take your number," he said and surprised himself. He didn't do phone numbers. That was the goddamned reason he couldn't talk to Roy!

Wilbur shook his head. "Nah. I don't think so. If I let myself think about that, then I'll sit around and wait for your call. I don't want to do that. You want me, you know where to find me. The Clan meets same time each month."

"Except next month. It'll be at your place."

Wilbur smiled. It was almost genuine at last.

"Yes. Check out the local gay papers. The information will be there."

Frank nodded.

"If you found out you wanted to come."

Frank nodded.

Wilbur started to get up, then didn't. Clutched those sheets in front of him, almost as high as his chest. He pointed at the floor. "Would you get me my sweats? My undies should be in them."

Frank reached over—they were close—and got them and handed them to Wilbur. Who then tried to put them on under the sheets.

No. Frank stood, knees popping, and reached out, palm open. Wilbur stared at his hand a moment, then took it. Frank pulled him to his feet, and the sheets fell away, and Wilbur stood before him, naked. Frank smiled. Told the truth. "You *are* beautiful."

You're just not Roy.

The thought surprised him—again—and he smiled, and Wilbur obviously thought the smile was for him. He surged forward and hugged Frank, and Frank let him. Hugs were nice. Especially naked hugs.

Even if they weren't leading to anything more.

In fact, right now, it was especially true. Who would have thought it could be so?

Frank stood and stepped back, gave Wilbur a chance to get up and…

"Ah…. Do you mind leaving while I get dressed?" He blushed.

Shit. Of course. Because even though they'd done what they'd done, everything was different now, wasn't it? He left the room and got a beer out of the refrigerator, and as he was taking the first few needed swallows, Wilbur came out and stood there, awkwardly, looking at him.

Frank sighed. "I am sorry, Wilbur."

Wilbur shrugged. "It is what it is."

"Want a beer?" Frank offered.

"I want about a case of them," Wilbur said. "But I think I'll do that at home. *All* by myself."

"You sure that's a good idea?"

Wilbur raised his eyebrows and looked at him with an "are you fucking kidding me?" expression and said, "I think it's about the *best* fucking idea I've had today. All week, even."

They hugged again, and this time it was really awkward. Then Wilbur was gone, and Frank finished his beer. Started another, and while he was doing it, the big red bear's words echoed through his brain.

"You didn't meet your mama? *My God! If I had ever had the chance to meet my brother…!"*

And then…

"Frankie…." His mother's voice. *"I'm in town…. And I wondered… is there any way I can see you? Would you see* me?*"*

Theo Gardener—his mother's husband: *"Your mother has been trying to find you your entire life. And he kept her from doing it."*

His mother: *"I've tried to find you for years."*

Theo: *"Frank. She loves you. She's never stopped loving you."*

And Wilbur again: *"You didn't meet your* mama? *My God! If I had ever had the chance to...."*

My God.

Frank put beer bottle to mouth again, tilted his head back, and finished it in one long draft. Closed his eyes. And knew what he had to do.

CHAPTER TWENTY-NINE

HER MOUTH tasted of beer and cigarettes. Ramona had taken up smoking again, and for some reason, Roy didn't *want* to kiss her. It was kind of grossing him out. The greasy feel of her bright red lipstick. How smashy mushy her big full lips were (hadn't he thought that way of kissing was hella sexy once?). And the way she used her tongue (it seemed so... big now, and she just jammed it in his mouth and let it sort of lie there), and the noises she made seemed more like someone who was having trouble breathing and was maybe in pain (instead of how erotic her gasping and moaning used to be).

Nothing like the way Frank kissed. Strong and powerful and as if he could take control, but never quite did. Let you kiss back, dared you to, leading and guiding and....

Ramona pulled back, looked at him. "Something wrong?" she asked, sounding cranky.

Bitchy.

Yes, there was something wrong.

"Nothing," he said, wished he was turned on, wanted desperately to be turned on, but wasn't.

How could he after everything she'd said to him moments before?

They'd sat on the porch ledge, a thing of cement and brick, straddling it—each with one leg on the porch side and the other brushing the shrubs in front of the house—and she told her story.

Instead of listening to his.

Instead of asking how he'd been and what it had been like for *him*.

"I wanted to go to Hawaii so fucking bad," she said. "And Pops wouldn't pay. I couldn't believe it. He's always paid. But he said *not* this time. And Chet was going. And Karen and Barb and Dominic and Caroline and... and Milo."

Milo, who moved right in on you the minute I was gone.

"Christ, Roy. I knew what it was going to be like and what they were going to be doing and the places they'd be going. *Drugs* people like *them* would be doing. I didn't want to stay home and be left out! Remember how we would be sitting by the pool or swimming in the ocean or eating one of those amazing meals in one of those amazing restaurants and how Milo would suddenly pull out his cell phone and call somebody and say, 'I'm in Hawaii, and *you're* not!' and then send them pictures? He does that whenever he goes some place cool! Well, I didn't want to be one of those people he called and said, 'Hey, Ramona, I'm in Hawaii, and *you're* not!'"

You're not, Roy thought. Not even mentioning him.

"And didn't we have a good time? Wasn't it fun? Wasn't it *gorgeous*?"

Gorgeous. Her word.

"Yes," Roy said quietly. Because it was true. He couldn't deny any of those things.

"Weren't the drugs *good*?" She did a little sitting (straddling?) shimmy—which is what she did when she was happy—that long red hair swaying as she did.

Well, he didn't do the drugs. He'd smoked some pot and was cajoled into a little coke, but the rest he'd stayed away from.

She wiggled closer to him so their knees were touching.

"And wasn't the *sex* good," she said, her voice throaty and rough. "*Really* good?"

Yes. It had been. Until Milo called him Ramona's "bitch." Called him "Sweet Cheeks."

"You know what *really turned me on*?" she asked, getting closer, knees between his, spreading them.

He shook his head.

"When Milo called you my *bitch*."

The words were like a splash of water to his face. But immediately on the tail of that was the realization, *Well, of course it turned you on.*

"Didn't it turn *you* on?" she asked. "At least a little bit?"

Roy almost got up and left then.

Really, Ramona? It turned you on when Milo degraded me? You thought it turned me on? Because it *hadn't*. It had humiliated him. Any part of him that might have enjoyed his submission to her did not also like being humiliated. Not in front of her hoity-toity friends and not here alone with her now.

She got even closer, their faces close with her hair hanging around hers like when she fucked him, and now their crotches were closer too, and she reached around either side of him and grabbed two handfuls of his ass. Her face was right up in his, and she kissed him. Then she clambered off her perch, stood next to him, leaned in, and kissed him again. She tugged at his hand, got him to swing his legs over, get off the wide railing, and stand, and now...

Now she was kissing him, sloppy, tasting of cigarettes, *not* sexy—*gross*—and all he could think was, *Does she think I'm turned on? Does she think she's making me hot?* After everything she had just said?

She pulled back. Whispered in a gravelly voice, "I want to fuck you."

She wanted to *fuck* him. Not "I want to fuck." She wanted to fuck *him* with one of her toys.

And Christ, he *wanted* to be fucked. Long and smooth and, toward the end, hard. But...

"But what about Milo?" he asked, and he wasn't asking because it was the moral thing. He was asking it as he would grab for a life preserver.

She stiffened. Took a step back. And when Roy said nothing more, she finally said, "I'm sorry about that too. When they arrested you, I was inconsolable. I cried for days. And then to my surprise, Milo called. He came over and let me cry. Then he did all those things you were supposed to be doing. Fixed things, like the garbage disposal. Checked my oil. Mowed the lawn. I was so grateful, Sweet Cheeks."

I bet you were. And for God's sake, stop *calling me Sweet Cheeks!*

"And then... then... one night we did it." Her voice broke on a little sob, except this time—*this* time—he caught something. Something *not* real. "I felt horrible. Not only had I not called you"—her voice broke *again*—"but then I *cheated* on you! I am such a horrible person!"

Roy's mind's eye widened almost in awe as he saw what she was doing.

She's faking. Oh God. She's playing me.

"And then...."

She was crying again. But now with marvelous clarity, Roy understood it for what it was.

Acting.

In his senior year of high school, he'd gone to the big end-of-year play because there was a girl in it he liked named Linda Bachman.

(And Joey was in it too, from his PE class, and for one whole scene he wore nothing but his boxer shorts. A few of the football team jeered at him, but not Roy. And had Roy heard there was such a scene and wanted to see that scene? Be able to look at Joey at least close to naked and not have to turn away? He wouldn't, couldn't, admit that then, but he saw the truth now.)

There came a part of the play where Linda had to cry. And she *did*. She stood under a blue-white spotlight and started to recite her lines, and then she began to cry. And Linda... well, she just seemed to *go away*, and her character was standing there instead, and soon people in the audience were crying. *He* was crying. There were stifled (and some not so stifled) sobs all around him (even football players), and Roy had simply been amazed how he'd been swept out of that high school theater and taken to a different place because of the magic she worked on that stage.

Afterward, he took her a rose backstage and told her how *good* she was and asked her how she did it. *How* had she cried like that?

She'd been so pleased by the rose and had hugged him, and when he asked the question, she seemed to glow.

"I look inside myself," Linda said, her eyes going away to someplace else. "And I find the part of myself that hurts and cries. I find it and grab hold of it and pull it to the surface." She said it breathlessly, excited and even a little in awe. Then her focus came back, and she looked at him and said, "It's *acting*, and it's everything to me."

It's acting....

Ramona wiped at her face with a sleeve. "After that I couldn't call you! I *couldn't*."

Shit. *Acting*. This porch was her stage, and she had reached inside herself and found that part of her that hurt and cried and grabbed hold of it and brought it to the surface. She was *acting*. With Roy as her only audience. A one-woman show playing for him alone.

Except she wasn't as good as Linda. Of course, she *had* fooled him before. Fooled him good, huh?

Ramona shook her head. "I kept *telling* myself that I needed to at least tell you I was seeing him—"

Seeing! Yeah, right.

"—but I was too chicken. And the more time that passed, the harder it got, until finally I couldn't, *couldn't*, tell you. I was too ashamed."

She began to cry again—*acting*—and he shook his head and reached out and touched her. Not to console her but because he couldn't stand to hear one more word. And she immediately looked at him, eyes a mess, mascara running down her cheeks.

"I forgive you," he said. Because damn. Why not? That and to get her to stop. And because, to his surprise, he found he really didn't give a shit what she had done anymore. How about that? Not even the fact that she'd never called him while he was in jail or after he'd been bailed out. Or been there for him those horribly short minutes before that horribly unsympathetic judge passed sentence.

"My cousin Janet told me she's sleeping with this guy named Milo," he'd told Demaine, who had nodded in sympathy.

"Yeah, that happen to a lot of dudes in here, man. I'm sure my Linzell ain't been true." He had laughed—more of a huff, a sad little sound—and looked at Roy. "He can't go no day without havin' his pussy filled, let alone wait till I get outta here."

Pussy? he'd thought in surprise but didn't ask. Roy said he was sorry, and Demaine shrugged and said, "You know, I really don't give a shit. If he gonna be that way, I don't want him."

And right now, this very minute, standing on Ramona's porch, Roy understood what Demaine had meant.

"You really forgive me?" Ramona asked, her eyes wide and stunned. She threw her arms around him, buried her face in his shoulder, and thanked him again and again.

"So what happened to Milo?" he asked.

Ramona froze and then let out a long sigh. "He broke up with me."

Well. What do you know?

"Sorry about that," he said and maybe gave a tenth of a shit about it, but no more. Because no one likes to be dumped, so he could sympathize even if it was only a smidgen, as his granny liked to say. And why not? Because what did it hurt for him to say it?

He could act too.

"I knew I had to call you then and beg you for forgiveness and see if you would take me back."

"Take you *back*?" The words were out of his mouth before he knew he was going to say them. Take her back? He almost staggered. What? Was she fucking *crazy*? "What?" he exclaimed.

She nodded. Smooshed up against him, dropped her hands to his ass again, and began to massage his cheeks. His "sweet cheeks"?

"Wouldn't that be great? You and me, together again? I never cared about Milo. I was *glad* he broke up with me. His friends made fun of me, and he never once said a word to defend me. He just liked that I fuc—" She stopped very suddenly. Paused. "I...."

"He just liked that you did what?" Roy asked, and even as the words left his mouth, he knew. *He liked it when you fucked him. With one of your strap-ons.* God. Roy shuddered. With one of the toys she'd fucked him with?

But then he laughed. He couldn't help it. "So Milo—Milo Giancarlo—was your bitch?"

"Huh? I... I...."

"Mister full-of-himself, hoity-toity Milo Giancarlo takes it up the ass? The guy that called *me* your bitch?"

Roy pushed her back, albeit gently. Laughed again. "Do you talk to him like you used to talk to me?"

"Yeah, Sweet Cheeks. You're lovin' that, ain'tcha? Going to make you my bitch."

"Roy. It's not like—"

"It's *just* like that." Why else would Milo have moved in on her so fast? He knew what she liked to do in bed. *All* his friends knew what Ramona had done to Roy while they were in Hawaii. What he had wanted her to do.

For Christ's sake.

"Roy," she said, and there was a pathetic little tone to her voice. "It's not what you think. I really *have* missed—"

"Ramona." He held up a hand, stopped her. "Just be honest with me. For once. You never really cared for *me*. You liked fucking my ass." Boy, the words were harsh when they were right out there, hanging in the air. But true.

She started to protest, but he went on. "I'm guessing it's not so easy to find a boyfriend who's into it, *although* I've read far more straight dudes like it than you would imagine."

She looked at him, eyes wide with astonishment. "You read *that*? Read it *where*?"

"And along comes Milo, and *he* wants it, and hell, I admit it. Milo is kinda sexy, if you're into really skinny guys. He's not really my type." My type! He said that? "Plus Milo has money. I get it! You traded up. You have every right."

"Roy! That's not true."

"Thing is, babe, ain't nobody better'n nobody else."

"What...? I don't underst—"

"But that doesn't mean I can't find better for *me*."

Frank.

"And maybe I have." *Oh, Frank!* "I'm not sure." *Frank isn't the settling-down kind.* "I can only hope." *Hope like hell.* "Ask him." *You never really know unless you ask.* His granny had said that enough times in his life. "And if he doesn't want me, then I'll find someone else." He stepped back again, turned, and started down the porch steps.

"Roy!" Ramona cried. "Where are you going?"

"To ask!" he called over his shoulder.

"Wait!"

He stopped, looked back.

She opened her mouth and then snapped it shut. Her wide eyes went even wider. "Wait a goddamned minute. *He*? Did you say *he*?"

"Yes," he said. "He. His name is Frank." Then Roy was going back down the walkway.

"You're a fag? You're a goddamned *faggot*?"

Roy climbed into his Jeep.

"Well, then why don't you call frigging *Milo* too! You all can have a fucking homo orgy!"

Part of him cringed at her shouting at him like that, out on the street. But another part? A bigger part? Just didn't give a shit.

"You know, I thought I loved you once," he called out after he'd started it up.

"You didn't love me," she screamed. "You just loved my strap-on!"

He shrugged. Thought about it a second. "I think maybe you're right," he yelled back.

And then he headed to Frank's.

CHAPTER THIRTY

FRANK DROVE without thinking. He knew if he *did* think, he'd change his mind. If he did think, the fear would take him back under that whirlpool of thoughts and emotions, and then he'd be lost.

Hell, he was scared to death with*out* thinking!

He pulled into the Meridian parking garage, despite the "Twenty-five Dollars after First Hour" fee, even though there was a garage only a block and a half away that was free this time of evening. A walk that far might give him a chance to think. And change his mind.

Frank went to the hotel lobby—surprised at how many people there were in the large open room—to make the call. If it disconnected while he was in the garage, he might—very well might—change his mind.

This was something he needed to do.

He pulled up the call logs on his phone and found the most recent right there at the top. Unknown Caller.

Unknown mother.

Only one way to change that.

What would Glen say if he knew? But Frank couldn't think about that either. He pressed the number.

On the fifth ring, about when he figured it would go to voicemail—and there was a part, a big part, of him that was relieved at the idea—there was a *bllrp!* and then, "Frankie? Is-is that you?"

God. Her. Same voice. *Her* voice.

Mama?

He almost said it, but instead said, "First thing. If you want me to talk to you, it's *Frank*. Not Frankie. You don't have the right to call me that."

There was a sharp intake of breath from the other end, and then, "All right. Whatever you say Fra-Frank."

For now, he thought and had no idea why he thought it.

"Second?" she asked, and that surprised him.

"I… I don't know yet," he replied. "I'll let you know."

After another long pause, he finally asked, "Wh-what room?"

"I—" Muffled talking for a second. "—it's 1018," she said.

"I'll be right up," he said.

"You'll be what?" *Complete* surprise.

"I'm in the lobby."

"You're in the *lobby*?" As surprised as Frank, maybe?

"Yes."

"*My God.*" More of that inaudible talking then, and finally, after what seemed forever but probably was less than thirty seconds, "Please. Come up."

Frank signed off without warning.

Somehow, he stood. The huge lobby tilted for a second. He closed his eyes. Steadied himself. Took a deep breath. *I'm about to see my mama.* Mother. *I'm about to meet my mother.* He looked up to where she would be. Was. Maybe a mistake. The huge kinetic sculpture moved, wires and large and small pieces of metal shaped like squares and circles and triangles in gorgeous but somehow muted colors, metallic on one side and fired ceramic glaze on the other. Moved in different directions, slow but crazy. It was hard to tell which way it all moved and why none of the parts crashed into each other, as close as some of those pieces—some of them also independently turning—were to each other. It made him dizzy, and he had to close his eyes again.

He took another deep, long breath. Then he opened them, steeled himself, and walked toward the bank of elevators.

It was the longest walk of his life.

Two couples waited at the elevator bank, and the Up button was glowing a soft yellow, one of them having obviously pressed it. A few interminable seconds later—time enough that Frank almost started thinking—the doors opened, and he went in with the others like a small herd of lemmings going up instead of charging off a cliff. Or at least he was.

The fucking thing stopped three times for passengers until there wasn't room for anyone else, and Frank realized they must all be going to Apogee to eat. *Where Glen and I ate dinner.* It certainly explained why everyone was so nicely dressed. He almost didn't get off on the tenth floor. And if he'd stood outside his father's door a long time earlier, if he thought that had felt like forever, standing outside his mother's was endless.

He almost didn't knock.

In fact, he was turning on his heel to leave—for sure this time—when finally something inside him took over, and he stepped up to the door and rapped on it three distinct times. Not too loud... and not too soft.

An instant later a man answered.

He was a tall man, although not as tall as Frank, with dark hair starting to go silver and deep dark eyes—probably about fifty-five or so. He had a mustache and a little soul patch like an inverted triangle just below his lower lip. Reminded him a little bit of MacGyver, but not quite. MacGyver's father?

"Frank?" the man asked. He had a deep voice.

Frank nodded.

"I'm Theo Gardener. I'm Marion's husband. We spoke on the phone."

Frank cleared his throat, then couldn't think of a fucking thing to say and nodded again instead.

"Won't you come in?" Thank God he didn't offer to shake hands. Frank didn't know what he would have done had that happened.

Theo stepped aside, and Frank, taking a deep breath, walked in as the man—his mother's husband—said, "Your mother is in the bathroom. She'll be out in a moment. She is understandably nervous. Hell. She's terrified."

She's terrified?

Theo closed the door, and Frank stood in the middle of the room, not sure what the fuck to do. Not sit on the bed like when he'd come up to see Glen. Besides, it was a little rumpled. Like they'd hastily made it. Had they gone to bed already when he called? It wasn't that late, was it? If he had a watch, he'd have checked. It seemed rude to pull out his cell.

He was glancing around for a clock of some kind when the restroom door clicked open. He froze. He couldn't help it.

A perilously long moment later, she stepped into the room. And for one blinding moment Frank thought he would burst into tears. Then, somehow, he got himself under control.

She stood there wearing a simple dark blue dress that stopped just above her knees and had a high collar. Her hair was indeed dark brown—almost black—not quite shoulder length, sort of parted to one side, with only the tiniest shimmer that spoke of the silver days coming. Her eyes were… God… lovely. Also brown. A warm brown neither light nor dark but a lovely color in between. She was wearing a bit of lipstick somewhere between pink and red, and she smiled, a big bright smile, but she was standing very stiffly, and there was fear there. In that stance. In those warm eyes.

She trembled. She was fighting it. But he saw it.

Mama….

"H-hello, son," she said finally, when he hadn't said a word. He couldn't. "May I call you that?" There was a flicker in her eyes, and her smile wavered. "Maybe I should call you Frank?"

Her voice had an English accent, although more what Frank thought of as Helen Mirren rather than Spice Girls.

He started to open his mouth, then took one more breath. He didn't want to—couldn't—let his voice break. Stutter. He had to be in control here.

But the memory came back. The hazy memory. Her voice…

"Every Who down in Whoville…."

The hair. It was the same. The eyes…. God…! That smile.

Mama.

It was her.

"You left me," he said, and then clenched his hands into fists, the nails cutting into his palms.

Her smile vanished, and pain came into her eyes.

"She didn't leave you, Frank," Theo said, stepping almost between them. "It was your father—"

Frank turned his attention on the man and threw every single iota of anger he had at him. If this were some kind of urban fantasy, the man would have burst into flame. *Do it. Say one fucking word.*

"Theo! Please."

The man, her husband, turned to her.

"Go. Downstairs. Upstairs. Go for a walk. I don't care."

"Marion!"

Frank could hear the hurt in his voice. He didn't care.

Her eyes were still on Frank. "Please." So much pain. And determination. *"Please*, darling."

Darling.

Theo stiffened, his shoulders went high and his spine straight, and then... they relaxed. Slumped. He turned back to Frank.

Frank ignored him. Looked past him and through him. At the woman behind. Tall and beautiful and... trembling in her perfect dark blue dress.

Theo Gardener stood straight again—Frank saw that too out of the corners of his eyes—and then he walked past Frank. He expected the man to shove past him, but he didn't.

I would have.

There was a click as the door closed.

The woman who was his mother looked away long enough to pull a chair out from under a desk and motioned to it. "Sit down?"

She stepped back.

Frank went to the chair—the type with wheels that could be found in any office—and sat down.

"May I get you something? I can call room service. Tea? Something a little more... substantial?" She turned to a cabinet under the flat-screen television. "I think I saw those itty-bitty bottles of alcohol. And I've got some bottled water."

"I don't need anything," he said, a little harsher than he intended. He took a breath. "Sit down."

After a moment, she did. She straightened her dress first, then sat. She had long legs that were surprisingly shapely. She had to be fifty. She looked good. Surprisingly good. It made Frank feel proud.

CHAPTER THIRTY-ONE

ROY FOUND it unexpectedly easy to get into the secured apartment building. He just moseyed along the walkway out front and waited for one of the residents of the Oscar Wilde to go through the lobby doors; then he slipped right in behind them. He even held the door for an elderly couple of men. Stopped and watched them a minute, his heart racing, a smile on his face.

Surely they were a couple. A couple that had lived through hard times to be able to be together. Why, compared to the tiny bit he knew about what gays and lesbians had been through, the world today was easy, could be his oyster.

Then before they could disappear into the elevator, he quickly crossed the lobby and joined them. Pressed the sixth-floor button.

Please let him be there.

His heart was more than racing now. It was *pounding*. Hopefully the two old men next to him, a little foldable shopping cart with groceries between them, were hard of hearing!

Please let him not mind that I'm here!

Roy did not want to be a guy that Frank had to break things off with. Well, not break, exactly. Didn't you have to be going out together to break things off?

He didn't want Frank to tell him they couldn't get together anymore. God, not yet. Not after what he was discovering about himself. He didn't know if he was bisexual (gay?) enough to want a boyfriend. But Frank could help him figure that out. Navigate those waters, so to speak. He wasn't ready to seek out male sex partners either. God no!

When he got to Frank's door and reached out to knock, he thought of something else.

Please let him not be with anyone. Oh God, please!

Because being a friend with benefits with Frank didn't mean Frank was going to be only with him, did it?

"I am a gay man, baby. I can't even imagine how many men I've had one kind of sex or another with. Hundreds, Roy. And I plan to have hundreds more while I'm good-looking enough to get them."

Roy felt that sting again. Recognized it for what it was. Jealousy. Stupid! He hardly knew Frank. And he'd known ahead of time that Frank didn't do relationships. If Frank suspected he was feeling anything like that he would… *end things*.

Roy's stomach clenched.

He liked that idea far worse than the one about Frank being with another man.

And fuck! Hadn't he just been at Ramona's? Hadn't he almost fucked her? Well, let her fuck him? Wasn't that why he went there? To see if he was only a little bit gay? Or bi? Or what-the-fuck-*ever*?

Oh, this was going to complicate things, wasn't it? Figuring out the whole universe of how men and women worked was insane enough! Did he want to join the whole universe of how men and men worked as well?

Then he thought about the man who lived on the other side of that door. The bed. The sex. Hell! Sitting naked on his balcony. And he knew the answer.

Yes.

Yes, yes, yes, *yes*!

He knocked. *Please let him be there.*

But after a moment, there was no answer. *Oh no.*

He knocked again, a little harder. If Frank was out on his balcony (naked?) listening to Pink Floyd, he might not have heard, right? Or if he was taking a shower? Or if…. The thought of another man hit him again. Frank in that bed with another man and ignoring the knock.

Please not another man. Please? Not yet.

He raised his hand to knock once more, and froze. Did he want Frank to open the door a crack, obviously naked, and tell him he was busy?

No.

No, no, no, *no*!

A door open, not Frank's door, and a voice said, "Hello?"

Roy jumped, jerked his head in the direction of the voice, and felt guilty for some reason.

A man stood looking through the open crack of a door down the hall, but he wasn't naked. He had short curly hair and was peering at him with brown eyes behind black-framed glasses. "I don't think Frank's at home."

"Oh," Roy said and felt *crushing* disappointment.

"You okay?" the guy asked. He opened the door a little farther.

Roy faked a smile. "Sure. I was just in the neighborhood, and—"

What was that look on the guy's face?

He sighed. *Knew* what that look was. The stranger was feeling sorry for him. Roy's stomach flipped. Jesus. Am I about the fiftieth guy he's seen standing outside Frank's door looking like a little lost puppy?

Roy steeled himself and took a few steps in the man's direction. He looked to be about Frank's age, around thirty, but plump.

"Okay, I wasn't in the neighborhood." He shrugged. "I've just spent the… well, a couple days with Frank."

Plump Guy nodded knowingly. In the background, Roy could hear what sounded like a television.

"I was invited back. Wednesday."

"It's not Wednesday," Plump Guy said.

Roy gave a halfhearted, you-caught-me-didn't-you? laugh and blushed. "No. It's not. But I made this decision… and I wanted to tell him."

"You didn't decide you want him to be your boyfriend, did you?"

Roy's eyes went wide. "Oh God no." He sighed again. "Frank made it clear he didn't do that."

Plump Guy half smiled. "Good." He opened the door still farther. He was barefoot, wearing loose shorts and a T-shirt with a silhouette of a bear with the word "COLT" within it, whatever that meant. The animal *clearly* wasn't a horse.

Roy had taken a few more steps while he talked, and he could tell for sure now that a TV was on in the man's apartment. Some woman was talking while music played in the background. It sounded like *Entertainment Tonight* or something similar. A man called out, "Harry! You gotta see this!"

Roy didn't know what to say now. He suddenly felt pretty stupid. And really embarrassed. Maybe a little pathetic. "I bet leaving a note would look pretty desperate, huh?"

Harry—that was apparently his name—twisted his mouth in that way that said, "Yup, it sure would." But what he actually said was "I wouldn't if I were you. If he wants to see you before Wednesday, he'll call you."

"But that's the thing!" Roy cried. "He can't. He told me to call him if I couldn't make it Wednesday, and I realized I don't have his number."

That look again.

Roy sighed once more. "I know what it looks like…."

"Harry!" came that voice from within the apartment. "Some prince has disappeared."

Roy shook his head. "Sorry. I should probably go home." God, he didn't want to. "Instead of looking like a lonely matchstick girl out here in the hall. He did tell me to call if I couldn't make it and—"

"You can't?"

Roy's face really heated up at that. "No. I can."

Harry laughed softly. There wasn't a mean note in it. "You were just hoping maybe to see him *before* Wednesday?"

Now Roy's face was burning.

"Harry!"

Harry turned around and yelled, "I'm talking to somebody here!"

"He's the prince of some little country called Monterosia, and—"

"I don't give a *shit* about some prince in Monty-whatever!" Harry turned back, shaking his head. "My lover is *addicted* to that stuff," he explained. "I've never even heard of fucking Monterosia, have you?"

Roy shrugged. "Nope."

"You know, it probably wouldn't be a horrible thing for you to leave him a note. Want to come in? I got paper and pens and tape and—"

"That would be *great*," Roy said, and his whole *body* grinned in response.

Harry stood aside, and Roy entered. It was a nice small apartment, filled with furniture, and a slim man sat curled up on a couch watching a medium-sized flat-screen television. "Cody, this is—" Harry stopped. "What is your name?"

Roy told him his name. Harry told Cody. Then told Roy Cody's name.

"Nice to meet you," Cody said without looking away from the television. P!nk sang while a pretty blonde woman talked. The story had apparently moved on from the missing prince of Monty-whatever.

"Nice to meet you," Roy said.

With a bob of his head, Harry led Roy into a kitchen that was only partially separated from the living room. The place wasn't as big or elegant as Frank's. It was still nice, though, and neat. There weren't even any dishes in the sink.

Harry pulled a little pad of paper from the door of the refrigerator—it was something a magnet *could* stick to and nothing like Frank's—with a pen and handed it to Roy. Roy started to write and then… didn't know what to say. Harry was *standing* there, and….

"Oh! Sorry." Harry turned away and headed over to the couch.

Roy looked down at the blank pink pad. Stared at it. What *did* he say? Just something casual and his phone number. But did he want to leave it on the door for anyone to see?

He took a few steps into the living area. "Um, Harry?"

Harry looked away from the screen. The story had already moved from the P!nk ad and now showed a boy band dancing and singing on stage. A bar at the bottom of the screen said "Electric i Tour Coming Back Home to USA!"

"Yeah?"

"I don't have a clue what to say. Do you see him very often? Maybe I can just leave it with you?"

Harry nodded enthusiastically. "I see him all the time. I'll be glad to give it to him."

"That way I can just leave my name and number and not some pathetic-sounding note."

Harry smiled. "Yeah. Phone number *good*." Then he frowned. "Pathetic-sounding note *bad*."

"You think?" Roy asked, a little bit relieved. "Even that won't be too much? I mean, I did only meet him this past week. I won't sound—"

"Wait a minute!" Harry's eyes went wide. "Are you Orange Jumpsuit Guy?"

Roy froze. *Orange Jumpsuit Guy?*

"You are, aren't you?" Harry jumped from the arm of the couch where he'd been perched and came right to Roy. "Oh man! Did Frank say some nice things about you." He was grinning. And then he winked. "Oh boy!"

So it wasn't so much "nice things" as nice *sexual* things.

"He did, huh?" Roy said when he could find his voice. He could feel his face warming again.

"Oh. Oh yeah! He finally found him an Orange Jumpsuit Guy! He's been talking about that fantasy for-fucking-ever!"

"Harry! For God's sake," Cody cried from the couch. He was actually looking away from the flat screen. "Maybe the poor man doesn't want to talk about what he does in bed! Just because Frank likes to doesn't mean Roy does."

Now Roy's face was on fire again. "Frank told you what we did?"

Harry nodded… then shook his head. "Well, not much, dammit. But oh! He was so excited to meet you. Have you done it yet? Did you wear the orange suit?"

Roy gulped, and now the heat drained from his face instead of warming it. "Wh-what?"

Harry leaned in and said in a conspiratorial way, "I bet it's his number-one fantasy. Cody likes that UPS man, so I bought a uniform and wore it for him. Had one of the best nights we've had in *years*! I told Frank to order one of those prison uniforms online and get someone to wear it for him. But he says it wouldn't be the same thing. But if you—"

"God damn, Harry!" It was Cody, and his sudden approach made them both jump. "Can you not see you're horrifying the poor guy? God, Roy, I am so sorry for my dumbass man."

Roy tried to respond, but his tongue wouldn't work. He had no idea what to say. It was the uniform? That was what Frank wanted? Wanted him to wear it so they could have sex in it? Wear a symbol of his hated time behind bars?

The expression on Harry's face suddenly seemed to melt. "Oh shit," Harry said. "I'm sorry."

"He's sorry!" Cody exclaimed, cocking a thumb at his lover.

"I didn't mean it that way." Now he looked horrified. And now *he* was blushing.

Roy, however, only wanted to bolt. Because he was suddenly afraid he might cry. And he didn't dare do that in front of them. Now that would be pathetic.

"I think I better go," he said. He started for the door.

"Roy!" Harry cried.

Roy was already at the door when Harry's hand came down on his shoulder. He started to shrug it away, but then Harry gave him a gentle little squeeze. He looked back.

"I am really sorry. I was being an ass." He looked quite contrite.

"*I'll* say," said Cody.

"Frank really didn't say anything. I was telling you the truth. Not really. He *started* to. Then he didn't." He got a curious faraway look on his face, then came back. "Yeah. He told me a different story instead."

Cody joined them.

"It's just he's been talking about this guy he saw on the side of the highway for *weeks*. Couldn't stop. Then he was all excited because he actually met you, and—"

"And maybe the 'guy' doesn't want to talk about what he was doing there, Harry," Cody said very quietly. "Maybe it's none of our business."

A whole new level of horror passed over Harry's face. "Oh God."

"Yeah," said Cody. "*Oh God.*"

Harry shook his head. "I am so sorry. I didn't mean anything by it. And I am sure you've paid your debt to soc—"

"*Harry*! Can't you quit while you are *so* far behind?"

Harry's mouth snapped shut.

Roy just blinked at them both. Wondered what was going on in their minds. Was it the same thing he was getting from everyone else? That he was some kind of Al Capone or Ted Bundy or Birdman of Alcatraz? Teflon dude?

But then to his surprise, Cody said, "I think Frank likes you."

Roy stepped back in surprise. What? "Huh?" It certainly isn't what he thought Cody was going to say.

"I'm not saying he is going to get down on his knee anytime soon… or ever. But I do think he likes you."

"Really?" *Because I really like him.* But then he remembered. He sighed. "He did say that he isn't the monogamous type."

"Maybe. Yeah. But I still think he likes you. And I think if he was worried about you, he wouldn't have invited you back to his place, even *with* his little fantasy."

"Because you weren't wearing the orange jumpsuit," Harry added.

Cody gave him a fierce look.

"No, *really*," Harry said. "If it was the orange fetish only, why invite you up when you weren't wearing it?"

"More important, Frank doesn't ask people to come back," Cody said. "He's pretty much a one-night stand kind of guy."

Harry nodded.

"He did say he thought he might like a friend with benefits," Roy said. "And I'd be happy with that." *Liar.* "You know… until I figure this all out. The gay thing? If I am gay."

"You don't know?" Harry asked him, eyebrows raised. "Really?"

Roy opened his mouth to answer and then let out a long breath instead. "I…. I'm thinking I probably am."

Harry and Cody smiled.

"Look," Cody said, "you want to stay awhile? I make great cosmopolitans. We could sit on the balcony. It's a lovely night. And if you have any questions about being gay, we'd be happy to answer."

"We sure would," Harry agreed—eagerly.

Roy smiled. It sounded nice. Really nice. But, "I can't tonight. Can I take a rain check?"

"Of course," the duo chorused.

"Even if he gives me the boot?" Roy asked.

"Especially then," Cody said.

For some strange reason, that made everything better.

Completely impulsively, he hugged Cody. Hard. Then gave Harry one as well.

He left then. Watched them right until the elevator doors closed.

And even though he went home alone to an empty bed, he was a little bit less lonely.

CHAPTER THIRTY-TWO

Neither Frank nor his... nor *Marion*... said a word for about a thousand years. At least that's how it felt. Time had seemed to screw itself up since somewhere around when Wilbur left his apartment.

Now here he was. Sitting with his mother.

His mother.

And God, she really did look a little like Princess Stephanie of Monaco. She had to be in her early fifties. But she was... she was pretty. Even beautiful.

Frank had a thousand thousand questions of course. But where to start? How to start? He couldn't even talk. Realized that if he tried, he very well might lose it completely. And he didn't want to do that. Didn't want to be weak in front of her. He felt that he had to be in control here. *Had* to be.

He opened his mouth to ask her where she was from—England, or had she gotten the accent from living there?—but the words wouldn't come. His throat closed up and seemed suddenly to be as dry as a desert. A sort of half cough, half rasp was all that came out.

The woman leapt up—"the woman" because he still couldn't bring himself to actually call her Mother—and opened the cabinet she'd indicated before, then opened the little refrigerator and pulled out a bottled water. She quickly handed it to him and then asked, "A glass? Would you like a glass?"

He shook his head, screwed the lid off, took a sip, and then chugged down half of it. It was like he was only now getting something to drink after hours of crossing hot sands. Then he coughed and coughed again, and she whirled around behind him and slapped his back.

Just like a mother.

Frank held up a hand—*enough!*—and dared one more swallow. It did the trick. "Thank you," he said and then wondered that the first time she had ever touched him was to smack him. *Ridiculous. Don't even start thinking that way.*

Or he would leave.

"You okay now?" she asked him, and he nodded and she sat, tentatively, as if expecting she might need to get up again.

He asked the question he had meant to before—for lack of anything else to say.

"England born and raised," she said, and her voice—it was musical. Lovely. Deep and feminine and melodic all at the same time. "We're in Wales now, actually. My husband is a doctor. A cardiologist."

Frank nodded. They had money. So they could afford this place, then, no problema. "What brings you to the States?" he asked.

She looked at him in outright surprise. Even astonishment. "Why, you, Frankie." Then, holding up a hand, "I mean... *Frank.*"

Now it was Frank's turn to be surprised. "You came all this way to meet me?"

She gave a single slow nod. "Yes, dear. Of course I did. I'd have flown to the moon."

"Maybe you should have called first? What if I hadn't seen you? Wouldn't that have been a complete waste of your time?"

She shook her head. "It was worth it just to hear your voice on the phone. I've wondered for so long what you would *sound* like. Your voice. What it would sound like."

Frank saw now that her eyes were shimmering. Wet again. A tear spilled out, and she quickly wiped it away.

"And?" he asked.

"Wonderful," she replied. "So much a *man*. Not the *boy's* voice I recall at all." And then two more tears ran down her cheeks. This time she didn't try to wipe at them. She just let them go, either not noticing or not caring.

He felt his own tears threatening, and he cursed them and hurled them back from whence they'd come. *Don't you dare*, he told himself.

"Well, I am a man," Frank said. "I'm not a boy anymore. I haven't been in a long time."

"A *long* time," she echoed. "Such a long time."

"Then why *now*?" he snapped. "After all this time?"

"Because," she said, "I've just recently found you! Or Theo did. I'd pretty much given up." She shook her head. "No. I never gave up. Not really. But I'd just about given up hope."

"Wh-what are you talking about?"

"She dumped you, Frank."

"Looking that long," she said. "After a while, you run out of energy. You think it's never going to happen. Everyone tells you to give up. And a few times... I almost did. But—"

"I've tried to find you for years. I finally all but gave up. Twenty-five years ago, ten years ago, there was no Facebook. I would find traces of you, and then...."

"—I couldn't. I'm your mother. Whatever you may think of that. But I couldn't. I couldn't give up hope."

"She's a bitch, Frank! And she's going to fill your ears with all kinds of shit to get back at me."

"I would find traces of you, and then, well, your father would.... No. I won't *say that. I won't say anything bad about your father."*

"But... your father." She stopped, looked away, looked back.

"Frank! She dumped you!"

And a decision seemed to come to her then. He saw it in the flash of her eyes.

"Your mother has been trying to find you your entire life. And he kept her from doing it."

"Your father didn't want me to find you, Frankie. He stayed one step ahead of me all the way. Every time I would find you and get the money to come looking for you, he would go. He'd be finished with the home or villa or whatever he was working on, and then he would leave. And I never understood it. I never understood why."

"She wanted to be a nurse or some fucking *thing. She said she would come back, and she never did."*

"Glen said you left us to become a nurse," Frank said.

She nodded. "I wanted a way to take care of you. I didn't have any skills. So I asked him if he would take care of you while I was in school, and when I was done, I would take you."

"Then several years later she started contacting me, telling me she wanted to see you. After she dumped *you!"*

"I know I made a mistake. I should have found a way to keep you while I was going to school, but I was nineteen when you were born. A... a kid. A stupid kid. I made a bad mistake, and I've paid for it all my life."

Frank shook his head. "I... I don't get it."

She took a deep breath. Let it out. "I would come and see you while I was in school. Sometimes he'd let me have you for the weekend. Those were the best times. Oh God. And the worst." The tears were still running down her cheeks, but her voice stayed almost steady, with only a tremble now and then. "Because when I had to leave you, it was total torture. I would cry all the way back on the tube."

Spying a box of tissues, Frank stood, picked it up, and took it to her, careful that she didn't touch him. That he didn't touch her.

"Thank you, darling." Her eyes went wide. "Sorry. I-I can't help it. It is taking everything out of me not to grab you and hug you with all of my might. You're right there—right there in front of me—and I can't touch you!"

It was all Frank could do then not to reach for her. He wanted to. God, he did! He really wanted to.

"I look at you now, and I can see you back then. My little boy. Your eyes and your hair.... Not quite curly but those little waves. How I would brush them!"

"Why did you leave me?" he cried.

Her eyes went wide yet again. Dark eyes opened so wide they were surrounded by the whites. "I didn't, Frank. Your father did. I came to see you one weekend. It was my weekend. And there was no one there. I knocked, and there was no answer. So I knocked again and again, and then I looked inside, and there was...." Her voice cracked. "There was nothing there! Some furniture. But I could tell. I could tell you were gone."

And then she cried. The sobs would rise up as she tried to speak and would break up her words so he could barely follow them. "I-I g-got the land... the landlord to open the door. He knew... he knew me. And sure enough. All the clothes—his... y-yours. Were g-gone. Books. All of his... t-tools."

She got to sobbing so hard then, she couldn't force words out at all, and he just sat there, having no idea what to do. He could see that she was trying to get herself under control. And he remembered the British.

Knew this had to be embarrassing her. So he didn't say a word. He sat and watched.

Finally she seemed to regain some sensibility, and she looked up with red, bloodshot eyes, and she said, "The man. The land… landlord. He was so mad. He said your father owed him a month's rent and tried to get me to pay it. But I didn't have any money. I was going to school full-time and working two jobs and getting no sleep. But I lived for my weekends with you, and then…." More tears. "God, Frank. I saw it! I saw me living a lifetime without you. I didn't know how I could do it. How I could bear it. And the only reason I did was my *hope* of finding you!"

Now Frank's eyes were filling with tears. Any second he would be crying. He hated it. "Why did you leave him?"

She looked at him in confusion, and then with the light of understanding. "Your father?"

Frank nodded.

Her shoulders slumped ever so slightly, and she let out a long and slow sigh. "Come on, Frankie," she said. "You know."

And he did, of course.

Of course he knew.

"I didn't mind him looking. I was nineteen when we met and I got pregnant. *I* looked. But Frank—and I am not trying to say something mean about your father—"

"Oh fuck that," he replied. "I do know my father. He did a lot more than look, didn't he?"

She didn't say anything at first. Then she nodded. "Yes," she said very quietly. "And the first time… and the second, I forgave him. I remembered the boy I met in high school. A nice boy. And I thought if I stayed with him, he would change."

"You think I don't know about your father? I know about your father. I know just what kind of man he is. Lo so."

"And I forgave him a third time."

"Your father? He is a man who loves the women, and I don't see that any woman will ever tie him down."

"Then I found out I had… a disease."

"A disease," he asked, sitting straight up in his chair.

She winced. "A… *sexual* disease," she said, dropping her voice on the last two words. And with that lovely voice, it sounded *so* wrong. As if she shouldn't be saying such things at all.

Not as wrong as it must have felt for a young woman in love, though. A young woman who had hoped her husband would change.

"…and I don't see that any woman will ever tie him down."

"I know it was wrong for me to leave you in his care, but I couldn't live with him after that! And my mother, who never liked the American boy who came as a foreign-exchange student but never left, was so pleased I was leaving. But she wouldn't let me come home. If she had, I could have done it. She could have watched you while I was at school, and then we would have been together all these years."

She quivered, and Frank figured she was a hairsbreadth from sobbing again. But somehow she didn't.

"I love you, son. I have never stopped loving you. I will never stop loving you. Is there any way you can ever forgive me for what I've done?"

"I love you, son."

The words seemed otherworldly. Unreal. Something he never thought he would hear. *She loves me?*

He could hardly believe it.

No such thing as love.

But then why had she spent a quarter of a century looking for him, then?

"What about Theo?" he asked and fought the sarcastic tone that wanted to take over his voice.

She looked at him curiously. As if she had no idea what he was talking about.

"I suppose you *love* him too?"

Her brows came together. "Of course. I don't know what I would have done without him all these years. He saved me. And he never stopped supporting me while I looked for you. I love him very much."

Love? Really?

"I don't understand why you couldn't find me," he said, but even as he spoke the words, he knew. If all she said was true, Glen had run off with him before Myspace and Facebook, even the internet, were active.

"It wasn't like I could hire a private detective. And when I met Theo, he was in his residency. So there was no money, for one thing, and your father was international with you. Believe me, what money I could spare, I did use looking for you."

Frank shook his head. He still couldn't believe it. "Why would my father do that?"

She shook her head. There was an ocean's depth of I-don't-know in her eyes. But as he asked, he knew the answer to that too.

Pride.

Simple pride.

Not only in the chip-off-the-old-block sense, but worse. A woman had left him. And she'd left him to make her life better. He hadn't been able to stand that, had he? Not for one minute. And as time had gone by, why, he'd probably used little Frankie as woman bait. What woman could resist the devilishly handsome single father whose bitch of a wife had left him with a five-year-old kid?

Dear Christ. Was I always bait?

How many times had he heard it? "You know, this one just might turn out to be your new mama!" And how many of those times had the woman in question blushed and then spoiled not just Glen, but Frankie—*especially* Frankie—rotten?

No. No, please no.

"Frank? Are you all right?"

Concern. For him.

Then he cried. He couldn't help it. The tears came, and a moment later she was holding him, and he was letting her, and then he was holding her right back.

His mama.

CHAPTER THIRTY-THREE

FRANK AND his mother sat and had tea she had made, and they talked.

About how she'd met Theo and fallen in love with him, and how he'd loved her back and cherished her.

Glen would never have cherished anyone.

No woman, that is.

And did he even really cherish me? Or am I simply a way he loves himself?

But despite the fact that Glen had given her reason to hate him, she was sticking to the facts.

"I'm sorry, but I don't have any lemon."

"Lemon?" he asked.

"For your tea."

He shook his head. "I don't like lemon in my tea," he said. In fact, he rarely had hot tea as it was. Probably hadn't had any that wasn't part of a hot toddy since he was in his teens.

"Me either," she said—pronouncing it eye-ther and making Frank smile for the first time.

There was a knock on the door and then it opened. It was Theo, of course. And she looked at him with such love that Frank's heart seemed to stop for a moment.

"Frank," Theo said and this time offered his hand.

Frank started to rise and the man—doctor, his mother's husband—waved for him to stay seated. He sat down next to her on the end of the bed.

"I see you're doing one of our traditions. Hot tea to calm the nerves."

"Instead of some scotch," Frank said.

"Oh, we do that too," Theo said with a nervous smile. "Want some? I'll bet we—"

But that reminded Frank of the afternoon with his father, and he didn't want to repeat that. Sober seemed the way tonight.

"You two are married, then," Frank said. "How long?"

"We've been together for nineteen years," Theo said.

"Eighteen," she corrected. "He's counting the year he tried to get me to go out with him."

"We did go out," Theo said.

"Tea on our breaks does not count as dates," she said.

"I don't know why not," he replied. "I paid, didn't I?"

And they smiled at each other, and Frank was suddenly reminded of Harry and Cody and began—to his surprise—to wonder something.

"Nineteen or eighteen years is a long time," Frank said.

"My parents have been married for fifty," Theo said.

Frank could only shake his head. And think about how maybe he was wrong. Maybe Harry and Cody weren't doomed. Because they looked at each other like these two.

"Mother," he said… and froze. So did she. So did Theo. It was like they were all three on pause there for a moment. "God." That was what he said next.

"Yes?" she asked him, albeit with caution in her tone.

He looked at Theo. "Sorry for me to ask this in front of you…."

Theo held out his hands, palm up. That's the way it is.

"If Glen—Dad—wasn't such a…."

"Womanizer?" Theo suggested. And even though that was a kind word, Frank still couldn't help but give the man a quick look when he said it. "Sorry."

Frank looked back at his mother—*my mother!*—and asked the question. "If Glen wasn't such a womanizer, do you think you would still be together?"

"Oh honey…." She gave him a gentle smile. "Who knows? I was in it for forever."

"You *really* believe in forever?"

"Well, I've been with Theo for nearly twenty years," she said and reached out and touched her husband's hand.

"As I said, my mother and father have been married for fifty."

Frank shook his head. Fifty? Of course he'd heard of such things, but now….

"And I love you forever," his mother said. *Mother!*

"Mama." The word was out. There was nothing he could do. It was out.

"Son."

Then they were crying again. This time much more gently but holding each other all the same.

And something happened.

Something inexplicable.

He became... lighter. It made no sense, but it was true. As if something really were lifting off of him. And as if some beast that had been hiding in deep shadows behind him, ready to attack, simply... went away.

It. Was. *Amazing*.

Mysterious.

After a while, still holding her, he whispered, "How can you be sure you love me?" Frank said, and when the word "love" passed his lips, he shivered. Love. Really? Love?

Love.

"I just do." She stroked his hair. She gave a stifled little gasp and squeezed the back of his neck. "Oh, I do."

"You don't know me."

"It doesn't matter," she whispered.

"You don't know what kind of person I am."

"Doesn't matter."

"What if I'm a murderer?"

"I would *still* love you."

He pulled back a little. "And if I was—"

"Gay?" she asked.

He pulled back farther and looked at her.

"Your father told me that too. As if that would make a difference."

His heart stirred. Stirred in a way it hadn't before.

He heard his mother's voice then, reading *How the Grinch Stole Christmas*. And he took those famous words toward the end of the story and thought, what if love—just perhaps—might be something more?

Frank looked at her again. He wanted to believe.

"What if I was just like my father?"

She shook her head.

"What if I'm a chip off the old block?"

She sighed. "Then I would still love you."

"What if I treat men just like he treats women?"

"I'd ask you why. But I would still love you."

He trembled. "It's because I didn't believe in love."

Her eyes filled again. "Oh," she said, her voice so small he could hardly hear her. "That makes me sad. Because I think you deserve a man who can love you. And treat you like Theo loves me. Someone for you to love like I love Theo."

He shook his head. "Do you really think?"

She nodded.

"You really love me? Even though you don't know me?" His heart had begun to speed up as they spoke, and now? Now it was pounding.

"With all my heart."

Aha! "*But*"—and he pointed at her—"then how can you love Theo when you love me with *all* your heart?"

She smiled. And God. It was radiant!

"Oh, honey! Love isn't an *amount*. It doesn't run out. There aren't portions to be divvied out and then there's no more."

She reached out and took his other hand. "Love is like an ocean. Like the whole world. That's why I could fall in love with Theo after I left your father. It's why I can love you with all my heart and love my husband just as much."

"Except…." This was Theo.

They both looked at him.

"Except you're her son. And there is no other love greater than that."

She smiled again and shed another tear, and she looked at Frank and nodded.

Maybe there was a little bit more to this love thing after all.

Frank took a very deep breath. Then he said, "You know, I could use a drink after all."

FRANK KNOCKED on Glen's hotel room door.

It opened a moment later, Glen's face radiant. "Frankie! You're back!" He was wearing only a pair of jeans.

"Yeah."

"Ah… thing is… I've got a little company."

Of course he did. He was the block, after all.

"That's okay."

Glen grinned. "Thanks for understanding, son."

"But that's not why I'm here anyway. Can I borrow that Lagavulin?"

His father was clearly surprised. "You want to *borrow* it? You drove back here to borrow whisky? Wouldn't it have been easier to pick up your own?"

"If I hadn't already been in the hotel, yes," Frank agreed.

"Oh." He looked at Frank as if waiting for an answer. Frank didn't give him one.

"*Glen*!" came a female voice. "What are you *doing*?"

Glen looked over his shoulder, "I'll be right there... ah... honey," then back at Frank. "Okay." He shrugged. "Sure."

He closed the door and was back in less than a minute. He handed Frank the square-shaped bottle. "Here you go, Frankie."

Frank smiled. "Thanks, *Pops*."

Glen's eyebrows shot up at that.

Frank started down the hall (didn't have to go far) and pressed the elevator call button.

A moment later Glen called out, "Frankie?" Frank knew Glen wouldn't be able to resist. To be fair, maybe he wouldn't have either. Wait. *Would* he have cared what Glen needed a bottle of whisky for? Nah. Not at all.

The elevator doors opened.

He stepped half in. "Yeah?"

"You meeting somebody or something?"

"Already have," he called back. "Mom and her husband. We wanted to celebrate."

Glen's eyes went wide.

"She's in the same hotel. Can you believe it?"

Frank stepped back and the doors closed.

THEY TALKED for over two hours, and then Theo suggested they have dinner the next evening.

"Or lunch," his mother said. "You can spend the whole day with us."

Frank asked if they could just make it dinner. He had a lot to process.

Stories of her schooling. Of meeting a handsome young man working to be a doctor. His courting of her. His winning her. Their marriage. Her insisting she stay working for a couple of years, especially while he was in residency.

Sadder stories.

Two attempts to have children, both ending in miscarriage, and then a need for a hysterectomy.

"It was a relief in one way. You disappearing and then two more children taken away from me before I could even hold them. I thought maybe I wasn't supposed to have children."

The words had broken Frank's heart.

He talked as well. Told them of his career.

"Following in your father's footsteps," she said.

That made him think of his sex life and suddenly he didn't want to think about that.

He told them how he decided he wanted to stop traveling the world with Glen and settle, and how it wound up being Kansas City of all places—

"It really is a beautiful city," she exclaimed. "What little we've seen of it. You hear Kansas City and you think Dorothy and the Wizard of Oz, not the beautiful downtown and your modern trolley and the museums. Theo insisted we see the memorial for the First World War. And we had dinner at Union Station."

—and that it was now considered one of the ten most cultured cities in the United States and there had been quite a call for what he did.

He told them about the Oscar Wilde, and how he'd already changed apartments twice and was getting to the point where he thought it might be time to change again.

"Or stay?" she'd offered. "Really set down roots. Or for that matter, buy a house? Make it totally your own?"

"It's nice being with so many other gay people. I don't know if that makes sense but...."

"It makes perfect sense. But still.... You could find a place close, maybe? Then you'd be able to see your friends but have more privacy."

"A house is a lot more maintenance than an apartment," he said. "I don't have to worry about the plumbing or the lawn or any of that at the Wilde."

"That's the truth," Theo said with a laugh. "A house is a lot more work!" He gave Marion a gentle nudge.

"Then you need someone to help you," she said. "A companion does more than keep you from being lonely or filling your bed."

An image of Roy flashed to his mind, but he dismissed it quickly enough. He didn't know the man. Roy didn't even know if he was gay!

Theo rolled his eyes. "She's like this with all our single friends. Figures no one is happy unless they're happily wed."

She shook her head. "That's not true." Theo nodded over her shoulder. "I just care about you, and I want someone there to watch out for you. Take care of you."

"I've done pretty well on my own."

"Nevertheless…."

He started to tell her why he slept around. Why he had such strict rules on how far he would allow a man into his life. How the minute a guy used the L-word, he was done.

But suddenly it seemed stupid. And he didn't know why.

It was a big reason why he found he needed to get away. He had other things that needed to be done.

CHAPTER THIRTY-FOUR

FRANK WAS letting himself into his apartment when the door to Harry and Cody's apartment door opened. It was Harry. He was in his boxers.

"What are you doing up?" Frank asked.

"Waiting for you," Harry said.

Frank pulled his keys out of the lock and crossed down to his friend. "Why?"

Harry gave him one of his silly little smiles. "You had a visitor earlier. Or someone looking for you anyway."

Roy?

Don't be silly.

"Who?" he asked.

"Orange Jumpsuit Guy," Harry said. And blushed.

Frank eyes went wide. Partly in horror. "You didn't call him that, did you?" *Please say you didn't.*

But the look on Harry's face told him all he needed to know.

Harry held up a hand while at the same time looking like a puppy caught with a chewed-up shoe. A Louis Vuitton. "I didn't *call* him that. But I did blow it and out him as your fantasy."

"Oh for Christ's sake, Harry!" Frank's stomach flopped over. *God, Harry. Why? Now I'll never see him again.* And that made him inexplicably very sad.

"It's okay! We saved it. Cody and me. We invited him in."

Invited him in?

"He's okay with it. I apologized like a motherfucker. And he doesn't hold it against you."

Thank God.

Harry raised an eyebrow ever so slightly as the door opened farther, and Frank saw Cody standing there in a pair of black briefs. "I'm pretty much the one who saved the day," Cody said.

"Maybe so, maybe not," Harry said.

"*Definitely* so," Cody replied.

Harry rolled his eyes comically. Frank was still uneasy, but now a part of him wanted to laugh.

"Really, Frank. It's okay." Cody nodded.

Frank almost smiled.

"He likes you," Harry said. He waggled his eyebrows.

"He doesn't even know if he's gay or not," Frank said.

Cody nodded again. "Oh, he's gay all right."

"Maybe this is the one!" Harry exclaimed excitedly, and surely he had to know how peculiar this conversation was, the three of them standing here like this, two of them in their underwear, apartment door open. The two of them trying to tell him that Roy might be "Mr. Right."

But then, he might be a pretty good Mr. Right Now.

"Good night, guys. Go to bed."

He turned. A hand touched his elbow.

Frank looked back. It was Cody. He was standing in the hall. In his briefs.

"He *likes* you, Frank."

Frank didn't know what to say.

He likes me. The thought made his heart speed up.

And then he heard his mother. *"Love isn't an amount. It doesn't run out...."*

But hadn't he seen differently? Had his father ever loved anyone? Really?

"Love is like an ocean. Like the whole world."

Could it be?

"Frank. She loves *you. She's never* stopped *loving you."*

Could it?

I thought she abandoned me. That's what Glen said.

His brows came together. There was going to be a good conversation there.

"Guys," he said. "I don't even know how to find him. I don't have his phone number. I meant to get it, and somehow...." He shrugged. "It didn't happen."

Harry got a curious look on his face. "Yeah... us too! We meant to get it. He was going to write it on a note and have us give it to you. But after we talked, he just sort of got away."

"So it will just have to wait until Wednesday," Frank said. Which would give him time to think. Because where this was going....

"You don't have to wait until Wednesday," Cody said.

"Huh?" What?

"He said he was helping his granny with a garage sale."

"Yeah...?" So what?

"In Roeland Park, right?"

Harry was grinning.

"Yeah...?"

"Roeland Park isn't a very big suburb," Cody said.

Harry was grinning.

"Yeah...?" Frank said for a third time.

Harry was grinning as wide as the Cheshire Cat in the Disney animated movie *Alice in Wonderland*.

"You could probably go up and down each street in the whole city in a half hour," Cody replied.

Frank gave a little twitch.

"You want, we could go with you."

"You do know that Cody is the garage sale queen of Kansas City, right?" Harry asked.

Now Cody was smiling.

He looked at them both. "You want me to drive up and down each street in Roeland Park looking for garage sales and looking for him."

They nodded as one.

And now *he* was smiling. He didn't even know he was doing it until the deed was done.

Crazy. It was crazy!

"I don't know if I can...," he said.

"It's easy," Cody said. "You get in your car and—"

"Not that," Frank said, cutting him off.

"What?" Harry asked.

He looked at them both again. If he said it they would never understand. They really believed that just like that—*snap!*—he could suddenly change?

What if he did go looking for Roy? And he found him. What would happen then?

"Love is like an ocean..."

"Love isn't an amount. It doesn't run out...."

He started to shake his head. Saw their hopeful looks.

I can't change overnight. What if I hurt Roy? Then he said it out loud. "What if I hurt him?"

Cody shrugged. "Sometimes first love hurts."

And if I try this… it would be my *first love.*

Now he did shake his head. "No. I think it would be better for us— him—if I just skipped it."

But then Frank saw that face once more in his mind's eye. *Roy's* face. Those eyes.

And oh God…. To wake up to that every morning. See that sleeping face next to his.

Impossible….

But he couldn't help it. He was smiling again.

CHAPTER THIRTY-FIVE

FRANK WOKE up, and Roy wasn't there. Bathroom?

Sure, he thought and scooted closer to Roy's side of the bed. A smile tickled his mouth. *Now* Roy wouldn't have much room. They'd have to snuggle very close. And very close could lead to morning sex. His cock, which was already half-hard from sleep, shifted. He inched a little closer to Roy's side of the bed and...

Roy's side was cold. Frank's eyebrows gave a little tick. *Where is he?*

Making coffee? Frank's nostrils flared. He couldn't smell anything. *Where...?*

Frank started to sit up to get out of bed and go look for Roy when it hit him. He would have laughed at himself but—*oof*—the disappointment was *crushing*.

Roy wasn't here.

Frank had dreamed it.

Dreamed first a bunch of rest-interrupting dreams, one after another, of him going to dozens and dozens of garage sales trying to find Roy. But he kept seeing, and for some reason picking up, total kitschy crap, even asking for prices, asking if they'd take a dollar, fifty cents, less, on a clock or a broken wristwatch or a Princess Di plate or an *NSYNC doll or a shamrock beer stein or pool sticks or a pair of old jeans or a birdcage or a Christmas ornament or baby clothes or an old laptop—"Does this work?"—or garden tools or a McDonald's Happy Meal toy... and never finding Roy.

He'd wake up and know it was a dream and feel all itchy and twitchy and groan and roll over and go back to sleep, only to be back at another garage sale picking up a piece of carnival glass or a useless VHS videotape.

And looking for Roy. Yelling at a very large woman with her hair up in huge curlers and wearing white shorts and flip-flops and a T-shirt with the inexplicable words I Call Woo Woo On You.

"Where's Roy live?" he screamed. "Where?" And she threatened to call the police.

The only reason—"Oh God," he said aloud, remembering—he finally *did* fall into deep sleep was that he, at last, dreamed he found Roy and strode up to him and kissed him hard right in front of a very skinny, very old woman with cat's-eye glasses. Roy's grandmother?

Granny. He calls her Granny.

In the dream, he'd actually scooped Roy up into his arms and carried him away, and the only thing that was missing was Jennifer Warnes and Joe Cocker singing about love lifting them up where they belonged.

He didn't question it. It was that real. So real he actually thought Roy had spent the night with him.

I need coffee.

Frank rubbed sleep out of his eyes. Stretched enough—arms out wide—that his back popped. Yawned. Scratched his balls. And then looked back at the empty half of the bed with lonely longing.

This is because of Mama, he thought, and then marveled at *that*.

I've met my mother....

Wow.

He sat up straight with a little jolt. He'd met his mother! *That* wasn't a dream.

Frank had met his mother, and she wasn't the beast waiting in the dark shadows behind him, ready to attack, ready to prove she was everything his father had ever said she was. He had believed it. Frank's shoulders slowly fell loose. *Of course I did. What else was I supposed to believe?*

Anger threatened then. A different kind of beast ready to claw up out of the dark. Anger that would make him hate his father.

He almost let it.

And then he decided it was too early in the morning, he needed coffee, and he would rather bask in this... glow. He could *feel* her then. Her arms around him. Her hands stroking his hair. *Mama.*

"I love you, son. I have never stopped loving you. I will never stop loving you."

For a moment, Frank didn't know whether to laugh or cry. Maybe both at once?

Coffee!

He stood up, and as he glanced back, he saw how big and empty that mattress was. With its white sheets, it looked like an arctic plain of ice and snow.

"A companion does more than keep you from being lonely or filling your bed."

Frank went and made the coffee then and found himself growing impatient for the damned Technivorm Moccamaster to *hurry up and get the job done already*! A Mr. Coffee might have been faster.

He decided to shower while he was waiting, and he did so, quickly, perfunctorily, skipping the normal jerkoff and *getting the job done already* instead. He checked his cell phone while he dried and found that it was going to be a perfect day. Then he picked out a pair of cargo shorts and a T-shirt that wouldn't embarrass Roy (that made him smile) and brown boat shoes, but before he got dressed, he filled a travel coffee mug—because he had some traveling to do—and stepped out on his balcony and drank some of it, naked, in honor of Roy.

He wished Roy were here now.

Imagine that!

Then he dressed quickly and left. He did not stop at Harry and Cody's apartment. He could do this alone. He had to do this alone.

Heart pounding, he was on his way.

As it turned out, there were a lot of garage sales in Roeland Park.

CHAPTER THIRTY-SIX

IT WAS a busy Saturday. The weather was wonderful. Sunny and only a few fluffy clouds in the sky. Warm but not hot, with a cool breeze. Perfect for a garage sale. And nice enough for shorts and a T-shirt (this one with the caption "That's What I Do. I Grow a Beard and I Know Things").

Roy was happy because Granny and Mrs. Kelly were happy. *Kelly.* She wanted him to call her Kelly.

They were doing a brisk business. That was good because he wanted to keep his mind occupied. He helped carry things out to cars. He charmed old women. Gave kids—with their parent's approval—cookies to help keep them quiet. Granny didn't have much stuff of interest to children.

He couldn't stop thinking about Frank. He knew it was stupid. Frank wasn't the kind to settle down. He didn't want a boyfriend. Only a "friend with benefits."

But that could be enough, right?

He was smiling. He couldn't help it. He felt good. Almost giddy.

Maybe it was the beautiful weather. The smell of some kind of flower, heavy and sweet on the breeze. The feel of the sun on his skin. Watching Granny and Kelly. So in love.

He wanted to be in love like that.

And he didn't want to wait his whole life to find a love like that. They had. Spent their whole lives living as heterosexuals. What might things have been like for them if they had started a life together years and years ago?

I don't want to do what they did. I don't want to waste all those years. I want to find someone to love me now.

A man.

He shivered.

Frank. He would love it to be Frank. He didn't need to go to bed with hundreds of men to find the one he wanted. He'd found the one he wanted. He'd found him when they'd locked eyes along a hot highway.

Roy helped his granny and Kelly, and he was nice to people and people were nice to him. All of that made him feel even better.

But while he did all those things, Roy couldn't help but indulge in a little fantasy. What it might have been like if he and Frank had started the day making love. Then showering together. Arriving here, maybe with doughnuts from Lovin' Oven, and helping Granny and Kelly together.

He couldn't help but pretend. Nothing wrong with that, right? Pretending?

"Roy?"

He froze.

No. It couldn't be.

But even as he told himself how impossible it was, he knew that voice.

Roy turned. There stood Frank. And he was smiling.

Roy didn't know what to say.

Frank did. "Just *how* many garage sales are there in this little town?" he asked.

"What?" Roy asked. How many garage sales?

"It's Roeland Park's annual area-wide garage sale," Granny, who had seemed to come out of nowhere, told him.

Frank nodded absently and held up a piece of paper. "Yeah. I got the map. Been checking them off."

"Anything in particular I can help you find?" she asked.

Frank shook his head. "No. I just found it." His smile widened.

"Oh?" she asked.

With a nod, Frank walked straight up to Roy. Roy's heart was racing. *Kiss me*, he thought. *Please kiss me.*

And Frank did.

Just a gentle one at first. One that made Roy's blood zing in his veins and then warm his face. Then Frank glanced from side to side, looked back with eyes that clearly asked if it was okay?

Roy kissed him back as his answer. This time it lasted a *little* longer. The kiss ended with them touching foreheads, noses, gazing at each other.

"You came looking for me?" Roy asked.

"I did," Frank said, very quietly, his voice breathy.

"I take it this is the gentleman you were telling us about?" Granny.

Roy stepped back a moment and turned to her. "Granny, this is Frank."

She came to them, wiping her hands on her apron. "I'm Billie Dee, young man." She held out her hand. "What was your last name?"

Frank took her hand, didn't shake it, but gave it a little squeeze. "Sinclair."

She nodded. Let go of his hand and then, to Roy's further surprise, Frank put that hand on Roy's back and dropped it to his waist, arm now around him.

"You going to treat my grandson right?"

"I am going to try." Then he gently pulled Roy so they were facing each other again. "I'll try if you want. I might fuck up. I probably *will* fuck up. I know I will. This is all really new to me. And who knows? In a week or so, it's possible neither one of us will be able to stand the sight of the other."

"I don't think that's going to happen," Roy said. His heart was now skipping rope. He trembled, terrified. And overjoyed. It was like a dream. The very one he'd been creating all morning. "But I might fuck up too. I don't know anything about being gay, Frank. I'm just starting to say the word out loud." He shook his head. "I wouldn't allow myself to think about it, not really, until a few days ago."

"Stuff like this doesn't usually work out. It's a first for both of us. I don't know if it can work—"

"Oh balderdash," Granny said. Kelly was standing beside her now. Granny took her hand. "First love happens all the time."

"We just met, ladies," Frank said.

"Love at first sight happens all the time." Kelly looked at Granny with utter joy.

"Well, I don't know if it was love at first sight," Frank said and pulled Roy against him. "More like lust."

"That works too," Kelly said.

"Can it be confusion at first sight?" Roy said.

Frank smiled at him. "Yes. That I believe." Then he kissed Roy again, and Roy couldn't feel the ground beneath his feet.

"What's wrong?" Granny burst out. "Haven't you ever seen two people kiss before?"

They separated to see a little woman turn and leave.

Roy didn't give a shit.

"You staying for dinner?" Granny asked.

Roy's heart gave another little jump. This was all surreal. But real. It was like everything had led up to this, and everyone was taking it completely in stride. But then, who knew? Maybe everything had been.

"Sorry, ma'am. I can't. I have other plans."

Roy's heart sank.

Frank tugged at him. "But Roy, I sure would like you to join *me* for dinner."

Roy looked at him curiously.

"I'd like you to meet my mother." Then he grinned wide, and it was so beautiful.

"You called her?" Roy asked.

Frank nodded. "And I met her."

"And…?" Roy couldn't believe it! Frank had done it? He'd met her?

"We spent a couple of hours together. It was wonderful."

The joy surged back. "Oh, Frank! That is so wonderful!"

"It really is," Granny said, and Kelly nodded in agreement.

"Will you come with me?" Frank asked.

Roy nodded. With his heart threatening to leap out of his chest, he nodded again.

"I am so glad." And then Frank kissed him again. This time it lasted much longer. Sweet and long and soft and as if this were the most normal thing in the world—for a man to kiss another man in the backyard of a garage sale in front of two elderly ladies.

When the kiss ended, Roy said, "Me too."

They stayed for lunch, though. Cold-cut sandwiches and potato chips and potato salad—red-skinned and homemade this time—and iced tea. They stayed until closing and helped put everything in the garage. With two men wrestling the tables, it didn't take any time. Plus, there wasn't a lot left. Sales had been good.

Then Frank asked if he could take Roy away, and the ladies gave their blessings. They drove to Roy's mother's house because Frank wanted him to leave the Jeep and ride with him. Said he couldn't wait to touch him until they got back to the city. So that was what they did, and Roy went in to tell his mother he might be spending the night at a friend's.

"Could I meet your friend?" she asked.

So, heart in his throat, he brought Frank in. His mother's eyes went back and forth between their faces, and Roy had no idea what was going on in her head. The two of them, Frank and Mother, talked a few moments, but Roy's heart was pounding so hard he hardly heard what they said.

Frank then asked again if he could take Roy away, and Roy's mother said, "Why, of course."

As they left, his mother touched his arm, and he stopped. Turned back. Unable to breathe. What was she going to say?

"I like him much better than Ramona," she said. "Already."

Roy had to fight to keep his mouth from falling open.

"He's better-looking too." Then she kissed his cheek and told him to hurry, his gentleman friend was waiting.

Roy went to Frank's car, realized he hadn't brought anything for spending the night with anyone, and told Frank that.

"Well, you're not going to need any clothes once we get back to my place," he said as matter-of-factly as if he were talking about the weather. "And we're close enough in size that I think I can find you something to wear. At least a nice shirt. Your jeans will do."

For some reason the idea of wearing Frank's clothes set Roy's blood to racing again. He nodded and got in and away they went.

For half the trip, neither said a word. At a red light, Frank looked at him. "My heart's pounding," he said and gave a little laugh.

"Mine has been since you got to Granny's house."

They gazed at each other, and then after a long moment, Frank kissed him again. "This really might not be easy."

"I understand. But God, I want to try."

"Lord help me," Frank said, "so do I."

A beep sounded from a car behind them. The light had turned green. Frank didn't flip them off. He just waved.

And they were off.

EPILOGUE

1

IT WASN'T easy. Not at all. They clashed.

But they never fought. Not really.

The first days were them getting into each other's way just as much as making love. Why, there were nights when one or the other of them said they wanted to be alone that night. But it was always followed by a very early call in the morning.

It got easier.

They made mistakes. Big ones.

Frank found he still liked to look at men, although to his surprise, he still didn't really want to touch (not even six months into their "trying this out").

Roy found he had a streak of jealously heretofore unknown. It surprised him because he wasn't in the least bit bothered by the fact the Frank had been with so many men before him. Well. Not much. It did make him wonder if one day Frank would decide this monogamy thing—which they had fallen into without talking about it—wasn't for him. It was most certainly what Roy wanted.

They worked it out.

2

ONE THING that happened early on—just a month or so after they started their little experiment—was that Frank showed him his shop, the back three-quarters of the building where he and his two employees—one was going to be leaving in a little over a month—worked on the cabinets and shelving and other woodwork for the homes Frank was restoring. Wooden pieces that were being brought back to their original beauty, or new ones that Frank designed himself, specifically for a customer.

Roy was in awe.

He touched the wood. Ran his hands along a board that had been sanded to a sensual smoothness. Marveled at the feel. Loved the smell of the sawdust and the stains. And suddenly…

"Remember always to measure twice *and cut* once.*"*

Grandpa!

"Because if you measure wrong and cut wrong, the board is ruined."

He remembered that day helping to make the shelves for Granny's kitchen and how he'd loved it….

"Ooh…. This is wonderful*!"*

"Really?" Frank asked.

Roy nodded. "Oh yes."

He watched in awe as a big, muscular man cut a board in a wavy shape on one side—it was probably the decorative part of a cabinet. After a few moments, the man asked if he wanted to try. Roy did.

An hour later he was shocked to find out how much time had passed without him noticing.

Something sweet turned wonderful that day. It added a powerful needed foundation to what was clearly becoming a real relationship.

Now their time apart would be spent because Roy was working in the shop—he took over the job of the departing employee smooth as could be—and Frank was out meeting customers. The rest of their time was spent together installing the units.

Or at home.

3

FRANK HAD given Roy a key to his place a month before he asked him to officially move in. Roy agreed before the words were barely out of his mouth.

Roy's uncle stopped telling faggot jokes.

"Not as funny once you find out your nephew is gay, are they?" he overheard his Aunt Audrey snap over Thanksgiving dinner at Granny's.

Gay.

That word.

Over and over, Roy was surprised by the word and told Frank so. But he went from fearing it to taking pride in it. They made plans to go to the next year's Gay Pride. Granny and Kelly made sure the two of them knew the ladies were coming as well.

That Thanksgiving dinner had almost caused a problem. Frank liked to cook. He didn't want to be served dinner. He wanted to be a part of it. And Cody and Harry had expected them both to come there.

Granny had been adamant. "I do not know how much time I have left on this earth, boys," she said, "and Thanksgiving has always been here and always will. Understand, Frank?"

He begrudgingly agreed. Only if he could bring his stuffing. To which she consented. And everyone loved it.

They had pie at Harry and Cody's. Well, a second slice of pie.

Granny said she would consider having Christmas dinner at their place.

Their place.

Later, when Roy told her how much that word had thrilled him—and he wasn't even trying to talk her into an exchange of venues for Christmas dinner at the time—she wound up deciding that if they agreed, no arguments ever, that Thanksgiving would always be at her place, then she thought that maybe "their place" would be all right for Christmas.

The family had loved the apartment.

There had been a growing tickle of unrest over the issue that Frank was thinking it was about time to move into another apartment in the Oscar Wilde and start another total renovation. Roy did not *want* them to move because this was the place that their love affair had begun. He wasn't even relieved by Frank's assertion that the new place really would be theirs because they'd do it together, instead of Roy moving into a place that was a *fait accompli*.

That was until they saw a nice little house, which would certainly need work, just three blocks from the Wilde.

They couldn't help but look at each other in excitement at the idea.

They worked things out.

And they certainly had no lack of people to lend an ear and a plethora of advice. Roy's mother. Granny and Kelly. Frank's mother, only a Skype call away.

They both only had one real problem apiece.

4

FRANK'S WAS his father.

Glen did not approve of Roy.

He wasn't even classy enough to speak in a voice Roy couldn't hear. He and Frank were on the balcony, and Roy was inside making dinner.

"I just don't understand, Frankie."

"*Frank*." He was getting tired of "Frankie." From anyone except his mother. That, he liked.

"How can you? We Sinclair men weren't meant to tie ourselves down!"

"It's not like we didn't have one of your women living with us at one time or another through the years," Frank snapped. Lots of them. He thought of Caterina again. He'd thought of her a lot lately.

"Temporaries. Just *temps*. Like a secretary you hire from a service for a while and then let go when the job is done."

The job is done?

Frank's stomach soured at the words. So much of what his old man had said for years now seemed horribly gross and offensive. He'd ignored it (mostly) growing up. His father had been the center of his life. But the more he heard Glen talk about how much he loved women, the more clear it was that he *didn't*. Not really. He was a misogynist. He liked tits and ass and pussy. But not *women*. It was a big part of why Frank had stopped being his father's "Boy Wonder." Why he'd settled in Kansas City. It was easier to love his father from afar. So easy to care about someone who wasn't there most of the time and that you didn't have to think about every day. Didn't have to think he might not be the hero "Frankie" had always thought he was.

Now?

Now the man disgusted him more and more.

And Frank hadn't appreciated it when he'd shown up at the door unannounced and asked if he could stay a day or so on his way to his next—amazing!—job.

"You don't want to stay at the Meridian?"

"Seems like money foolishly spent, especially when I can stay right here with my boy."

"Especially when Mama isn't in the same hotel?"

Glen had started at that. Then scowled. All but bared his teeth.

Frank had to fight himself not to bare his own right back.

"How you can have forgiven that bi—"

"Glen!" he shouted. "Don't even go there." The man was pacing. Could he have forgotten that Frank knew the real story now? Could he? It seemed impossible. But then, wasn't it true that if you lied about something long enough, even you began to believe your conjured tales?

Frank's hands were in fists at his side, and he had to take a deep breath, *will* them to relax.

Glen had brought whiskey. Jameson. Not as good as Lagavulin, but still quite nice, It went down smooth. Thing was, though, Frank wasn't really in the mood. Although it might be all that calmed him down enough not to belt his father.

Father.

The word seemed to mean less these days. And it was fortuitous that the man had insisted long ago that Frank call him Glen and not Dad or Father or any of those paternal terms.

"I can only guess at the lies she told you. The awful things she must have said!"

"She tried not to say anything bad about you, Glen." *More than I would have done in the same situation.* God! What would his life have been like if he'd been raised by his mother instead of this man?

Better? In some ways certainly. Not in every way, to be fair. He *had* seen the world.

I'm still trying to defend him.

Glen had stopped pacing. Was looking at him in such a way that Frank had no idea what he was thinking.

"I really think it's best if we don't discuss her at all," Frank told him. "Because you're only going to have to explain why you wouldn't let me see her. Let me meet her."

"She abandoned—"

Frank glared him into shutting up.

"Frankie...," he said with a sad sigh and suddenly looked completely defeated. "She would have taken you. The courts would have allowed it. Handed you over like a fast-food order and wouldn't have cared one whit for all I did for you." He sat down on the ledge of the balcony. "I had no idea how much I would love you when it was just you and me. I was a typical father when you were a baby. I hardly paid you any attention. We fathers didn't in those days. That's all new-age stuff. Lamaze classes and all that *hee-hee-hooooo* shit. Fathers taking maternity leave. No way!" He drank his whiskey. "But then when it was just you and me? Something happened to me."

He looked up and damned if there weren't.... No way! Tears in his eyes?

Glen stood higher. "I kinda fell in love with you, kid. And I... I didn't want to give you up. I traveled the world for a living. When would I see you? Once or twice a year? I couldn't stand the idea!" He slashed his hand down through the air.

"But you didn't have to stop me from seeing her!" Frank cried.

"I did! I did! Because they would have taken you away!"

They. It sounded rather paranoid, didn't it? Like men in black or government agents bombarding the public with gamma rays or putting fluoride in the water to give everyone cancer.

"It's true!" Glen turned away and wiped his face with his sleeve, and when he turned back around, finally, he had completely and totally regained his composure. Frank would never have known he had looked—only a moment ago—like he was on the edge of completely losing it.

Not long ago, Frank would have hated that. But that was because Glen had taught him things like "Big boys don't cry." Now that he'd cried some? Why, he found it wasn't a weakness at all.

When he'd cried with his mother, it had been the complete opposite.

It had been healing.

Empowering.

And yet.... And yet now he could almost understand. Glen had done what he'd done out of love. Or at least the only way he knew how to love, even though it was selfish. True love would have been if Glen had done what was best for *Frank*. Real love wasn't keeping Frank to

himself like a pet when Glen and Frank's mother broke up. More than
once Frank had seen that one person keeping the dog when a couple split
was more about hurting the other person than because there was any real
bond with the animal. If the dog or cat was lucky, the vengeful keeper of
the pet wound up actually liking it.

*Is that what I was? A pet? One you wound up liking instead of
wanting to take to the pound?*

"She didn't deserve you!" Glen said. "A lot of women work and
go to school and keep their kids. I had to raise you all over the world.
Some of those places didn't even have a real doctor within five hundred
miles!"

*If you want any chance of me not dumping you for life, I suggest
we change the subject.*

Glen did. But as it turned out, that was a bad idea too. Glen didn't
pick a better topic of conversation. "Is that why you decided suddenly
you wanted a boyfriend? Because your *mama* told you that *love* was
real? And that you weren't complete without one?" He shook his head,
downed his drink, and reached for the bottle. "Let me tell you something
about love. It's bullshit!"

Frank nodded. "Yeah, Glen. You've told me that all my life. And
now you're turning around and saying you loved me…."

Glen froze.

"You say you've never fallen in love but you fell for me."

Poured some Jameson.

"You're pathetic. You know that?"

"Your *boyfriend* is pathetic," Glen said. "*Beneath* you. *Jesus*. Can't
you do better than that if you're going to get you a temp?" Glen looked
at him. "Do you have some more ice?"

"Dad…?" Frank surprised himself that he used that word. "Whatever
happened to Caterina?"

Glen cocked his head in confusion. "Who?"

Who. Of course.

"Caterina. She lived with us in Tuscany. She went with us when we
went to France."

Glen's eyebrows furrowed together. Then relaxed. "Oh. Caterina."
He smiled wistfully. "She was lovely, wasn't she?"

"For a while there I thought she might really become my mother."

Glen gave him a look that said, "Really, Frank? Really? Please!" And then...

"She told me she was pregnant."

Frank froze. Wait. What? Pregnant? Did... did that mean...?

"Then she got an abortion."

It was as if Glen had punched him in the stomach. Frank nearly doubled over.

Later he told Roy, "I don't know why it hurt so bad. I hadn't even... you know... it hadn't even sunk in that I'd almost had a brother or sister. And then I found out it was dead. I know it's stupid, but it hurt, Roy. It *hurt*!"

And Roy pulled him into his arms and told him he understood. That it wasn't stupid. God, Roy had tears in his eyes, and Frank had never felt so safe as when he was in those arms.

"When I told her I was glad she got the abortion," Glen continued, "she left. She walked right out the door. You were off fishing or something. I don't know. And when you got back, I told you she was gone."

Frank closed his eyes. Christ.

"Thank God she did it," Glen said. "If she even was pregnant. I think maybe she was lying. Trying to tie me down. That's what women do. You ever see some really good-looking young man with some ugly pig of a woman? They've got a baby, and she's pushing the stroller along, and he's following about five or so paces behind looking like he's walking with all these chains and weights on him? Looks haunted and trapped? *Doomed*? And you *know* exactly what happened. He was a horny teenager, and his girlfriend, the cheerleader, kept her legs locked and told him he had to wait. But Available Alice, she spread hers wide and told him he didn't even have to wear a condom. So he turned out the lights and pretended he was drilling Buffy or Kendall or Valerie or whateverthefuck her name was, and then what happened? She got pregnant. And he is trap—"

"You know, Glen," Frank said, making a decision, "I think you should leave now."

Glen tilted his head. Looked at Frank in disbelief. "Huh?"

"Go. Please."

"You're making me *leave*?"

Frank nodded. "Yes. And if you don't walk out on your own, I'll show you the way out."

Glen's mouth fell open.

"Go, old man. *Go.*"

His father closed his mouth with a snap.

"If you ever want there to be a chance to see me again, go now." And then, again, *"Please."*

Glen stared. Nodded once. Threw back the whiskey in one gulp. And walked off the balcony and into the apartment. Frank followed him.

His father passed Roy, who was standing in the kitchen, not moving one inch. Glen stopped. Looked at him. Shook his head. Sneered. Then he went to the guest room and came back with his suitcase.

He looked back and forth between them.

"You'll learn," he said. "And then you'll be sorry."

"Out, Glen," Frank whispered.

"There is no such thing as forever love. You'll come to me and say, 'You were right, Dad—'"

"*Glen.* Leave."

Glen did.

When the door closed, Frank staggered, and to his forever relief, Roy was there in an instant. Helping him stand. Helping him to the couch. Pouring him some Jameson.

Holding him. Just holding him.

For Frank, *that* was when he knew that maybe love *did* exist.

If you found the right person.

The right man.

5

FOR ROY there was only one more demon he wanted to conquer.

It came immediately after Demaine was set free.

Apparently, it wasn't any harder for Demaine to get into the "secure" Oscar Wilde than it had been for Roy. When Roy answered the knock on the door, there he was, all six feet and more of him, all dark-chocolate brown, corded, powerful slabs of muscle, filling up the doorway.

"Demaine! Holy shit! You're out. Why didn't you tell me?"

"Wanted to surprise you, brother." He grinned, and Roy threw his arms around him, amazed himself by doing so. He could never have done this seven months ago. Roy backed up. Looked up and up and up.

"My God it's good to see you."

"Good to see you too, man. You gonna let me come in?"

"Oh!" Roy laughed. "Sure."

He stood aside—*way* aside—and the mountain walked in. He was carrying a big flat box, which he laid on the couch. Didn't say a word about it. Roy took the cue and didn't say anything either.

It was driving him crazy, though.

"So where is Mister Man?" Demaine asked.

"He's meeting a potential client. A big one. We'll make a tidy sum if he can get the lady to sign the contract."

Demaine smiled. "We. I love it. Listen to you!"

Roy blushed.

"Look at you. Couldn't admit you were gay seven months ago, and now it's 'we' with another man."

"I couldn't admit…. You knew?"

Demaine raised an eyebrow. "Yes. I knew."

"Then why didn't we—"

"You weren't ready, for one thing. Besides, I already told you that. Sorry."

That's when Roy remembered Demaine saying that his boyfriend had a pussy. Frank had explained that to him, much to his embarrassment and confusion.

"Did your boyfriend wait for you?" Roy asked. "Sorry, I can't remember his name."

Demaine sighed. "Nope. She found her someone else right away. I knew it would happen. And that's okay. I want someone true. That loves me and not just mah big dick."

"You have a place to stay?" Roy offered. He didn't know what he'd say if Demaine said no and that he sure needed one. Frank had only started to get used to him being there twenty-four seven, and he wanted Roy there. A houseguest?

"No. That's okay. I'm stayin' with my auntie. And she needs me. She fell jus' last week and broke her hip. Am'blance had to take her in without me. If she hadn't been standing on a chair to change a lightbulb, this wouldn't have happened. One week. One week she coulda waited. She knew I was gettin' out."

"Will you stay for dinner? I'd love you to meet Frank."

"Another time, child. Another time. I just brung you somethin' I thought you might like. From one of our little conversations on the phone?"

Huh? Roy couldn't imagine. They'd talked on the phone several times in the last few months. He'd even gone to visit. But he hadn't asked for anything.

He went to the box. Opened it. Gasped. Lost color.

Orange.

It was an orange jumpsuit. The kind he'd had to wear for six months.

"You said your man gets all hard over peels. I won't tell you how I got these out for you. And one your size."

Roy looked up. "God." His stomach twisted.

"No. I ain't God. But he does work in mysterious ways. And sometimes he uses a big black man to do his will."

Roy shook his head. "I-I don't know, Demaine. I mean, I didn't ever want to wear one of these again."

"Even if it gets your man—" Demaine narrowed his eyes, sighed, grabbed at his crotch. "—all hots and bothered?"

"But it's all about…."

"All about what, brother?"

"Me being inside!" Roy cried.

Demaine took a step toward him. Stuck out a finger and poked Roy in the center of the chest with it. Several times. "Boy! You ain't inside. You're out! The only inside you in is your man's heart. And his bed. So tonight, you put this thing on and give ol' Frank the fuckin' of his life, you hear me?"

"But…." Roy's stomach was still tied up in knots.

Now Demaine put a hand on his shoulder. "You are out. And I don't think you ain't ever goin' back in. Right?"

"R-right," Roy said. And then, "I haven't even told him what I was in for."

Demaine's eyebrows came crashing together in a big knot. "You what?"

"I haven't—"

"You ain't told him why you went to jail? Hasn't he asked?"

Roy shook his head. Frank hadn't asked. And he loved him for it.

"Well then, you have a good man."

Roy smiled, and his stomach began to unknot. "I… I think I do."

"I know you do."

Roy's smile broadened.

"You a top or a bottom?" Demaine asked.

Roy blushed. "I'm…. We're both versatile."

"Yeah, yeah. Whatever. But which one makes you feel alive! Like you were born to be doin' it?"

Roy blushed all the harder. "When… when he…."

"Is inside o' you?"

Roy nodded.

Demaine did too.

"You wear that tonight," Demaine said. "You have him fuck the hell out of you. And I'll tell you something else. Chains that you can take off have no power over you. Maybe it's time for you to stop lettin' that orange have any either."

Roy's mouth fell open. Then he closed it. And wondered on all his friend had said.

"Okay," Demaine said. "I am ret to go!" He turned and headed to the door. He stopped right before grabbing the knob. Turned. "I'm happy you're happy, my friend."

"But are you happy?" Roy asked.

Demaine grinned. "Honey? I am out of that place! And I'll tell you something." He slapped his chest. "This brother ain't ever goin' back in. You believe that?"

Roy nodded. Grinned as well. "I believe."

"Then praise Jesus," Demaine said, winked, hugged him, and then his giant of a friend was gone.

Roy was left alone with the open box and the orange jumpsuit of a prisoner. And a big decision to make.

6

ROY PLACED one foot and then the other into the legs of the jumpsuit. Then he stood, pulled it up his torso, and a certain dread passed over him as he slipped his arms into the sleeves and tugged the garment up onto his shoulders.

He trembled, found he couldn't even zip it up. In his mind, he could *see* the bars of his cell, see the closed doors, the tiny cot, the lidless metal toilet, and the ugly matching sink. He saw the corridors, was hit in the stomach with the cramps of always having to watch over his shoulder. The men there. They liked his eyes. Told him he had a "pretty mouth," just like in that movie.

He found that there were quite a few inmates that thought he was "pretty." *Pretty as a girl*, they'd said. It was a huge part of why he grew the beard. To try and avoid looking girlish in any way. It was also why he'd begun working out so much, to help protect himself if Demaine had not been able to.

Protecting himself was why he served his full six months instead of the four everyone, his lawyer included, thought it would be. The powers that be didn't like it when you got into fights.

He shuddered.

And then he heard Demaine's words. *"Chains that you can take off have no power over you. Maybe it's time for you to stop lettin' that orange have any either."*

Time to free himself?

He took a deep breath. Let it out through his mouth. Wasn't that what that guy inside who was into yoga said? Deep cleansing breaths. In through the nose. Out through his mouth.

Roy opened his eyes.

Out of the corner of his eye, he caught a flash of bright orange. He jerked his head that way. It was the mirrored doors of the closet, of course. He was looking at himself.

He trembled again.

Turned. *Stared* at himself. Took a step. Another.

And saw himself with a gay man's eyes, not those of the man he used to be when he was afraid to look at a man's body. Knew that it would turn him on.

His body had changed so much since the days before he "went away." His waist had narrowed. His shoulders had grown wide. Look at how big his chest had become. And with that zipper all the way down and the hint of pubic hair showing, how deep into flesh his abdominals had been carved.

God. He saw then what *Frank* must have seen. Recognized how tantalizingly his pubic hair drew the eyes with his zipper pulled down so far. A gay man would be wondering about what he could *almost* see and would want to see *more*. And finally, Roy noticed how blue his eyes really were. Why, he'd never thought about them. They were the eyes he'd seen in the mirror a trillion times. But he never actually *saw* his eyes.

Until now.

Maybe it was the dimness of the room. Maybe the contrast with the orange uniform; he didn't know for sure.

But that must've been what Frank was talking about when he went on and fucking on about his eyes.

Roy's cock shifted. His eyes widened. He laughed. *I'm frigging turning myself on!* He laughed again.

He felt… why… good.

Really *good*.

A half hour later, he made a phone call. He'd had an idea, and he needed a little help.

His friends were only too happy to oblige.

7

FRANK WAS home and happy about it. He had dinner in two grocery bags—the strong fabric ones that Roy's granny had made for them—on one arm as he fished his keys out of his pocket. He'd stopped by the grocery store and grabbed a Carlisle Free Range Chicken. He'd been given some wonderful fresh vegetables, picked *right* out of the garden of the lady he'd signed on as a new client today. He'd even gone to Lovin' Oven and bought a loaf of the bread Roy had come to love so much. And a single rose. He couldn't wait to see Roy's gorgeous blue eyes flash when he handed it to him.

Red. For love.

Love.

Who would have imagined? Not Frank, that was for sure. And any time he doubted it, all he had to do was look at Roy. No, simply *imagine* him, and this new and wonderful feeling would bubble up inside in a rush, and he knew. *Knew.* This was love.

Sometimes it scared him. What if it went away? He'd seen it happen to couples, gay or straight, his whole life—and just forget about his *father's* relationships. What if these feelings were just some kind of hormones or chemistry or the need to breed that even gay men felt? What if Glen was right? What if this *wasn't* real?

Worse. What if Roy realized it first? Fell out of love with *him*? Left him while he was feeling this way? He'd seen that too. Friends bereft. Devastated. Inconsolable. Practically suicidal. Finally *hating* their exes. Did he want that? To have love turn to hate?

God no.

But then something had hit him. Hard and fast. Just today.

Harry and Cody. Who he had given six months to go before their relationship was kaput. Why, they were still together, weren't they? He and Roy had spent the evening with them last night. He'd watched them and been struck with the idea that they seemed to be even *more* in love. In fact, they hadn't been bothered at all that he no longer told them his sex stories. He didn't have any fresh ones, after all, and he certainly wasn't telling them what he and Roy did. Didn't talk about their sex life even when Roy wasn't with him. Oh *no*. That he wasn't sharing. He kept those stories all to himself. Roy wasn't some nameless trick he'd picked up in a bar. No. Roy was…

Roy was *wonderful*.

Then something else hit him on the way home while he was anticipating how the bread and rose would make Roy happy.

God—I am… I'm in love! This is what it's about. All I want to do is make Roy *happy.*

These feelings, they weren't going away. Six months and they were waxing, *not* waning.

Both of them had carefully evaded using that infamous L-word, although he could tell Roy *wanted* to use it. Nearly had at least a half-dozen times.

Oh my God! Am I going to be the first one to say it?

His heart *raced* at the thought, and he grinned and wondered what Roy would say, would think, *when* he did.

"Roy, I love you," he said aloud in the (empty) elevator, trying it out. He shivered in delight. It felt good!

The elevators doors opened.

"Roy, I think I'm *in* love with you."

Goose bumps popped out all over his arms.

He stepped out into the empty hall.

"Roy, baby? I… I've *fallen* in love with you."

He laughed out loud it felt so good!

And then he noticed the apartment door was ajar. What in the world?

When Cody called out to him, he nearly dropped his groceries. He spun. "What the fuck, Cody! Scare the shit out of me, why don't you?"

Cody's eyes went very wide. "Sorry, man! I heard you laughing out here, and I thought I'd tell you what I just heard on the television."

Christ. Cody was always sharing something he'd seen on television. Which celebrity couples were breaking up. What the Kardashians were up to. What dumbass thing the president had done.

And how *rarely* had Frank given a shit about that any of that stuff. But, oh well, that was a part of who Cody was. Why fight city hall?

"What did you hear, Cody?" he asked, only half paying attention.

"Well…," Cody said hesitantly.

"Go on! You got me curious now." Which wasn't really true. He was thinking of the door again. Roy wouldn't have left it like that. He'd gotten to enjoy being naked when he was home, but he was still way too paranoid about anyone *seeing* him.

"Some convict escaped from jail," he said.

Frank looked back. "Huh?"

Cody nodded, looking *very* serious. "Yeah. They think he got out in a laundry truck."

"Laundry truck? What kind of idiots let a prisoner escape in a *laundry* truck?" He shook his head. "That's the oldest trick in the book. It's almost corny."

Cody spread a hand over his chest. "Hey, I just pass the stories on. I don't report them."

"*Somebody*'s getting fired," Frank said.

"No doubt," Cody replied.

Frank thought for a moment. "Did they say what he'd done?" And glanced at the door *again*.

"Well, I don't think he's a murderer or anything like that…." Cody looked vague, as if he didn't know the details. Which wasn't like him at all.

"I think it was burglary." That was Harry. The door had opened a little wider, and he was standing there behind Cody.

"Burglary?" Frank repeated, and eyed his slightly ajar door once more. *Don't be stupid*, he told himself. An escaped convict wouldn't hide in the Oscar Wilde Apartments.

"Oh! And a rapist!" Harry cried with great exuberance.

"Huh?" Frank said, glancing back at his neighbor.

Harry nodded. "I heard he's a rapist."

Cody glared at him.

Now Harry looked a puppy who had been caught piddling on the floor. "Well, that's what I *heard*."

But Frank had turned back to the door. He reached for it, only now burdened by the dead weight of the bags of groceries. He let them fall to the floor. Opened the door. Stepped in.

8

THE APARTMENT was dark. Which it shouldn't have been. Roy *should* have been home. He wasn't working today. Roy would have called him and let him know if he was going out. Maybe Roy *had* called, and he'd missed it? Frank pulled out his cell and, nope, no missed—

That's when, fast as a flash, someone came surging out of the shadows, grabbed Frank's arm, and pulled it around behind his back, sending his phone clattering to the floor.

He almost peed himself.

Then he felt cold metal at his throat and knew instantly it could only be the barrel of a gun. He only dimly heard from the hall…

"A rapist? *Really*, Harry?"

"I thought it added the right—"

"You're an idiot!"

Frank could only think of one thing about his friends. He wanted to shout to them for help.

"Don't say a word" came a raspy growl.

Sweat broke out across Frank's forehead, and his pits went wet.

"I—"

"Did you hear me?" the man hissed, because yes, it was a man.

"Down the hall. Now."

Fuck! He didn't move. His arm was pulled higher and there was pain (a little), and then he was being guided. Guided down the hall.

Think! Think! What did he do? Hadn't he heard never to fight? Or had it been that he was *supposed* to fight? Like stomp on their foot or….

He was stopped. Pushed into his bedroom.

Bedroom? Why? God. Out of the corner of his eye, in the mirrored closet doors, he saw the orange jumpsuit. Holy fuckin' shit! It *was* the escaped convict! And Harry said he was a rapist.

"Take off your clothes," the man said, and Frank got a chill. The voice was garbled, as if the man had a hand over his mouth.

Then the man was behind him. *Directly* behind him. Another chill passed through him, and to his surprise, he whimpered.

Now the man's whole body was touching his. He could feel a beard against his neck, wanted to look in the mirror to *see* the man, but was afraid. If he saw the man's face, would the man kill him? He was shaking now.

Then…

"Baby?"

Frank froze. And…. Wait. Roy? Was that Roy? But how could…?

An arm went around him. "Y-you know it's really me, don't you?" came Roy's whispered voice.

Frank didn't know whether to laugh or cry. Now he dared look in the mirrors—really look. And God, it *was* Roy. Oh, and his expression! Shit. Holy shit! Roy looked like he'd done something wrong.

Oh God. *He's playing my fantasy for me.*

You sweet beautiful man. The *courage* it must have taken Roy to do this. And he was wearing his orange jumpsuit. Frank had hinted that they might play with one, had even pointed out a pair of prison oranges at the Halloween store back in October. Roy had actually gone pale, so Frank had never suggested it again. Of course he wouldn't want to do anything like that, Frank realized. *That must have been the worst thing that ever happened to him, and I wanted him to make it a game?*

And now that was what Roy was doing!

Oh my God, I love you. He startled himself with the thought and then wanted, once again, to both laugh *and* cry.

So this is love, he thought. And decided it was good.

"Please, please," he whimpered. Or hoped it sounded that way. "I'll do whatever you want. Just don't hurt me." He pulled his shirt off, slowly, leisurely, the way he knew Roy liked it. Liked how his skin was revealed, inch by inch. Chest. Back. Roy loved both.

Roy gave a little gasp and then growled in his pretend escaped-convict voice—

Don't laugh!

—"Now your pants. Get out of those fuckin' pants."

Frank got out of his fucking pants.

Another gasp.

He can't help it. Frank grinned. *He loves my ass.* Frank fought to hide a grin. Roy could see his reflection as well. He'd almost ruined this little game. Better not try for a second time.

He still couldn't resist shifting from one hip to the other, flexing the muscles of his ass.

There was a growl. "Bend over the bed!"

"You're... you're not going to... to fuck me, are you?" Frank asked, voice rough. Not at all damsel in distress. "I've never... no one has ever done that." This time he really had to fight to keep from laughing. Yeah. Right. *He'd* never been fucked before. *If you could see me now, Kostas.*

The thought only turned him on more. Oh, and he *was* turned on. With a little tug, tug, jerk, his cock stiffened to full straining erection.

"I'm... I'm not gay," Frank said.

"Then what's *this*?" Roy said and reached around him and roughly grabbed hold of his hard-on. Jacked it. Frank moaned. Then was glad Roy let go of him down there. One or two more of those and he'd cum just like that!

Roy still had the jumpsuit on. Frank could feel the fabric and the cool metal teeth of the zipper against his back. He shivered again, but this time in anticipation. He could feel precum running down his shaft.

"Bend over" came Roy's voice again. But Frank changed the story a little bit.

"No," he said and turned. Revealing his body. His hard cock.

But now it was Frank's turn to gasp.

Roy stood there in that orange jumpsuit. The zipper was pulled down as far as it would go, showing muscled flesh, chest, chiseled abs, and *his* cock, rising from the V at the bottom of the suit's opening. His balls were out too, and it was all Frank could do not to fall down to his knees and suck his lover off.

Instead he fell on the bed, scooted back a little, and raised his knees, grabbed them with his hands and spread his legs wide to expose his hole.

"If you're going to fuck me, I want to see the man who *takes* me."

9

ROY THOUGHT he'd cum right then. Seeing Frank like that. On the edge of the bed. Knees high. Legs spread.

Oh, and his hole. A lovely maroon. Just like his nipples. His *hard* nipples. Maybe the story Frank had told him was true. Maybe you *could* tell the color of a man's asshole by looking at his nipples.

But the only asshole he was interested in was his beloved's. And he *did* love Frank. Loved him beyond anything he'd ever dreamed possible. He'd come so close to telling Frank that too, but he'd been afraid. Afraid if he did, the magic would be broken like a soap bubble.

He couldn't think about that now, though. This was all about Frank's fantasy. He took the few steps to bring him between Frank's legs. What he wanted to do was fall to his knees and kiss and lick and suck on Frank's hole and send Frank to heaven using the tongue his lover had taught him to use so well.

But would that be a prisoner kind of thing to do? From the experience of his incarceration, and the scene Frank wanted, he didn't think so. He also didn't want to think about what his life had been and been like. *That* would be a hell of a mood killer! So he turned his thoughts away from such things. Because right now, he was turned *on*. He was so fucking hard, his cock was aching. How could it be any other way with his frigging gorgeous man before him, legs spread, eyes begging?

Roy felt a tickling on his balls, and when he reached down, he found they were slippery wet, and *whoa*, he couldn't believe it. It was his precum, running like a leaky faucet down his shaft and down his balls!

It was the most carnal he'd felt since that first time they'd had sex.

"Fuck me," Frank's eyes said.

Roy moved a little closer, nudged his cockhead against that hole, and then—oh!—why it slipped right inside. There was only the tiniest wince on Frank's face, and then he locked his legs around Roy's waist and pulled him closer. To Roy's astonishment, he slid farther in.

But wait! Condom! He wasn't wearing a condom.

"I'm ready, baby."

Ready? Really?

They'd started talking about this in the last few weeks. Roy had been unable to believe that Frank brought it up. The man who said to never, ever let a man fuck you without a condom. Frank said there was one way it was okay. That was if two people were monogamous. And had tested negative. Frank had surprised him one morning in the shop and told him to take a break. They'd gotten in Frank's car, and when they stopped, it was in front of Kansas City Health Clinic.

Roy had looked at his Frank with wide eyes. Shocked. Frank *meant* this.

So they'd gone in and done it. Gotten tested. And through no mountains of surprise, both tested negative. Yet they still hadn't gone home and thrown away the condom box. Frank wasn't quite ready. Roy was. He had been since that first time. Had wanted to know what it was like to feel a man's cum pumping into you. What it felt like to bear it inside of him.

But he'd waited. Apparently for today.

Frank pulled him in deeper, and he slid into the furnace-hot depths of his man, and *God*, nothing, nothing had ever felt like this! So wet and tight and scorching and *exquisite*. And this was one more time that he didn't resent Frank's past—his sexual experience. Frank knew how to relax. There was no way he would be able to take Frank so easily, so fast, even after the countless times Frank had fucked him.

He really should get some lube, though, he thought, and glanced at the bedside table, but *God*, he did not want to pull out so he could get it.

"Baby?"

Roy snapped his eyes back and looked at Frank. Baby?

"Fuck me. Fuck me. *Fuck* me!"

"But…."

"Fuck me!"

He nodded. And he did what Frank asked. And by God, his own natural lubrication was flowing so copiously that Frank seemed to have almost no trouble taking him at all.

Then a little of the devil got into Roy. *Think that's easy, do you?* he thought as Frank used those locked legs to control the depth and speed of their fucking. *How about this, my man?*

He grabbed Frank's knees and spread them *wide* and pushed them back, and he started to *fuck*.

"Fucking you," he said, his voice raspy with desire. "Fucking you! Fuck you like you've never been fucked." And while he couldn't know that, of course, one thing he *could* know: Frank hadn't been fucked bare in a lifetime of fucking. Not since he was a teen. That after all these years it was *Roy's* bare cock that was inside of Frank. That *he* was fucking Frank like *he'd* never fucked anyone before.

He pounded into him. Fucked hard and fast and rough and oh, oh, oh *Christ*, so good!

Then suddenly, shocking Roy, Frank shouted and started cumming! He hadn't touched himself. Roy hadn't touched him. Not *there*. But the semen was spurting in great white ropes over his tan skin, leaving great splashes of pearlescent pools, and the sight, the very sight of that, sent Roy over the edge, and he came. He felt like he was pumping his very life into Frank's fiery depths, his marrow, his *soul*.

"*God*, Frank! Oh my *God*!"

How could anything be like this? Anything?

It seemed to go on and on, stretching, stretching out on and on and forever.

There had never, never, *never* been anything like this at all.

10

THEY WERE curled tight, and funny that after that it was Frank who held Roy tight against him, Roy's back to Frank's front.

Frank held him and sighed and sighed again and kissed his neck, and Roy had goose bumps and wondered if maybe they could do this again. But this time with Frank fucking him. So he would finally know what it was like. He wiggled his ass against Frank's cock, trying to get it to take interest. Surely it wouldn't take much?

"I love you," Frank said, and Roy's eyes flew *wide* open, and he froze in shock and astonishment. "Is that okay?" Frank asked.

Was it okay?

Roy shifted a bit so he could turn his head comfortably and look into Frank's eyes. "Is it *okay*?"

"Yes," Frank whispered. "Tell me it's okay. That I haven't ruined it."

Tears sprang to Roy's eyes. "Oh my God, Frank! No, you haven't ruined it. I'm in love with you. I've wanted to tell you forever. But I was afraid that if I did, I'd break the magic. That I'd scare you away."

"Oh, baby," Frank said. "I'm not going anywhere."

A tear rolled down Roy's cheek.

"You okay?" Frank asked.

Okay? Was he okay?

"Oh, Frank. I'm incredible! I'm happier than I've ever been in my life. I didn't know I could feel this way. This whole. This complete."

Frank pulled him closer. "God, Roy. Me either."

They kissed and then kissed harder and then they made love again.

This time Roy found out what it was like.

It was wonderful.

11

THEY WERE sitting on the couch, and Pink Floyd was playing on the stereo. Frank wished they were naked out on the balcony, but January was hardly the weather for that.

He was happy. So happy. He didn't know he could be so happy.

He shook his head in wonder and simply looked at Roy and knew he was in love. He couldn't wait to tell his mother.

But then he noticed a curious look on Roy's face. It…. It…. "Is something wrong?"

Now it would happen. Roy had changed his mind. Frank had finally done it. Fallen in love and now—

"There's something I need to tell you," Roy said.

Frank's stomach sank. "Y-yes?"

Roy swallowed. Frank saw his Adam's apple bob once, twice. Roy took a deep breath and then said, "Checks."

What? What did Roy say? It sounded like Chex. Chex? Why was he talking about breakfast cereal?

"Bad checks. I wrote bad checks."

Frank shook his head. He still wasn't getting this. Roy wrote some bad checks? Who hadn't ever done that?

"On *purpose*. I knew I didn't have the money to cover them. I wrote them anyway."

Frank sat up straight. The words were starting to make more sense now, but *not* at the same time. They strung together in a way that meant something, but at the same time, Frank had no understanding of where this was coming from. *Why* Roy was saying it.

"I… I was seeing this girl…."

"Ramona?" Frank asked. Roy had long since told him about the strap-on dildo. He hadn't been surprised. He'd known Roy had taken him far too easily that first time.

"Oh! That's right. I told you about her." Then he blushed, and Frank smiled. He couldn't help it.

Roy's mouth turned into a grim line, and Frank's smile vanished.

"Well I didn't tell you this part. She talked me into going on a trip with her to Hawaii with these rich friends she had. They'd started letting us hang out with them. Or letting her, anyway. I think I was the loser they put up with."

"Hardly a loser, baby." He reached out to touch Roy's leg, but Roy held up his hands. A clear no, not yet.

"It was so fucking important that she go with them. Her father usually paid for anything she wanted to do, but not this time. So she talked me into paying for us both. I didn't have the money."

Finally, Frank began to catch on. "You wrote checks to pay for it all, and when it came time to pay, you couldn't."

Roy shook his head. His face was ashen. Ashamed. "It was a lot too."

Frank nodded. Trips to Hawaii certainly could be expensive.

"With the hotel and food and the day and night we stayed on Maui so we could see the black sand, it was almost ten thousand dollars."

Frank nodded. He supposed that was right. It was less than he thought Roy was going to say but no paltry amount. He bet the Meridian was near two hundred dollars a night, and that was Kansas City, not Hawaii.

"And you didn't have the money to pay it all back."

Roy shook his head. "So it was stealing. I stole that ten grand, Frank."

That was when it hit him. "That's why you went to prison."

Roy cocked his head. Looked at him curiously. "*Prison?*"

Frank nodded.

"I didn't go to prison."

Now it was time for Frank to look at Roy curiously.

"It was jail. I went to jail."

Still…. Not quite getting it…. *Again.*

"They didn't charge me with a felony."

Frank sat up straight.

"Is that what you thought?"

"Roy, I didn't think about it."

Now Roy looked offended. No. Hurt. No…. Angry?

"I trusted you," Frank said.

"Wh-what?"

"I trusted you, honey. I was never really worried." And he wasn't, was he? Somehow, he had just… known. He told Roy that. "I guess there was this part of me that thought maybe you had held up a convenience store or something, but…." He shrugged. He really never had *worried* about it. He'd been curious. But not worried. He told Roy that too.

Roy's mouth fell open. Then closed. "All this time I've struggled with this? With telling you? And you didn't care?"

"It wasn't that I didn't care," Frank said, not even knowing where the words were coming from. "I… I just *knew*. I knew you couldn't have done anything *really* bad."

The look on Roy's face was complete shock. "I…. I…."

"I love you, Roy."

And then something else hit Frank. Hit him so hard he gasped.

"Frank? Are you okay?"

Frank blinked. Blinked again. "Jesus. I just realized something."

"Y-yes?"

"*My God.* I think I fell in love with you that day I saw you on the highway." It was a self-revelation so *huge* it was…. Why….

This must be what enlightenment feels like.

Roy's eyes filled with tears. He went blurry because Frank's did too.

"Oh, Frank."

"Oh, Roy," he said and smiled, and the tears ran, and then they kissed. And made love again.

12

AND THEN after….

"We can't tell Harry and Cody," Frank said as they lay on the floor, bodies entangled.

"Tell them what?" Roy asked.

"About the checks."

"No way!"

"I mean…." Frank grinned. "We have to let them think it was *bad.*"

"It *was* bad," Roy said, hurt.

"I know, baby. I know. I'm not making light of what you did. But I'm saying…. We've got to let them think it was *horrible.*" He laughed. "Murder, maybe."

Roy raised an eyebrow. "You're terrible."

Frank laughed.

"Cannibalism?" Roy offered.

Frank burst into laughter. "Oh my God."

"That's why I didn't do life. There weren't any…"

"Bodies!" they chorused, and laughed and laughed and laughed.

And when they finally stopped, Frank pulled Roy closer. "I love you so much, Roy. I know that now, more than ever."

"I love you, Frank."

"You'll never have to worry about me asking you to do something you don't want to do."

Roy smiled. "Thank you, Frank. You don't know what that means to me."

But Frank *did* know.

More than that, it meant never giving up. Never letting go.

"She loves you. She's never stopped loving you."

"I love you son. I have never stopped loving you. I will never stop loving you."

And now he would never stop loving Roy.

He would love him *per sempre*.

Forever.

ACKNOWLEDGMENTS

SPECIAL THANKS TO ALL THE PEOPLE WHO HELPED ME WITH THIS BOOK!

Yes, I am starting a new tradition, and it's asking on Facebook for help with ideas, opinions, and research while I am writing. And so many people help! Here is the list for *Orange*. I hope I didn't forget anyone!

Oh! And in case you were wondering why it is that Harry and Cody believe in magic, then I suggest you check out their story. It's called *Christmas Wish*, and you can find it on the Dreamspinner Press website.

And now, in no particular order…

Emanuela Piasentini for the Italian.

Matthew Ryan for Apogee.

Denise Dechene for Nadir.

Elin Gregory for a perfect line.

Sue Brown and Beverly Jansen for Helen Mirren.

Lisa Lewenz and Kaje Harper for the "foldable" shopping cart.

Caroline Duffy and JL Merrow for the "bathroom."

And Chrissy Miles for a heaping helping of edits—my God!

Noah Willoughby for thousands of words of transcribing.

Brenna for her eagle eye, especially on names!

Of course, I have to thank Andi Byassee who is my indispensable senior editor and dear, cherished friend. Love you!

And Tippy, the world's most *amazing* copy editor.

And Dave Suntown for the *Orange* model and getting him to wear the orange!

Mr. Suntown's got a website you can subscribe to and see all kinds of lovely men. Check it out right here: https://onlyfans.com/suntownphoto

B.G. "BEN" THOMAS lives in Kansas City with his husband of more than a decade and their delightful dogs Sarah Jane and Oliver. He is blessed to have a daughter as well as many extraordinary friends.

Ben loves romance, comedies, fantasy, science fiction, and even horror—as far as he is concerned, as long as the stories are entertaining and about *people*, it doesn't matter the genre. He has gone to literature conventions his entire adult life where he's been lucky enough to meet many of his favorite writers. They have inspired him to create his own stories; it is where he finds his joy.

In the nineties, he wrote for gay adult magazines but stopped because the editors wanted all sex without plot. "The sex is never as important as the characters," he says. "Who cares what they are doing if we don't care about *them*?" But then he discovered the growing male/male romance market and began writing again. He submitted a novella and was thrilled when it was accepted in four days. Since then the romantic tales have poured out of him.

"Leap, and the net will appear" is his personal philosophy and his message. "It is never too late," he testifies. "Pursue your dreams. They will come true!"

Website/blog: bthomaswriter.wordpress.com

BLUE

B.G. THOMAS

Blue McCoy has lived on the streets for a long time, surviving by his wits and doing what he must, and he's not above using his youthful appearance and air of innocence to his advantage. It's not an easy life, but he's happy. He has everything he really needs: the clothes on his back, a house to squat in, a sweet dog. Everything except that special someone to love him.

Six months ago, John Williams's wife left him because she was bored. "Even your *name* is boring" were her last words to him before she walked out. Now he's by himself in a big house, trying to figure out what direction his life should take. He's never been so alone.

A chance encounter sets John on a new path, a path that becomes clearer when loneliness sends him to a local animal shelter to get a dog—and he finds an angel instead. An angel named Blue. A crisis brings them together, but it is something else that keeps them there. Could it be love? A love that can forever end two men's deep loneliness and bring them the support and sense of belonging they've searched for all their lives?

www.dreamspinnerpress.com

DREAMSPUN DESIRES

GETTING HIS MAN

B.G. Thomas

GETTING HIS MAN

A love story worthy of an old movie... with a new twist.

Getting His Man

A love story worthy of an old movie… with a new twist.

Artie needs a hero, a man like those he's always revered in Golden Age films. His drug-dealing jerk of a roommate got him arrested, and since his savior isn't likely to sweep in and save the day, Artie calls a bail bondsman.

August has always imagined himself a hero from a black-and-white movie, but he's never found a man willing to let him play that role—at least not until he gets the call from Artie.

Both of their dreams might come true, but not before August must use his skills as a bounty hunter as well as a bondsman. Artie is on the run for his life, and August must protect him and help him clear his name. Only then can they both finally get their man.

www.dreamspinnerpress.com

NEW
LEASE

B.G. THOMAS

Wade Porter spent his whole life in the shadow of a lover who doled out snippets of love and time as he saw fit—and who insisted that love stay deep in the closet. But now that man is gone, and Wade finds the oceanside cottage where they spent so many weekends together in the Florida Keys cold and empty. He has come one last time, not even sure he wants to keep living.

To his surprise, the house next door is occupied by another bereaved and lonely man. Kent Walker is an artist of romantic gay paintings who is open to the future—and determinedly interested in Wade. Kent wants to show Wade the beauty in being an openly gay man and the possibilities for a real relationship.

Maybe Kent can help Wade let go of the past and discover a better way to live—and love.

www.dreamspinnerpress.com

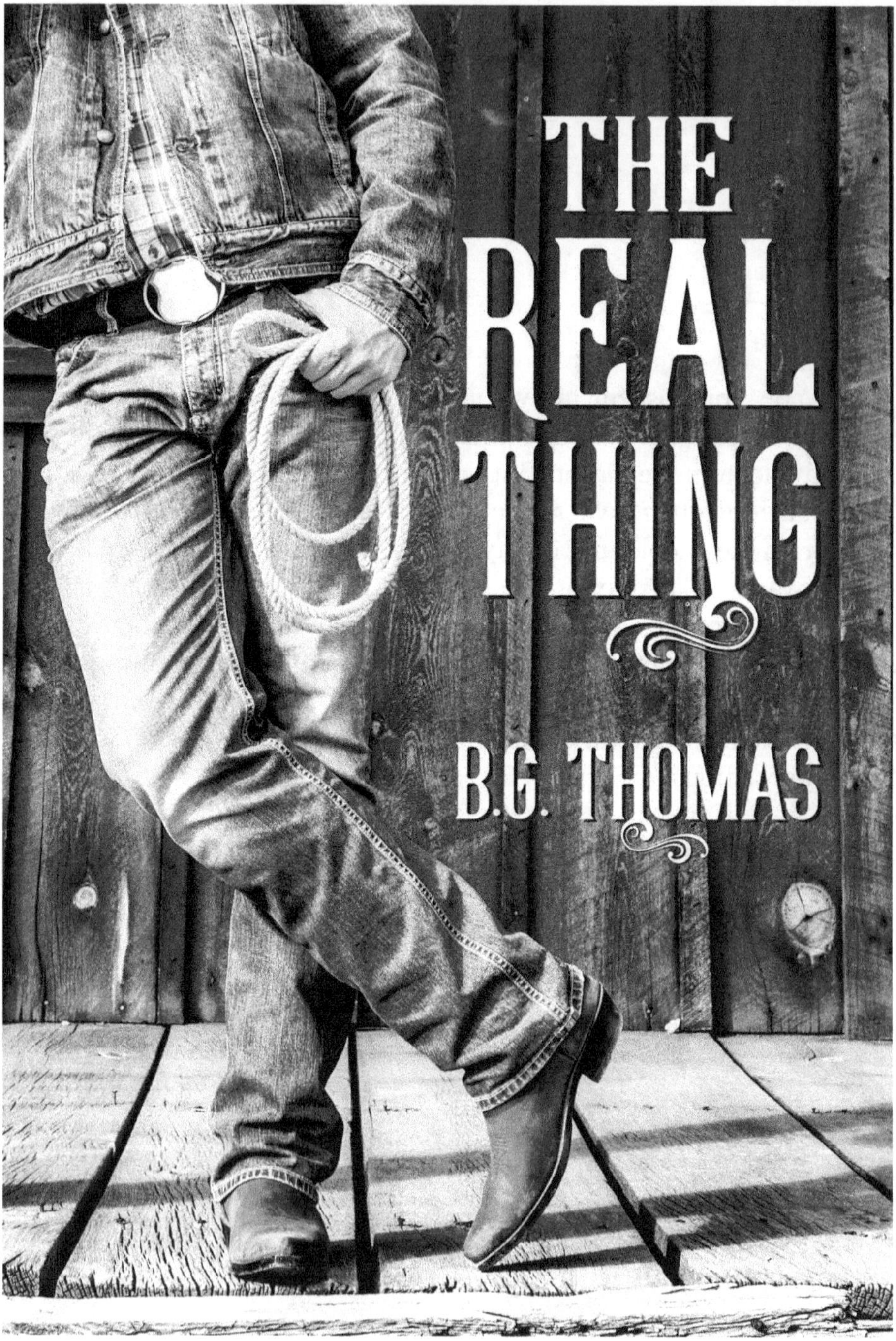
THE
REAL
THING
B.G. THOMAS

Bryan Mills has fantasized about cowboys all his life. Real cowboys, that is. He even dresses in what his roommate calls "cowboy drag" when he visits his favorite bar, in the hope of attracting the attentions of a genuine cowboy. But all he usually finds are posers and guys his own age.

Then one night, to his surprise, Curtis Hansen buys him a beer, and Bryan has no doubt this is the real thing. Curtis is a rugged, gorgeous man who is every bit a cowboy. He even owns his own ranch. What follows is about the most amazing night of Bryan's young life.

But can they move beyond a night of incredible sex when Bryan admits to Curtis that the only horse he's ever ridden was a birthday party pony? And that he's nothing but a poser himself? Maybe, just maybe, Curtis can find the real cowboy inside Bryan, and they can ride off into the sunset together!

www.dreamspinnerpress.com

SOMETIMES "MAN'S BEST FRIEND" ISN'T AT ALL WHAT HE SEEMS

B. G. THOMAS

SOMETIMES
THE BEST PRESENTS
CAN'T BE
WRAPPED

Ned Balding used to be a decent man—until the stress of seemingly countless responsibilities changes him, and he becomes cold and driven—the kind of man who considers firing an employee days before Christmas. The kind of man who kicks a dog…. But Ned's transgressions haven't gone unseen. A Salvation Army Santa witnesses his misdeeds and decides Ned needs to be taught a lesson.

When Ned wakes up the next morning, he's stunned to discover he's been transformed into a dog.

In the past year, Jake Carrara has lost his mother, a lover… even his dog. His boss came close to firing him just before the holidays. He isn't sure he's ready for another pet when he's asked to foster a dog, but Jake's good heart won't let him refuse. Little does he know, this isn't just any dog.

Through a twist of fate, two people with little reason to be friends might teach each other to rediscover the good—and the love—in life.

www.dreamspinnerpress.com

FOR MORE OF THE BEST GAY ROMANCE

DREAMSPINNER PRESS

dreamspinnerpress.com